Burn

The Firebrand Chronicles Book 3

J.M. Hackman

ISBN: 979-8-9921251-3-9

Cover by C.S. Hackman

Second edition printing November 2025

BURN

The Firebrand Chronicles Book 3

This book is dedicated to the Most High King.

Author's Note

Brenna James is your typical teen. She likes to hang out with friends, enjoys time off from her studies, and dreams of acing her history exam. But she struggles with impulsivity, time management, and poor choices. Why does she do the things she does? When is she going to "grow up?" Welcome to ADHD, Attention Deficit Hyperactivity Disorder.

ADHD is usually recognized as the child running around the classroom, yelling out answers without raising their hand, or incessantly picking on the classmate in front of them. But it's also the quiet, withdrawn kid in the back row, distracted and unable to focus on their classwork. It's called ADHD, Predominantly Inattentive (It's a sibling to the better-known ADHD, Combined—which includes a hefty dose of hyperactivity—and the lesser known ADHD, Unspecified). ADHD, Predominantly Inattentive affects girls more often than boys. In all three types, there's a lot of "noise" or extra information in their head, so that concentration becomes impossible. They have trouble focusing on tasks, tracking or managing time, and making (and keeping) friends.

But this condition is real—it's not an excuse for laziness or bad behavior, or something kids can control or grow out of. (ADHD children grow into ADHD adults who use techniques, coping mechanisms, exercise, and/or medication to help them focus.) These children are also bright, creative, and determined. They're not broken—they just learn and process the world around them differently.

If you'd like to learn more about ADHD, check out www.additudemag.com or chadd.org.

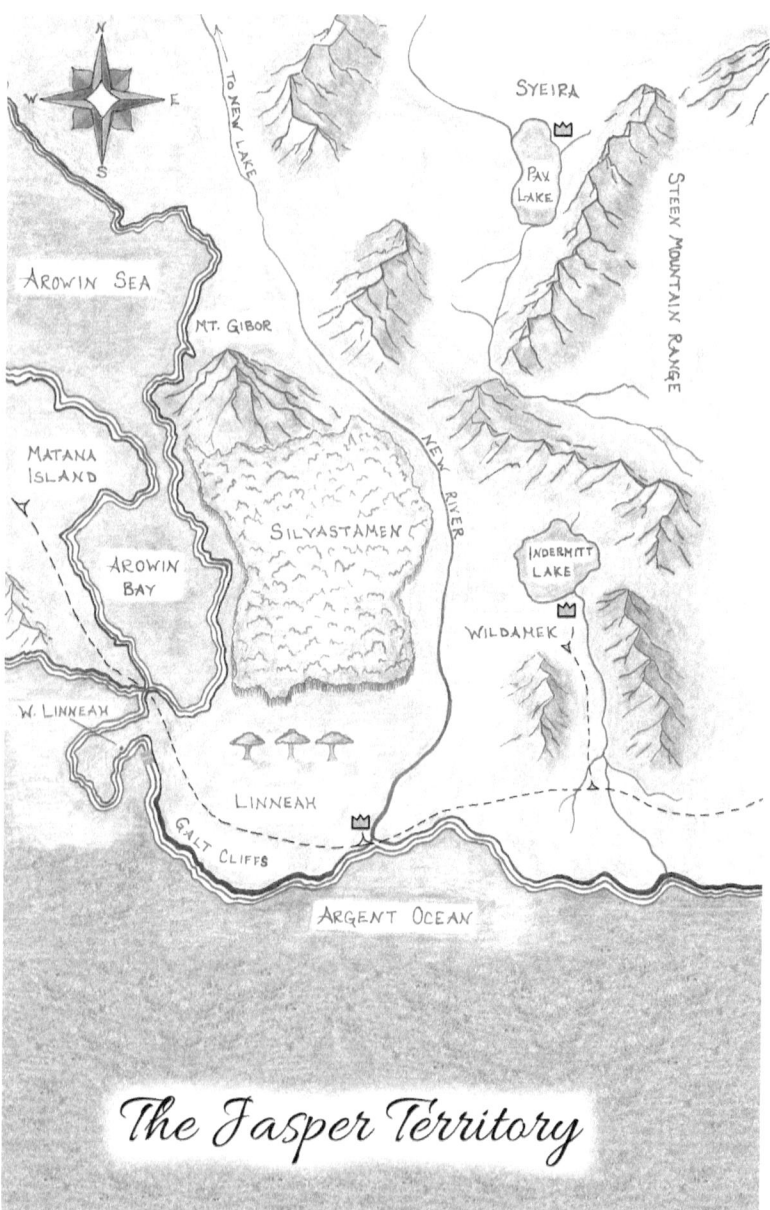

The Jasper Territory

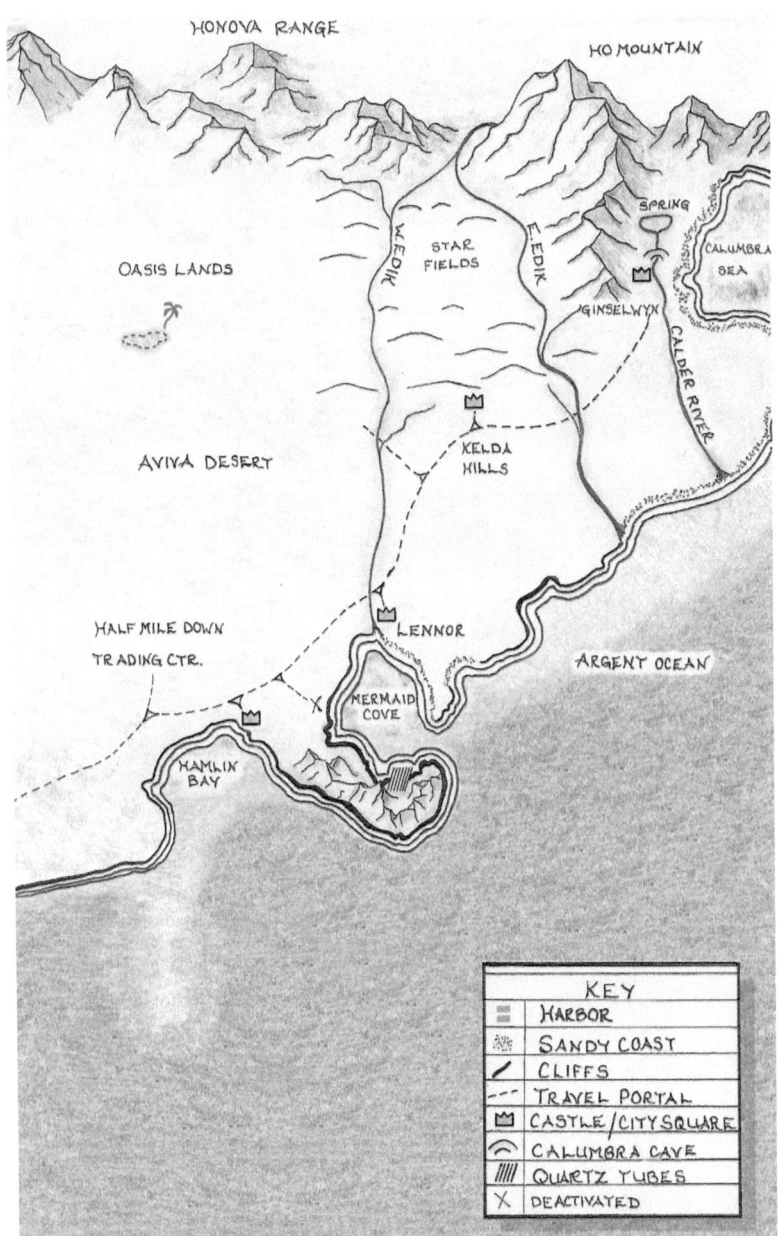

THE FIREBRAND CREED

Elyon within,
Guides my soul,
Leads me on,
Makes me whole.
Fire within,
Ignites my heart,
Lights my way,
My counterpart.

Prologue

THE GUARD, EVAN, SNATCHED Mom's bag and hurried her down the castle hallway as the battle horn sounded again.

"Get my family out too. Harrison? Come on, Brenna." Mom snapped orders like a general as we rushed to evacuate.

Dad popped his head into the hall from a nearby room. "We're leaving now?"

She jerked her head once. He disappeared down the hall, calling my grandparents' names.

Two more guards came running from the other direction. A third, louder call from the horn penetrated the thick stone walls.

"Now! Evacuate the castle!" shouted another guard.

My heart raced, and my stomach cramped. Where was Baldwin? "Baldwin?"

Mom called out, "Contact your griffins!"

I grabbed my bag and headed for the hidden staircase at the end of the hallway.

On my way, I veered into a few rooms, calling Baldwin's name, but one of the guards pulled me into the main hallway and herded me toward the back exit.

"Do not worry, Lady James. No one will be left behind." He led me to a decorative set of shelves hiding the exit.

Arvandus? We're evacuating now. Rune's forces have broken through. Meet me on the back side of the castle as soon as you can.

Almost immediately, he replied, *I am coming, Raven.*

Down the staircase and then through the storehouse, our footsteps stomped like a million feet at a concert. The sound pounded through my chest, mingling with my heartbeat. To my left stood elevated ledges full of containers, keeping preserved goods away from potential water damage. Drying herbs hung from the ceiling, their scent filling the storage area.

More footsteps joined ours, and I glanced back.

Baldwin and another guard clattered down the steps at the very back of our group, and a wave of relief washed through me. The guard at the front pointed to our group. "Put your hoods up. Expect enemy soldiers to be waiting. We will eliminate them while you mount your griffins and cross the river."

Baldwin drew his sword. "I am willing to help."

The guard eyed him for a minute before nodding. "Thank you, Baldwin Marek. You and Evan will cover the queen's family."

At his words, Dad pulled a sword from the scabbard hanging at his waist, and I stared. He saw my expression. "What? I've been taking lessons."

The metal rasp of unsheathing blades rang through the room. Above our heads, raucous yells and boots stamping filtered down to our hiding place. My chest ached. They'd breached the castle.

I sucked in a deep breath before following my grandparents. Several guards flanked Mom and Dad. Baldwin and I followed, shadowed by two more guards. The door leading outside waited in front of us, a portal to freedom. Grandma pushed it open and led us out of our hiding space. The rushing of the New River thrummed in my ears, and we headed north, using brush as cover. Where was the crossover?

Half a dozen Linnean soldiers emerged from a copse of trees, breastplates glinting. "Follow us, my Queen." One of them pointed toward the castle. "The enemy is headed this way."

I peered around Grandpa Takacs. My skin crawled, tension tightening my shoulders. The soldiers drew close, their breastplates wavering, shifting in the fading light. When one lifted his head, a flash of dotted lines became visible before they disappeared, his face once again smooth.

"No! Don't follow them." My voice carried on the evening air, and everyone in our group slowed.

"Someone here is an Illusionbrand." I scanned the group of soldiers. Which one? "And they're using Shadow Power."

"Brenna?" Mom hesitated, her voice strained.

Grandma flipped back her cloak hood, and storm clouds rolled in, their bottoms black and threatening. "I believe her. Evan, Baldwin, protect the Queen!"

The closest soldier growled. "You're mine, old woman." He charged, his Linnean breastplate evaporating. In its place glimmered bronze armor, a palm-sized medallion displaying a gem-encrusted serpent. It looked a lot like the one Baldwin and I had battled a year ago. The insignia of Rune's army.

Grandpa Takacs stepped forward. "Over my dead body." One hand clutched a dagger; the other wielded a bladed bo staff. He blocked the soldier's first thrust.

His sword drawn, Baldwin narrowed his eyes, focusing on the enemy soldiers. I helplessly clutched my sword and waited for one of the soldiers to attack. The loss of my Firebrand talent gaped, a giant hole in my heart.

Rune's soldiers began glowing with a blue light, Baldwin's gift in effect, their swings and thrusts slower than usual. As my grandparents were drawn away from our group, another soldier with dark eyes moved forward, focused on Mom, sword ready.

His movements slowed as he parried my mother's guard. Hail bombarded our group, striking enemy soldiers' heads. In seconds, it evaporated into raindrops. Hmm, there must be a Waterbrand here, too.

Grandma Helen reached up, a sparkling staff of lightning materializing in her grip. She swung it around, and the lightning rod sliced across a soldier's breastplate, a line of glittering sparks in its wake. The rain ceased, and the man stumbled back before renewing his attack. I frowned as the sparkling line faded. He should be dead, but he fought on undeterred. The scent of ozone filled the air.

Fear crawled up my spine.

As one we moved forward, swords flying, deflecting attacks. With a particularly vicious thrust, Grandma Helen sliced through the man's left leg. He crumpled. Without hesitation, she stabbed him in the back before leaving him to die. Grandpa Takacs took down another soldier, his blow knocking aside the enemy's sword before bringing the pommel down on the man's temple.

The four remaining soldiers fought the two guards and us. The other Linnean guards lay dead behind us, dark blood pooling beneath their bodies. A low screech rent the air, followed by a bone-shaking roar as our griffins arrived.

Lev, Campion, and Arvandus each wore a white banner rippling in the breeze. With their massive wings spread, they swooped at Rune's soldiers, who ducked and swung their swords in a useless attempt. One soldier escaped and turned, his eyes finding me like a homing beacon. With a vicious smile, he pulled back his arm and released a throwing star.

Baldwin shoved me aside, and I toppled to my knees. My breath caught in my throat. The star seemed to slow. Each point and angle glinted, defined like a stop-motion shot.

Baldwin raised his sword to knock the star aside. It exploded before it even made contact with his weapon. Fine dust, like sand, swirled around his face. His green eyes dulling, he staggered, then collapsed. As Baldwin's gift disappeared with his consciousness, his attacker gave a triumphant grin and sprinted forward.

The soldier slipped on the damp grass, and the snake medallion on his breastplate fell to the ground. His eyes dark with victory, he ignored it and raised his sword over Baldwin's chest.

"No!" My scream was a living thing, defiant and wild. I moved in, fear blurring my vision. In desperation, my blade found the unprotected side of the soldier's torso, and I plunged the sword in. The soldier's eyes went wide, and I yanked my steel out, blood gushing from his side as he fell. By the time my father reached me, the soldier was dead.

All my anger drained away. I dropped to my knees next to Baldwin's still form.

His cheek was warm against my blood-flecked hand, his eyes closed. Searching, I found the pulse beating in his neck.

My father knelt next to me. "Is he—?"

"He's alive." The words eked past the thickness in my throat. Tremors shook my shoulders, horror taking hold.

With a quick nod, he picked Baldwin up. "I'll take him on Lev, if he permits it."

My grandfather grabbed Grandma Helen's hand. "We will meet you there."

With a swipe of his bladed staff, a glittering split rent the air. I blinked as purples, blues, and sparkling vivid pinks swirled in the void. He waved, and then he and Grandma Helen stepped through the opening and disappeared. The split melted away as if it had never existed.

My heartbeat drummed loud in my ears. What had just happened? It must be shock—had to be.

Mom's voice broke through my daze. "Arvandus is here. Follow us to Syeira, Brenna." She mounted Campion while Dad slung

Baldwin onto Lev before climbing on himself. The two griffins leaped into the air.

Arvandus waited nearby, thousands of silver sparks discharging from his wingtips. *Raven? We must go. Now. More soldiers are coming.*

The gem-encrusted medallion at my feet caught the light. Something made me grab it, and I ran a thumb over the glittering gems. When a tingle zipped through my fingers, I shoved it into my bag. Giving the dead soldier a wide berth, I hurried to Arvandus and climbed on. My griffin launched into the sky.

My mind whirled. What had Grandpa done? His gift must deal with space-time, although I didn't fully understand how it worked. But I'd never seen anything like it. He'd cut the air like fabric. Where it opened, a strange and beautiful space waited.

I winced at a stinging throb in my bicep. Blood dribbled past my elbow and dripped off my wrist. *Arvandus, I'm bleeding.*

How badly?

Um—I'm not lightheaded. I'll wrap a strip of fabric around it to staunch the flow. I curled my hands into the white banner at Arvandus's neck. *What's with the white scarf?*

It marks us as friends of Syeira. The archers will not shoot if they see the material.

Good. One thing I didn't have to worry about.

Ripping off a piece of the scarf, I bound the cut. Despite the relief over my family's safety, my limbs trembled. Baldwin wasn't dead. And that throwing star...it'd been filled with weird yellow dust. Had it been a drug? A poison?

My mind spun for hours, filled with random images, until twilight stole into the dips and valleys of the landscape. The time in the air had done me no favors, nothing to do but think, worry, and obsess over what had gone wrong. Was Baldwin still unconscious?

Brenna, do not worry. Baldwin is a strong young man.

Hey, are you reading my mind?

I do not need to. Your anxiety covers everything like a heavy cloak.

"Well, excuse me for being concerned," I mumbled, low enough so he couldn't hear me.

Clouds shifted, covering the moon in wisps. Weariness stole over me. My eyes drifted closed, but I forced them open, blinking several times. The adrenaline rush had vanished, leaving behind deep fatigue. I focused on the horizon. Just needed to stay awake...

Raven!

I jolted, my eyes flying open. Grabbing the fur at Arvandus's neck, I righted myself. *I'm exhausted. How much farther to Syeira?*

We have several more hours.

I groaned.

We must keep going. Tie yourself to me with the white banner if you must.

I made a mess of it, but I managed to secure myself, then spent the next few hours nodding off.

Brenna, wake up. We are here.

I opened bleary eyes.

Dawn pinked the sky, Pax Lake a small glimmer on the horizon. The water turned a liquid peach as the sun rose. Syeira's thick walls came into view, emerging from a mountainous rise. At its base, a moat-like valley was filled with fog.

I stretched a little. "That's a big city. Is the rest of it in that valley?"

"Only inside the walls. They cannot build in the surrounding valley."

"Why not?"

"Everyone builds on the mountain. The valley holds a thick mist filled with fierce beasts. Or so the stories say."

As we drew closer, the dense mist shifted in the valley but never dissipated. We flew over the city's white walls topped with leafy gardens. Archers stationed among the trees on the roof watched our approach but turned away as Arvandus's white scarf fluttered in the breeze. In the distance, the wall stretched on, encompassing miles of farmland, stone residences, and thriving businesses. An enormous stone castle thrust its turrets into the sky, looming over the smaller buildings clustered at its feet.

It was hard to take it all in—my eyes wanted to do nothing but close.

Arvandus landed near the castle, and a guard approached as I dismounted, his silvery helmet looking like an upended mixing bowl. "Welcome to Syeira."

"Hi. I'm Brenna James, and this is my griffin, Arvandus."

"Ah, the queen's daughter. She will be happy you've arrived. Arvandus, the griffins have been given a field on the northern side of the city. You should have no problem finding it."

Arvandus nodded. "Thank you. I am interested in a long nap."

The guard turned back to me. "My lady, your family arrived earlier and is resting inside the castle."

"Go." Arvandus nudged with his nose. "We can talk later."

I gave him a quick hug before falling in to walk next to the guard. Flat stone sidewalks led to the castle steps.

"Would you like a room, my lady?"

"Yes, please. I'm exhausted. And I need to have someone look at my arm."

He glanced at the pinkish rag wrapped around my bicep. "Hmm, yes, treating your wound should be our first priority."

A servant waited at the main entryway to the castle.

The guard gestured to me. "This is Brenna James, Queen Sarah's daughter. Take her to the infirmary for wound care, then please leave a message for Queen Sarah informing her of her daughter's arrival."

As the guard left, the servant girl turned. "If you'll follow me, please?"

Archways, staircases, and white stone blurred as she hurried me through the castle to the infirmary. At one of the doors, she finally stopped, knocked, and then pushed it open.

A bald man looked up, his eyes unfocused behind a pair of thick glasses, beige jacket hanging open. "Yes?"

"One of the exiles, Brenna James, is here for wound care."

"Ah, of course. Have a seat." He gestured to the nearest bed.

I dropped my bag near the bed and sat. The room seemed empty save for one bed with its white curtain drawn.

"Welcome to Syeira Castle, Brenna James. I am Dr. Winward. Can you tell me what happened to your arm?"

I closed my eyes. So tired. "When we left the castle, enemy soldiers engaged us. One got me with his sword."

"Mm-hmm." He removed the dirty bandage and inspected the long gash. "Well, the bleeding has slowed, but it needs to be cleaned." He gathered supplies. "I'll clean the wound, cover it with salve, and then rewrap it. We'll check it in the morning. Have they given you a room?"

I shook my head. "Not yet."

"We'll have you stay here for the next twenty-four hours for observation, then."

It was just a cut, but if he wanted to keep me here, I wouldn't stop him. After all, the bed was so comfortable. And these sheets...I ran my hand over the petal-soft fabric.

I lay back as instructed. He cleaned and rewrapped my cut with a snowy-white bandage. I must've fallen asleep because I when I woke again, bright sunlight had replaced the glow of dawn. Dr. Winward puttered around the room, muttering under his breath, while another man stood at the foot of the other bed, the curtain slightly open.

"Did they say what happened to him?" he asked.

Apparently, hair was frowned upon here, because every single guy I'd seen so far, including this guy, was bald. He looked at the doctor, his dark brows drawn into a frown.

Dr. Winward glanced up. "Hmm? Oh no, they didn't. Only that it was an unusual weapon filled with strange dust the young man inhaled."

"Not a fatal toxin?"

"No. I'm sure he'll wake up in the next several days. He'll be able to tell us more then."

The doctor turned, and the bald man stepped to the side to write something in a notebook, giving me an unobstructed view. In the bed, Baldwin lay still. His face was pale, and for just a second, I feared he was dead.

It's all my fault...

I slammed my eyes shut as if I could block the thought. But it was. He'd pushed me out of the way—I should be the one in that bed. Curling my fingers into fists, I shoved the thought away. He'd be fine. What had the doctor said? He'd wake up in a few days.

With a jerk, Baldwin sat, opened his eyes, and looked straight at me.

My initial joy faded. Something was wrong, wicked wrong.

No recognition, no emotion, his face completely gray—he looked like one of Rune's men.

A Life Shade.

Chapter One

In the dark night sky, the Petrus Rings blurred while the stars whirled in slow circles. Nitis, my new Syeiran friend, tripped but managed to tumble down gracefully next to me. I took a drink from my bottle and sighed, tension draining from my shoulders.

Just beyond the black metal fence of the public park, two anonymous musicians played drums and an unidentifiable stringed instrument. Singing and music drifted through the darkness.

Nitis shifted next to me. "My father'll never miss these from his store, so drink up. Masdravik!" She clinked her bottle against mine and took a large swallow.

Pressing the bottle to my neck, I sighed as the glass cooled my skin. I was seventeen, legal drinking age. And it wasn't like I was going to drink and drive. In this bottle lurked a fuzzy, comfortable slide that made everything okay, even though nothing was. I took another gulp, the burn scorching my throat before cloying warmth took over.

Nitis pointed her finger at me. "You want me to beat you again tomorrow?"

I snorted at my sparring partner. "Tomorrow night." She'd crushed me this afternoon, but I had plans to return the favor.

Despite getting drunk here only a few times, I told myself it wasn't going to become a habit. Not that anyone noticed.

After the first week of adjustment, Mom and Dad disappeared into meetings with important people—Syeiran royals, generals, and military strategists. I filled my time with sword training, flights with Arvandus, and daily visits to the dungeon. After Baldwin had awoken from the effects of the drug, he'd been confined to a cell.

The Syeirans weren't taking chances with a Life Shade.

Nitis tossed her hair back, blonde curls bouncing. "You know, Deen's planning to stop by tonight. That'll be fun, right?"

His overly round face came to mind. As Syeiran tradition required, he'd recently shaved his head for his eighteenth birthday. It wasn't a particularly good look for him, and he kept offering to allow me to rub his bald head. Ew.

"Fun?" I squinted, noting there were now two of her.

She gave me a sly smile and raised her eyebrows. "Deen said you're pretty. Maybe you could get to know each other."

I took another drink. Baldwin's gray face flashed in my mind. "No, I'm good."

"Hmm." She pressed her lips together. "You still consider that Life Shade your boyfriend?"

Swallowing the defensiveness blocking my throat, I looked away. "He's not a Life Shade. Not really." Even if he wasn't the person I remembered. Even if he was only like that because he'd been protecting me. Stupid, pathetic me, who'd lost her talent and her home.

Tears pushed at the back of my lids. Sheesh. And we'd now reached the emotional part of our evening where I'd cry on Nitis's shoulder. Time to go.

I pushed up and wobbled for a minute, the world unsteady. Through the trees, the bleached stone wall surrounding the city fuzzed into the shadows. I blinked to clear my vision.

"Brenna, forget it. We don't have to meet Deen. We can just relax here."

"No, I've gotta go. See ya tomorrow." I raised the bottle in an awkward salute and turned toward home.

I stumbled up the path leading to the refugee camp, which is what I called the Linneans' temporary houses. They'd been built quickly, although many of them were starting to look more livable. Ours looked the same as it had the day they'd thrown it together. Its rough-cut boards, slanted ceiling, and cramped spaces made for tight living. In rainy weather, the wind whipped under the roof's waterproofed sheeting, and it often came loose.

A stench hit me like a wall, and I held my breath as I passed the large building off to my right—the public restrooms all Linnean refugees shared. It stank until three in the morning, when the city's sanitation system kicked in. Welcome to my new life.

Our house, if you could call it that, was between my grandparents' and Baldwin's parents' houses. Since Grandma Helen and Grandpa Takacs had mended their relationship, they now lived in the same house and often had me over for lunch.

After our flight from Linneah, I'd learned Grandpa Takacs was a Traveler. His gift allowed him to cut and mend space, as well as repair portals. When we'd escaped from Rune's soldiers a month ago, he'd grabbed Grandma, sliced a cut in space, and slipped through it to arrive here quickly.

Reaching our front steps, I sat. It was too late to visit Baldwin, and I wasn't ready to be penned up inside the small-framed building like a rat in a cage. Thankfully, tonight a mild breeze blew. I didn't know what would happen when winter came in a couple of months. Would we still be here?

"Having trouble sleeping?"

I jumped. Baldwin's father, Keel, sat in the shadows at the far corner of his house.

"Something like that."

He shifted in his chair. "I understand."

Keeping my inebriated state to myself, I nodded. I stopped as the dark shadows blurred into smudges.

The small amount of moonlight illuminated Keel's dark hair and brows, which were now furrowed in thought. "I appreciate you visiting my son every day. He hears you. It will bring him back to us." He said it like it was true, a result from repeating it often enough. Maybe he was right.

I shrugged. "I don't mind. I—" I swallowed. *I wish he recognized me. I wish it wasn't my fault. I wish I could've done something to prevent this.* "I just miss him."

"I know, Lady James. I do, too."

We stayed that way for a long time before he rose and went inside. I stayed outside a while longer, content to pretend I was somewhere normal and happy. Anywhere but here.

Our house lay still and quiet, indicating Mom and Dad weren't inside. On a small rise, the castle glowed against the dark night. Helli lights blazed in the many windows, the alcohol distorting the bright squares. Yesterday, my parents had spent their evening holed up in meetings with the generals of the Linnean army. Wherever they were training, it had to be better than this place.

After a few more minutes, I swayed to my feet, and my stomach twisted. I bolted to an area far behind our house and vomited. Dry heaves wracked me until I finally managed to take a deep breath. Why did I do this, when I knew this would be the end result? Just like my questions about everything else, I had no good answer.

When my stomach settled, I stumbled toward the house, up the steps, and into my small bedroom. I took a few sips of water from my canteen before dropping onto the bed. If only the room would stop spinning.

The next morning, I woke late, bright sunlight slipping past flimsy curtains. I lay still in the quiet, my head throbbing. After gingerly getting up, I checked Mom and Dad's sleeping area. The bed's wrinkled blanket implied they'd slept here. I tugged loose the note tucked in the door frame.

I'm sorry we've not been home much, sweetie. Still trying to make arrangements with the king and queen. Should reach a resolution soon. We'll see you tonight. Love, Mom

Make arrangements? What kind? Permanent ones? My heart dropped. I didn't want to stay here forever—this wasn't home. Home was Linneah. As my stomach roiled, I searched the stash of snacks Mom had put in a small cabinet. Jerky, nuts, crackers. I opened the box of crackers and ate a couple. When they settled okay, I swallowed several mouthfuls of water and a dose of medicus syrup for my headache. Another handful of crackers followed. Breakfast was finished.

I carefully hitched my bag onto my shoulder. It held my soap, toothpaste, deodorant, and a myriad of other products that made me presentable. A bathroom stop, a shower, and a good teeth scrubbing would hopefully make me feel more human.

After finishing, I headed back to our cabin. Visiting Baldwin was my first priority this morning. Late evening visits didn't work. I'd come home more depressed and lay awake for hours, dark thoughts whirling. As I drew closer to our shack, someone stood from their lounging position on the steps.

It was Anna.

My mouth dropped open. It'd been weeks since we'd parted ways in Ginselwyn, and I'd thought of her often, wondering if she was okay. I ran up and threw my arms around her.

"You're here! I was so worried, but I couldn't contact you. How are you? How's your family?"

She returned my hug with a fierce one of her own. When she pulled back, tears welled in her eyes. "The island—Rune took it all. Every last inch." Her breath hitched, and she swallowed. "But my family's okay."

I breathed a sigh of relief. "How'd you escape?"

"I stayed in falcon form for as long as possible. My family shifted too and avoided Rune. He was whitecapped because there weren't more people on Matana Island. So he started catching animals and torturing them." Her tears spilled over.

My stomach tumbled. "Wh-what happens when Merripens are tortured?"

She swiped at the tears on her face. "Only the strongest Merripen can withstand pain while holding a shift. Rune killed or imprisoned those who broke their shifts. My parents snapped their scales, and when they found me, we skimmed the blue to Kelda Hills and left everything behind."

I gave her another hug. "I'm so sorry. At least you and your family got out. I would've contacted you, but I couldn't send a fo-li." The light wolves, or foslykos, used to send messages hadn't been in Linneah anyway. The company had evacuated weeks earlier.

She shrugged. "I probably wouldn't have gotten it. Things are storm tossed."

She followed me inside, looking around with interest. "Ooh, it's a tiny house! I always wanted to live in one."

Dropping my bag next to my bed, I screwed up my face. "It's no fun in real life, though. I try not to spend much time here. I need to head to the castle. Want to come?"

"Sure. What's at the castle?"

I gestured for her to follow me outside, and she dropped into step next to me as we hurried up the path toward the massive stone building. "Um, Baldwin."

Or at least someone who looked like him. I forced the explanation past the lump in my throat.

"When Rune invaded Linneah, we tried to escape but were attacked outside the castle. Baldwin inhaled a weird powder, and now he doesn't respond to anyone. But I've been visiting him, hoping I can help him remember stuff." Although it hadn't worked so far. So why did I keep doing it?

"Aw, that's a rogue wave. Did you guys ever make up?"

"Yeah, right after I got home. We talked, and it's all good. But now—" I shrugged, unwilling to verbalize how much I missed him.

Anna gave my shoulders a squeeze. "Don't give up. You guys are perfect together, no drift about it. Do you know if Erhardt is around?"

Speaking of perfect together... I gave her a sideways look and swallowed my smirk. "Why?"

She blushed, but a small smile emerged. "Just wondered."

I pointed north. "He's probably training by the griffin field. He arrived yesterday to meet with the king and queen. Mom and Dad have been talking to them, too. She mentioned discussions about an arrangement with the royals, whatever that is."

"You're skimming the blue anyway, right? For training with Abira."

I bit my lip. Only a few people knew I'd lost my ability to create fire. Baldwin had pulled the secret out of me, and Arvandus knew, but I hadn't shared with anyone else. Going to Kelda Hills to train with Abira didn't make sense if I didn't have my talent anymore. "I'm not sure. I'm planning about five seconds in advance."

She gave me a thumbs-up. "Like waves, all shimmer."

As we climbed the steps to the castle, the sun gleamed off the white stone. At the top of the stairs, two guards waited in gray uniforms and silvery helmets. A design like two intersecting half circles was stitched on their chests. Each man kept one hand on the hilt of his sword.

I gave them a smile, but the tall one on my left stopped me. "Who's your companion?"

"Oh, sorry. This is my friend, Anna."

"We've increased security, Lady James. She may wait here while you visit the dungeon."

"But—"

"Salt it down," Anna said before I could begin pleading. "I'll find Erhardt and catch you later."

"If you're sure."

"Later, wavekeeper." With a nod, she headed down the steps. The guard escorted me through a white filigreed archway and past a tiled courtyard filled with emerald ferns, curtained alcoves, and a sparkling blue pool.

When the guard deposited me at the double doors, the servant girl offered me a friendly smile. After so many weeks of this familiar routine, she permitted me to find my own way to the lowest floor.

Two curved staircases leading to the second floor flanked the airy entryway. White and cream mosaic flooring, as smooth as glass, stretched down the hallway. The same pattern repeated throughout the castle. A helli lantern chandelier hung from the high ceiling. The sun coming through the arched windows made the hanging crystals sparkle and dance.

My footfalls echoed in the quiet hallway. Part of me dreaded this and the other part clung to the ridiculous hope Baldwin would be back to normal. At the end of the corridor, a set of stairs waited. Dodek, the guard stationed at the entrance, gestured me through. I'd gotten to know him well, and as with the servant girl, he permitted me to visit without a supervisor.

A cool breeze smelling faintly of cinnamon wafted through the stairwell. My steps slowed as I heard a voice coming from below. Since Baldwin hadn't spoken for months and he was the only prisoner in this part of the dungeon, he apparently had a visitor.

I hesitated, not wanting to share my time with him. But curiosity drew me.

Padding down the last few steps, I peeked down the corridor. Dread filled me at the gleam of blonde hair. Gari. Of course.

I stalked toward her, anger rising as I noticed her holding his hand through the bars. "Excuse me? I hope I'm not interrupting anything."

She jerked, then schooled her expression into disdain. "Of course not. I am helping Baldwin remember."

Slack jawed and gray, his face held no recollection. In fact, he didn't look at her at all, just stared at the floor.

"It's time for you to leave."

She turned toward me, her hand still clasping his. "Why do you think you can help him remember? The two of us have a history."

I clenched my hands so tightly, my nails bit into my palms. "But we're paired. So I'll ask you one last time to step away before I make you."

Sniffing, Gari dropped his hand. She stepped toward me and offered me a sad smile as she took my fingers instead. "I only wish to save you the heartbreak."

Don't touch me. I opened my mouth to offer the nasty response, but it never materialized. "What do you mean?"

"The Baldwin we know is never coming back. This is who he is now. Are you ready to spend the rest of your life with him in this state?"

My stomach plunged. She was right. He was never, ever going to be the guy I fell for on the castle balcony so many months ago. But we were paired...

Her eyes filled with compassion. "He needs someone willing to invest in his long-term care. I fear you may not have the resources to do so. I can arrange for someone to keep him comfortable, maybe even help him improve, although he will never recover completely."

Tears pushed behind my lids. "You don't know that." I could barely get the words out.

"True. But Life Shade reversal is almost unheard of. Perhaps with a gifted healer, some progress could be made."

Of course. Her father probably had access to the best healers. What if they found a cure? If Baldwin was with me, he wouldn't get better.

"So maybe it would be best if you discontinued your daily visits? I will let him know you are thinking of him, and if improvement occurs, I will be sure you are notified."

"Right. Thanks." I slid my hand from hers, suddenly tired, and turned toward the stairs.

They stretched before me, a towering climb away from the gloom of these cells. The love in my heart would have to be locked up, forgotten. I could never take care of Baldwin the way she could.

My lethargy shifted, the numbness falling away. I cocked my head. But why would I think she could do more for him than I could? As queen of Linneah, my mother could get Baldwin any healer in the Jasper Territory.

Gari's gift! As an Affector, her ability to influence someone was rare and powerful. With a simple touch, I'd been ready to just leave Baldwin here with her.

I spun back around. "I don't think so. Nice try with your talent, Gari, but I'm not leaving. Don't *ever* do that again."

Her features twisted. "He deserves someone better than a crossbreed."

My hands fisted at the racial slur. "He made his choice. I'm done with your interference. He's told you, and now I'm telling you. Leave us alone."

With an eye roll, she brushed past me, her lavender scent swamping me. Her retreating footsteps grew fainter as she climbed the stairs.

Releasing a shaky sigh, I looked up. Baldwin's clear eyes were fixed on me, something close to approval on his face. Was he in there?

As I took a step closer, he did too. His hand reached out.

CHAPTER TWO

"BALDWIN?" MY VOICE CRACKED.

His eyes clouded, and his hand dropped.

My fingertips brushed cold steel bars. "Are you..." My words trailed away as he turned his back on me.

My heart splintering, I stepped back and leaned against the wall. My eyes watered. Back to square one.

More footsteps on the stairs disturbed the moment. It was like Grand Central Station in here.

Ahmik, the physician's assistant, shambled down the steps before stopping at the bottom of the stairs, a black bag in his hand. "Oh, terribly sorry. I didn't realize there were visitors. I'm here to examine the prisoner."

"Well, I just got here. I suppose I could get something to eat and then come back, although I'm not really hungry..." I let my voice trail off, hoping Ahmik would let me stay.

He opened his bag. "Thank you. That would give me ample time to complete the examination."

Up the stairs and back into the hallway, my steps dragged toward the kitchen. King Ohin and Queen Tala had made every effort to make sure the Linneans were taken care of. And although my family hadn't been invited into the royal dining hall, they allowed us to eat in the kitchen. It was better than the setup back at the shack. There, a sheltered cooking area sat off to the side for two families to share. We often shared several meals with Baldwin's parents or my grandparents.

At the kitchen, I snagged a small sandwich from a tray, then continued toward the courtyard. Despite the delicious smell of roasting meat, I wasn't hungry. Seeing Baldwin often had that effect on me. His Life Shade state was just another reminder of everything he'd been, another way I'd screwed things up.

The servant at the door gave me a polite smile, and I stepped onto the white tiled area. I popped the last of the sandwich into my mouth and headed toward the pool. A cerulean blue, it waited in the center of the courtyard, a waterfall splashing at one end. Sheer canopied curtains hung from the four archways surrounding the water. Comfy chairs sat tucked into secluded nooks, bubbling water a pleasant backdrop. A latticed roof kept off the worst of the sun and gave the climbing ivy plenty of real estate.

I fingered a glossy leaf before dropping into a cushioned chair. Disappointment wrapped its fingers around my throat. I struggled to take one breath, then another.

Baldwin was the same every day. Seeing the flash of clarity disappear in his eyes was crushing. Would he ever truly get better? And did I stay with him out of love or guilt? Probably both. If Baldwin didn't recognize me, what did that do to our relationship? I couldn't imagine what his parents were going through.

A woman's voice slipped through my dark mood. "It's been a long time, but it's good to be back for a visit."

My ears pricked. I knew that voice. What was Abira Edan doing here? Wasn't she supposed to be waiting for me to show up in Kelda Hills? I pressed into my seat in an attempt to hide. But in these white upholstered chairs, I was as conspicuous as a pimple on a nose. I wasn't ready to see her, to explain why I'd stayed here instead of going to Kelda Hills like I'd promised.

"Thank you for the escort." She followed the guard to the door, her steps slowing as she caught sight of me. "Brenna? How convenient. You're just the person I wanted to see. How are you?"

I'm living in a shack. My boyfriend is a Life Shade. I lost my gift four weeks ago. "I'm fine. How'd you get here?"

She settled into a nearby chair, her keen eyes studying me. "Outside the city, there's a company that rents hippogriffs to travelers. I flew in on one."

"Oh, well, it's nice to see you." I forced the lie and a smile, my cheeks aching.

"You too. I wondered if you'd forgotten our agreement. A lot's been going on, but I became worried."

"Sorry. I kinda forgot." The second lie slipped out like it was coated in oil. Maybe it became easier to lie every time you did it. Abira deserved more, but I didn't know how to tell her the humiliating truth.

"I also came to visit your mother. Is Queen Sarah here?"

I waved a hand toward the castle. "Probably. I haven't seen her this morning, but her note said she was in talks with the king and queen."

"I'll see if someone can let her know I've arrived. Would you like to have dinner together tonight?"

No. "My friend Anna just arrived this morning."

She stood with a smile. "Well, bring her along. The more, the merrier. I'll see you then."

After she disappeared inside the castle, I sat, mulling over the impossible problem. There was no way I could train with Abira. I'd have to tell her what happened. Yeah, not happening.

I shifted in the chair, and something poked me, digging into my bottom. Reaching into my back pocket, I pulled out the medallion I'd picked up off the ground so many weeks ago. Even with the sun hidden behind the dark-bottomed clouds, the rough crystals glittered. I'd carried it around with me, almost like a good luck talisman.

Unfortunately, it hadn't worked yet.

Brushing off lint, I let my fingers trace the dazzling serpent. I wanted to hate it, especially since it was from one of Rune's soldiers. But the tiny gems were gorgeous. As I brushed my fingers across the sparkling design, an electric tingle shot through my palm. Flinching, I studied the medal before giving up. They were beautiful crystals, but that was all. Maybe it was dumb hope that caused me to keep it.

I slipped the medallion into my pocket and wandered down to the dungeon, hoping Ahmik was done. Although dark-gray clouds promising rain littered the afternoon sky, in the dungeon, several helli lanterns were lit. Their soft glow lent the dark room some warmth.

As I reached the bottom of the stairs, Ahmik closed his bag. "Impeccable timing, Lady James. Unfortunately, I have bad news. Lord Marek must be transferred to a different facility. There are so few treatments for those in his condition."

The words slammed into my stomach, hollowing me out. "But—but you can't. I mean, there's got to be something that will help."

The assistant glanced away before looking back at me, his eyes sorrowful. "The only known treatment, a Remembrance Ceremony, is rare and dangerous. He must link with someone close to him who knew him well."

Hope streaked through my heart like a blazing comet. "How does it work?"

Ahmik stroked his chin before walking to Baldwin's cell. Baldwin stared at the brick wall, his back to us. "During the Remembrance Ceremony, he and the other person, called a Connector, join hands. We place a bowl of healing herbs on Lord Marek's chest. Then the Connector links their energy and memories with his. The connection sparks the neurons in his brain to help him regain what was lost."

Silence fell in the dungeon, and tension tightened my shoulders. Sounded like a bunch of bunk, but if it worked...

His voice interrupted my thoughts. "The mental condition of the Connector can be severely compromised if the ceremony is unsuccessful. So you can see why it's not attempted often. Our only other option is to have him transferred." He turned to walk away.

"Wait." I couldn't let Baldwin be moved. Something deep inside told me I'd never see him again. "I'll do it."

Ahmik's heavy brows climbed his forehead. "You'd do this for him?"

"Yes. If you think it'll help him. But—"

"Yes?" The assistant's eyes never wavered.

I frowned. "Why didn't Dr. Winward ask his parents?"

Ahmik cleared his throat and lowered his eyes. "They are, uh, elderly. The Remembrance Ceremony works best with younger participants. Usually siblings. Despite the lack of a family link, your regard for him should be enough. Are you available to do it now?"

I nodded, pushing aside thoughts of being brain dead. This was my way to pay him back for saving me. If he hadn't pushed me out of the way, I would've been the Life Shade. Glancing at his cell, I flinched. His hands white knuckled around the bars as he laser focused on us.

The assistant's voice pulled my attention from Baldwin. "I'll call for a guard to transfer him to the infirmary immediately, then."

After a brief wait, a guard with no neck and massive shoulders unlocked Baldwin's cell and escorted him to the infirmary, Ahmik and I trailing behind.

The empty infirmary offered plenty of room for our entourage. In the sterile room, the guard helped Ahmik secure Baldwin to the bed with straps. The patient wasn't happy about it. His teeth clenched, Baldwin strained against the binding, his muscles bulging.

"Baldwin, it's fine." I stepped closer.

His glare would've peeled paint off a building, but I reached out a hesitant hand anyway. He grabbed my wrist and yanked me close.

I gasped, and the guard seized Baldwin's arms.

A sneer twisted Baldwin's lips before he released my wrist and turned his head away.

Ahmik shook his head. "I don't believe this will work. The patient is too erratic."

"No, this will work." I turned to Baldwin. "Please, I want to help you. Just let us do this so you can get better." My voice cracked on the last word.

He stilled. His eyes were the same, clear emerald green. But his skin remained gray and dead. Most of all, the person inside, the responsible, thoughtful, humorous guy who could set me at ease with a simple phrase was gone, buried under layers of poisonous dust.

I gave the guard a shaky smile. "Let him go. Maybe he's calmed down enough."

Rain slashed against the windows of the infirmary, and water came down in sheets outside. Ahmik hurried to the counter to gather ingredients.

The guard looked at me, hesitant. "You sure, Lady James?"

Baldwin's stare was unrelenting, but my fear eased. He wouldn't hurt me. "Yes. Go ahead."

The guard slowly released his hold, then pointed to the door. "I'm not moving beyond this doorway. He's too dangerous."

Ahmik spoke up. "I'm terribly sorry, but when we begin the ceremony, you'll have to stand outside the door. Only those involved should be in the room."

Fidgeting, I ran my fingers over the medallion hidden in my pocket. If I ever needed a stroke of good luck, it was now. After an extra minute, Ahmik strolled over and carefully placed the bowl of herbs on Baldwin's chest.

Baldwin stiffened, his nose wrinkling.

I sniffed, the scent sharp and pungent. "What's in the bowl?"

"Healing herbs. Lavender, bacopa mint, and trill root." The assistant gestured to me. "You stand here, behind his head, and hold his hands."

I did so, Baldwin's fingers closing over mine in a firm grip. I hoped he couldn't see up my nose. Right. Like that mattered.

Ahmik gestured to the guard. "Please wait in the hallway."

The guard shot him a glare before he looked at me. "If you need me, Lady James, I'll be on the other side of the doorway."

I nodded. As he left, silence fell.

With a reassuring smile, the assistant continued. "Now, I want you both to close your eyes. Lord Marek, try to clear your mind of everything. Imagine a blank canvas for all of Lady James's memories."

I shook my head. "Not all."

"What?" Ahmik gave me a dark look.

"He doesn't need all my memories. Not all involve him."

"Oh." The man's face smoothed. "Of course. But you need to open your mind, to be a free channel for him. All his neurons need are a push from you."

A trickle of unease slid down my neck. Being anxious about this was silly. After all, Ahmik was a doctor's assistant. Baldwin needed this. I couldn't heal him without my talent, but this ceremony was the next best thing.

Closing my eyes, I allowed the thrumming of rain against the window and the sure grip of Baldwin's hands to relax me. Open and free.

"Your mind is very cluttered, Lady James. Break down those mental walls. You need to share your memories with Lord Marek."

I cracked open one eye to glare at the annoying assistant. "Working on it, okay, bud?"

"My name is Ahmik."

Right.

Closing my eyes, I tried again. Clear and accessible. Like the travel portal tunnels, only instead filled with all the times Baldwin and I had shared. The memories burst forth—when we first met on the balcony, sparring together as I learned how to wield a sword, the trip through Silvastamen, both of us at the Shaverim Festival, the look in his eyes before we kissed.

The memories surged like water through a dam, and anxiety bit down. Too fast. What was going on?

Trying to slow the gush of thoughts, to think about something else, became impossible. Somewhere in the background, Ahmik muttered a swirl of dark words. An ache built at the base of my skull, sinister magic piling up in the room. Tendrils of agony spread, and I clenched my jaw. A moan slipped from between my gritted teeth.

At a crash from my right, my eyes flew open. My stream of memories slowed, sluggish drips leaking to another dimension.

"Stop!" Abira stood in the doorway, her eyes as bright as the twin balls of orange flame in her hands. Behind her stood the guard, his eyes wide.

The assistant stopped speaking. Images began flowing in reverse, filling the dead spaces in my mind with blurred colors and words, memories running together.

She unleashed one fireball near Ahmik. He ran for cover, even as the fire died a quick death on the tile floor. The guard cornered him near an empty bed, where Abira clutched his shirt and dragged him to the center of the room. As soon as she released him, she freed the other ball of fire, which morphed into a fence of flames. He clutched his arms to his body as the fire flickered around him.

The guard moved closer and unsheathed his sword, his steely eyes fixed on Ahmik.

She hurried over to where I stood next to Baldwin, our hands linked, then reared back as she caught sight of Baldwin.

"Saints and sinners, what did he do to you?" Grimacing, she removed the bowl from his chest before turning to me. "Brenna, are you injured?"

"Ungh." My fingers stuck to Baldwin's, my mind numb. My tongue didn't work.

Moving closer, she danced her fingers over my skull. Whispered prayers of healing wrapped around me as her fingers sifted through my hair. After a minute, the agony melted away, my mind cleared, and memories clicked into place. Without warning, my knees buckled, but she caught me, placing me in the nearby chair.

She then turned to Baldwin and pressed her hand to his brow. Several minutes passed as she muttered, her eyes closed. She undid the straps holding him to the bed and brushed a hand over his forehead. I caught her quiet words. "Elyon help you. Just rest."

Baldwin said nothing.

With a quick glance at me, probably to ensure I hadn't dissolved into a helpless puddle, she stalked over to Ahmik, who cowered in the circle of endless flame.

"I wonder if King Ohin and Queen Tala know they have an infiltrator in their employ."

The man's eyes flashed. "I did nothing wrong."

"Wiping the minds of two young people clean is your idea of innocent behavior?" Abira's hands curled into fists.

He gave her a malevolent glare. "They would have thanked me. I foresee their deaths, excruciating and bloody as they fight a losing battle for the wrong king. What about you, Abira Edan? Are you ready?"

At his words, a shudder wracked my frame. Without Abira, Baldwin and I would be empty husks. But was Ahmik telling the truth? What was waiting in our future? My head throbbed as dread settled across my shoulders.

"Abira!" Dr. Winward walked into the infirmary, his eyes widening. "How did—what happened?"

"Jivin." With a small smile of surprise, she met him and gave him a hug.

His cheeks flushed. "It is so good to see you. It's been too long."

"It has. But you look as handsome as ever."

I raised my eyebrows. Abira had a boyfriend? Or was he an ex? Maybe I was hallucinating... I rubbed at the ache lingering at my temples, my thoughts wispy like spun sugar.

Jivin's flush deepened, and he cleared his throat. "I assume you are responsible for the fire surrounding Ahmik."

"Yes. Your assistant just attempted a Forgetting Ceremony on this young man and Lady James."

Dr. Winward's face went pale. "Ahmik, why would you do that?"

The man said nothing, his face set in stony lines.

With a twitch of her wrist, Abira sent the flames higher, some of them licking close to the assistant's face. "Who are you working for?"

"No one, argh! You're burning me." Ahmik twisted, pulling away from the flames.

Abira's gray eyes glittered. "Tell me, or you'll suffer worse."

Chapter Three

Baring his teeth, Ahmik grunted. "The only true lord of this world, Prince Rune."

At his admission, Abira dropped the height of the flames but kept the fire fence intact. She turned to Dr. Winward. "We must notify the king and queen. Can you call for another guard?"

"Yes, absolutely. And my dear, your firework is fabulous, as always." He squeezed her hand before leaving to find help.

In moments, two muscled guards led a sputtering Ahmik down the hallway. I didn't move, just relaxed in the chair and allowed things to happen around me. Baldwin sat up and ran a hand over his face. I couldn't help but notice his face was less gray, his cheeks tinted with color.

When Dr. Winward and Abira retreated to a corner to talk, Baldwin shifted toward me, his legs over the edge of the bed, our knees almost touching. He cleared his throat. "I, uh, I am not sure what happened. We are in Syeira, right?"

Despite the relief filling me, my mind was oatmeal. I rubbed my forehead. "You gotta give me a minute." After a few seconds, I released a sigh. Longest day ever. "Okay, what's the last thing you remember?"

He was quiet a moment. "I have a lot of missing pieces. I remember a throwing star filled with mist. I think I blacked out. The next thing I remember is being in a cell. And anger. An all-consuming anger at everyone and everything."

"Rune turned you into a Life Shade. The mist was poisonous dust. I saw you wake in the infirmary, but you were already gone. There was no recollection in your eyes."

He frowned. "I remember your visits. You were crying."

Sheesh. Of all the things to remember, he remembered that? "You didn't seem to recognize anyone."

"It was weird, like someone or something else was controlling me. I had two sides—the normal me and the angry me. The anger seemed to grow stronger every day. Probably because of the medication Ahmik gave me."

My mouth dropped open. "What?"

Baldwin's mouth twisted. "Every time he examined me, he gave me an injection."

"I'm so sorry. I didn't know."

"You do not have to apologize." He reached for my hand.

I recoiled, then placed my hand in his.

He bit his lip. "Did I, um, did I hurt you?"

"No." I hurried to explain. "But I never knew how you would react. Sometimes it seemed like you recognized me."

"I did. But talking was impossible. The drug gave me plenty of energy but warped my thoughts."

Already the skin stretching across his palm had more color, his nails flesh colored as the gray receded. Joy and anxiety fought for dominance in my chest. "I'm glad you're back. I missed you."

He didn't have time to answer. Abira walked over. "Jivin says the powder only blocked memories. It was yellow, right?"

Baldwin took his time answering. "Yes. I think so. You should check his bag, though. He was giving me injections with every examination. I assume it is a different drug."

She frowned. "Rune has developed plenty of new drugs. Rumors are the dust is being used to abduct men to fight in his army. I'm sure Ahmik planned to wipe Brenna's mind with the ceremony and deliver you both."

I shuddered. I'd never seen a female Life Shade, but I was so glad I didn't get to be the first.

Baldwin tilted my hand back and forth. "Your hands are shiny."

"What?" Welcome to Stupid Central. Information seeped in, only to register minutes later.

"Your hands," he repeated. "They are sparkling."

Twisting my wrist back and forth, I watched the particles reflect the light. "Your hands glitter, too."

Abira grabbed our hands and rubbed them. "What did he put on your hands? A connective tonic?"

"No, nothing."

After a few brushes, she released them. "Were you touching something glittery that perhaps transferred to your hands?"

"Um...oh!" Reaching into my pocket, I pulled out the medallion. A familiar tingle zipped through my fingertips, clearing my mind like a brisk fall breeze. I handed it over. "I picked this up from one of Rune's dead soldiers weeks ago. For some reason, I couldn't leave it behind."

Abira turned it in her hands, running a finger over the sparkling design, before pulling away. Glistening dust shimmered on her fingertip. Her eyes widened. "Well, now I know why you two recovered so quickly. These crystals are filled with power."

"Another one of Rune's toys?" I asked.

Abira shook her head. "It's strong. It feels a bit like the power stored in jaspers."

I tilted my head. "Where would his army get something like that?"

Baldwin's eyes lit up. "The Stones of the Spring. Rune took them. Maybe he divided them among his fighters. Would these medallions give them more strength in battle?"

Abira handed the ornament back to me. "That would be my guess."

While Baldwin and Abira continued to talk, I clutched the medallion in my fist. If Abira was right, these powerful gems should be able to heal me. I closed my eyes and focused, imagining a fireball in my palm. When nothing happened, I tried again, sandwiching the medallion between both hands.

A black void of nothingness met my concentration. No return of power. I was freakishly alone, a dull stone in a world full of jewels. My boyfriend and my teacher had already forgotten me as they talked. My talent was gone and wasn't coming back. I swallowed hard.

Tears dammed up in my throat, and I stood to leave. I wouldn't cry in front of everyone, regardless of what Baldwin had already seen.

Dr. Winward joined Abira and Baldwin's conversation, and I slipped out the infirmary door. Forcing the lump down my throat, I hurried for the seclusion of the courtyard. One section farther away from the pool held tall, leafy plants and long curtains offering shade. It would be the perfect place to fall apart.

To my relief, it was empty. I slumped into a chair and buried my face in my hands. Would I ever get over losing my gift? Unlikely, since the loss reduced me to tears. Every. Time.

I blotted my face with my sleeve and leaned forward, my long hair like another curtain. Maybe I should contact Arvandus for a ride. But even that held little appeal.

Minutes later, footsteps caught my attention, and I froze like a rabbit. I didn't know why I bothered. It never worked for rabbits.

Abira slipped into my secluded alcove and sat next to me. "This is a relaxing nook."

"Hmm. Yeah." Or it had been until she showed up.

"Jivin is keeping Lord Marek in the infirmary until tomorrow for observation."

I nodded but remained silent. Maybe if I didn't encourage a conversation, she'd go away.

That hope dissipated like fog on a sunny morning when she leaned forward. "Why didn't you come to Kelda Hills?"

I kept my face blank, hoping she wouldn't notice my tears. Discomfort crawled through my stomach. "I told you. I forgot."

"Of course. I'd forget a promise like that, too. Especially since someone was expecting you."

"You're not my mom." I snapped the words.

"I didn't say I was. But we made arrangements, and then I heard nothing. I was worried."

"Life got a little more complicated than I expected."

"Yes, I understand. That's why I waited before coming to see you." Her voice sharpened. "But here you are, with nothing but time on your hands. So maybe I misunderstood your level of commitment to the training?"

Anger flooded my chest, with only one way to go—out. "It doesn't matter, because it's gone, okay? Gone. I have no talent, no ability. I'm just a freak, with a weird streak in my hair that means nothing!" I thrust the chair back as I jumped to my feet, and it fell with a clatter. "So I can do whatever I want, wherever I want, for however long I want. Cause it doesn't matter!" *I don't matter. I. Don't. Matter.*

It repeated with every beat of my heart.

She stood. "What do you mean you have no talent?"

Arms crossed, I turned away and bit my lip. After a few moments, I managed a deep breath and faced her. "When I removed the second Dunamis in Ginselwyn, something happened. Now I can't do anything—I can't heal, I can't produce fire. Nothing."

Abira's eyes went wide. "Perhaps you needed time to recover. Have you tried recently?"

Setting my jaw, I held out my palm. A warm breeze danced past my arm, and a tingle fizzed across my fingers, but my palm remained empty. Standard operating procedure. I dropped my hand and turned to pick up the chair.

Abira pursed her lips. "When you use your gift, what goes on in your head?"

I stared at her for a second, then shook my head. "Nothing. I just do it."

She cocked her head. "Have you always used your talent that way?"

"I think so."

She gestured to the chairs we'd just vacated. "Have a seat."

Puzzled, I sank into my chair. Where was the disbelief? The yelling? Instead, she gave me curiosity, questions, and a calm acceptance.

"Your missing gift has nothing to do with the Dunamis or the depression you're dealing with."

"I'm not depressed."

She raised one eyebrow. "Of course not. As I was saying, its absence doesn't have anything to do with your current situation. Have you changed your mind about training?"

"No, but I can't do anything. I'm useless." I could barely get the words out.

Her gray eyes were steady. "No. Even if you never use your gift again, Elyon still considers you valuable. When you would attempt to heal, Brenna, where did the power come from?"

Duh. "From Elyon. Right?"

"That's correct. So you asked Him for the power every time?"

I snorted. "If I was in trouble or trying to stay alive, there wasn't time."

"Yes, but what about when you were working in the infirmary?"

"Well, the talent was just there."

She paused. The silence built. Then, "Brenna, when was the last time you asked for Elyon's assistance rather than relying on your own physical power?"

"All the t—"

"Stop. Think about your answer, because it isn't 'all the time.'"

I opened my mouth. Closed it. Thought back. And couldn't remember when I'd specifically asked for help healing or fighting.

When I looked at Abira, she shook her head. "You can't do it all on your own. You have a natural talent. But if learning more Firebrand skills is the path you want to take, it will require a massive amount of power, more than you have."

The yearning I'd pushed aside for months roared back, so intense my hands shook. "It's what I want."

"Then acknowledge the Author of your talent. When you can, connect to the power available to you. If you want your ability to return, my guess is a simple 'I'm sorry' will suffice. Forgiveness is Elyon's specialty." She patted my knee, then stood. "See you this evening."

Openmouthed, I slumped into my chair as she walked away. No way would it be that easy. Hadn't I asked before? My thoughts raced back to the battle last year. There had been a lot of attention and admiration from the Linneans for the way we'd handled the enemy soldiers. Maybe I'd begun to think I was a Big Deal.

Raven? I need to stretch my wings. Would you care to join me?

My griffin's message pushed aside my conversation with Abira. It had been awhile since I'd seen Arvandus or flown with him.

Sounds good. I'm coming.

The hole in my heart where my talent resided gaped with an almost physical ache, driving home how much I'd lost. I reached in my pocket for my jasper as I headed for the griffin house. Aside from some pocket lint, my fingers came up empty.

Of course. Because I'd stopped carrying the reminder of my AWOL ability.

After I'd used it on the last Dunamis, I'd worried it had been damaged. But the gem had glittered as usual, its facets sparkling. I frowned, casting back to when I'd seen it last. Maybe a week ago. I'd put it in my bag for safekeeping. Even if it didn't work, I didn't want to lose it.

I drew close to one of the gates. The Syeiran's wall had eight securely locked gates, spaced evenly throughout the city. Everyone, even the smallest child, knew the stories of what existed beyond.

The Beasts of the Mist stories varied—they sported sharp teeth and glowing eyes, or four-inch claws and a shadowed face, or long fur matted with the scent of blood and decay. The stories always ended with someone's injury, disappearance, or death.

Thankfully, I'd never heard of an incident inside the city. But the horrifying stories, along with the mist, made this spot an out-of-the-way, secure place to plan our return to Linneah. If that's what Mom was doing.

Each gate looked like the next—black iron bars with a heavy latch set in a white marble arch. At shoulder height, a fist-sized padlock secured the latch. Beyond, mist swirled and ebbed, hiding terrifying creatures.

Before I hurried on, a glimmer pierced the mist. Hesitating, I edged closer to the gate. What shone beyond the gloom? Was someone crazy enough to walk through the mist with a lantern? I squinted.

What if it was a glowing monster? I hadn't heard of that variation, but there was always a first time.

A scream lodged in my throat as a form detached from the haze. A muscular man with long white hair and an even longer sword strode toward the gate. His simple shirt and pants gleamed, the light surrounding him blazing. Without pausing, he marched directly *through* the iron bars, his eyes fixed on me.

My heart raced. I was so dead.

The Beast of the Mist was a warrior, ready to pillage cities and take prisoners.

Chapter Four

THE WARRIOR HELD OUT a hand to keep me from bolting. "Greetings, Brenna the Firebrand. May Elyon's blessings be yours."

My mouth opened, but it was a second before I squeaked a coherent sentence. "Who are you?"

"I am one of the Sahale, Elyon's messengers. You are to train for the coming evil. Elyon needs fighters."

I shook my head. "Sorry. I don't have my gift."

The warrior tilted his head. "The raven's share may strengthen or weaken, but it never disappears. Elyon's gift to you will always be enough." He held out his hand. In his palm blazed my jasper, its red center a living fire. "It is available, as is Elyon's forgiveness. Do you desire them?"

How did he get that? My mouth opened and closed, but I only held out my hand. The warrior dropped the jasper and its glistening chain into my palm.

I clenched my fingers around the jasper and bit my lip. After so many disappointments, I was afraid. But this was different. If I'd been forgiven, my gift would be there. "I'm sorry. I screwed up."

The warrior's eyes glowed silver. "Elyon loves you. You only need to trust Him."

With a deep breath, I slipped the jasper over my head. I closed my eyes, searching for the reservoir of power that used to lie within. *Please? I'm sorry, and I messed up, but I'm trying. Really.*

Moments later, a small, warm flame filled my hand. It was Christmas and Easter and several birthdays all wrapped into one shining, amazing moment. I stared at the gift that had rested beyond my reach for months. Letting the flame wink out, I bit down on my welling emotion, my insides quivering.

The Sahale's eyes were a gray fire. "The mission will be dangerous. Do you accept this call?"

"Yes." My stomach dropped. I'd already faced a lot of dangers, including a few that had almost killed me. What else was waiting for me?

"Be strong, Brenna the Firebrand." With nothing more, the warrior turned, passed through the gate like a ghost, and disappeared into the mist.

I headed toward the griffin house, my thoughts whirling. Since my gift had returned—and I still felt tentative about it—I had no reason to delay my trip to Kelda Hills with Abira. When I fought Rune next time, I needed to be ready.

As a fellow Firebrand, he was lightyears ahead of me. His trainer had probably been some super-genius Firebrand, who had hopefully moved far away or was dead. No way could I fight two powerful Firebrands like that in battle.

Arvandus rested outside the griffin house. Made of distressed wood, the weathered structure stood two stories high. All the griffins had their own stall, although the quarters were smaller than what they were used to.

I approached him. "Hey. Ready for a short flight?"

His nose twitched. "You reek of alcohol, Raven."

My intention to tell him about the Sahale warrior's visit vanished in a flare of irritation. "What?"

He shook his head. "When you drink to excess, the stench seeps from your pores. This is the second time this week. I cannot make you stop, but it is troubling that you continue your destructive behavior."

I was already tuning him out. "Are you going to lecture me, or can we fly?"

He knelt. "Would you like to talk about it?"

"I'd rather not. It's just something I do to relax."

"To forget, you mean."

I jerked, stunned into silence as we took to the air. *That's not why I do it.*

Yes, it is. You are sad. Things have not been easy. But Raven, drinking does not make things better. Your problems will still be waiting when you are done.

Rather than respond, I redirected. *Speaking of problems, two have been resolved. Earlier this morning, Abira arrived. After a heart-to-heart, I found a Sahale. Or rather, he found me and offered me a second chance. So now my talent's back.*

That is excellent news. I know the exodus of your talent worried you.

By the way, how would you feel about going to Kelda Hills?

For more training? I have heard rumors of many people journeying there for training. I think it is a wise move.

The next nugget of information would tick him off, but he needed to know. With a deep breath, I told him what had happened this morning in the infirmary. Silver sparks trailed from his wings like tiny comets as he climbed higher.

His response didn't surprise me. *If I see Ahmik, I will eat him for supper.*

You can't go around eating people, Arvandus. The king and queen will take care of him.

Late afternoon sun gilded the city, touching everything with a golden sheen. To the west, farmers harvested crops of vegetables and late-season grain. A herd of small cows called *vaccarus* grazed in a nearby field. Even with the sun, fog obscured the landscape beyond the thick city walls. Archers kept watch at their wall-top stations. We remained within the city's boundaries since Arvandus wasn't wearing the white scarf that marked us as friends of Syeira.

When we were done with our flight, he dropped me off at the castle.

I dismounted and turned to him. "If you see Anna, can you tell her to meet me at the house?"

"She is here?"

I buried my fingers in his thick fur and scratched his neck. "She stopped by for a visit. She's living near Kelda Hills now. I'll see if I can find Mom and Dad to tell them about leaving."

At the castle entrance, I was escorted across the courtyard and permitted inside. I turned to a nearby servant. "Can you tell me where Queen Sarah and Advisor Harrison are?"

The young boy gestured down the hallway. "They are still in conference with the royal family. Is it an emergency?"

"No, that's okay. I'll visit the infirmary." Baldwin needed to be told about my plans, too. I didn't like leaving this quick after his recovery, but he'd understand. As a Time Reeler, he'd probably be interested in learning more about his talent too.

When I entered the infirmary, Baldwin stood in an empty bay. His body flowed like water as he moved through a series of martial arts stretches.

Dr. Winward shook his head. "I don't know if I can keep him here for twenty-four hours. He doesn't want to rest."

Baldwin paused. "I rested plenty in that disgusting cell." He finished the set, then gave me a warm smile. "I wondered where you went."

My heart fluttered. I'd waited weeks to see that expression. "I went for a ride with Arvandus. I came back since I didn't want you to be bored."

Dr. Winward made a couple of quick marks in a notebook. "Oh, no chance of that. Lord Marek has been very popular."

"Really?" I narrowed my eyes when Baldwin blushed.

"Kersen stopped by." He mentioned his best friend and shrugged. "And after he left, Gari showed up."

Already? I'd only been gone an hour. "That's nice." Not.

At my flat tone, he took my hand. "It was awkward, and she left shortly afterward. I still do not know why she stopped by."

Because she was annoying and hard to get rid of. Like a fungus. I bit my cheek and tried valiantly not to say anything nasty. Why wouldn't his ex give up already? She didn't listen when Baldwin had told her weeks ago he wasn't interested, and she hadn't listened to me.

"I don't think I need to answer that for you. You're a smart guy. But I wanted to let you know, I'm probably going to leave with Abira for training."

"And what about, you know? Did it come back?"

"Yeah." I shot Dr. Winward a side glance, unwilling for this stranger to hear everything. "I'll tell you about it later."

"When do you leave?"

I shrugged. "I'm not sure. I haven't told Abira about my decision. I wanted to find Mom and Dad to ask them about it."

"I can walk with you, although no races through the hallways."

I grinned. "Got it."

He glanced at Dr. Winward, who nodded his approval. "Return immediately if any symptoms resurface."

Baldwin agreed, and we hurried from the room. We fell into step side by side, our footsteps echoing in the long corridor.

After a moment, Baldwin glanced at me before studying the hallway. "Thanks for visiting as often as you did."

I bit my lip. "Your dad was sure you could hear me."

"I could. I just was unable to reply. It was the worst part. That and being unable to hold you when you cried." He cleared his throat. "I hated that. It tore me up."

My breath caught, and I squeezed his hand in reply.

Before we could say more, a door on my left swung open. The guards on either side stepped back, and Mom and Dad exited, followed by King Ohin and Queen Tala. None of them looked very happy.

As Mom spotted the two of us, the pinched look on her face disappeared. "Baldwin! Praise Elyon! You've recovered."

He bowed. "Thank you, Queen Sarah."

She smiled. "We should celebrate. Would you both like to come to supper with us?"

"Can Anna come too?" I asked, remembering my previous plans.

"She's here? That's good. Is her family here as well?"

"No, but they all escaped and are living in Kelda Hills."

The approach of another person captured Mom's attention. "Abira Edan! It's nice to see you."

Abira gave an elegant curtsy. "A pleasure, Queen Sarah. I came to see you and Brenna about further training. I'm sure the last month has been chaotic."

Mom glared at the disappearing figures of the king and queen of Syeira. "Yes, it has."

Dad stepped forward and blocked them from her gaze. "It appears we have a lot of people here. Why don't we throw together a picnic at our house?"

I smiled. "That sounds like a great idea."

Chapter Five

By the time Dad and Grandpa Takacs returned from the market with several bags of food, a small gathering milled in front of our ramshackle house. Grandma Helen and Baldwin's mother Mariel shaped the meat into patties, while Abira cut thick slices of bread and talked in low tones with Mom. Erhardt and Anna hadn't arrived yet. I cut a large block of cheese into chunks while Baldwin put out plates and utensils.

We soon found a private spot away from the crowd with Lev and Arvandus. After we settled, I told them about my visit from the Sahale.

Baldwin's eyes went round. "Amazing. Was it the same one who told you about the First Prophecy?"

"No, this time it was a warrior guy with a huge sword."

"Very cool."

"Yeah. It kinda worried me, though, when he mentioned danger. I mean, we attacked a serpent, fought Talus, and battled Rune's forces. What's next?"

Baldwin leaned back. "You cannot worry like that. Perhaps he only meant war is dangerous. Just do your best while training with Abira."

After a while, the aroma of roasting meat floated on the breeze. Arvandus growled. "The scent of the roast is powerful. We must hunt."

"They're burgers."

He gave me an impassive look, and I waved him on.

With a leap, Arvandus and Lev took to the air, their powerful wings carrying them higher until they were mere specks in a blue sky.

Baldwin put an arm around my shoulder. "As soon as I regain my strength, I might travel to Kelda Hills as well."

"Really? What for?"

"I have been considering training too. An instructor there is looking for Time Reelers." He frowned and looked at the ground.

"That's a good thing, right?"

"Yeah, but—I am sure it is nothing." He attempted to smile. "Being in a cell for four weeks did me no favors."

"Well, today was rough. You'll bounce back. I'd be thrilled to have you in the same city."

He kissed my cheek. "That affects my decision as well."

"Dinner is served!" Grandpa Takacs's voice carried to our spot behind the house.

We filled up on sliced bread, roasted burgers with a tangy cheese sauce, crunchy veggie crisps sold by the bagful at the market in town, a fruit platter, and an entire tray of Kunkelsteuchen for dessert, which made my taste buds do the happy dance.

Afterward, as darkness fell, everyone talked and visited, using blankets, chairs, cushions, whatever they could find as a seat. A small fire flickered in the center of the gathering. Baldwin sat on my left, talking to Erhardt and Anna, who'd arrived right before the meal.

Abira claimed the other seat next to me. "If you're still interested, I'd like to start your training."

"Right now?"

She rolled her eyes. "No, but I'd like to leave tomorrow. After we arrive, we'll review, then go over a few new skills. We don't have time to waste. Rune's planning more invasions."

"How do you know?"

"When he realized he could negotiate a better sentence, Ahmik talked. The king's still trying to determine if the information is accurate."

I shrugged. "Probably. Doesn't Rune want to control everything?"

"It's more complicated than that. A family promise fuels many of Rune's goals."

The implication of her words hit me. What? "And you know this how?" I raised an eyebrow.

She lowered her eyes, but her words were firm. "It's a long story, one for a different time."

My imagination sprang into overdrive. I wanted that long story. How much did she know about Rune?

Muttering from my left interrupted the questions for Abira gathering in my mind. Baldwin's mother, Mariel, shuffled over to where I sat.

"Beyond the portal, beyond. The key lies beyond." Her eyes zeroed in on me, staring through me like a laser. In the darkness, her eyes glowed.

I shivered. Keel hurried to her side and held her shoulders as her body shuddered. When she spoke again, her voice held the power of a commanding officer.

"Beyond the Portal that is no more,
beyond a cloudy, mysterious door,
find the treasure that lies within,
and release it from the place of sin.
To seek and find, go farther on.
Find the key before Skeleton's Spawn."

Eyes rolling back in her head, Mariel slumped. Keel caught her and lifted her easily. "I will put her to bed."

"Do you need help?" Grandma Helen asked.

At Keel's nod, she rose and followed him into the house.

"What just happened?" I asked Baldwin. My hands trembled in my lap.

He sighed and stood. "Another prophecy. They wipe her out every time. I should go help. I will return."

My mom settled into Baldwin's empty spot. When I shivered again, she hugged me to her side. "It's okay, sweetie."

"That was terrifying. Does she have to go through that every time?"

She gave my shoulder a comforting rub. "I don't think so. I've only ever seen her give one other prophecy. I'm sure she'll tell us more about this one after she rests up."

Like that would help. "But I was going to leave tomorrow with Abira."

Mom patted my hand. "We can send you a message if it pertains to you. But I wouldn't worry. It probably involves someone else entirely."

When Keel emerged from their house a minute later, she left to talk to him.

Abira leaned forward. "Did any of that make sense to you?"

"Oh yeah, it was crystal. No, of course not. Why are you asking me?"

"That prophecy was for you, regardless of what your mother thinks. My guess is she knows it as well but doesn't want to alarm you."

Too late for that. Adrenaline, worry, and fear zipped through my bloodstream, urging me to stand up, grab my sword, and fight. Or run. That was a good option, too.

I jiggled my leg up and down instead and picked at a hangnail. "I have no clue what all that was." It would take a degree in Prophecy 101 to decipher it.

Abira dropped the subject. Eventually, my grandparents turned in, and Erhardt left for his house. Abira departed, turning down my mother's offer of a place to stay, although I wasn't sure where Mom had intended to put her since our rooms were so small. Anna planned to fly out with us in the morning, so I agreed to let her sleep in my room despite the close quarters.

Baldwin turned to me before leaving for next door. "I cannot see you in the morning. Dr. Winward may have released me, but he wants me at the castle early for an examination. But when I come to Kelda Hills, I will find you. It should only be a few weeks."

I laid my head on his shoulder. "I hate this. Every time I think I'm going to get some time with you, we either end up apart or busy."

He rubbed a hand down my back, his caress warm through my shirt. "Things are crazy. So we have to fit the time in when we can."

"Yeah. I know."

"Goodnight." He leaned in slowly, giving me time to move before he brushed his lips across mine. After a gentle squeeze of my hands, he walked away.

It was weird. We were so tentative with each other. Although we'd dated for months, it felt like we were starting over. Maybe in a way, we were. He'd been someone different for a few weeks. I only hoped that angry stranger was gone.

As my parents, Anna, and I cleaned up the remainder of the picnic, Mom pulled me aside. "Abira talked to me about your training. Your dad and I think it's important for you to learn all you can with her."

They certainly seemed eager to get rid of me. "I haven't seen you that much anyway." The words came out whiny, the tone of a spoiled brat.

She pursed her lips. "I know we've been busy, but who's been coming home at one or two in the morning, hmm?"

"Uh..."

"Yeah, I know about your late nights, Brenna. You're supposed to check in with your grandparents. Grandma said you were late coming home almost every night this week."

I scowled. "How do they know? They go to bed early."

She shook her head. "Grandma Helen stays up until you come home. And last week, she heard what sounded like you getting sick." Her gaze was steady. "She checked on you, but you waved her off. Said you were fine. Grandma said the odor of verum could've been detected in the Steen Mountains."

Her stare weighed like an anvil on my chest. I didn't remember any of that.

"I don't care how old you are, that behavior stops now. You have too much promise to ruin yourself like that." She sat on the steps leading to our house.

I had no idea Grandma Helen stayed up for me. I settled on the steps, guilt a leaden ball in my stomach.

As the stars came out to glitter among the Petrus Rings, shadows deepened across the treetops of the city. Mom put her arm around me, and I leaned into her embrace.

"I miss the nights in Linneah. Here, the night falls fast like a dark curtain." Her voice was quiet.

"Will—" My voice broke, homesickness feeling like grief. "Will we ever go back?"

"Yes. Don't doubt it." Mom's voice firmed. "We are strengthening our forces, although the Syeirans denied our most recent request for support."

My mouth fell open. "What? Why?"

"They are pacifists. They're willing to offer sanctuary, but they won't contribute military aid. No men and no weapons." She sighed. "We'll reclaim our home, with or without their help."

That would be just a little tough with no soldiers. "I haven't seen any of our soldiers. We still have the Linnean guard, right?"

Mom rubbed a soothing hand up and down my back. "Yes, they've been moved to a secret training facility in the Steen Mountains. They're safe from Rune and his forces."

"Safer than here?"

She smiled a cat-that-ate-the-canary grin. "Several of our Wisdom Trainers and Illusionbrands teamed up to create an excellent cloaking technique. No one can spy on us with spiegel globes. It's the perfect setup, and our army is growing and becoming stronger."

Her arm around my shoulders was a safe place, and I snuggled in deeper as she continued.

"I don't want you to worry about us. I'll send a fo-li if I need to contact you. Listen to Abira and learn all you can. I love you."

I slid my arms around her waist. "I love you too, Mom."

This trip wasn't like a week of summer camp or a trip to a friend's house. The darkness pressed in, isolating the two of us. I breathed deeply, hoping her floral scent would erase the uncertainty lodged in my throat.

The next morning, I crammed everything into my bag and forced it closed. Apparently, packing efficiently wasn't in my skill set. I grabbed a leftover Kunkelsteuchen from our tiny kitchen and met everyone outside.

Grandma Helen handed me several more wrapped pastries for my trip. "I'll miss you, but Elyon's got amazing things in store for you." She grinned. "Just think of the stories you can share when we see you again."

I gave her and Grandpa Takacs a hug, as well as another one for Dad and Mom. Arvandus waited nearby while I said my goodbyes. He'd agreed to allow Abira to ride to Kelda Hills, even though the flight would take longer carrying two people.

Anna walked up to me. "I'll follow you until you stop for lunch, then ride the curl to Kelda Hills. My mom's probably whitecapping since I've been gone this long."

"You did tell her, right?"

"Yeah, but there's lots to do. Getting settled, installing the new stones, finding—"

I tilted my head. "You found a set?"

"Yeah, we had to. I heard Rune busted up the old ones."

"I found a medallion he created. Each of his soldiers wears one." I pulled it from my pocket and handed it to her.

She studied it. "That's the stones, no drift about it." With a shrug, she handed it back. "Keep it. Maybe you can use it for something."

"Visit me when you get the chance, okay?"

"Absolutely." With a smile, she gave me a quick hug before disappearing behind our house. She flew out in Steen falcon form, the brown-feathered raptor a favorite of hers.

As we rose into the air, I waved goodbye to my family, a lump growing in my throat.

We planned to travel straight through to Kelda Hills, stopping for only lunch and bathroom breaks. Weeks ago, when we'd flown in from Ginselwyn, it had taken all day, so I was prepared to spend most of the day in the air.

With Abira quiet behind me, my mind turned over the words of Mariel's prophecy. The Portal that is no more...the treasure...the key...Skeleton's Spawn. None of it made sense.

Arvandus, thanks for agreeing to let Abira ride with us.

It is the most practical solution. And I am more than strong enough to carry two.

Hmm, he was in an egotistical mood this morning. *Last night, Mariel delivered a prophecy.*

Interesting. What did it concern?

Well, me, maybe, although that's up for debate. She mentioned a treasure, a key, a portal that is no more, and Skeleton's Spawn. I thought you might be able to help me decipher the prophecy.

He was quiet for a long moment before he spoke again. *Do you remember the exact wording?*

Surprisingly, the words were implanted in my chaotic brain like an extra megabyte of memory. I recited the prophecy for Arvandus.

He gave a small growl. *None of it sounds familiar. Perhaps we will discover more in time.*

Around noon, my stomach reminded me about lunch with a loud rumble. I leaned back to speak to Abira. "Are you hungry?"

With a wince, she shifted forward. "We should probably stop. My muscles are stiffening up."

Arvandus, can we stop for lunch?

You are fortunate. I have found the Aviva Desert Oasis on the horizon. We can stop there.

I squinted. The landscape revealed only tan, undulating waves of sand. *What do you mean you found the oasis?*

It is never in the same place twice. It disappears and reappears within a one thousand-mile area called the Oasisland.

An oasis that moved? I leaned forward, hoping to see it. After another minute of flight, a green patch came into view. Arvandus headed for the bright pop of color against the sandy terrain.

I waved goodbye to Anna, who tipped her wings and flew on. Arvandus circled once before alighting gracefully next to a stand of trees. Abira and I both found a secluded, friendly bush, then met each other near a palm tree. Out of the shade, the sun was like a blast furnace.

In the distance, thick columns stood alone, collapsed steps leading to missing floors. Several crumbling structures survived, a testament to a great civilization now gone. An angular dark-blue building rose above the ruins, the rock's metallic flecks glittering under the sun's glare. A tattered purple banner hung above the massive doors, and white stars glowed against the faded violet backdrop.

I pointed out the building to Abira. "What's that? It's gorgeous."

"The temple. They worshiped the heavens."

With a building like that, I could believe it.

The oasis itself contained a massive cerulean pool ringed by lush ferns. On one side, emerald bushes crowded the shore, each shrub holding huge colorful blooms of crimson, eggplant, and fuchsia. On the other side, several paths wound through thick foliage before ending at the water's edge. Stately palm trees offered shaded areas for relaxing near the water.

Arvandus interrupted my quiet observation of the oasis. "I do not need to eat since I had a delicious deer last night. If you do not need me, I would like to take a quick nap."

"I'm good."

He settled under the tree.

Abira and I found another palm tree closer to the water and sat on a blanket to enjoy our lunch.

She drank from her canteen. "I'm curious. Why didn't you tell me what happened in Ginselwyn?"

Shrugging, I focused on unwrapping my Kunkelsteuchen. "At first, I thought it would come back. I would recover and the gift would too. When that didn't happen, well, I was embarrassed. I'd never heard of anyone losing their gift. And then with everything that happened when I arrived home, I just kind of gave up. You can't force something like that."

"True. But I could've helped you through it."

"I thought I was finished. Why would you care about a Firebrand without fire? So I just planned to hang out at home and figure something else out."

A gentle zephyr blew, a small mercy in this arid landscape.

"Well, you were wrong about one thing. I'd care even if you couldn't create fire." She offered me a wry smile. "You're kind of like me—opinionated, headstrong, don't know when to quit. The world needs more of that persistence."

The water rippled under the light breeze, and I returned her smile. My positive traits were often overlooked. In school, I was constantly reprimanded for not paying attention, for fidgeting, for forgetting things. Some teachers didn't understand or believe ADHD was a real thing.

Yeah, try living in my head for a day. I took another bite of Kunkelsteuchen. "Did you know Arvandus said this place moves? Isn't that weird?"

"It's definitely not a natural occurrence. Would you like to hear how that happened?"

Nodding, I leaned forward.

"This place used to be the major city of the great kingdom Aljania. The citizens used the water for drinking and essential daily needs, of course, but thirsty, desperate nomadic tribes would come in at night, kill citizens near the pool, and then take as much water as they could carry. After several attacks, the king created a spell to move Aljania's location, and then he destroyed the portal leading directly to his city.

"The nomads never found the oasis again, and the Aljanians were safe. Unfortunately, not having the same location meant their allies couldn't find them either, and explorers often never returned. For one reason or another, the kingdom died off, but the Aviva Desert Oasis continues to shift its location."

"It's too bad we'll never know what happened."

She raised her eyebrows. "One common theory states the nomads finally found them and massacred them all."

Sheesh. Happy, happy. "Remind me never to ask you for a bedtime story."

With a grin, she packed away the remains of her lunch.

I found Arvandus napping under a palm tree. He looked so relaxed—well, as relaxed as a winged black panther could look. But since I wanted to be in Kelda Hills by nightfall with an actual bed, I woke him. "Arvandus?"

He didn't move.

"Big guy, we have to go."

One golden eye slitted open. "I just lay down."

"No, you've actually been asleep for close to an hour. We need to get going."

Abira walked up and dusted off her pants. "We're not that far away. We're heading to my brother's inn."

I glanced at her. "Oh. Why?"

"That's a surprise." She turned to Arvandus. "Do you know Declan Edan's inn south of the Starfall Fields? It's northwest of Kelda Hills."

He sat up. "That used to be a nomadic settlement area."

"It still is. It's called Starfall Rim."

"I can get you there before suppertime." He rose, stretched his legs, then extended his wings once and folded them against his body. "I am ready."

We climbed on, and Arvandus took to the air.

Chapter Six

True to Arvandus's word, we arrived near Starfall Rim at suppertime. Several tents dotted the landscape below, outdoor cooking fires little dots of yellow and orange. As we drew closer, the inn's windows glowed with warm light in the barren landscape. To my surprise, half a dozen large buildings had sprung up around the inn.

Abira leaned forward. "Can you direct Arvandus to my brother's inn up ahead?"

After I shared the information with Arvandus, he landed in the inn's backyard. We removed our bags and stretched.

His nose twitched. "I smell foslykos."

I grinned. "Declan raises them, both the colored and invisible ones."

He growled, his eyes becoming yellow slivers.

"What? You don't like light wolves?"

His ears twitched. "We have an uneasy peace."

"Well, you're not allowed to eat the host's livestock."

Arvandus didn't respond, just sat, his tail flicking.

I hoisted my bag onto my shoulder. "I'll ask about accommodations and meals for you."

"That's unnecessary. We're home." Abira grinned.

The inn was awash in yellow light, voices and music trickling outside from the bar area.

I wrinkled my nose. "We're living in the inn?"

She pointed to a long two-story structure made of timber. "Welcome to my home and the new Firebrand guild."

My mouth dropped open. "A guild? What do you need a guild for?"

She gave me a sideways glance. "Where else do you expect to train? Do you have a problem with being a Firebrand guild member?"

"No." I guess. Uneasiness threaded through my stomach. This sounded like school, something I wasn't fond of and tried to avoid. "Are all the talents coming here to learn?"

She gestured to another new building, a few of its windows glowing with light. "Because they're rare, Time Reelers and Travelers will be housed together in the Dominion guild. We also have a Waterbrand guild, an Illusionbrand guild, and a Warrior guild. Many of the Builderbrands are constructing the guild houses. More guilds will spring up as time passes. We're going to do them right this time around. We'll work together. Come on."

She motioned for us to follow her, and Arvandus and I trailed in her wake while studying our surroundings.

As we climbed the Firebrand's guild steps, she pointed to a tall, unfinished structure in a field to the right. "That will eventually be a griffin house, Arvandus. The builders expect it to be finished in a week or two. You can stay on the porch or in Brenna's room until then."

"Thank you. I will be here, resting, if you need me." He padded to a far corner of the porch and curled into a black mound of fur and feathers.

The broad double door held an artistic stained glass panel of a phoenix in shades of saffron, burnt orange, and cerise.

After unlocking the door, Abira dropped her bag in a nearby chair before opening a few windows. "Unfortunately, I don't have a lot for dinner. We'll have to eat at Declan's tonight. I'll purchase provisions tomorrow."

The sizeable living room, decorated in shades of blue, opened into the dining room. Stairs led to the second floor. A spacious kitchen lay straight across from the entryway, a tiled farmhouse table in its center and encircled with wooden cabinets. A bathroom with a tiny shower and sink was tucked into the space under the stairs, and at the thought of more students, I prayed for a larger bathroom on the second floor.

Abira gestured to the stairs. "All the bedrooms are on the second floor. You can choose which one you want later. For now, leave your bag, and we'll get something to eat."

"Let me get some water for Arvandus." In the kitchen, I found a bucket, filled it with water, and placed it on the front porch.

Declan's inn was as I remembered it—stairs and windows carved from rock, cool air in the entryway, the empty registration desk just beyond the front door. We headed right toward the swinging double doors and entered the bar area. A mirrored glass cabinet set against the wall gave the illusion of more space. The room burst with people, conversations swirling with the scent of spices and roasting meat.

Abira and I waited for fifteen minutes before two seats became free at the bar. We slid onto the vacant spots, and Johnson, the Welden bartender, turned to us.

His aura glowed brilliantly as recognition brightened his face. "Hi, Abira. Hey! Brenna, right? How did Starfall go?"

I smiled. "I found a star. And I didn't die, so I'd say it's all good."

He chuckled. "Good for you. What can I get you?"

Abira leaned forward. "Two fruit sips. What's the special tonight?"

"Rason stew and Keldan wheat dumplings."

Abira gave me a questioning look.

My mouth watered. "Sign me up."

She turned back to Johnson. "And two specials. Is Declan around?"

"Probably. I'll see if I can find him."

"Thanks, but no hurry."

In seconds, he placed our fruit sips in front of us. I took a swallow, the mild, fruity flavor soothing my dry throat. I studied the room behind me by viewing the reflection in the mirrored cabinet. Travelers relaxed in chairs throughout, identified by the cloaks and bulky bags at their feet. At a large table, a group of adults talked and ate dinner. Waiters and waitresses hurried among the tables, refilling water glasses and serving meals.

"Your brother's inn is packed tonight."

Abira waved a greeting to a group of adults before responding. "The guilds have been good for his business. Some instructors don't like to cook."

"Is that why you built here?"

"No, he donated the land for the guilds." She eased back in her seat and released a relaxed sigh.

"Are there any other members coming?"

She took a sip of her drink. "Three are coming in several weeks, and two more next month. But for now, it'll just be the two of us. We'll get some one-on-one study."

Which meant I'd have to work like a dog.

Johnson delivered our meals, and I dug in, finding the stew flavored with an unfamiliar herb. The meat melted in my mouth, and I sponged up light-brown gravy with hearty biscuits. Maybe nobody would notice if I kidnapped the cook.

Declan showed up behind the counter as I pushed away my empty bowl. He placed a piece of pupkissberry pie in front of me. "Welcome back."

"Thanks." Smiling, I took a large bite, enjoying the sweet mixed-berry flavor.

Abira gave him a mock frown. "Where's mine?"

"You'll have to wait until tomorrow night. That was the last piece."

She looked around before turning to him. "I thought maybe Brenna would like to see the fo-lis before we headed back to the guild."

"Ooh, can we?" Last month, while staying at Abira's, a light wolf had delivered a message to me. I was eager to see more of the beautiful animals.

Declan leaned against the counter with a smile. "I was doing paperwork, so I can use the break."

After I finished my pie, we walked outside and around to the new addition's entrance. The inn's square footage had doubled due to the L-shaped room. Declan led us through the main door, and the musky smell of wild dogs filled the air. The building's dirt floor held dens spaced about six feet apart. Several wolves rested in them, peeking over the edge when we entered.

"I have four common foslykos now, and two of the invisible breed." He gestured to the back of the structure.

"How can you take care of them if they're invisible?"

"Normally their fur is white. It's when they're running a message that they become invisible. They're perfect for sensitive or classified letters."

He stopped at the edge of a den and knelt down. "This is an invisible fo-li, Clearwater."

My breath caught. The wolf's pure-white fur glowed with aurora borealis colors. Green, blue, and red eddied and swirled. "Go ahead and pet her. The fo-lis are trained to respond to humans."

Kneeling, I ran my hands along her soft fur, colors shifting and spinning as I stroked the wolf's neck. She touched my palm with her wet nose, and I scratched behind her ear.

Declan stood. "Would you like to see the pups?"

With a final pat for Clearwater, I stood. "I'd love to."

In the other corner of the building, a mother wolf had dug a large den holding four pups. Three slept on, oblivious, while the fourth snuggled against its mother. She whined and nosed him as he struggled to get comfortable.

"These are common foslykos, and this is Luna. She had these pups shortly after you visited several weeks ago. Her partner, Blaze, is out on a mission."

The shifting colors blended in the traditional grayish-brown fur. As the pups and mom cuddled, the blending colors settled into a glowing mosaic, like light through stained glass. I wanted nothing more than to pick up a wolf pup and nuzzle it, but the watchful expression in Luna's eyes stopped me.

"They're absolutely adorable," I said.

"Ashka, Avi, and Baron are sleeping," he said, pointing at each one. "Copper's curled up under the mom's chin."

While Copper had a white tuft of fur between his eyes, his siblings had white tufts above their eyes like eyebrows, lending them a surprised look even while they slept.

After a few more moments, we headed back outside. Shadows lengthened, and a sliver of moon rose over the smudged mountains in the distance. The Petrus Rings brightened as night fell, and stars winked on in the twilight.

Abira covered a yawn. "We need to get back. One of us will stop by in the morning to buy from the traveling market. Don't let the seller leave. I know sometimes he's eager to move on."

He shrugged. "I'll do what I can."

I turned to him with a smile. "Thanks so much for showing me your fo-lis."

"Sure. If you ever want to help, stop by."

"I'll be keeping her busy. New training starts tomorrow," Abira added.

Remembering the exhausting work of training a few months ago, I stifled a groan.

My expression must've shown my thoughts because Abira grinned. "Time to get back to work."

We waved and headed to the house. Tomorrow would *not* be fun.

The following morning, dawn woke me. Early morning light slipped past the heavy curtains, and I slid from bed. Moving the curtain aside, I checked out the scenery.

My corner bedroom on the second floor offered a view of many of the buildings in this new community and Declan's inn. Most of the other bedroom vistas were different versions of tan mountains and sand.

After a knock on the door, Abira peeked in. "Oh, you're up. Good. There's some nut bread on the counter for breakfast. Come to the backyard when you're done. We need to get started."

Maybe I could get a few more minutes of relaxation. "What about your trip for groceries?"

"I already ran a list over to Declan. He'll pick up the essentials for me."

Darn. I washed my face with cool water, combed and braided my hair, and dressed, opting for a white tank and lightweight pants. Downstairs, nut bread waited on the counter as Abira had promised. I finished several pieces with a tall glass of milk, took a deep breath, and headed outside to my doom.

"Have a seat." Abira sat under the large porch that ran the width of the house. She gestured to the chair next to her.

The backyard held a mix of pale, sandy dirt and stubby grass, a rock garden, and a few leafy sweet nessian trees offering shade. Already, the sun baked the backyard. A corner of the yard lay devoid of grass, bare earth peppered with rows of green sprouts. A white globe rested in the center.

"Hey." I pointed to the white orb. "You've got a watering system for your garden."

"Declan gave me one as a housewarming present when I moved in." Smiling at the memory, she leaned forward and placed her elbows on her knees. "So, each member of the Firebrand guild must learn the creed."

Ugh. Memorizing. "How long is it?"

Her lips quirked. "Eight short lines. I think you can manage it. *Elyon within, guides my soul, leads me on, makes me whole. Fire within, ignites my heart, lights my way, my counterpart.* Now you try."

I repeated it, stumbling over the unfamiliar words.

"Practice that often, preferably before each training session. The Firebrand Creed helps us remember why we practice and learn and where our power comes from."

"Are you making me memorize it because I lost my talent?" The memory stung.

She shook her head. "No, every Firebrand needs to learn it. Say it again." After I fumbled through it three more times, she stood, apparently satisfied with my less-than-stellar recall efforts. "Let's review the basic skills."

I took a deep breath and proceeded to do everything she asked: healing, producing fire, then enlarging a flame, flamer beam, and fireballs, as well as the newer skills of heat retrieval from water and earth. By late morning, after several rotations of old fire skills, sweat soaked my skin.

She dropped next to me on the stubbly grass. "Well, you're rusty, but the skills are still there. Go drink two glasses of water and then come back out."

"What about lunch?"

She smirked, her gray eyes sparkling. "We can get at least an hour more of practice in."

I bit back a groan and walked inside to drink several glasses of water. After a five-minute break, I headed back outside.

She clapped her hands, ready to teach more. Where did she get her energy? And how could I get some? Despite the time of day, I was ready for a nap.

For the remainder of the day and the rest of the week, I practiced all the old skills I hadn't touched for weeks. I pushed away the occasional twinges of guilt—when my gift had disappeared, I'd been clueless how to get it back.

Arvandus kept to himself, exploring the surrounding countryside, hunting, and napping while I trained. He was the lucky one. For him, this was a vacation.

CHAPTER SEVEN

TWO WEEKS AFTER I arrived, during breakfast, Abira turned to me. "I'm going to start timing you."

Dread expanded in my chest, and I swallowed the remainder of my rainfruit juice. "Why? I'd rather learn something new."

Standing, she put her dishes in the sink. "You need to master those skills you find so boring. They should come to you as easily as breathing."

"They do, but they're still boring." I followed Abira's lead and put my dishes in the sink, then followed her outside into the sweltering morning sun.

She held out her arms, palms up. "There's plenty of heat here to play with. Produce a flame as quickly as possible."

I breathed in and created a fireball.

Abira frowned at the glowing orb. "That's your best effort?"

Not really. I released the fireball and tried to drum up some enthusiasm. Maybe I'd learn something new if I could slaughter the speed challenge. My next effort was better. But apparently not good enough.

"Again, please."

And that was the pattern for my morning.

Before lunchtime, I drank several large glasses of water and then washed up. Wisps of hair escaping my braid were plastered to my forehead, and my tank top clung to my back.

After a simple lunch of crusty bread with sliced meat and cheese, Abira wiped her mouth. "You did very well this morning. You can have the afternoon off."

My mouth fell open. "Wow. Really?"

Her lips twitched. "I'm not unreasonable. You'll have to be back at it tomorrow, but you can do whatever you want this afternoon. Return in time for supper."

Arvandus? I dashed outside to find him. During this past week, we'd talk before bed, but our flying time had been cut back to nothing. Hopefully we could remedy that.

He strolled around the side of the house, his tail flicking. "Raven, I was about to fly. Do you need something?"

I grinned. "Want a sidekick? Abira gave me the day off."

"I would enjoy that. We have not seen each other much."

The cloudless sky boasted a bright sun. A perfect day for flying. "I can't believe how much training she's having me do."

Arvandus shot me a stern glance. "I have missed our time together, but you must focus on completing your training."

Sighing, I leaned against his warm side. "I know."

I rubbed the area on my shoulder blade where a half-finished tattoo waited. Three pieces of the scrolling flame guild mark stained my skin. If I passed the next two tests, I'd receive the other two pieces to complete the design. It would identify me as a level-five Firebrand, the highest level attainable, although Abira claimed there was always more to learn.

That thought was slightly depressing.

"Remember why you are doing this, Raven."

I remained silent and scratched behind his ears. I didn't like to think about why. Rune was best tucked far away in the corners of my mind. After several minutes, I slid my arm around his neck. "Ready to fly?"

He stood, stretched, and then knelt for me to climb on his back. "Of course."

As he took off, the rush of warm air pulled hair from my messy braid, and I squinted against the brassy sun's glare. Everything grew smaller as we climbed, blue sky stretching to the horizon.

Not far from the guild houses ran a thin river, its dark, graceful curves slicing through the desert landscape.

I guessed that's where the guild houses were getting their water supply. The Honova Mountain Range surged up to meet the sky to my right, and the Aviva Desert Oasis was somewhere ahead, hidden miles away among sand dunes. While plants and trees grew to tiny smudges below, the Starfall Fields became a rolling landscape of tan bumps.

Tiny figures of a nomadic tribe trudged west with their livestock, the travelers a slow-moving dotted line. I turned my gaze back to the sky, enjoying the wind in my face.

As we circled back toward the guild, a dark speck marred the endless blue, and I shaded my eyes. It was bigger than a bird, and as it drew closer, it appeared to be something large with wings—almost as big as Arvandus.

Do you see that thing, Arvandus? Should I be worried?

No, unless you have suddenly grown fearful of Lev.

Lev? Baldwin's here?

In minutes, Baldwin flew abreast of us and waved, his familiar grin making my heart leap. I couldn't prevent my answering smile.

Would you like to land? Arvandus's question captured my attention.

Do you mind?

Arvandus's chuckle rumbled through my mind. *No, it has been a good flight. I am sure you would like to greet him.*

In seconds, Arvandus landed near the guild buildings, Lev directly behind him. I slid off and turned to find Baldwin had dismounted more quickly than I had.

He looked fantastic. Apparently he'd been training outside. Aside from the healthy color in his cheeks, no trace of gray remained in his tanned skin. His shoulder muscles were broad, and his biceps nicely toned. Very nicely. My cheeks heated, but I couldn't look away.

He pulled me into his arms, his lips warm against my ear. "I missed you."

I shivered at the light contact. "I missed you too, although Abira's been training me hard. This is the first break I've had for weeks."

Keeping our hands linked, he pulled away. "Which building is yours?"

I pointed to the door with the stained glass phoenix. "The Firebrand guild is here, and you're not far away." I gestured to the Dominion guild hall.

Baldwin's face grew serious.

"Hey, it's not that bad. You can't be nervous. Are you?"

His somber expression disappeared as if it had never been there. "No, only eager to get started. My instructor said to meet him at Declan's. Do you know where that is?"

"Sure." I gestured to the building, which was quiet for the moment. "Declan is Abira's brother, and he owns the only inn here."

"If I can get Lev in the griffin house—"

"There isn't one, at least not yet. Maybe in a week? It's taking longer than they thought."

Lev spoke, his voice a rasp. "Baldwin, I will wait with Arvandus while you meet your instructor."

Both griffins walked to the shaded porch to relax and wait.

Baldwin shifted his bag higher on his shoulder. "When Dr. Winward cleared me for flight, I had no reason to wait in Syeira."

"I'm glad you're here. But I'm not going to hang around while you meet your instructor. Do you want to reconnect after supper? I could show you the fo-lis."

He gave my hand a gentle squeeze. "Okay. I have seen fo-lis before, though."

"Have you seen pups?" When he shook his head, I grinned. "They're really cute. Even a too-cool-for-cute guy like you will think so."

"What do you mean too cool for cute? I like cute. After all, I like you." He gave me a wink.

My heart melted a bit, even though it was an obvious line. "Flattery. Nice. I meant cute as in adorable. And they are. You'll see."

As hard as it was, I left him at the inn's door and walked to Abira's. Finally, Baldwin was here. Maybe, just maybe, we could spend some time together. If we could just avoid the arguments and quests and poisonous dust and all the other things that kept causing problems.

After a shower, I helped Abira prepare supper, which was bread pockets filled with savory meat stuffing. I think it was rason but didn't ask. Instead, I embarrassed myself and ate four.

After dinner, one hour stretched into two, then three. No Baldwin. Lev was still on our porch when night fell.

I stepped onto the porch to give both griffins some water before I went to bed. "Thanks for the flight, Arvandus. I hope we get a chance to do it again soon, but—" I shrugged.

"I understand. As I stated previously, your training is paramount."

I turned to Lev. "Do you know where Baldwin is? I didn't expect him to be gone this long."

The griffin's voice was quiet in the dark. "His teacher showed him the guild hall and then took him to the inn for a late dinner."

My heart fell. Maybe we'd get less time together than I thought. "Oh. If you'd like to stay the night here, that's totally fine."

Lev inclined his head. "Thank you. If he does not return, I will stay."

In my bedroom, I opened the window to let in cool night air. A few high clouds hung in the dark sky, sliding past the Petrus Rings and glistening stars. Declan's inn still glowed from the chain of helli lanterns lining the entrance. I rested my chin in my hand and watched the night shadows shift until I felt sleepy.

The next morning, Lev was gone, as was Arvandus. Maybe both were hunting. A note covered in a familiar scrawl had been tucked in the doorframe.

Sorry for not coming back tonight. Niklos likes to talk. A lot.

My eyes went wide. Niklos? Wasn't he the head of the Warrior guild? I kept reading.

Since no students are in the Dominion guild, I will be placed in the Warrior guild for now. Niklos said my sword skills were remarkable and feels I will be an asset. Before I left Syeira, I was training with alternate weapons and am interested in learning more.

Niklos has a big day planned for me tomorrow. Although I had hoped for some time together before training started, he is ready to begin. I will try to see you tomorrow after supper. Love, Baldwin

Despite the confusing news regarding his guild placement, my eyes stuck on the next-to-last word. Love? He'd never used it in his letters before. And I'd never told him I loved him, although I'd admitted it to myself.

It wasn't a casual thing for me, the way some would say, "I love pizza." What I felt went far deeper than my favorite food. Is that how he meant it? Maybe it wasn't a serious thing for him. Maybe he'd said it to Gari.

Maybe I should stop obsessing.

Scanning the letter again, I frowned. So Baldwin was going to be working hard with little free time. Sounded like someone else I knew. Abira had jumped right into serious training as well. No down time, just a nice meal at the inn, and then *wham*, right into skill review. Almost as if there wasn't enough time to cover everything.

My skin prickled despite the warm sun. If the guilds were just starting, why were the instructors pushing the new arrivals so hard?

Abira sat in the backyard, pulling weeds from the garden. When she saw me, she stood and dusted off her pants. "Time for a new skill."

"Finally."

"I hope you'll pick this one up faster than you completed the speed training."

The criticism stung. I propped my hands on my hips. "You're pushing me really hard. And Niklos is pushing Baldwin hard, too."

Her brows rose. "He's here?"

"Yesterday afternoon. He flew in on Lev, but we didn't get much time together since the two had to meet."

"Hmm, I wonder why Niklos took him on..." She stood and threw the weeds onto the discard pile. "You'll get plenty of time together."

"When? Because I've been working nonstop since I arrived."

"It's called training, Brenna." Setting her jaw, she walked toward the shaded porch.

"Right. But my schedule goes like this—breakfast, train until lunch, have a break to eat, then practice until supper. Although I'm happy to be learning, the schedule feels a bit relentless." I followed her and dropped into a chair, waiting for her reply.

After a few more seconds of silence, she sighed and sat next to me. "Rune's been sighted in other alternities. It appears he's looking for something."

"Other alternities?"

Abira gave me a half smile. "There are other alternities other than Earth and Eventyr. Most of our portals link to Earth, but there are others. Rune's been searching them."

At the sick flip of my stomach, I swallowed hard. "What's he looking for?"

"We're not sure. Some think he's looking for the Lost Children."

"Who are they?"

Her eyes were steady. "Talents from the Jasper Territory who went missing. Some live on Earth."

I twitched, studied her serious face. "You mean I'm not the only one?"

Abira shook her head. "Not even close. How much history of the Jasper Territory do you know?"

Leaning back in the chair, I shrugged. Grandma Helen had given me a history book months ago, but I'd forgotten a lot of it.

"I'll assume that shrug means not much. During the Fifty-Time Guild War, many of the talents escaped through portals. When the war was over, some returned. Others never did, their families blending in on the other side. We don't know how many are still there, coping with gifts that make them different from everyone else."

Sounded like fun. Not. When my talent emerged, I'd thought I was going crazy. "Did anyone search for the missing?"

"The Jasper Territory's a big place, and it was unclear whether they stayed on the continent or left for another alternity."

The thought of those missing people made my head spin. Where were they? Earth? Another alternity? They wouldn't travel far from a portal, would they?

Abira's voice broke into my thoughts. "But I believe Rune's looking for something more important, more powerful that will give him an advantage."

Like he didn't already have a boatload of advantages already? "An enormous suitcase of Shadow Power?"

She frowned. "You know, people don't usually joke about this."

I crossed my arms. "I don't know, okay? And thinking about it makes me nervous, so I make dumb jokes."

Thankfully, she let it go rather than lecture me about inappropriate comments.

"He stole the Sacred Veil from Linneah, which you retrieved. Then he took the Stones of the Spring. There's one more object of great power—the Caelestis Staff. And if Rune finds it, it'll be impossible to stop him."

CHAPTER EIGHT

MY HEARTBEAT SLOWED. *THUD-THUD. Thud-thud.* I swallowed the sour taste in my throat. "You said *if* he finds it. Is it lost?"

Abira grimaced. "Nobody has seen the heavenly staff for many times. It was hidden long ago. Explorers searched faraway lands and wise men studied prophecies, but all came up empty."

"If it's that hard to find, maybe we don't have to worry." That was a reassuring thought. I'd go with it.

"Hmm. Maybe."

"Is that why you're training me so hard? I don't think you answered that question."

She crossed her arms. "I don't have to. But I'm feeling generous. Any skills you master will help. Rune isn't resting. You shouldn't either. You'll have the remainder of your life to rest if you'd like. But right now, times dictate guild members need to work hard." Great. Abira's eyes were like flint, the set of her jaw carved from granite.

Two glasses of water waited on the table nearby. I took a drink from one, then stood. "What's the new skill?"

Standing, she held out her palm. A flame flared to life. The orange flames blurred then shifted, transforming into a red apple, its

edges defined. Another moment passed before the apple morphed into a yellow flag flapping in a stiff breeze. She squinted,
and the flag became a small orange man, swinging miniature
fists at an unseen opponent. She flicked her fingers, and the
man winked out of existence.

I closed my gaping mouth. So. Cool. I'd seen her do it once
before, but I would never tire of seeing the skill.

She allowed another flame to dance on her palm. "This is
called pyrocharisma. It requires intense focus and stamina.
Although it looks like it's just for show, it has practical uses.
For example, fire can be used as a distraction." The flames shot
horizontally and became a Steen falcon, wings spread in flight.
"Or a vicious predator." The flames danced higher, becoming
a three-foot tall dragon.

"A dragon?" I grinned at her whimsical choice.

Abira nodded. "They live in Fallon, on the next continent
over."

My smile died. "You're not kidding."

"People from Earth don't believe in them?"

"Not really. They're viewed as a myth." The dragon hung
next to her, mouth gaping wide, tail whipping the air.

She flexed her fingers, and the dragon disappeared in a puff
of smoke. Wiping her brow, she blew out a breath. "In battle,
the flames can be used to create weaponry—a sword, an ax, bow
and arrows. Really anything you prefer to use."

"Do the weapons work? Or is it just a scare tactic?"

"No, they'll work even better than traditional weapons because you're the creator. If you focus, the weapon you're wield-
ing will find its mark every time."

If you focus... One of the worst things to say to someone with
ADHD. Focus was a wish and a dream unless I was chewing
fypex gum. I tuned back in to what Abira was saying.

"...hold in your mind the item you want the fire to become. You can't be thinking of fifteen other things. Imagine only one item, let it take shape. Start with static, simple profiles."

What was an easy shape? I created a flame in my palm. A clam shell came to mind, and I clenched my jaw, concentrating on the scalloped edges. The fire puffed out like a red balloon before blobbing into an oval, its edges wavering, and sweat broke out on my neck.

I huffed out a breath, and the flames returned to their normal shape. When I tried again, the fire flattened, the flames sizzling in their compressed state. They managed to become shell-like, but nobody would've been fooled. I allowed the fire to go out.

Abira blinked. "That was...interesting. I think you need more practice."

Thanks, Einstein. I pressed my lips together and tried again.

An hour later, I drained my glass of water and flopped onto the chair next to Abira. She'd patiently watched me struggle the entire time while offering comments on form and technique.

"I don't think pyrocharisma is in my skill set."

She waved away my comment. "Everything else came easily. This is a challenge. Work at it. I know you'll get it."

The lack of focus was killing me. Too much was going on in my head—thoughts of a key, a portal, the Caelestis Staff, wondering where Baldwin was, followed by the puzzle over why he was in the Warrior guild, and oh yeah, what Arvandus was doing right now...

I held up a finger. "I'll be right back."

I hurried to my room and grabbed a piece of fypex gum from my bag. One of the natural ingredients was something like caffeine, and it helped me concentrate. I hurried outside, passing Abira in the kitchen. As I chewed, other shapes to create came to mind. Two tries later, the crude form of a sword glowed in my hand, basically a pointed stick with a crossguard.

Abira returned from the kitchen and set two more glasses of water on the table. "Very nice." A pleased smile graced her lips.

Releasing my focus, I allowed the sword to dissolve and grabbed one of the glasses. "Thanks."

"I'm proud of you for not giving up. Continue to practice so it comes more easily. If you master this skill and your speed, you can receive another piece of your mark."

I took several large swallows of water, draining half the glass. That's what I was counting on.

"I'm going to get lunch ready. You can stay out here, relax, practice, whatever." She left.

Sipping my water, I settled in a chair. A brush of desert air scented with warm sage cooled my skin. Despite the exhaustion settling into my limbs, life was good.

The afternoon sped by in yet more training as I practiced new and old skills. As suppertime approached, Abira stopped me. "Very, very good. Your persistence is paying off. Why don't we eat at Declan's tonight? We can celebrate your progress."

I perked up at the thought of a meal at the inn. After a quick shower, I changed into a clean set of clothes. As we walked over, the sun hung low, already on its path to the horizon. A lovely golden haze settled over the landscape.

Behind the Warrior guild was an empty field with a target set up. Someone out of sight, a very good shot, released arrow after arrow into the center. Was it Baldwin? What was he doing over there? Yes, he was a good swordsman, but he was a Time Reeler.

The Builderbrands had finished building the Dominion guild, so an instructor was probably around. The excuse about the lack of students didn't make sense. After all, I was the only Firebrand so far, and I was being trained. Maybe I could walk over to the Warrior guild later tonight and get some answers. But if other students were there, it'd be weird.

I frowned. What was the etiquette for our situation?

Declan's bar area held fewer patrons tonight, and we found an empty table immediately. While debating between stew or a sandwich, a shadow blocked my light. I looked up. "Hey!"

Baldwin grinned. "Mind if I join you?

"Aren't you eating with Niklos?"

"No. Tonight I am on my own."

"Please, have a seat." Abira gestured to the seat beside me. "I'm getting a crick in my neck looking up at you."

Baldwin smirked and sat. A waiter came by, poured water into the waiting glasses, and took our order.

In minutes, Declan showed up at our table and settled in the remaining chair. "Mind if I eat with you? Business is slow tonight, and I haven't eaten anything since breakfast."

Abira shook her head. "You need to take breaks."

He waved off her comment. "It was too busy. I had a handful of nuts a few hours ago. Besides, we had an interesting visitor come in around lunchtime. Johnson talked him up a bit."

Something in his voice drew Abira's gray-eyed gaze. "And?"

"The traveler had just come from the Linnean coast. Said it was trickier than a star's curse to leave with all the soldiers patrolling the borders. The Linneans living there now claim Rune's no longer in power."

Anxiety swirled through me, and I took a drink of water to hide it. Rune was in power somehow, even if he'd put a puppet on the throne.

Leaning forward, Baldwin voiced my thoughts. "Of course he is. Whenever he invades, he takes over."

"True, but the rumors coming out of Matana Island and Linneah say Rune left and never returned. The Skeleton King's now ruling."

Uneasiness snaked through me, and I rubbed my temple. Where had I heard that before? Declan stopped speaking as the waiter approached with our meals. The tense silence grew, engulfing our table while the waiter placed our plates on the table. Despite the delicious aromas scenting the air, my mouth was dry.

After the server left, Declan continued. "Terrified residents try to escape, leaving everything behind. Those who can't leave stay locked in their homes."

Abira bit her lip. "Do the rumors say where Rune is?"

"One is that the Skeleton King killed Rune. Another claims Rune left on a recruitment mission."

A memory pushed at my mind, and my eyes went wide. "The Skeleton King?" I choked on a piece of bread.

Baldwin took my hand, concern creasing his forehead while I tried not to cough up a lung.

Abira leaned forward. "Take a sip of water and try again."

After a few swallows of water, I took a deep breath. "What if the Skeleton King is the Skeleton's Spawn? You know, from the prophecy."

Baldwin's eyebrows shot up. "Could be. But what about everything else mentioned?"

I pursed my lips. "Don't know. The key? The place of sin? The portal that is no more? All a mystery." As I turned to my meal, the words and meaning meshed. I gasped. "The portal! The portal to the Aviva Desert Oasis. Because it was destroyed, right?"

Abira took a drink. "It fits."

"Yes!" I gave a fist pump. "But then, should we go? We should go." I put down my fork, my leg bouncing beneath the table.

Baldwin laid a calming hand on my thigh. "Stop, please. That makes me nervous."

"Sorry." I settled for wiggling my toes.

Abira took a bite of her carmeil salad and chewed slowly. "Maybe, but something like this isn't to be rushed into. After all, the prophecy wasn't clear. We don't know what we're looking for."

Mental facepalm. Treasure, just liked the prophecy said. But I didn't say anything.

Declan shook his head. "What's this about a prophecy?"

Baldwin briefly filled him in and recited the words burned into my brain. "But none of it makes much sense."

I shook my head. "Can't we just go snoop around? I mean, the oasis isn't that big."

The image of the temple rose in my mind. That's where the treasure was hidden, and I bet the treasure was the key. Where better to hide treasure than in that impressive temple?

After my idea was dismissed, talk turned to trivial matters. Why was nobody excited by my genius idea? I picked up a piece of bread and pulled at the crust. My brain wouldn't leave the thought alone. Between the yearning to look for the oasis and trying to puzzle out the other important phrases of the prophecy, I missed Baldwin's question.

"Brenna?"

"Hmm? What?"

"Are you done?" He pointed at my plate littered with bread crumbs. "Declan said we are welcome to visit the fo-lis."

"Oh, sure." I laid the sad piece of shredded bread aside. I hadn't been eating it, just decimating it while the beginning of a plan spun in my head.

The four of us headed outside, the night air darkening into twilight. Baldwin's hand found mine, and I breathed out a happy sigh, thoughts of portals, oases, and staffs floating to the back corners of my mind.

In the fo-li house, male light wolves prowled the area while mothers stayed in dens with their cubs. After introducing Baldwin to the fo-lis and repeating all their names, I sat at the other end of the building with Copper while Baldwin ended up petting Clearwater's pups. The adult wolves scrutinized our movements, but after a few questioning sniffs, left us alone.

Declan cocked his head and gestured to Copper, who had nestled between my crossed legs. "I've never seen wolves take to anyone as fast as you. You ever think of being a fo-li instructor?"

I grinned and shook my head as Copper's sharp teeth scraped my fingers. "Hey, ouch! No biting." I pulled my hand away and scratched behind his ears.

After a few minutes, Abira followed Declan out of the building. "I'm going back to the guild, Brenna."

"We'll come back when we're finished here."

After a while, Baldwin wandered away to talk to the caretaker, who had returned from supper.

Copper settled down, willing to sit quietly while I petted him. "You're such a good boy."

He whined and panted, almost grinning.

"But of course he is."

I whipped my head up, looking for the owner of the mellow voice. Nobody lurked nearby. The caretaker and Baldwin still talked in low tones at the other end of the building, filling water bowls.

"Right in front of you, Raven."

Luna nailed me with her golden eyes, and for a moment, I forgot how to breathe. "You—you can talk?" I squeaked out.

She gave me a wolfish smile, her sharp teeth showing. "To those we respect. You have such compassion and gentleness for my young ones."

"Have you talked to Declan? Or the caretaker?"

A whine slipped from her throat. "Declan cannot hear us. Not everyone can. The man who cares for us can hear but thinks he is losing his mind. If you listen, Raven, all living things speak. I often hear you talking with your griffin. He is an honorable creature."

I shook my head slightly to clear it. "He claims you have an uneasy peace."

"In the distant past, yes. But we have no problem with him or his tribe."

At least I wouldn't have to worry about separating a fighting fo-li and a griffin. That job would probably kill me.

Her smooth voice interrupted me. "The pack is aware of the evil that infects the territory. You will need to be very careful. But we are your friends. We will help you in whatever way you need."

"Thanks—wow. Thank you. Why?"

One of Luna's pups whined, and she gave him a reassuring nudge. "Because all creatures benefit from a pack helping one another. You are interested in a peaceful world, just as we are. But that peace is being threatened. So we must work together, and we must be careful."

I nodded, still a little weirded out from talking with a foslykos.

"My youngest needs to eat. Could you put him in the den with me?"

I deposited Copper next to his mother with a last scratch behind his ears. "Thanks, Luna. Goodnight."

Baldwin waited for me outside. "Well, you were right. They are cute. Too cute for me, in fact. Because I am so cool." He kept a straight face for a full second before a mischievous smirk lit his face.

"Oh, shut up." I bumped his shoulder with mine. "Did you know light wolves talk?" The words coming out of my mouth sounded ridiculous, and I mentally winced.

"I have heard of that happening. Why? Did you have a long, meaningful conversation with them?" With a half-grin, he raised an eyebrow.

"Um, kind of. Luna offered the pack's help if we needed it."

The smile slid from his face. "You are serious."

"As a heart attack." I scratched the back of my neck and turned toward the guild houses.

"Wow." He fell silent, and I chanced a look at his face. The serious look he usually wore had returned.

"It's not a big deal," I said, hoping to remove his grave expression.

"Actually, it is. To have the help of the pack could be very beneficial—for whatever." His brow furrowed, his normally bright eyes dark.

Uncomfortable silence pressed in. What was he thinking? Lately, it was impossible to tell. "Okay, you're upset. What's wrong?"

"Light wolves offer help to humans only if a threat is serious. Did she say anything else?"

"Only to be careful."

"Good advice." He shook his head as if to clear it and changed the subject. "You seem calmer than you were at dinner."

And just like that, his words reminded me of my half-formed plan. I could check out the temple and be back before anyone noticed I was missing. What if the key, or better yet, the Caelestis Staff were hidden there? What if I found them *both*?

I looked at him. "Not really. Now that we know the location, we should go. Really. It wouldn't take long."

Baldwin rolled his eyes. "Brenna, you do not even know what to look for."

"I saw a temple at the oasis. It's huge and beautiful. If you had to hide treasure, wouldn't you hide it in a place like that? Especially since the oasis is never in the same place twice? It's perfect. We can go in, search the temple, get the treasure, come home."

He shook his head before I even finished speaking. "It is a bad idea. Just wait. We can learn more and then search the oasis with more information."

Learn more? That would take forever. By then, Rune would've found the staff, and we all could say hello to the apocalypse. Biting my tongue, I shut down my reply. I refused to sit around and paint my nails. He didn't see the genius in my idea? Fine. I'd do it myself.

"I will see you tomorrow." He gave me a kiss goodnight, but I didn't linger, still annoyed.

Arvandus wasn't on the porch or in the backyard. I'd have to message him. I turned to head back to the front of the guild when I heard voices. Abira and Declan's voices filtered through the open kitchen window.

"I hope you know what you're doing. The last time you did this, it was catastrophic," Declan said.

"Yes, thank you for the reminder." Abira's words bore sharp edges.

He muttered a curse. "It's not your fault. You can't blame yourself."

There was a long moment of silence. "No, I should've seen—"

"You're not a Sensitive. You did a good job, but you can't save them all. And you seem to be trying to, which is why I'm concerned."

"This is different." Her impassioned words carried. "Brenna may be impulsive, but she isn't brainwashed with the One Territory Philosophy or some other garbage. The instructors must gather every student, especially the more powerful ones. Every bit of instruction we give them can help stop Rune and his forces."

"What about the Skeleton King?"

I took a step closer to hear her quiet answer.

"I don't know who or what that thing is, but it's not good. With the way problems are multiplying, the instructors could use help from other talents. Like you. You're the most powerful Communicator I know."

His heavy sigh drifted to my hiding place. "The light wolves are just a side business."

"It doesn't have to be. You could be part of this. Your contacts are invaluable. And we'll need fo-lis, especially invisible ones like Clearwater, to send messages. We need to be ready."

For a long moment, the night filled with only the sound of chittering insects.

"Please, Declan?"

After another deep sigh, he said, "All right, but I can't afford to offer the service for free."

"I don't expect you to. Your help means communication is one thing I don't have to worry about."

After a beat of silence, he spoke. "What other things are you worried about?"

"We don't know where he is, Declan. All my attempts with the spiegel globe were useless."

"Maybe he's dead," he offered.

"Or maybe he's hiding."

Their voices drifted away as they moved to another room. I turned to sneak around to the front door and jumped. Arvandus sat at the edge of the yard, watching me. Sheesh. He was like a ninja.

When I approached him, he blinked once. "Eavesdropping again, Raven?"

"Nobody tells me anything, so I get my information where I can." Although it hadn't been nearly enough. What had happened in Abira's past? What was the One Territory Philosophy? I wanted the complete story so much, it was like a craving for a thick Belgian waffle drenched in maple syrup.

"You need your sleep."

"Yeah, maybe not." I hesitated. Maybe I should take another griffin. I didn't want him to get into trouble. "You're free to decline, but how would you feel about a midnight run?"

"Explain, please."

I shared with him the conversation we had over dinner. "So it's possible the Aviva Desert Oasis is 'the portal that is no more,' while the Skeleton King is probably the Skeleton's Spawn mentioned in the prophecy. I bet that beautiful temple's hiding something—if not the key, then maybe the Caelestis Staff. If I could get there, I'd find it before Rune does."

Arvandus tilted his head. "Are you sure this is the best way to proceed?"

Definitely not. But... "I know it seems crazy, but if Rune's out there looking, which he probably is, the last thing I should be doing is sitting here. And like I said, you're welcome to sit this one out. I could probably find another griffin to take me."

Flashes sparkled from his wingtips, a growl lacing his words. "That is an extremely offensive idea. Why would you ask another griffin?"

"Abira won't be happy. I don't want you to get into trouble."

"We travel together, Raven. Always. Regardless of any unusual idea you formulate, I am more than willing to fly with you. Someone must keep you safe."

I gave him a quick hug. "Thank you. I'll pack my bag. We'll leave after they go to sleep. Let's shoot for midnight."

CHAPTER NINE

UPSTAIRS, I LISTENED. DECLAN eventually left, Abira's footsteps died away, the house fell silent. I threw a few essentials into my bag. After tucking it into a dark corner of my bedroom, I scrawled a note to Abira and waited for midnight.

I scurried down the hallway, then crept down the stairs. Despite the house's new construction, the fourth step squeaked. I used the railing to lift myself over it and almost choked when my bag strap cut across my windpipe. Elegance personified.

As I stole to the edge of the porch, the slivered moon offered light to see by. Arvandus waited a good distance from the house near a stand of trees.

He stopped pacing when he saw me. "We must hurry. I cannot guarantee we will find the oasis as easily as last time. We may have to search a great distance."

"I understand. But we've got to try." My whispered words seemed too loud in the dark.

"Unbelievable." A familiar voice cut through the shadows. Baldwin emerged from the darkness, arms crossed. "You are leaving?"

"What are you doing here? It's late."

Scant moonlight silvered his face. "I had this weird feeling you were planning something. Whatever it is, it is a bad idea."

A scathing reply burned on my tongue, but I swallowed it. "We're just going to search the temple. I'll be back after we're done."

"It makes no sense!"

"I have to do it, Baldwin. Every minute wasted here is another minute Rune has to find whatever he's looking for."

His jaw jutted. "I think you should stay here."

Anger flared. "I think you should shut up. I didn't ask for your opinion. You don't like my decision? Fine. But you don't get to tell me what to do."

He huffed out a breath. "Then I will come with you."

My mouth dropped open. "What?"

"Lev and I will fly to the oasis with you. We can search for, well, whatever it is we are searching for, then fly back. It will go faster with two."

"But you think it's a bad idea," I pointed out.

"Yes. But I want to go with you. Wait here. I will get my bag." He disappeared into the shadows.

So weird. Why would he want to go with me...? I gave up trying to figure him out and paced the small clearing. A glance toward the guild confirmed Abira was still asleep. Why was I waiting? I didn't have to. But a small part of me wanted him on this adventure. We could find the treasure together—just like we'd faced Rune's army together so many months ago. When we worked together, we were a great team.

A few minutes later, Lev landed, Baldwin sitting tall on his back, the two of them gray-silver silhouettes in the dim moonlight.

I climbed onto Arvandus, and in seconds, we were airborne. The night air cooled as we climbed, starlight gilding our faces, the Petrus Rings seemingly within our grasp. Wisps of clouds laced the sky, dampening our cloaks when we soared through.

While we flew, Baldwin and I didn't communicate. Combative, prickly words lurked in the back of my throat. Instead, I told Arvandus about my conversation with Luna. I capped the story with a reassurance. *So you don't have to worry about fighting her.*

I am not worried about fighting her.

Well, sor-ry. I just meant she likes you. She called you honorable.

But of course. It is nice to be appreciated.

Shaking my head, I stroked the ruff of his neck and enjoyed the starry night.

It was hours later when he spoke again. *We have reached the border of Oasisland.*

Unfortunately, dawn waited offstage, and the land lay like a dark smudge of black below. *Can you see anything?*

The moonlight is enough. I will do my best.

An hour and a half later, the griffins had dropped in altitude, yet we still searched. The sky lightened, dawn casting pink, purple, and peach streaks across the horizon. Shadows and fog dusted the landscape below, and I squinted, hoping for a splash of green. A half hour later, my optimism had dwindled to a hard kernel of disappointment. We'd traveled all this way, but we'd have to go home empty-handed. Baldwin's full-arm wave caught my gaze. He pointed ahead, his eyes intent on the horizon.

I messaged Arvandus. *Baldwin or Lev sees the oasis.*

I will follow.

As Arvandus dropped behind Lev, my stomach fluttered with expectation. Or maybe it was just hunger.

Minutes later, we dove toward a familiar splotch of green and blue. We dismounted at the water's edge. Both griffins drank from the oasis while we stretched our muscles. Clear as glass, the water barely rippled. Rocks, pebbles, and the occasional frog or salamander covered the pool's bottom.

I looked at Arvandus and Lev. "You guys did a great job. While you hang out here, Baldwin and I will search the buildings."

Arvandus scanned the area, his golden eyes keen. "Lev and I will serve as lookouts. The two of you must also watch for each other. Be safe."

We left the griffins by the shaded watering hole. I dug a handful of nuts out of my bag and munched on them as we walked.

"What is your plan now that I have found this place?" Baldwin threw his shoulders back and took in the landscape as we headed toward the buildings.

I rolled my eyes at his arrogant statement. So much for humility. "We need to check each building. I don't want to miss anything." Even though every bone in my body wanted to head straight for the impressive temple. Was it locked? If it wasn't, what was it like on the inside?

Baldwin gave me an impassive look but said nothing.

Irritation simmered under my skin. "Okay, Sherlock, what do you think?"

"Your plan is just fantastic."

Wow. Pushing down indignation from his drawled comment, I stopped in the middle of the path and propped my hands on my hips. "Look, if you're going to let all your snark out of the box while we're here, you can find Lev and leave."

"I am not sure what a snark is, but I am not leaving you here alone."

"It's being snide or condescending. Being less than supportive." Something I hadn't expected from him. "And I'd be fine. Arvandus is here."

He wouldn't look me in the eye. "Sorry. I would just do—"

"You'd do things differently. Yeah, I got that much." I bit my lip, hoping he'd say something, *anything* encouraging.

He pressed his lips together, obviously struggling not to say I was an idiot.

Disappointment filled my stomach. He didn't get it. In the early months of our relationship, I'd avoided in-depth discussions about my ADHD, but I couldn't escape it any longer. The urge for him to understand swept over me.

I tapped my head. "There are a thousand ideas in here, and sometimes, I want to try them all. I've told you I have ADHD. Even though I usually handle my symptoms, sometimes I'm not very successful."

"You said it was like being distracted."

I wrinkled my nose. "That's a very mild description. It's like having a million conversations at low volume. I get distracted or zone out. But sometimes I see a solution no one else sees, because my brain works differently."

"And your solution was to travel here?" He gestured to the landscape and shook his head.

Hurt bloomed in my chest. I'd heard variations of them before. But coming from Baldwin? I blinked back the stinging in my eyes and turned away. *Thanks for understanding, pal.*

I headed to the first broken-down building. We veered off the path and headed for the porch. With my first step, wood crumbled beneath my foot, rendering the entire staircase unusable.

Baldwin walked to the crushed wall and looked over. "It is just a shell. No floor or anything."

The inner walls had fallen away, too. After a quick walk through the town, we discovered other buildings in the same state of deterioration—no mementos, only splintered wood, broken pottery, and collapsed floors. They were the remains of another life, previous occupants long gone.

We left the residential area. Excitement fizzed through my bloodstream. I pointed to the indigo building rising above the town. "What we're looking for has to be in the temple."

Baldwin and I approached the dark-blue steps, cut from the same sparkling stone as the building. Despite the collapsing rocks around the perimeter, the steps took our weight, and we climbed the stairs all the way to the surrounding rock patio. The building was in the shape of a star with five wings, the stone walls glistening with gold and copper glints. Broken stained-glass windows bracketed the etched wooden door. Small windows perched high on each wing provided a bird's-eye view. The massive door to the temple stood ajar, doorknob missing.

Baldwin laid a hand on my arm. "Be careful. Inside, it could be as bad as the other houses."

We entered, the high ceiling soaring and open, pane-less windows allowing natural light, bugs, and sand to enter the rooms. The other houses had wooden floors. Here, the stone walls and floor eased my worry of falling through to the basement. A broad staircase made of the same blue stone swept up to the next floor, but I focused on the small wings on the lower floor.

Sand coated everything, shushing our footsteps as we moved from wing to wing. A spacious room with beautiful tile work on the ceiling could've been a meeting room—it was hard to tell without furniture.

I passed through an empty kitchen which held carved stone basins and broken crockery. In the next massive room, the few remaining chairs were broken into sticks.

Baldwin met me near the entrance. "I just checked the last wing. An empty study or library, and another room that was probably an armory. Only a few intact cabinets remained, and they were empty. There is nothing left."

My heart sank. I'd expected to find the Caelestis Staff in the armory. I pushed the sad thought aside. It could be somewhere else. Or maybe the key was stashed in a locked cabinet or under plated glass or in a steel vault—anywhere. "All right. I'm heading to the next floor."

He sighed. "Brenna, this place is abandoned. The people took what they needed, and it has probably been looted since then. There is nothing here. No treasure, no key, and definitely no staff."

Turning away without a response, I headed for the stairs. Why did I invite him again? Oh, that's right. He invited himself.

The steps led to a walkway that ran the perimeter of the building. Each small wing was accessible through a beautiful wooden door etched with stars. The second floor held more rooms in each wing just like the first floor, basic and empty.

I hurried to the third floor. The solid steps had less sand covering them, but the metal scrolled railing wobbled back and forth like an unsteady toddler. Staying close to the blue stone wall, I climbed the staircase and entered the first room.

Minutes later, Baldwin joined me. A cabinet door hung open, a few empty jars stacked on the shallow shelves. I tilted my head. Why build shallow shelves in such a large cabinet? The depth didn't look right. I thumped the back, stunned when my fist punched through the brittle wood and into a hidden compartment.

"Baldwin, look!" From deep within, I pulled out a leather-bound book and a jar filled with liquid. I grinned. "Treasures."

He moved to my side and thumbed through the book. "It seems to be a medical textbook or doctor's notes."

A cold sensation slammed into my throat, icing my collarbone. I touched the jasper, its surface like an artic kiss. Fear settled deep. The last time my jasper did this, Rune appeared.

Voices from below paralyzed my limbs. My eyes widened. It had to be Rune, but how had he escaped the griffins' notice?

I pulled Baldwin closer, his familiar scent of leather and citrus calming my anxiety. "There's someone down there. I think it's Rune."

"Relax, Brenna. You cannot know that."

"I can too know that. We need to leave."

I peeked out the doorway and peered through the latticed railing. A man's head bobbed into view as he trudged over the sandy floor. Hundreds of small, black braids ran down his back, the familiar sword tattoo on his cheekbone making my blood run cold. Taurin Trennen, who had abducted my mother, stolen Linneah's Sacred Veil, and then started a war in my adopted country of Linneah. Psycho.

Cold prickled up my neck. Why would my jasper ice up at Taurin's arrival?

"Who is it?" Baldwin whispered as he peered around my shoulder.

"Shh."

"My lord, where would you like to search first?"

Rune stepped into the entryway, a black cloak billowing behind him. Black satin ribbon striped his black shirt, and his pants flaunted crisply folded seams. Totally ridiculous for exploring an abandoned temple. "I will search the first floor. Look for a subfloor, Taurin, and bring back anything useful."

"I might be more useful if I helped you search the first floor. After all, the old woman only shared the first line of the prophecy before you killed her."

The bottom dropped out of my stomach as Baldwin gasped. I gripped his hand. It couldn't be Mariel. It. Just. Couldn't.

Rune's face morphed into a dark mask of anger. "I did not ask for your opinion." His cloak and black suit shifted, becoming transparent, the air around him shimmering. "Do what I ask, nothing more and nothing less. Do you need a reminder of who's in charge?"

I rubbed my eyes and squinted. Rune's body seemed to be covered in vines or ribbons, the illusion fuzzy. He stepped closer to Taurin, and the man backed up. One step more and the pair moved out of sight. I nearly groaned. What was happening down there?

Taurin's voice shook. "Please, my prince, forgive me. My mistake." He appeared again, hurrying away as if being chased by a rabid dog.

Thrusting the book and jar into my bag, I tried to back away from the doorway. Baldwin's body blocked me. After shoving him back into the room, I lowered my voice to a harsh whisper. "What are we gonna do? He'll head up here when he's done looking around down there."

Baldwin set his jaw. "Follow me."

Peeking around the doorframe, Baldwin checked left and right before hurrying to the room at the farthest wing. We stepped lightly, our boot soles quiet. Once inside, I checked the view from the single window in the room—the ground fell away in a sheer drop. Trapped.

Linking his hands, Baldwin made a stirrup. "Climb on. I will hoist you out."

My eyes bugged. "Onto what?"

"The ledge. It is small but big enough to hold us both. I called our griffins."

When I hesitated, his voice sharpened. "Come on. He will come up those stairs any moment."

As if on cue, shuffling steps came closer.

I slipped my foot onto the stirrup and grabbed the top edge of the window frame. No way was I going out headfirst. I shoved one leg out and pulled the other leg through, parking my rump briefly on the window's edge before dropping to the ledge. My bag clunked against the frame. I bit my lip.

Baldwin followed me out, his face tight with worry. "I hope he did not hear that."

"Is someone there?" Rune's voice floated through the open window. Had he skipped the second floor altogether?

The griffins soared around the corner of the temple, Arvandus's wings trailing silver sparks as he flew toward the window, then hovered. *Raven, you must jump. I can get no closer.*

I shook my head, denial my new companion.

Baldwin spoke near my ear. "Jump onto Arvandus's back."

The ground tilted, shifting farther away. "What if I miss?"

His eyes were serious. "Do not."

"Come out so we can greet each other." Rune's smooth voice came again, this time close. Too close.

I jumped.

My outstretched hands grabbed Arvandus's fur, my stomach slamming into his side. My griffin went into a glide, his wings impeded by my hanging body. I squeezed my eyes shut, my fingers clutching handfuls of my griffin's fur. A fully grown scream lurked in my throat. After slinging my leg up and over his body, I grappled my way into position on his back.

My heart pounded as I sent a message to Arvandus. *Fly around the side of the temple. Rune was in the hallway, and I don't want him to know we were here.*

As Arvandus put on a burst of speed, Lev pulled even with him. Baldwin sat on his griffin's back as if he jumped from temple windows all the time. I threw a look behind me. Rune was nowhere to be seen. We cleared the pointed wing of the building, and the griffins climbed higher, putting us well above the temple's flat roof.

Nearer the oasis's edge, Lev let out a few chirps.

Lev wants to know if you prefer to land here before continuing home.

We'd better, just for a moment.

Gesturing to Baldwin, I pointed toward the ground. He frowned and shook his head, but I ignored him. This wasn't a request. I needed a friendly bush before we flew the many hours home.

After landing and dismounting, Baldwin met me. "We do not have time for this. He could be on his way here to find us."

I held up a hand. "I need a bathroom stop. This is my last chance before we go home. I'll make it quick."

Muttering under my breath about difficult males with steel bladders, I found a large, bushy fern and did what I needed to do.

When I returned, Baldwin knelt by the pool, his face pale. At my approach, he averted his face, but a thin, shiny trail on his cheek caught the light.

"Are you okay?"

He shrugged. "Sure."

Taurin's words slipped through my mind. *The old woman only shared the first line of the prophecy before you killed her.* I knelt next to him and nudged his shoulder. "Liar."

He cleared his throat. "I am fine."

"The woman Taurin mentioned isn't your mom. There's no way Rune could've made it into Syeira."

He glanced down at the water. "My head knows that, but my heart..." He swallowed and didn't continue.

Fear lay heavy on both of us—Rune wouldn't hesitate to kill the people we loved. Squeezing my hand, he stood and helped me onto Arvandus before mounting Lev. We took off. In the air, I pushed aside dark thoughts and allowed myself a deep breath. My pulse rate had settled a bit, but disappointment shadowed me.

Despite finding the jar and the medical text, I'd been sure this temple was hiding the key or the staff. We hadn't thoroughly searched the oasis, but my intuition told me Baldwin was right. If anything had been here, it'd been taken a long time ago.

The flight back gave me plenty of time to think—about the real "portal that is no more," Rune, the jar I'd found. By the time the sun painted the air gold, the edge of Starfall Rim came into view.

We landed behind Declan's inn, and I slid off, my muscles stiff. Close to eight hours of flying would do that. "Thanks, Arvandus. I appreciate your going with me. And, um, for saving me."

Arvandus growled. "You are fortunate I was there. And as usual, Raven, please do not do that again."

"I'll try." I turned to Baldwin who was stretching his back. "I'm sorry. The trip was a bust. You were right."

"Not about everything." His face lay in somber lines, his eyes dark. "You do find different solutions to problems, ones I would never think of. You described how you think differently, and in return, I was a jerk. I cannot say I understand exactly how you feel. But I want to. I am sorry. Thanks for explaining."

The knot lodged in my chest loosened, cool relief washing through me.

Grasping my hand, he continued, his fingers warm. "But I still worry one of your impulsive solutions is going to hurt you, badly. What if Rune had caught you?"

"He didn't."

"But what if he does?" Baldwin shook his head. "That thought keeps me up at night."

"You don't need to worry about me." But my heart was a bird in my chest. *Worry about me, just a little. Please love me like I love you.* My cheeks hot, I turned to remove my bag from Arvandus's back. That needy voice needed to shut up.

Unaware of my lovesick thoughts, Baldwin continued. "I can be the voice of reason to your impulsiveness. But solving this problem will not be quick. The situation with Rune is a process."

I sighed. "I hate this. All these problems... On top of not finding the key or staff, we still need to find the right portal, determine what's going on with Rune, and figure out what's in that jar I found."

"What is wrong with Rune?"

"Didn't you see what he did? It looked like an illusion. He became almost transparent. Is it possible he's developed an Illusionbrand talent, as well as being a Firebrand and a Traveler?"

Baldwin rubbed his jaw. "Maybe. He could have used his Traveler talent to get Taurin and himself past the griffins."

I was still thinking on Rune's possible new talent. "Probably. Did you see his illusion?"

Baldwin shook his head.

I squinted. "It was weird. His clothes became see through, but vines or something covered him. He wasn't naked." Which was a terrifying thought all by itself for other reasons. Ew.

"You have forgotten one more thing."

Great. I really wanted another problem, because of course, the mountain of issues I had wasn't large enough. "What's that?"

"You do not have to do this all by yourself. I would like to help."

The anxiety twisting my stomach released its hold. "But as you said, I'm impulsive. Sometimes my ideas don't make sense. Are you sure you want to help?"

"Oh, right. Well, forget it then." He smirked, and his gaze dropped to my mouth.

My stomach dipped. Oxygen vanished, but who needed to breathe, really? If I took one little step forward, his lips could be on mine.

He shifted closer, his hands finding my waist and his breath brushing my cheek. "Brenna, I—"

"There you are." Declan came around the side of the inn. Baldwin stepped away, and the moment disappeared.

I gritted my teeth. The man had lousy timing. "Hmm, yes, we are. Here, that is. Because, you know, where else would we be?"

Declan grinned. "Nice try. Abira is not happy. You'd better find her before she gets angrier."

Baldwin shifted his bag. "I left Niklos a note."

"I left her one, too. But apparently, well..." I threw my hands up. Even though I left a note so she wouldn't worry, it didn't matter. I was in trouble anyway. Why did I bother?

Baldwin and Lev headed for their guild while Arvandus and I walked toward the Firebrand guild. Abira waited on the porch, and my steps faltered. With her arms crossed and set jaw, she looked like an angry statue.

When we drew close enough, she glared at Arvandus. "I expected more from you. What were you thinking?"

Arvandus sat near the porch, his head high, his tail flicking. "She would have found a way there. I took her to keep her safe."

"I'm not sure that excuse works. Either way, you'll be pleased to know the griffin house is finished. You're still welcome here, but you can get a place there if you'd like."

I stroked his neck. "Thanks again. I'll see you tomorrow."

He nodded once and padded toward the building.

I envied his ability to walk away.

Chapter Ten

Silence built in the space between us. I could handle it. Let her stand there all day. I'd gone to the oasis because I had to, and I wasn't going to make excuses. No way. My note wasn't enough? Well, too bad.

I sighed. Ugh. "Sorry."

Her face didn't change. "And why are you sorry?"

Good question. "Because you're mad, although I'm not sure why. I left a note."

Her eyes rounded. "That's it? You leave in the middle of the night, with only a scrawled *I'll be back*, and you think I shouldn't be upset?"

A surge of anger flashed through me. "I had to go. And do you know why? Because Rune was there, searching. I told you he might show up, and he did."

"Don't change the subject. Even though I explained why we should wait, you didn't."

There'd been very little explaining. "I'm an adult—"

"In my house, you follow my rules. If you're not interested, you can go back to Syeira."

My stomach twisted. What would Mom say if I returned? I pulled in a difficult breath.

Abira squinted at the landscape as if the answer to her problems was written on the mountains. "I've prepared supper tonight, but for the rest of the week, you'll be responsible for the meal."

"For the week?"

"Do you want to extend supper duty to a month?"

Slamming my mouth shut, I clamped down on my anger and followed her into the guild house.

"Go wash up and then help me get supper on the table, please."

Upstairs, I grumbled under my breath and deposited my bag in my room before using the bathroom. I washed my hands and then ran a damp rag over my skin to cool off. I exhaled—heaven.

In the kitchen, she handed me plates and silverware before turning to the marble counter to slice vegetables. "Did Rune see you?"

"I don't think so. We escaped on the griffins."

"How could you search if you didn't know what to look for?"

It seemed so obvious. "I assumed we were looking for the key or the staff. That's only two things. The temple was the most logical place to look. And to answer your next question, no. We didn't find a key, or a staff, or anything that might explain the prophecy."

She continued to slice vegetables but said nothing.

Maybe Abira could find something helpful in what we'd discovered. "But we did find a journal and a jar full of a weird liquid. They were hidden behind a false back in a cabinet on the third floor. I didn't have time to examine them because right after that, Rune and Taurin arrived."

"Taurin Trennen?" she asked.

"You know him?"

After sliding vegetable slices onto a platter, she scattered a sprinkling of herbs on top. "He's been with Rune since the early days."

I tilted my head. "You seem to know an awful lot about Rune. How come?"

She placed the platter on the table but didn't meet my eyes. "What's that saying? Know your enemy? I've picked up information over the times."

Narrowing my eyes, I crossed my arms. "No. You told me once you knew why Rune did the things he did, but that was a story for another time. I think that time's here. If I want to be better prepared, I need to know the enemy too." The questions I'd put aside days ago came roaring to the front of my mind.

To my surprise, she didn't push back. She gestured to the glasses on the table. "Pour our drinks. Supper's almost ready. This kind of information goes down better with food."

By the time we sat down to eat, the anticipation was killing me.

I took a sip of water and looked at Abira. She appeared to be avoiding our talk. After getting up to get butter, and then napkins, and then another serving spoon, she finally settled at the table. Despite the tight set of her jaw, she looked me right in the eye.

"I know Rune well. Too well. I was his Firebrand instructor."

All the air left the room. My mouth fell open. "You? Why? Why would you do that?"

She glanced down at her plate. "Things were different then. Looking back, I can see all sorts of signs I missed. But that's the funny thing about hindsight. It's so much clearer when you look back."

My appetite fled. This person I trusted was the super-genius Firebrand who had taught Rune everything she knew.

Although I wasn't hungry, I loaded my plate on autopilot. Vegetables, meat kebabs, a fresh roll, don't forget the butter—all items that had no appeal for me. After seasoning everything with an herb blend, I waited for her to continue. There had to be a good reason for this.

She held up a hand. "I'm only going to share this once. The memories are painful enough, and I don't enjoy the telling."

Without waiting for my response, she continued.

"Rune's father hired me as his son's instructor. I'll admit I was influenced by the obscene amount of money." Her lips twisted. "But Rune was an eager student. Although he didn't make many friends, he became close to a boy from town named Rexson and spent time with his family."

"Rexson, as in Emperor Rexson?"

She took a drink of water. "Yes, although he became emperor much, much later. Rexson's father, who was a Healer, taught Rune about herbs and plants."

She gave me a mirthless smile. "I really thought it would make a difference in him, but his father changed that. As times passed, he visited often and indoctrinated his son with his beliefs, namely the One Territory Philosophy."

I'd heard that phrase when I'd eavesdropped the other night. "What's that?"

She pushed a lock of hair over her shoulder. "It was a powerful group that championed joining the Kasek and Jasper Territory under a one-man rule. His father's visits affected Rune's behavior. He became aggressive and looked for ways to surpass what I could teach him. Meanwhile, cracks formed in Rune's and Rexson's friendship—they were so different. When Rune was nineteen, his father fell ill. On his deathbed, he pled for his son to create the One Territory."

I took a bite of vegetables, barely tasting them. Abira's meal sat untouched before her.

She cleared her throat. "With no money and no resources, Rune stole all the supplies from Rexson's father and escaped to the Kasek Territory. Not long after, strange drugs started being sold in the underground."

"Like Shadow Power?"

"That showed up about ten times later." She finally looked at me. "It's believed he used some of the early batches of Shadow Power on himself. Rune gathered his father's influential friends, set himself up as prince, and began campaigning for the One Territory." With a visible swallow, she turned her attention to her plate.

"So Rune's still trying to fulfill his father's deathbed request?"

She forcefully stabbed a veggie slice. "Yes, two territories under a one-*man* rule. Rune's first step will be to kill Queen Tala."

Although Abira didn't mention it, Rune would kill my mother as well. I struggled to swallow the food in my mouth. The conversation I'd overheard between her and Declan the other night made more sense now.

"Did you teach Rune everything you knew?"

"No, he left before I could complete his training. But I'm sure he picked up the rest of it somewhere. There are plenty of teachers, some less scrupulous than I. And of course he's added more gifts to his repertoire, although I'm not sure how."

My thoughts whirled, trying to fit the pieces of information together.

After a long moment of silence, she gave me a quick glance. "Any more questions?"

I pulled some meat off a skewer. "No. Maybe later."

Although she tried to hide it, relief filled her eyes. She buttered her roll. "After you eat, I'd like to examine what you found at the oasis."

While I tried to finish my meal, my thoughts kept my appetite at bay. If she'd trained Rune, there was no chance I'd be able to beat him, especially with the other gifts he now had. He'd know what to expect.

I bit my lip. Weird things happened all the time. Maybe he'd step outside his house someday soon and get hit by a falling meteor. It could happen.

We cleaned up after supper, and I went upstairs to retrieve the jar. Inside, the viscous liquid swirled and sparkled, the mysterious contents in a sluggish dance. It had an unbroken wax seal, and *Res-*

piraqua had been scrawled on the top in a shaky hand. I grabbed the soft leather book too and carried the items to the kitchen.

To my surprise, Baldwin sat at the kitchen table with Abira. I gave him a smile. "Hey, stranger. I didn't hear you come in."

He pulled the chair next to him back from the table. "I saved you a seat. When I stopped by, Abira invited me to study the mysterious jar."

I slid into the chair. "I haven't had a chance to study it either. It's still sealed with wax."

He leaned forward. "I am surprised it is still intact."

"And labeled too, for all the good it does us." I handed the jar to him and the book to Abira. I had leafed through the leather-bound book earlier, although most of the markings looked like gibberish. A few words jumped out—*fever, apoplexy, hives.*

After studying the fragile pages, Abira tapped a page and relaxed. "Here it is, the recipe to make the contents of the jar. Respiraqua, made from the roots of the Pulnoma lily. The compound allows a person to breathe underwater."

I grinned. "Really? That's so cool." The smile slid off my face at the thought of what we'd left behind. "What if we were supposed to search the oasis with that?"

Baldwin's eyes widened before he shook his head. "No, you could see all the way to the bottom of the pool. It would be impossible to hide something there."

"But what if it was concealed in a nook somewhere?"

Abira pointed to the notes. "Before you start with the gloom and despair routine, there's another note. Apparently, they mixed this compound to sell. A few nomads would come through and buy it, especially a Kell named Baz who was a cheat. They charged him twice as much."

That information made me feel a little better. "Any other information you can make out?"

She shrugged. "Baz was from Lennor, near Mermaid Cove. Aside from the dosage, that's it."

I thought of all the "mythical" creatures that truly existed in the Jasper Territory—griffins, centaurs, and fauns, just to name a few. "Let me guess. There really are mermaids in Mermaid Cove?"

Baldwin didn't blink. "I have never seen one, but others have."

Right.

"How much do you take to breathe underwater?" I asked Abira.

She squinted at the notes again. "One teaspoon? Or is that two? I can't tell. It's blurry." Sitting back, she studied us both with pursed lips. "I've been thinking about what you told me, and I believe the key is intertwined with the staff. You two need to search by following the clues of the prophecy."

Unbelievable. I clamped down on my frustration and spoke through gritted teeth. "That's why we went to the oasis."

"Yes, but you did it on your own, without clearing it with me. You can't make autonomous decisions that put you at risk."

I bit my cheek and tried not to let anger color my words. "So now what? The prophecy mentions a key and a cloudy door and a bunch of other stuff. We don't know what any of it refers to."

She shot me a look of disapproval. "That certainly didn't stop you earlier."

Grr. Giving her a glare, I sat back, my left leg jittering up and down. Baldwin laid a calming, firm hand on my thigh. Pressing my legs together, I tried to relax.

Abira stood. "I'll need to speak to Niklos and explain my idea. As for the prophecy, let's treat it as a starting point. It's what Rune's following, so that tells us something. We can think about it tonight, then meet tomorrow and discuss it more."

I stifled a sigh. As if another night thinking about the prophecy would help.

After a few more minutes of small talk, she headed upstairs, leaving Baldwin and me alone at the table. I sneaked a glance at him and noticed his grim face. His new default expression—serious, gloomy, troubled. Where was the flirty guy from months ago who stole kisses when others weren't looking?

Maybe Rune's poison had changed him irrevocably. I swallowed hard. "Why the solemn expression?"

He jerked and gave me a fake smile. "Just thinking."

I rolled my eyes. "Right. This is me you're talking to, not your mom or dad. You've been awfully grim when you thought I haven't been looking." I remembered my questions from a few days ago. "Does it have anything to do with the fact you've been put in the Warrior guild?"

His eyes slid away from mine. "Kind of. My talent is, uh, gone."

Déjà vu. "Gone?"

He continued as if I hadn't said anything. "And before you ask, this has nothing to do with what you experienced. I have been unable to manipulate time in any way, shape, or form since I woke up."

"I'm sorry." I laid my hand on his. "Is it because of the poison?"

He pulled his hand away and rubbed the back of his neck. My fingers cooled. "Rune is involved somehow, but no one knows exactly how." He gave a sharp, mirthless laugh. "Of course, my father would be thrilled to learn I am in the Warrior guild. Maybe I should send him a fo-li."

I frowned. "What are you talking about?"

Baldwin slumped in the chair. "My father always wanted a son who was a Warrior. He was less than pleased to learn I was a Time Reeler."

"Did he say that?"

"Not in so many words. Instead, he continually encouraged me to be like Erhardt." He lowered his voice in an imitation of his father's. "'Erhardt is a natural born leader. Follow his example, and you will go far.'"

It didn't sound like Keel, but then who knew what went on behind people's closed doors? I scrounged for something to say, but it didn't matter.

Baldwin's expression flattened. "So I have begun training as a Warrior. I will learn everything I can about axes, polearms, maces, hand-to-hand combat, and whatever else I can pick up. I may not have a gift, but I will train so hard, it will not matter."

I rolled over in bed and shoved the pillow into place. Why couldn't I sleep? My day had started way too early: getting up before dawn, riding for hours, running for my life...I should be exhausted. Yet I lay wide awake, worry filling my head as a crescent moon tracked across a dark sky.

Baldwin's dogged determination bothered me. Gifts mattered, and he knew it. But after his confession, he'd shut down and wouldn't talk. No amount of worrying would help that situation, so I was praying for a miraculous fix.

The prophecy loomed in my thoughts. Abira and Baldwin were just as confused as I was. And we were running out of time. Although Rune had only heard the first line of the prophecy, it wouldn't be long before he learned all of it.

What would he do to the Jasper Territory? What about my mom and dad? Would he kill them? Maybe they'd be able to escape. But I knew my mom—she wouldn't leave her people behind. Tension stiffened my already-tight shoulders.

I got up and, using the moonlight, found my bag in the corner. Slipping a hand in, I searched the depths of my bag. A notebook was in there—maybe journaling would calm me. My fingers brushed cool glass. I pulled out the bottle of verum I'd stashed there weeks ago. When I held it up to the moonlight, the blue liquid shone ink black.

Just a small swallow would settle the clamor in my head, and hopefully, help me sleep. After the day I'd had, I deserved that much.

The first swallow burned, and I took another, feeling the warmth swirl and slide the whole way down.

Minutes passed, and the moon continued to create shadows on my wall while I drank from the bottle. My thoughts wandered to the phrases of the prophecy. What connection did a staff have with portals, keys, doors, and treasures? I closed my eyes, my head spinning. Impossible. As a dribble tracked down my chin, I swiped it away. I should've grabbed a cup from the kitchen.

My head fell back, and I studied the ceiling, my thoughts going fuzzy. Oops—too much. I giggled. After a few tries, I corked the bottle and placed it on the floor, my movements overly careful. Sleep would be easy to find at this point. I hadn't solved the riddle, but it would be there in the morning. I snuggled into bed, letting sleep take me.

I woke to darkness. Something had roused me—a sound?

The sheet trapped my legs while my mind fought through a tired fog. I struggled out of the covers. Another sound came through my open window—a short bark that ended in a howl. Others joined in. I hurried to the window. Clouds covered the moon, adding more shadows to the landscape. Nothing moved. A sixth sense threat caused gooseflesh to pebble my arms.

After yanking on a shirt and pants, I hurried down the stairs, my stomach pitching.

With every movement, my head pounded. Outside, the bark-howls grew louder, more insistent. A breeze blew, pushing clouds across the night sky. Even the Petrus Rings were partially hidden. Shadows moved, thickened. The lights in the fo-li house flared to life. Dread tied my lurching stomach into a hard knot.

When I reached the door of the foslykos house, a strange scent hit me. I drew back, my mind racing. Woodsmoke tinged with iron. The caretaker sat several paces from the entryway, mute and shaking as he leaned against the wall. His long, dark-blue hairstreak was vivid against his pale face.

Declan knelt just inside, cradling a growling light wolf named Spirit. He turned, his eyes wet, and held out a hand. "Brenna, get Abira."

As I took another step, he pushed me back.

"No, you can't—just go. Get help, please." His voice cracked.

I hurried back to the guild and climbed the stairs, calling Abira's name. She appeared in the hallway, her long white nightgown rumpled. "What's wrong?"

"Something bad with the fo-lis. Declan needs your help."

When she nodded, I turned and jogged to Baldwin's guild. Declan had asked for help, and Baldwin was a clear thinker in a crisis. Skidding to a stop near the Illusionbrand guild, I cradled my stomach. Bile gathered near the back of my throat. I swallowed hard and then breathed deeply, forcing everything down where it belonged.

When the urge to throw up passed, I hurried to the Warrior guild. I knocked on the door, palms sweating, shoulders stiff. The sound of feet on a wooden floor creaked inside before a middle-aged man opened the door. His dark hair stuck out at odd angles.

He gave me a bleary-eyed glare. "Yes?"

"Um, Baldwin needs to come to the fo-li house. Declan asked for help. It's an emergency."

His expression softened, and he pulled back. "Wait here. I'll get him for you."

In minutes, Baldwin came out, pulling on a shirt as he walked. "Are you all right? He said it was an emergency."

"Declan needs you. Something's wrong at the fo-li house, but—" My throat grew thick as we turned toward the inn. "Baldwin, it's bad. He wouldn't let me in."

His eyes narrowing, he picked up the pace.

When we arrived at the fo-li house, Abira sat with the caretaker, her hands bracketing his temples as she prayed over him.

Johnson stood at the entrance with Spirit, who still shook, growling, his ears laid back. Baldwin and I approached, and Johnson shook his head. "You don't have to go in."

"We came to help." Baldwin entered first, his gasp hitting me one second before the strange smell did.

Four wolf pups and two adults lay dead on the blood-drenched floor, dark-red liquid staining fur as it pooled beneath them.

Chapter Eleven

I GAGGED AND DASHED outside to empty my stomach. Acid burned my esophagus, and I choked, my eyes watering. After a minute or two, I steeled myself for the carnage and ventured inside the fo-li house again.

Clearwater and a regular fol-li, Gray Breeze, had been slaughtered, their throats carved open. Two invisible fo-li pups were nearby, dead from several long cuts across their throats, their white fur stained scarlet. Two of Luna's pups, Avi and Baron, lay near the far wall. The mother huddled under a low table, whining, staring at her dead pups. I scanned the room. Where were Ashka and Copper?

Declan handed Baldwin a pile of fabric. "Help me cover them, please."

Baldwin walked to the far corner with Declan, both of them covering dead wolves with old sheets as they passed. His face had paled, his movements wooden.

I knelt near the table, tears blurring my vision. "Come on out, Luna. It's okay." Lies, all of it. It wouldn't be okay, not ever again. I swallowed hard, trying to breathe through my mouth.

Luna shifted, and Copper squirmed out from under her, his little body shivering. Luna's ears flattened, the fur around her neck spiked. "Where is he?"

"Who?"

She growled. "The bone man who killed my pups."

Bone man? "I haven't seen him. He—he must be gone." I hoped.

"I hid Copper, but my other pups followed my mate."

She crawled from under the table as if her joints hurt. "I'm so sorry, Luna." As Copper tumbled into my lap, I sunk my fingers into Luna's neck ruff. Wet warmth met my hand. Pulling away, I gasped. Dark red coated my palm. "Luna, you're hurt."

"It is nothing. Where is Ashka?" She whimpered.

"We'll find her. You need healing. Stay still."

I laid my hands on her fur, but the pleasant haze of healing didn't come. I closed my eyes. Not again, please not again. My gift was back. I'd seen it, so where was it now?

After a frustrating minute with no change, I inspected her wound. The bleeding had slowed, but it hadn't knit together as usual. I frowned. What was going on?

"Why do you call him the bone man?" I asked.

"I could see his bones through his skin."

Ew. A shudder wracked my body. "Let me get you cleaned up." I stood and walked to where water and feed were kept. But the water bucket lay empty, overturned near the wall. I interrupted Abira and the caretaker's quiet conversation. "Excuse me. Is there any water for flushing wounds?"

"I used it to put out the fire. The creature tried to burn down the fo-li house." The man gestured to the gaping hole in the wall, its edges charred black.

"I'll get you some, Brenna." Abira stood, retrieved a bowl and a rag from a cupboard, and left. She returned a minute later with a full bowl, then pulled a medical kit from a wall cabinet and handed everything to me.

After cleaning Luna's wound, I attempted to heal it again. Its appearance remained unchanged. Despair settled in my stomach as I applied a thick layer of ointment to her wound. At least the bleeding had stopped. I finished, and Blaze sidled up next to her with Ashka. The adults nuzzled each other in greeting, their two pups crowding their legs.

I crawled to my feet, terror clinging to me like cobwebs. Baldwin and Declan continued cleaning the area, so I headed toward the entrance of the fo-li house.

Abira still sat with the caretaker who was talking, his voice shuddering. "—should be out there, searching for that, that thing. But I cannot."

"No one is expecting it of you, Luister. Johnson and a few Warriors are searching the perimeter. Can you tell me what you saw?"

Luister swallowed, his eyes wild, his voice a cracked whisper. "This monster was bony like a skeleton. He was carrying two blades. I managed to escape the swipe he took at me, but the creature never slowed. Headed right for the wolves. He butchered them when they tried to run. The stronger ones attacked, giving the little ones a chance to escape. I pulled a blade to stop him, but the monster released a fireball. I threw water on it to prevent it from spreading, but I was unable to save them. Clearwater, Gray Breeze, the four pups..."

Abira shook her head, her voice calm. "You did what you could. You saved some of the pack. And the bump on your head will feel better tomorrow."

I couldn't sit next to him with the horror fresh in his face. Once I stumbled outside, a cool breeze jettisoned the scent of death trailing me. But Luister's words and Luna's information replayed in my mind. It had to be the Skeleton King. Where had he come from? And why would he want the wolves dead?

After a few minutes, I took a deep breath and returned. Abira still sat with Luister while he rested. I leaned close. "Is there anything I can do?"

She looked up, her voice calm. "Check the other wolves for injury. Hopefully Luna was the only one."

After checking Blaze, Ashka, and Copper, I found Clearwater's mate, Ice, had a seeping cut on his neck. He refused to let me touch it and wouldn't leave his mate's lifeless body. Grief filled the room like a heavy silence. Unshed tears burned my eyelids, and a lump stuck in my throat.

After ensuring the wolves' well-being, I left and walked to a large sweet nessian tree beyond the guild houses. I slid down the trunk and wrapped my arms around my knees. My head throbbed. It'd grown to a full-size hurricane, but the hurt in my heart spilled over, corroding its edges. No amount of medicus syrup would ease the pain.

After a few moments, I wiped my eyes with my sleeve and tried not to think about the images seared into my brain. Clearwater, Grey Breeze, the four pups, their blood like a macabre Rorschach inkblot—I shook my head. *Stop thinking.* Dwelling on the images made everything hurt more.

On impulse, I headed to my room. The corked bottle of verum waited on the floor next to my bed. In the darkness, I uncorked it and took a huge swallow, warmth flooding my system. Several more large gulps followed, and I prayed the liquid would push out the pictures replaying in my mind.

Out my bedroom window, the wolves' wing of the inn glowed with helli lanterns. If I squinted, the light haloed around the scene, softening the edges. I took several more swallows, already sick of the taste but finding a weird familiarity in it. Corking the bottle, I headed outside. They might need me, and I didn't feel right hiding in my bedroom.

Unable to face the carnage in the fo-li house, I veered off course. I sat at the base of the nessian tree and tipped my head back to peer at the sky through the leaves.

"Hey." Baldwin appeared out of the pre-dawn shadows, his face drawn.

I jerked to the present, my thoughts slow to focus. "Oh, hey. Are you done?"

"For now. Just a break, though. I told Declan I would help him bury the wolves. What is that smell?" He wrinkled his nose as he sat next to me.

"Um, what smell?"

"Is it—is it you?" His expression darkened.

"Well, that's romantic. 'Hey girlfriend, you stink.'" I forced a laugh, the sound fake even to my own ears.

Baldwin's eyes narrowed. "Verum. Why do you smell like verum?"

I searched the horizon. Dawn hadn't arrived yet, but the promise of it was a pale-yellow glow where mountains met sky. "Um, it's just something to take the edge off. Tonight was wicked horrible."

His next question was quiet. "Do you drink often?"

"No, it's not like that. I won't be able to fall asleep like everything's fine." My voice broke on the last word. "The verum helps."

"I see." His voice dropped, and his lips pressed together.

Cheeks burning, my nails scored my palms. After tonight's nightmare, I didn't need this. An awkward silence filtered into the space between us.

"I had better go. Declan needs help digging the graves." He gave me a brief kiss on my cheek before he stood and dusted off his pants.

"See you in the morning." I tried to fake a nonchalant wave.

He gave me a long look before walking off. I frowned at his back, the churning in my stomach having nothing to do with alcohol.

I didn't wake until noon. My head throbbed, and I rushed to the bathroom to throw up. Luckily, Abira also woke late and was unaware of my hangover. After a dose of medicus syrup and some crackers, I dragged myself to the kitchen to help her get brunch on the table.

She played with her eggs and rason sausage before pushing the plate away. "I guess I'm not very hungry this morning."

Yeah, death would do that to a person. I winced, her clinking silverware like a gong. I swallowed the last of my rainfruit juice and took my dishes to the sink. Her next words surprised me.

"Why don't you work on your pyrocharisma this afternoon on your own? I have to talk with Niklos and check in with Declan. I'll be back in time for supper. Remember, you're on duty."

When she left, I breathed a sigh of relief and rubbed my temples. The headache had receded to a dull roar, and I'd avoided a lecture. After last night's events, a theory lurked at the edges of my mind. I needed privacy to test it.

Once in the backyard, I took a deep breath and focused, intent on creating a static ball of fire. A small flame flickered before it winked out. I tried again. A flare of light with some earsplitting pops, but that was it. I walked into the kitchen and drank a large glass of water before returning to the backyard.

Several more tries brought various unimpressive results—a wobbling, fiery blob that looked like red gelatin, a flame that appeared then dissolved from top to bottom over and over, and a spray of sparkles like pixie dust. There wouldn't be much pyrocharisma practice today. My gift was there. Maybe. I just couldn't trust it.

"I hoped you would be here." Baldwin came around the corner of the guild house, his hair mussed, his green eyes glittering.

"Hey." My headache melted away.

"We need to talk." His words were flat, bitten off.

Nerves fluttered in my stomach. Heart drowning, I walked to the porch and dropped into a chair, needing its support. This was so, so bad. "Never thought I'd hear a guy say that."

He sat across from me, his face serious. "I had a hard time falling asleep last night. I, well, I care about you, but I kept thinking about your drinking."

"It's not *my* drinking. It just helps me relax." Irritation sharpened my words, and I bit my lip.

His eyes flashed. "Do you know what it does to talents?"

I shrugged, unwilling to share some of the weird things that had happened last night and this morning. It was just a fluke.

"It kills them." A muscle jumped in his jaw. "My grandfather was a classic case. An alcoholic. He drank himself to death."

I shut my gaping mouth. "I, uh, I didn't know that."

"Yeah. 'Hi, I am Baldwin, and my grandfather was a drunk' is a real conversation killer. The point is, he was a gifted Story Shaper, but as time passed, he continued drinking, stopped writing and creating, and became an angry, bitter man. It was rough on my whole family, but especially my grandmother."

My voice dried up in my throat, my tongue like parchment.

"So I am having a difficult time understanding why you would willingly do this. I would give anything to have my talent back." His last sentence was so low I almost didn't hear it.

Baldwin made it sound like I was one step away from Alcoholics Anonymous. But I wasn't anything like his grandfather. I could stop whenever I wanted. "I'll be careful."

He gave me an incredulous look before he glanced away. "I see. I thought you should know."

"Thanks." After some brief, stilted small talk, he left. My stomach knotted tighter. At least he hadn't given me an ultimatum.

Pushing the whole awkward conversation aside, I focused on some pyrocharisma exercises. I managed a few positive results, then decided to quit for the day. Although Arvandus had declared the griffin house in Linneah more comfortable, I wanted to check out his new residence.

I headed to the building, tension leaking out as the sun warmed me. A fruity cactus flower scent drifted on the breeze.

Broad double doors of the spacious wooden house stood ajar. A special pulley mechanism opened windows for fresh air. The wooden stalls were typical of those in Linneah, and the smell of hay permeated the air. Since I didn't see Arvandus, I walked inside. Only a few griffins lay on the far side, napping. Arvandus rested in his stall.

I peered around the doorjamb. "Hey, want to fly?"

His nose twitched. "Greetings. You smell again, Raven."

Favoring him with my darkest glare, I leaned against the doorframe. "Thank you for that astute observation."

"Raven." Arvandus's voice was low, gravel wrapped in tissue paper. "You are capable of amazing things. But this? This path is damaging."

Blah, blah, blah. He sounded like a broken record. "Baldwin already told me what it did to his grandfather."

He got up and stretched. "You need to stop. Be present. Feel the pain, the sadness, instead of dulling it. I need to walk. Would you like to come along?"

Ooh, yes, please. I loved getting lectured. "I guess."

I followed him outside reluctantly, ready to make excuses if he continued his sermon. Heat waves warped the distant landscape.

A flock of birds flew overhead, their bodies dark flecks against a background of blue.

Arvandus padded at my side, and I turned to him. "Did you hear what happened last night?"

"Riothamus mentioned it this morning."

It took me a moment to place the name. Oh, the griffin leader. I shaded my face from the sun's glare. "That creature sounded like the Skeleton King. But why would he want the wolves dead? And is working with Rune or alone?"

"I cannot answer your questions. Everything is based on assumptions. Perhaps the Skeleton King is trying to silence Declan."

A harrowing thought grabbed my lungs. "Or he's trying to silence the guilds."

Arvandus's golden eyes met mine. "If there are no foslykos, there is no way to carry messages, and no way to ask for help."

CHAPTER TWELVE

ABIRA ARRIVED LATE FOR supper, which was a good thing. The *easy* grilled rason salad I'd intended to serve? Yeah, not so much. After picking greens and other veggies, I washed said veggies, chopped them, grilled meat, and then made it into a functional salad instead of a chaotic explosion of ingredients on the counter. I'd just finished assembling the salad when she arrived. As she washed up in the kitchen, I poured us both glasses of rainfruit juice.

Over supper, she shared more news on Declan. "He plans to eventually introduce a new wolf or two into his pack. He hopes, in time, one of them will breed with Ice."

It would be a while. Ice had stood next to Clearwater's dead body for a long time.

"And I talked to Niklos. He's giving Baldwin time off from his training to help you search for the key. Because we both believe the prophecy and the staff are connected, he offered a book from his personal collection that might help."

She retrieved the book from the living room and slid it across the kitchen table. *Secrets of the Staff.* The gold letters seemed to glow against the black background.

"It's the best book written about the staff. It mentions legends and sightings, that sort of thing."

"When are we supposed to leave?"

"As soon as possible," she said with a definitive stab at a piece of rason.

"Tomorrow, then."

Abira leaned forward, her face set in serious lines. "Yes, and I'd like you to come back when you find it. You've still not completed your training."

"Sure." My stomach felt queasy. There was so much I didn't know. I'd need every skill, every trick, tip, and technique to fight Rune. Even then it might not be enough.

Later that evening, I headed to my room to read, still exhausted from the last few days. The book's foreword wasn't exactly encouraging.

No eye has seen the Caelestis Staff for over three hundred times, although clues, prophecies, and legends abound. Within these pages, clues will be shared, prophecies expertly interpreted, and legends analyzed in the hopes that one day, the Caelestis Staff will be discovered.

The opposite page held an illustration. The staff's length was a slender blend of curves, cutouts, and decorative stars. Underneath, the small print read *Artist's illustration of staff.* I rolled my eyes. That was *not* a functional staff. That was a fantasy dreamed up by a frustrated artist.

I flipped through the pages of theories, suppositions, and maybes. Tossing the book to the end of my bed, I flopped onto my back. The "expert" author didn't know more than anyone else. A sound outside pulled me toward my window. I opened it, the moon a disc of light. The sound came again, louder. Sorrowful howls of half a dozen wolves, mourning the loss of their pack members, filled the night. I stood near the window, cool air glazing my skin. Unshed tears burned my eyes.

I returned to my bed and picked up the book, newly determined to learn about the elusive staff. While I read, the prophecy danced in my head, but any connections between the prophecy and the staff were as impossible as holding on to sea foam.

After turning down the helli light, I placed the book on the floor and snuggled into my soft sheets. The howls had fallen silent an hour ago, and the house lay still. But my mind wouldn't shut off. Of course. Because that was what my nights had become.

Maybe some verum would help. As I reached for the bottle, the memory of Baldwin's angry expression filled my mind. Maybe not. It's not like I needed it—I'd skip this time.

I turned my thoughts to the prophecy since that was our starting point. What portals did I know about? The ones connecting the Jasper Territory cities to places on Earth. Other portals to alternities I wasn't aware of. A travel portal which provided exits to all the major cities in the territory except the ones they'd never finished like...

I shot up in bed, a gasp lodged in my throat.

The deactivated entrance in the travel portal! Gareth had hidden Tiny and me there weeks ago. After she'd fallen asleep, I'd gone exploring, because I didn't want to wake up to giant, man-eating bugs. Instead, I'd found a wall of a hazy, silvery-slick substance. A portal that is no more...because it was never listed on any map. A cloudy, mysterious door...made of a weird, opaque material. That was it.

I jumped out of bed, ready to share my discovery. But everyone was asleep. Gah! Of course. I figured out the puzzle, but nobody was available to talk to.

Grabbing the notebook from my bag, I wrote down everything I could remember, just in case I forgot about it in the morning. I was a master of short-term memory loss. After lying back down, I closed my eyes. When I opened them again, morning sun blasted through my window.

In record time, I washed my face, braided my hair, and threw on a layered outfit for traveling. I shoved extra stuff in my bag—the jar, the leather book, the small notebook I'd scribbled my ideas in last night, an extra set of clothes. After picking up my bag, I grabbed my sword on my way out of the bedroom.

The kitchen was empty, save the golden rays of sunlight illuminating dust motes on the kitchen counter. A note lay on the kitchen table.

Gone to talk to Niklos. Will return with Baldwin. Have breakfast, then be ready to go. ~Abira

A loaf of nut bread with Bora fruit glaze sat on the counter, and I cut myself a thick slice before washing the whole thing down with a glass of milk. Delicious. A slice of that would make a good snack, so I wrapped up a few for my trip.

Arvandus wouldn't be able to go with us. We couldn't reach the deactivated portal entrance from outside, and I didn't know where it led. After storing slices of nut bread in my bag, I walked over to the griffin house to break the news.

Arvandus lay outside, his eyes slits as he soaked up the sun.

"Hey, big guy."

"Raven, you are dressed for traveling."

"Abira wants Baldwin and me to leave this morning, but you can't go with us."

That statement got his attention. His golden eyes flew open, and his ears pricked forward. "Why not?"

I sat on the ground next to him. "Late last night, I figured out the location of the portal that is no more. Remember me telling you about my trip in the travel portal with Tiny? She needed to recover after going overboard with her talent. Gareth found a safe deactivated portal entrance for us to use while she rested. It's possible that's the location."

"How sure are you?"

"Hmm, about seventy percent. But I'm betting Abira and Niklos don't have any idea. They'll send us someplace, but it'll be a guess."

Arvandus was silent for a moment, his voice a touch grouchy when he spoke. "I could fit in the travel portal."

"Not if we don't want to stand out. And I don't know what's on the other side of that deactivated entrance." Just saying it out loud made me want to take him with me.

He tilted his head. "Unfortunately, you are right. But not for the reasons you mentioned."

Of course not.

"I have heard rumors from other griffins and their bonded riders. The travel portal is being heavily monitored by Rune's soldiers. If you and Baldwin hope to travel successfully, you will have to go undercover. By the way, they have also altered Matana Island's and Linneah's exits into checkpoints, so avoid those places if possible."

I laid my forehead against his shoulder. "I wish you could come with us."

"If you need me, contact me."

I gave him a hug, then forced myself to pull away. "I promise."

After a few more minutes of small talk, I swore again to contact him if I needed help and left. Abira still wasn't back, so I went to the backyard and practiced. In quick succession, I produced and extinguished three flames, followed by a massive fireball.

After several repetitions, I switched to pyrocharisma. With pinpointed focus, I created an unnamed bird which morphed into a book with ruffling pages before it collapsed. Satisfied with my progress, I headed into the kitchen for some water. A minute later, Abira and Baldwin found me there.

Abira gave me an approving smile. "It looks like you're ready to go. Niklos and I have been discussing whether you should go to Ginselwyn or Lennor. Either location would be a good place to get more information."

I held up a hand. "Last night I had a breakthrough. I think the portal that is no more is in the travel portal. It's listed as an unfinished, deactivated portal entrance, and it's blocked by a glassy substance, like a cloudy door. We could start there. If we make no headway, we can go to Lennor or Ginselwyn. But it'd be dumb not to check it out."

Abira frowned and looked at the floor. "You know the travel portal has become dangerous since Rune took over two cities."

"I know. We won't go any farther than we have to."

Baldwin rubbed his jaw. "You could pretend to be Bob again."

Wincing, I shook my head at his mention of my disguise a few months ago. I had vowed after Starfall never to do it again. "You said I was a lousy guy."

"To someone who knows you, yes. But I am wondering if it would be better than nothing."

Abira tilted her head. "The extra measure of anonymity might help."

And that's how I found myself walking to the travel portal dressed like Bob, the alter ego I swore I would leave far behind me.

Arvandus and Lev had dropped us off at the main road out of Kelda Hills, close to One Maiden Chasm. We crossed the bridge, the trip a lot less scary this time than with Tiny, although some of the boards were still missing. I clutched the iron railing and watched my steps. Fewer people navigated the bridge and the road into Kelda Hills now that Starfall was over.

After the slight squeezing sensation of passing through the portal entrance, we entered the rock-studded tunnel. The porous stone walls connected to the main travel portal tunnel not far ahead.

I tugged the dark scarf higher over my mouth. This was so dumb. If I got too hot from all the layers, Bob would become a balled-up wad of clothing in my bag.

Baldwin leaned close, his voice low. "How far to the deactivated entrance?"

I blinked. "You're kidding, right? It's a couple of hours beyond the Aviva Desert Oasis, not far from the Half-Mile Down trading center."

"Figures," he muttered. "It will take forever to travel that far."

Shrugging, I turned right and stepped into the main tunnel. The air here hung musty and flat, and I wrinkled my nose.

Baldwin kept pace with me, his shoulders stiff.

After a few minutes, I swallowed my sigh. "What's wrong?"

"Nothing." His knuckles tightened on the straps of his bag.

"If you hold that bag any tighter, it'll disintegrate. Just try to enjoy the trip."

He mumbled something and continued to stomp through the tunnel.

I rolled my eyes. This was so fun. Not. "Bud, it's going to be a long trip if you're like this."

"I cannot get us there any faster. That ability is gone, remember?"

I drew back at his bitter tone. "Nobody asked you to. We'll be fine traveling at the normal rate."

He said nothing, his expression growing darker.

It was a long, long trek. I tried to talk with him. Baldwin continued to sulk, only answering with single syllables. I gave up. Were we there yet?

After we passed the Aviva Desert exit, the portal became busier. Fortunately, the travel portal here was well-maintained, the gutter clean and the helli lights spaced at regular intervals and working well. Our steps clicked with purpose on the cobblestone pathway.

A sudden disturbance caught my eye. Ahead, two muscular men in light armor seized a man's arm. After slamming him against the tunnel wall, they began to search him. Other travelers hurried by, giving the group a wide berth.

I grabbed Baldwin's hand. "What's going on?"

His dark brows drew together. "I do not know, but we should not delay."

We hurried past the trio, while the man being searched protested he had done nothing wrong.

Once we'd put some distance between us and the men, Baldwin turned to me. "Did you see their breastplates?"

"No, I avoided looking at them."

"They had a snake medallion attached to the front."

My stomach hollowed. The memory of Abira's words regarding the medal came to mind—*it feels a bit like the power stored in jaspers.*

Thrusting my hand into my bag, I curled my fingers around the medallion. I pulled it out and shoved it at Baldwin. "Here. Can you use this? Abira said the power feels like what's in jaspers. Maybe it could help us get to our destination quicker."

Baldwin gripped it in his hand, and his face brightened. "It feels like the same thing. But we should save it for an emergency."

Wasn't that what this was? I bit my tongue. It didn't feel right telling him how to use his talent. "Well, put it in your pocket in case we need it in a hurry."

Another hour passed as we talked about trivial things—the griffin house, the Warrior guild, his roommates. His improved mood made the trip more pleasant. Inside, though, I was frustrated. I couldn't say anything to make the loss of his talent better. When I lost mine, I felt like I didn't matter, that I was less. Was Baldwin struggling with the same thing?

As we drew near the exit for Lennor, the pounding of marching boots broke into my thoughts.

"Halt!" a voice yelled from behind, seconds before a beefy hand grabbed my arm and spun me around. Two broad guards, each with a medallion on their chest, inspected us. The tall one who'd grabbed my arm spoke. "State your reason for using this tunnel."

I ducked my head. At this close range, they'd notice I was a very effeminate guy.

Baldwin cleared his throat. "We are on our way to visit our sick uncle."

The shorter guard sneered. "What's his name?"

"Desmond Mazur," Baldwin answered promptly.

The taller guard moved in closer. "What's in your bags? They need to be searched."

Baldwin's face flushed, and his hands balled into fists. "Why? We are not carrying contraband."

I blinked once to keep my expression from freezing into horror. No contraband, but a whole sheet of paper with instructions and remembrances of a deactivated portal entrance. And an old jar of Respiraqua. And an ancient medical journal. We were dead.

The guard's voice dropped to a rasp. "Because I said so. Unless you'd both like to get up close and personal with my sword."

Chancing a glance up, my gaze snagged on the shorter guard. His eyes narrowed. "You look familiar. I know you..." His voice trailed off while my saliva turned to wood shavings.

I withdrew deeper into my hood, a gut-level warning stealing my breath.

Baldwin took a step closer to me and grabbed my hand. His other hand was shoved in his pocket. "We're in a *hurry*." His eyes met mine as he jerked his head toward our destination.

I got the message.

Turning, we both sprinted away. As my steps matched his, vertigo hit. Colors swirled. While Baldwin and I hurtled through the tunnel, people around us seemed to slow. Everything blurred. The guards were left behind, shouts to stop fading.

Holding Baldwin's hand, I continued to squint because the less I saw, the better my stomach felt. After several minutes, I tugged his arm, struggling to speak.

"Whatever you're doing, stop."

He slowed, then stopped, then stepped off to the side of the tunnel. A broad grin split his face. "What does Anna always say? Oh yeah, that was foamed out."

"Anna says a lot of things. I don't say them, and you shouldn't either." My vision cleared, patched holes and graffiti coming into focus. A broken helli light winked off and on above us. A thin trickle of liquid dampened the gutter.

He took my hand. "Are you okay?"

Mostly. I kept my other hand on my stomach, which still whirled like a blender. "Yeah. We passed Lennor a minute ago. Where's Half-Mile Down?"

"We are not far."

"The deactivated entrance was about ten minutes this side of the trading center, and the hole was large, covered with a mesh screen." I looked both ways, the tunnel empty for the moment.

"We are close, then." Rolling his shoulders, Baldwin started off down the tunnel.

I stayed on his heels, my hand resting on my sword. Tension settled heavy on my neck, cramping my shoulders. I pulled my scarf higher. Five minutes later, the tunnel was full of travelers. So much for secrecy. I tugged at my cloak again, withdrawing into the folds, and tried to mimic his walk. More up and down, less side-to-side sway.

After several glances at me, Baldwin touched my arm. "What is wrong?"

"Huh? Nothing. Why?"

"You are walking funny."

I huffed out a breath and gave up. He was right—I was a lousy guy.

Just ahead, a man in uniform caught my attention, a serpent medallion glittering on his chest. The lines of his face pinched into a menacing scowl. And behind him waited a huge hole covered with mesh screening.

Chapter Thirteen

Baldwin slowed and gave me a questioning glance. Yeah, not stopping. I continued on as though our destination was far ahead. After rounding a curve in the tunnel, we were out of sight of Mr. Mean and Nasty.

I turned to Baldwin. "That was the entrance. How are we going to get in with him there?"

He shook his head, a grim twist to his mouth. "We need a distraction, something to pull him from his station."

"Great idea. And how will we do that?"

"No clue. A good soldier does not leave his post."

I rubbed my forehead where the start of a headache gathered. "Maybe an emergency. What crisis would pull him from that spot?"

"A request from his commander." Baldwin crossed his arms, sure of his answer.

"That doesn't help unless you can impersonate Rune. What about a fire?"

"That might work."

My shoulders slumped. Fire, but no fuel. "The only fuel I've got is a small notebook, but it won't burn long."

Baldwin rummaged in his bag, pulling out a notebook of his own. "Here, use this too."

I ripped out a handful of sheets. "Let's crumple the paper, then lay the rest near the gutter."

He frowned. "Why?"

"Because we can't start a fire in the middle of the tunnel. It would make the most sense for it to start off to the side, like someone threw a match or a cigarette or something."

After a minute, Baldwin's hands overflowed with paper balls. "This is not working."

I shot him an irritated glare. Great positive thinking. "Well, I haven't lit them yet."

"No, I mean anyone coming around the curve in the tunnel will see us starting a fire."

"Oh. Hmm." I sat near the gutter, avoiding the questionable liquid dribbling in a thin stream. "Put the paper behind me. I'll cover it with my cloak until I'm ready to light it."

As I carefully fanned out my cloak, Baldwin stuffed a few pieces of paper behind me. I added my own, the pile growing behind me, mostly concealed by my cloak.

Putting a couple of paper balls behind me, he leaned closer to whisper in my ear. "We have company from your left."

I rubbed my knee as if I was hurt. "Seized up on me." I lowered my voice to its bottommost register.

Confusion colored his expression before he grinned. "You should have stretched before we started."

"I will be fine."

The travelers were two girls about our age who slowed a bit as they walked around us. The taller one glanced back at me, gave me a flirty smile, and winked. My cheeks heated. I might be a lousy guy, but I'd fooled at least one person.

As they continued on, I looked up to see Baldwin smirking. "Do I have competition?"

"Um, saw that, huh? No, she wasn't my type."

His eyes lit with laughter as he put the last sheets of paper under my cloak. "That is all of it."

"Okay, I'm going to light it. As soon as it catches, we hurry back and tell him. Let's hope it draws him away."

Baldwin looked both ways. "Wow. Right now, the tunnel is empty."

Before I could overthink it, I stood and released a small fireball. The paper lit, the white edges browning before becoming ash. A thin wisp of smoke curled toward the ceiling. We backed away and hurried toward the soldier. A sudden pop made me turn. While the paper continued to burn, the fire spread in the gutter, flames leaping in the liquid. Flammable. Great.

Baldwin's eyes grew round. "Fire!"

We ran toward the soldier, skidding to a stop next to him.

Baldwin pointed down the corridor. "My lord, a fire is in the gutter, coming this way!"

Mr. Mean and Nasty's expression grew darker before he hurried in that direction. Baldwin slipped behind me and slid the screen cover from the opening.

"Come on, Brenna."

After I rushed into the tunnel, he struggled to replace the screening. I held my breath. What if he couldn't get it into place in time?

"I need help," he said with a grunt.

I hurried to Baldwin's side.

"There are hooks on the other side," he explained. "The best we can do is prop this screen up. The guard will probably fail to notice. Can you help me pull it into place?"

I grabbed my side and pushed and pulled, wincing at the metallic screech. Maneuvering the grate was like herding an elephant into a refrigerator.

We hurried away from the opening, almost at a run. I checked behind us. The circle of light at the end remained clear, evidence the guard hadn't returned. Turning, we hurried farther into the dark tunnel, a small flame in my palm as a flashlight.

The interior was as I remembered. Filigreed silver brackets spanned the tunnel walls at regular intervals. Made of brown stone, the walls, path, and gutter remained clean and dry, even if the air carried a stale scent this far back from the main corridor.

Ahead, a glossy surface gleamed from the reflected firelight. I dashed forward, eager to show Baldwin my find from several months ago. We stopped in front of the silvery-white, glossy obstruction.

He touched it with a finger. "Cold, yet it gives."

"Not enough. I couldn't push through it."

The red flames in my palm contoured his cheekbones. He pointed to my scabbard. "What about your sword?"

"I didn't have one last time. It's worth a try."

Withdrawing his sword, he used both hands to swing it in a large arc. The sword sank into the substance, its progress slowing until it stopped. Baldwin yanked on the handle several times before his shoulders drooped. "Stuck. And I really liked this sword."

I'd thought about this substance for a while, remembering the look, the feel, and possible solutions to getting through this strange blockage.

I touched Baldwin's arm. "Let me try something."

I pulled off my cloak so it wouldn't be in the way and stowed it in my bag. Closing my eyes, I called up an image in my mind. I inhaled, then breathed out slowly, the words of the Firebrand creed an unspoken song in my heart. Power surged through my arms. I opened my eyes and gasped.

"Nice," he murmured.

A red, glowing ax, with a wicked sharp blade, blazed in my grip. Grasping it with both hands, I swung it at the glassy material. It slipped through like a hot knife through butter. With several more swipes, I carved out Baldwin's sword, the substance melting as the fiery ax touched it.

With a few more cuts, I'd sliced a hole big enough for us to climb through. Beyond the door, the tunnel continued, an unbroken hallway of stone and silver brackets. I collapsed the fiery ax and propped my hands on my hips. "Well, that was anticlimactic. Why would anyone block off more tunnel?"

"Not sure." Baldwin wiped off his sword with the hem of his shirt before slipping it back into its scabbard. He patted it with a pleased smile. "Thanks. I appreciate that."

Another flame flared in my palm for light, and we continued on, the tunnel walls narrowing and the stone path turning darker in hue. Bending down, I touched the ground, my fingers coming away damp. Where was the moisture coming from?

After a few more steps, Baldwin held up a hand. "Listen."

Plip. Plop. Plip-plip. Plop. Dripping water echoed in the corridor.

He checked the ceiling before pointing to the brackets. "The walls are wet, and the bracings are rusted."

"Where's the water coming from?"

"If we are under mountains, it could be runoff."

"Through the travel portal?"

He pursed his lips and shrugged. As we continued walking, rivulets of water trickled down the walls. An inch of water soon coated the path as we sloshed through it, full gutters on either side. The tunnel angled downward, a pinhole of light growing at the other end. The water rushed away from us, toward our destination.

We hurried forward, anxious to be out of the damp, drippy tunnel. Although Baldwin didn't say anything, he scanned our surroundings with one hand on his sword.

We cleared the tunnel and stumbled to a stop. Our path ended at a small cliff. A solid bluff of stone on each side anchored the portal exit. No way of escape presented itself.

I looked at Baldwin, stunned. "Now what?"

He leaned over the edge of the cliff and checked the view below. "I think I see a pool far below."

"Yeah, thanks. Not helping."

He held his hands up, palms out. "Just stating the truth. We have two choices. Either return the way we came or jump."

My mouth dropped open. "That's not a choice. That's suicide."

"I thought you knew how to swim."

"I do, but what if it's a tiny, shallow pool?"

He raised one eyebrow, almost like a dare. "It looks deep. And it appears to be our only way to discover what is down there."

"Then how would we get back up? What if it's not deep?" Across the valley, a mountain range disappeared into cloud cover. A glimmer caught my attention, my previous questions already forgotten. I squinted. "What's that shiny stuff?"

"Adamas Mountain. The entire face is composed of quartz tubes that disappear into Mermaid Cove."

The tunnel behind us filled with a sudden thundering roar. I whirled to look. A wall of water surged forward, funneling toward our vulnerable position on the cliff.

Baldwin grabbed my hand. "Jump!"

Sucking in a quick breath, I leaped, portal water surrounding us. The quartz face of Adamas Mountain glistened as we fell. In seconds, rock walls covered in greenery rushing to meet us blocked the view. Baldwin's hand, my lifeline, was snatched from my grasp, and we landed in a large pool, the water warm.

After sinking deep, I struggled to the surface with a gasp. "Baldwin?"

A second more and his head broke the surface, a grin on his face as he spotted me. The tight coils in my chest loosened. We located our bags bobbing on the water like buoys. After a brief struggle, I wrangled mine onto the bank.

The current tugged, pulling me away from the edge of the pool and into the center. I kicked against the flow, panting. Almost there. I reached up, the edge of the pool farther away than before. The water level was dropping.

"Um, we have a problem," I gasped.

"Keep swimming." He wasn't far behind me, the undercurrent pulling both of us away from escape.

My toes scraped the bottom. With brutal force, the water knocked my feet out from under me. A fear of being sucked down a drain, a phobia I'd outgrown years ago, surged to life. Arms flailing, my head went under, and I inhaled a mouthful of lake water.

The current tumbled me along the pebble-strewn bottom before slamming me into a grated hole. I pushed my face above the rushing flow, coughing and hacking. The water disappeared into the void, but I couldn't move, the force draining the lake greater than anything I'd ever felt.

In seconds, the tugging sensation stopped, and warm, dry air rushed from the grate. Still coughing, I braced myself on my hands and knees, air blasting my face. Despite my efforts to move away, it was impossible. An exquisite floral scent drifted over me. Pure bliss.

"Hold your breath!" Baldwin yelled over the sound of rushing air.

I beamed as he squished his way toward me. "But why? It smells like lilacs."

He hurried to my side, his jaw set. "Alucin gas. It causes a loss of consciousness and bad dreams."

Grabbing the wet scarf hanging near my face, he covered my mouth and nose and helped me stand. The warm rush of air followed us as we moved away.

We squelched to the edge of the lake bed. Baldwin boosted me onto dry ground, and I turned to offer him a hand. He took it, and as he began to climb, his eyes rolled back in his head and he went limp.

That cleared my head. "No, no, no," I whispered as he lay slumped against the bank. I tugged. He was a dead weight, and Superman wasn't waiting in the wings to help. Seconds dragged by as I tried to puzzle out how to get him out of the pool.

The sloshing of flowing water drew my gaze upward. Water shot from rock crevices, filling the pool like a tsunami wave. Great. Just super, because things weren't nearly difficult enough. As the pool filled, I desperately pulled with all my strength, my muscles burning.

Finally, his body shifted, and I dragged him out of the pool, over rocks and rough ground. I slumped next to him. He'd be bruised when he woke up, but he was alive.

The clearing lay hidden with high stone walls surrounding it. Four archways had been carved into the rock at equal distances apart. Clusters of trees and low-lying ferns filled the spaces between each arch.

Although my clothes were almost dry from the warm gas, my boots squished with every step. Baldwin seemed comfortable for now, so perhaps a fire would help dry our boots while I waited for him to wake up.

After a quick search, I located a good amount of branches and kindling. I cleared an area near Baldwin and started a fire. While the fire grew, I used sticks to make supports and spread our cloaks over them to dry. I pulled off my socks and boots and Baldwin's as well. Surprisingly, everything in our bags appeared pretty dry. Maybe the skins were waterproof.

While our clothes dried, I settled next to him. How long would he be out? Would we have to stay here overnight? I shivered despite the warm air.

Baldwin shifted, muttering a bit before his words became clearer. "Whether you like it or not, I am a Time Reeler."

Of course he was. I opened my mouth to respond but never got the chance.

"Father, I am not Erhardt. My talent lies elsewhere."

His eyes remained closed, so I prodded his shoulder, but he shifted away.

"I cannot follow in his footsteps. That is not my gift. But there is honor in each talent, not just in being a Warrior." He bit his lip, worry screwing up his face. "I will make you proud of me. I promise."

My heart broke as a tear leaked from the corner of his closed eye. Unfortunately, that wasn't the end of it. For the better part of an hour, Baldwin argued with his father or muttered nonsense. I spent some time brushing his hair from his forehead, an action that seemed to calm him.

Baldwin finally moaned and opened his eyes.

"Hey." The tight grip on my heart eased, and I brushed his hair back from his forehead a final time. "You're back."

"I keep passing out on you." He skewed his mouth into a grimace. "Sorry. Was I out long?"

"No, only about an hour." One of the longest of my life.

Rubbing his forehead, he sat up. "Wow. Some of those dreams seemed real."

I cleared my throat. "Really? What were they about?"

He looked away. "Just bad stuff. Like, really disjointed images."

My stomach sank. Well, I wasn't ignoring the white elephant in the clearing. Which in this case was his father. "Really? Cause you talked quite a bit."

His eyes shot to my face. "I did? What did I say?"

I bit my lip. "Um, you muttered and argued a lot, I think with your dad."

His shoulders drooped. "Oh."

Hesitating, I leaned close. I really didn't want to screw this up or make him shut down. "He's wrong, you know."

His gaze slid away. "About what?"

"About you. Erhardt's an okay guy, but he's not you."

Shrugging, he said nothing.

I ran through all the arguments in my head, but none of them sounded good. The fire popped, wood smoke scenting the air.

After several long minutes passed, I nudged him. "When you found out I lost my talent, how come you didn't ditch me? I mean, I was useless, especially as we escaped from the castle. I was just a weirdo with a hairstreak clutching her sword."

Baldwin's fierce gaze met mine. "Not true. You alerted the queen to the imposters using Shadow Power. You have good instincts and traits that have nothing to do with your gift."

"Yeah? Like what?"

"Your loyalty, your determination, your ability to solve puzzles." He ticked them off on his fingers, not even hesitating.

I poked at the fire with a stick before turning to him with a grin. "Gotcha. Just like you have abilities that have nothing to do with your gift. You know, a really cute guy, a Linnean actually, told me something important a long time ago. 'Just because someone says it, does not make it true.' Your father loves you. I'm not saying his comments didn't hurt, but I don't think your Warrior status makes you more valuable. Learn all you can about weaponry if it makes you feel better. But before you even discovered your talent, I thought you were pretty cool."

The words came easily, eking by the others lurking in my throat, the ones about how my life was richer with him in it, his voice was the one I dreamed about, and how his arms were one of the safest places I'd ever been.

I wanted to say I loved him. But I wasn't saying it first. No way. Not ever.

Amusement teased the edges of his lips. "Cool, huh? Even when I act like a jerk?"

I shrugged. "Everyone has those moments."

He reached out, capturing my hand. "You were supposed to say I could never be a jerk."

My side glance expressed volumes, and he chuckled. We sat quietly for a while, watching the fire dance and our clothes dry.

I finally spoke, content to change the topic. "So which way should we go—north, south, east, or west? Want to flip a coin?"

Baldwin rolled his eyes. "You are smarter than that. If we go that way"—he pointed to the archway behind us—"I think it returns to the travel portal at some point. I am guessing left and right will take us toward Lennor and Hamlin Bay respectively."

When he didn't say anything else, I pointed to the archway in front of us. "Where does this archway go?"

"The only thing in that direction is the mountainous region that leads to Adamas Mountain. Primitive."

"Is it explored?"

He shook his head. "Not really."

I sighed. "That's probably where we need to go, then."

He checked the inside of his boots. "Almost dry." He cast a wary glance at our surroundings. "I am not sure how safe this place is in the middle of the night."

The thought sent a shiver down my spine, and I tugged my cloak from my bag. We pulled on our socks and boots in silence.

After shouldering our bags, we headed toward the far archway. I arranged my now-dry scarf to cover the lower part of my face.

After a slight curve, a dense, tropical rainforest greeted us. The humid air pressed down, making me sweat. I spent all that energy and time drying out for this?

"Stop right there!" A guard strode over, his hand gripping the whip at his side. His lips curled into a sneer, and wrinkles stretched out from the corners of his narrowed brown eyes. "Who are you? Did the prince send you?"

CHAPTER FOURTEEN

"YES, OF COURSE," BALDWIN responded, his voice smooth and confident.

"Are you here to inspect the crop? I told him before he left it wouldn't be ready for another week."

When we didn't respond, the man gave a huff and hurried off, clearly expecting us to follow.

I widened my eyes at Baldwin and pulled down my scarf. *What are you doing?* I mouthed.

He visibly swallowed and shrugged.

The man trudged up a dirt footpath leading through gnarly tree roots and thick, glossy leaves. As his strides ate up the ground, we dashed after him. Through palm-like trees and ropy vines, I glimpsed the glittering quartz tubes of the Adamas Mountain emerging from the heavy cloud cover, their glistening lengths plunging straight into the horizon. Moss dripped from fern-like trees, and vines curled through the green undergrowth.

I adjusted the face scarf back into position. We crested a small rise, and I blocked the sudden burst of light with my hand. The facets of the tubes angled the sunlight onto the massive field in front of us. Plants with pale green leaves and striking red marks covered the ground.

The path encircled the field in a spacious arc, and rough-timbered houses, some with small garden plots, lined the track. With guards nearby, people in groups of two and three worked in the field, bending and disappearing from view before popping back up. The workers were of different ages and skin tones, their backs stooped and bent from their work.

Near the end of the row, a guard stood watch while two women worked. His whip split the air, and I flinched. A scent on the breeze stung my nose, a foul blend of cayenne, fennel, and ginger. Under my cloak, a drop of sweat slid down my neck.

The man gestured to the field. "Here, just like my report stated. The workers are stripping the foundation leaves. We'll dry them the day after tomorrow, but the rest of the plants aren't ready for harvest yet. We have a five, maybe seven, day wait."

After clearing my throat, I lowered my voice. "We're to check the rest of the place."

The man gave me a quizzical glance, then shrugged. "Fine. I can't imagine you'll want to stay long."

He spun on his heel and followed the path back to his post.

I glared at Baldwin and dropped my voice to a whisper. "Now what? How are we going to find out where we are, when we don't know who the prince is?"

"We can find out. Ask around."

"Oh yeah, everyone's super friendly." I rolled my eyes. "No one's going to say anything. The workers won't, that's for sure. And if anyone notices that melted portal door, they'll know we aren't supposed to be here."

"Hello there."

We turned at the raspy voice. An old Camlo woman stood by the open door to her house. She wore a simple dress of pale green, and a straw hat covered her head.

A network of wrinkles lined her face as she smiled. "Why don't you come in out of the sun? I have ice-cold rain fruit juice I'm willing to share."

A guard shouted in the field. I turned as his whip found the back of a nearby man. Cringing, my hands balled into fists. I shot a look at Baldwin and stepped away from the nightmare. "Thanks. Sounds good."

As we entered the house, the old woman placed her hat on a nearby table, revealing her bald head. Her kind expression shone against her rich brown skin. "I pull the drapes to keep it cool here. Why don't you join me in the kitchen?"

We passed through the simple living room decorated with only a low table, one chair, and a padded settee. The utilitarian kitchen held a counter, wood shelves stacked with mismatched dishes and mugs, a sink, and a dining table with four chairs.

"You settle here at the table while I get the juice." She tottered off down the stairs.

A minute later, she returned with a pitcher. She pulled three mugs from her shelf, and after pouring, passed them out. I couldn't take a drink, not with the scarf still covering my mouth. I set the drink on the table.

She settled next to me. "My name is Sorsha. And who are you?"

I opened my mouth, but Baldwin beat me to it. "This is Bob, and I am, um, Ben. We are here to check the prince's crop."

I wanted to strangle him.

Sorsha gave us another gentle smile. "Nice to meet you, Bob and Um-Ben. It was good of the prince to send you. Such a kind man, full of goodwill and caring for his community."

"Yes, we have found that to be true." A nervous tic twitched near Baldwin's left eye as he continued his improv routine.

Sorsha leaned forward, her glittering onyx eyes suddenly shrewd. "Really? Anyone the prince sent wouldn't have stopped to drink rainfruit juice with an old woman. So let me ask again. Who are you?"

My breath stalled in my lungs.

Baldwin swallowed, his Adam's apple bobbing. "I believe you have misunderstood—"

"Don't." I put a hand on his arm. "Just stop."

"What? She clearly has—"

I couldn't do much worse than he had. "I'm Brenna, and this guy who won't stop talking is Baldwin. You're absolutely right. We don't know the prince, and we don't know where we are." Ignoring Baldwin's huff of irritation, I pulled off my face scarf.

"Mm-hmm." Sorsha leaned back with a satisfied smirk.

The knot in my stomach cinched tighter. Would she call for the guard? Kill us herself? Had I doomed us by spilling it all?

"And how did you arrive here in the valley?"

As I hesitated, she added, "The truth. I'll know if you're lying."

"We were flooded out of a deactivated tunnel and ended up in the pool. I'm not sure how we'll return."

She grimaced, her wrinkles shifting. "Well, you're here now. I can keep you safe if the prince shows up."

I breathed out a quiet breath of relief. "Who is he?"

"His name is Rune, although he prefers to be called Prince Rune."

My mouth fell open. "What? How did he become ruler of this place?"

Sorsha's brown eyes filled with sadness. "Ah, I see you know him. Many families escaped to this unexplored valley during the Guild War. In the past, only miners looking for Adamas quartz came through, and they used the higher path through the mountains. So we remained safe and undiscovered for many times until Rune learned of us. He came in, killed the resisters, and took captive the able-bodied."

I leaned forward. "Are you one of the Lost Children?"

She frowned. "Lost Children?"

Baldwin's eyes lit up as he turned to Sorsha. "The families who disappeared during the Fifty-Time Guild War are called the Lost Children. Many Jasper Territory citizens searched everywhere. But nobody ever thought to look here."

Sorsha nodded. "My grandparents built a comfortable life here, never thinking we'd eventually be imprisoned."

"You don't look trapped." I arched an eyebrow.

"Appearances are deceiving. With my bad legs, I can't work in the fields, but I'm required to deliver babies, care for the sick. Things I would do anyway. Not everyone is so lucky." She took a sip of juice.

"And no one has attempted to escape?" Baldwin leaned back in his chair.

Sorsha shook her head. "The exits are blocked. Even if we could escape the guards, we'd end up trapped in the clearing. So why did you come here, Um-Ben?"

He flushed. "I prefer Baldwin, thank you. A prophecy led us here, claiming a treasure needed to be claimed and freed."

Sorsha leaned forward. "A prophecy? What does it say?"

I repeated it.

"It mentions a key?"

"Yeah." I fidgeted with my scarf. "That's one of the parts we don't understand—at least not yet. We were more focused on the treasures, hoping once we found them, we would get more answers."

Since I didn't feel completely comfortable with her yet, I didn't mention the staff.

The faint scent of fennel and ginger lingered in the house, a faint reminder of past unpleasant experiences.

"The crop outside is Shadow Power, isn't it?"

She gave me a side glance. "Aren't you a smart one? Yes, it is. And when the prince returns, he plans to collect it all."

My stomach sank. The massive fields contained plenty of the drug to give to his army. "Is there a way to stop him?"

Sorsha shook her head. "You don't say no to him."

That's what I was afraid she'd say. "Does he have any supporters here?"

She pursed her lips in thought. "Most of the guards are loyal since their families are promised safety."

Baldwin gave me an appreciative look as if he understood where I was going with my line of questioning. Good, since I wasn't so sure myself. I was just gathering information.

He took a sip of his juice. "How many guards are there?"

"Ten, but don't count Gerard at the tunnel. He puts up a gruff front, but he doesn't like the prince either."

"When's Rune supposed to return?" I asked.

"He left three days ago. So it'll probably be about five days before he returns."

"Probably?" Baldwin leaned forward in his seat.

"Relax, young man." Sorsha patted his hand. "The prince rarely stays long."

We sat in companionable silence before she stood.

"Since you're here, why don't you join me for supper? I have plenty, and I don't mind sharing."

I glanced at Baldwin. "If you're sure..."

"Absolutely." She turned to Baldwin. "Um-Ben, help me get some things out of the cellar."

Baldwin's cheeks flushed again as he rose to follow her.

I stifled a grin. "Do you need any help?"

"You just relax, Brenna." Sorsha's voice trailed up from the cellar.

Walking into the living room, I thought about where we'd spend tonight. Maybe there was an inn here. I snorted. Probably not. And leaving didn't seem like the right thing to do. The prophecy said to find and free the treasure. What was it? *Where* was it?

Baldwin peeled and chopped vegetables, then Sorsha pulled it all into a giant carmeil salad with a side of crusty bread.

As we gathered in the kitchen to eat, there was a knock at Sorsha's front door. "Sorsha?"

She hurried to the door and opened it. "Gerard, how can I help you?"

"Wanted to check on you. Saw those inspectors come in. Didn't expect them to stay so long."

"You worry too much. Come in."

Baldwin and I pushed back our chairs and stood. His hand grasped mine in a protective gesture.

The guard who had escorted us to the field walked in, his gaze sweeping the room. His shoulders stiffened as he caught sight of the two of us waiting in the kitchen doorway. "What's going on?"

Sorsha led him over to the chair in the corner of the living room. "The inspectors are these youngsters. They're following a prophecy that led them to us."

Perching on the chair's edge, the man licked his lips. "But the prince said—"

"Gerard, that man doesn't deserve your loyalty. Remember what he did to your sister?"

A flash of grief came and went on the older man's face. He swallowed and regarded us again. "Where are you from?"

Baldwin stepped into the living room. "We are both from Linneah. As I told Sorsha, many people from the Jasper Territory searched for you after the Guild War."

Sorsha shook a finger in the guard's face. "Don't you dare say a word to anyone about them. They're staying here until they decide to go."

Gerard rose and walked to the door. He gave us a searching gaze as he paused at the door. "I won't say anything. But I don't know how they plan to leave."

The closing door sounded like a cell slamming shut.

Baldwin leaned against the kitchen doorframe. "I am surprised he listened to you."

"He knows he'd better. I'm a Sensitive."

So that's how she knew we were lying. Her instant trust in us made sense, too.

After a filling supper, I wiped my mouth with a thin napkin. "That was delicious. Thank you."

She smiled. "You're welcome. I'd appreciate your help cleaning up the kitchen."

I pushed away from the table and stood. "Sure."

Baldwin made himself comfortable in the living room while I helped her clean the table and wash dishes.

As she filled the sink with soapy water, she looked at me. "Would you like to stay here tonight?"

I'd turned that problem around in my head during the meal but hadn't asked. She'd been so generous. "It would be a big help."

She dried a newly washed bowl with a soft towel. "One of you can sleep in the storage room and the other on the living room floor. I have a few blankets, but with the humidity from Mermaid Cove, I don't think you'll need many."

"How far away is the cove?"

Sorsha placed the clean bowl on the top shelf. "Just above the cloud cover. If it wasn't for the veil, we'd be underwater."

I stopped, my hands buried in soapy water. "What do you mean?"

She grinned. "You don't know anything about this place, eh? This is Undertown Valley. Mermaid Cove is above us, separated by only the veil."

I shut my gaping mouth. "A veil? Does it ever leak?"

"Not that I've heard or seen in my many times. We don't need rain for that rotten crop, just the sunlight that filters through the quartz. There's plenty of humidity in the air. Of course, it's good for our vegetable gardens, too."

I shook my head. So weird to live *under* the cove. Of course, if the clouds were usually as heavy as they were today, the residents would never be able to tell.

When we finished cleaning up, Sorsha told us to stay out of sight of the guards while she picked more vegetables from her garden. I joined Baldwin in the living room and shared Sorsha's and my conversation.

He put his arm around my shoulders and leaned against the padded settee. I laid my head on his chest, content to enjoy the sound of his heart beating.

His voice was a low rumble in my ear. "I have been thinking about the prophecy. What if the Lost Children are the treasure that needs to be freed?"

After a moment, I looked up at him. "How? They're trapped here." Just like we were. "And the guards...how would we get past them?"

"I do not know, at least not yet. But there has to be a way to help them escape."

I pulled away to get a better look at his face. "You're serious."

"They are valuable citizens imprisoned by an evil man. They should be free."

Standing, I walked to the window. Night had begun to fall. The shining light from the glittering quartz tubes faded. A dark-gray canvas, the sky held no stars or moon. No Petrus Rings either. As the wind blew, the scent of herbs tickled my nose. Baldwin's words hung in the room, a spark of hope.

"We'd have to evacuate everyone before Rune returned. But you know what else I'd like to do?"

Baldwin raised his eyebrows. "What?"

"I'd love to torch that whole field. Destroy the crop. Leave only devastation for him to find."

"Not that you are bitter or anything." His mouth quirked at the corner. "Seriously, though, it is a good idea."

"Do you think the people would be willing to leave?"

"We can ask Sorsha when she returns."

"Ask me what?" The older woman entered from outside, her hands full of vegetables.

Turning away from the window, I hurried toward her. "Let me help you with those."

Baldwin joined us in the kitchen as Sorsha and I brushed excess soil from the root vegetables before placing them in a wooden crate. "We were wondering how the residents would feel about a mass evacuation."

Her eyes grew wide. "I can't leave you two alone for a minute, can I? It's a bold idea, although I don't know how it'd be implemented."

Baldwin rubbed his chin. "How are the exits blocked?"

"A cloudy, wax-like barrier blocks the way to Lennor, Mermaid Cove, and Hamlin Bay."

I perked up. "If it's anything like that substance we encountered in the tunnel, I can get you out."

"What about the guards? They won't stand aside while people leave." Sorsha brushed the dirt off a round, purple vegetable.

I rinsed off my hands, then dried them on a towel. "That's a wrinkle we haven't ironed out yet. Do you have any ideas?"

She dropped into a kitchen chair, her eyes intent. "Tell me more, and maybe I'll think of something."

I slipped into the chair across from her. "If we could distract the guards, then we could evacuate everyone, get them to the neighboring cities. I would burn his crop to the ground. His Shadow Power drug has slipped into every city in the Jasper Territory, and it needs to be eliminated."

"He also uses it to strengthen his soldiers on the battlefield," Baldwin added.

Sorsha cleared her throat. "This strain of the crop is especially powerful, and therefore, valuable to him." She was quiet for a moment. "The people won't need much prodding to leave. As prisoners, many of them want to be free, to build a life away from this place. Gerard could help us with the guard situation. How do you plan to burn a crop of this size?"

I grinned. "I'm a Firebrand."

Sorsha's lips parted, the skin around them turning slightly gray. "Elyon help you. Don't let anyone hear you say that around here."

My heart dropped to my knees. "Why?"

"Because the prince killed all the Firebrands when he invaded. He intends to be the only one with that ability. Some families hide children who come into that talent, but when they're discovered, they're taken and never seen again."

The last Dunamis Rune left for me had been Marziah, Linneah's Firebrand instructor, wearing my jasper. Knowing she'd been chosen because of her talent was a bitter pill.

Sorsha continued. "He uses his gift to control, terrorize, and kill others. If he finds out about you, well, there's no telling what he'll do."

I stood and pushed in the chair, the salad a solid lump in my stomach. "He already knows me. And that's why I want to torch this crop before he comes back."

She sighed. "If you want to clear out the valley, that crop is the least of your problems."

Baldwin stepped closer. "What if we could neutralize the guards tomorrow? We could encourage people to leave, tell them there was an emergency, and they have to evacuate."

"You can't neutralize the guards in one day, but Gerard could." Sorsha propped her hands on her hips. "I'm too old for this. But this opportunity may not come again." She walked into her bedroom, muttering and shaking her head as she closed the door behind her.

Baldwin rubbed his neck and looked at me. "Now what?"

I shrugged. "No clue. But we can't do this without help." Disappointment filled my chest. "Maybe we've gotten carried away."

Sitting, Baldwin focused on her closed bedroom door with a gimlet stare.

Several minutes later, she came out of her bedroom with an armful of linens. "Here." She thrust the sheets at me. "Make up a bed for Um-Ben in the storage room and another for yourself here in the living room."

An etched, leather-bound book lay on top of the pile. A faded ribbon held the book closed. I placed the sheets on the sofa before holding up the book. "What's this?"

Sorsha stepped close, the scent of fresh earth and flowers surrounding us. "That's my great-grandmother's diary. You might find some answers inside."

I flipped through the book, the cover worn smooth.

She turned and pointed at Baldwin. "You're coming with me. Let's find Gerard and talk to him about your risky idea."

Chapter Fifteen

After they left, I made up a bed in the storage room for Baldwin. Not much was there—a dusty chair, boxes covered by an old sheet, and a couple of woven baskets, one of which had a broken handle. I spread out a few blankets and included a thick folded one for a pillow if Baldwin needed it. Five minutes later, I had a similar sleeping area for myself on the living room floor near the couch.

The diary lay on a small table in the living room. I eyed it as I made my bed, my skin itchy with the possibility of answers within the pages. After sitting down, I removed the ribbon holding the book closed and opened it.

The faded entries were written by a young Camlo girl living in the mountains of Wildamek—entries about her family buying their first rason to raise on their farm, about the boy she had a crush on, and about her grades at the conservatory.

While it was interesting, it wasn't what I was looking for, so I began skimming. About halfway through, the word "key" popped out from an entry.

My mother came home yesterday carrying a beautiful key on a silver cord. I've never seen anything so pretty. Mother won't tell me

*what it's for. I wonder if it opens the door to a gorgeous castle high in
the mountains? Or maybe it's a gift for one of the dragons of Fallon.
Or perhaps it belongs to the Midnight Unicorn.*

The entry ended. Despite my uncertainty regarding the Midnight Unicorn, there wasn't near enough information for me. Several entries passed before I found another reference.

*I should keep this secret, but I cannot keep it inside. My mother
has been entrusted with the key to the Caelestis Staff. She will leave
to find a hiding place for the key in a few weeks, and I'm going with
her! It shall be a grand adventure! My mother says for too long the
staff has lain unguarded. But with the key, the powerful staff will be
secure. I so wish we could see the staff itself, but our trip is only to find
a suitable place for the key, nothing more.*

Stunned, I sat back, my index finger marking my place. This had to be the key mentioned in the prophecy. It was linked to the Caelestis Staff, although I didn't know how. Maybe it unlocked the box where the staff was stored.

I flipped to another page and began searching.

Again, she filled the pages with reports of her daily life—until nothing. A blank page, then the entries began again, three weeks later, speaking of her life, her friends, her everyday routine. I could've cried. I skimmed the rest of the pages, hoping for another mention, but nothing.

By the time Sorsha and Baldwin returned, I'd had plenty of time to turn ideas around in my head while I got ready for bed. I raised my head from the pillow when they walked in the door.

Sorsha lifted a hand to cover her yawn. "I'm going to bed. Baldwin can tell you what happened at the meeting. Goodnight."

"G'night." Any questions would have to wait until morning. I sat up and crossed my legs while Baldwin settled on the floor near my makeshift bed.

He gave me a satisfied smile as he leaned against the settee. "The meeting went well. The same substance in the deactivated tunnel blocks the exits. I offered your services in eliminating it. Gerard has agreed to help by sharing a drink with his fellow guards laced with a sleeping agent. But if some fail to drink it, we may have to detain or distract them in other ways.

"Tomorrow, Sorsha will spread the news to the workers and their families. They will have the day to pack and prepare, then, the next day, we will help evacuate the people to the outlying cities of Hamlin Bay, Lennor, or the travel portal for those who wish to risk it. She is also sharing information about the guilds, so if they wish to join, they know where to go."

"Why don't we send them all to the guilds right off?"

Baldwin shook his head. "How? The travel portal is too dangerous. If Rune or his guards recognize them, they will be killed."

Disappointment filled my chest. No quick solutions, just a plan and a hope things went smoothly.

Baldwin continued. "The day after tomorrow, we will get up early, have breakfast, and head for the portal entry. Sorsha thinks a few families will be ready to go immediately. But we have tomorrow to prepare."

I took a deep breath. There was so much to do, but it would have to wait. "It's late. I should probably get some sleep."

He leaned close, brushing his lips against mine. Once, twice, and then he lingered, our breaths mingling. The dim lighting in the room, the warmth of his hands, his scent of citrus and leather—it all pulled me in. I moved closer as his mouth found mine again. His hands skimmed my waist, finding a bare strip of sensitive skin under my tank top. I gasped as his hands glided up my bare back and he took the kiss deeper.

All that existed was the two of us. I caressed his neck, sinking my fingers into the glossy hair at his nape. Baldwin groaned. I jerked away. Sheesh. I obviously didn't know what I was doing.

He grabbed my wrists, his fingers gentle. "Do not go. Please."

"I don't think I'm very good at this."

He raised an eyebrow. "You are so wrong about that."

Sorsha bustled in, and we jerked away from each other. She turned, her eyes wide. "You two are still up? It's late, you know."

"Sure. Right. Yes." Baldwin squeezed my hand and scrambled to his feet.

I closed my eyes in a long blink, heat climbing my cheeks, suddenly mortified at how senseless I'd been moments ago.

Leaning down, he winked and whispered, "Sleep well, love."

I twitched, stunned silent, as he walked into the storage room. My heart melted into a liquid glow in my chest while my mind spun. Love? He'd never called me that before. Confused, I slid into my nest of covers. My mind replayed his flirty wink and whispered comment in a looping reel, each replay as sweet as the first.

Although sleep came, dreams arrived with it. A bare-chested Baldwin rode a singing donkey, hiding from me while carrying a key as big as his arm. I woke an hour later, my blankets twisted around my feet. What was with that dream? A singing donkey?

Grabbing a blanket, I snuggled it around my shoulders, slipped out the front door, and settled on the front steps. Although darkness blanketed the community, the quartz tubes emitted a dull glow. The lack of stars and moon amplified the silence. Scents of fennel and basil rode the light breeze.

The door creaked open, and I turned.

Sorsha lowered herself next to me with a moan. "I used to be able to scramble up and down like a jungle rat, but now?" She shook her head. "Why are you out here in the dark?"

"I couldn't sleep."

"We have a lot to accomplish in the next day or two."

"I know, but—" I let the sentence die. Sleep showed up when it wanted to, sometimes complete with weird dreams.

"Did you read the diary?" At my nod, she pursed her lips. "You have questions. That's what's keeping you up."

Maybe. Or a hot boyfriend with talented barnyard animals. "The diary mentioned a key."

She focused on the dimly lit quartz tubes. "From the prophecy. You must find it."

I ground my teeth in frustration. "But your great-grandmother didn't write anything about the trip and never mentioned where it was hidden."

Sorsha snorted. "Of course not. News like that isn't scattered about like seeds. But a few secrets were passed down to me. I never had children, so they might have died with me. But..." Her teeth gleamed in the shadows. "It appears I will get to share at least one secret with you."

Any remaining restlessness evaporated, and I leaned forward.

Her voice was like fine-grit sandpaper. "To find the key, you must go to Mermaid Cove."

I waited, but she leaned back, finished. Shifting on the steps, I blinked once. "That's it? The cove is pretty big, right?"

"Yes, it is. You'll need help from the keepers of the cove."

Hope flared. The cove had a keeper? "Do the keepers live nearby?"

Sorsha chuckled. "Mermaids, lovey. Not a human keeper."

Of course. Because humans were just so ordinary. I suppressed an eye roll. "Well, at least the mermaids will help."

"Hmm. I've never heard them called helpful. They're a ruthless species, sneaky and capricious. But they're the only ones who can help you, so be careful."

Great. Nasty mermaids—sounded like a party.

"Come on, off to bed with you. I can't have you asleep on your feet tomorrow with all the work waiting for us."

With my most pressing question answered, I stood, weariness overtaking me. The rest of my sleep was dreamless.

The next day passed in a blur of activity. I helped Sorsha prepare to leave the small house. Afterward, she passed the news among the prisoners. It spread like wildfire, and I spotted a few groups of people whispering, their eyes shifting. I worried the guards would get wind of the news.

Sorsha shook her head when I mentioned my fears. "Unlikely. No one will risk the guards hearing. They know how rare this chance is. Elyon put you and Baldwin here for this purpose. With your help, we can escape."

I didn't say anything, my lack of confidence stealing my words. I hoped she was right.

The next day dawned bright. The Adamas quartz tubes glowed extra bright, refracting the sunlight onto the valley, the fields and most of the tiny houses drenched in a buttery glow.

Baldwin and I were on our own for breakfast, since Sorsha had headed out an hour earlier to gather the early risers. After dressing, I returned to the kitchen to find a loaf of bread sitting on the table with some spreads and a pitcher of rainfruit juice.

I shared with Baldwin what she'd told me about the location of the key late last night. "So we should head to Mermaid Cove after everyone's evacuated."

He finished spreading jelly on a thick slice of bread, then cleared his throat. "I have a bad feeling we are running short on time."

"What do you mean?"

He rolled his shoulders. "I cannot explain it, just this anxiety in my stomach. When you clear the blocked exits, can you put our bags in the clearing?"

Ice cold gripped my chest. "You're kinda scaring me."

Giving me a hug, he said the magic words. "Everything will be all right. But we should be prepared for anything. If things go wrong—"

"If things go wrong, I'll meet you at Mermaid Cove. I promise."

With a long look, he squeezed my hands and turned away. We finished breakfast and cleaned the dishes. As I wiped the last one dry, Sorsha returned with two men and a woman.

She made introductions. "This is Dade and Corwin."

The two Welden men gave us a single head bob, their gazes curious. The Weldens' glowing auras, where their legs should have been, filled the room with light.

She gestured to the woman. "And this is Asha."

The Linnean woman gave us a friendly smile, her teal hairstreak glimmering.

Sorsha took a seat with a sigh. "They're going to help with the evacuees. Dade will guide people to Hamlin Bay, which is the portal on the left, and Corwin will assist those heading to Lennor, which is the archway on the right. The rest of us will help the residents get to the clearing. Do you have any information for those who wish to journey through the travel portal?"

"Are there many who wish to use it?" Baldwin asked.

Asha shook her head. "No, maybe half a dozen. Most wish to find the guild houses for training."

I crossed and uncrossed my legs, the nervous energy in the room a living thing. "They'll need to go to Declan's inn at Starfall Rim. But Rune invaded Linneah and Matana Island, and his soldiers are patrolling and harassing portal travelers."

Asha took a deep breath and exhaled slowly, her face pale.

Sorsha clapped her hands. "Let's move. We have a community to evacuate."

Outside, clusters of people waited near several houses, their belongings stuffed into bags. These families looked ready, their expressions ranging from anxious to determined.

"Where is Gerard?" Baldwin scanned the field.

The fields were empty, and expectancy shivered in the humid air.

"He vowed to keep the guards occupied for a few hours, enough to get the first round of evacuees on their way. We'll have to think of something after that." Sorsha turned to talk to a family of four.

I gawked at her. No plan? How could we keep the guards from noticing empty fields, the lack of workers, and residents leaving?

Baldwin patted my shoulder. "Have faith. We can always lock them in the drying shed."

I hoped we didn't have to resort to that.

While Baldwin gathered the first group of evacuees, I hurried ahead to clear the tunnel entrances. I dropped Baldwin's and my bags behind some rocks in the clearing before heading to the Hamlin Bay opening. True to the reports, the slick wax filled the entrance.

After taking a moment to create the fire ax, I swiped it through the substance, the material melting in seconds. I cleared the tunnel to Lennor and Mermaid Bay the same way. Curious, I ventured farther into the corridor until it forked. Two signs hung high on the stone wall, marking Lennor to the left and Mermaid Cove to the right.

When I returned, I joined Asha. We moved quickly among the homes, gathering early risers who were ready and reminding those who weren't where to go.

For the first two hours, things went smoothly. Over one hundred residents were sent on their way, and a handful of travelers heading to the travel portal were given a map with directions.

At one point, I turned to Asha and pointed to the tunnel behind the waterfall, the only passageway that remained a mystery. "Where does that end up?"

Asha tilted her head. "We believe it links to a massive storage room behind the trading center. The prince uses that entry point." She grinned. "But Elyon willing, we will be gone when he arrives."

The crowd of evacuees traipsed through the clearing, children fussy, men and women talking in low, worried tones. While guides assisted the people moving into tunnels, we helped Sorsha spread the news and aided families preparing to leave.

Gerard suddenly appeared, breathing heavily. "Half of the guards took the drink and are asleep. The remaining guards will be returning in several minutes. I couldn't delay them any longer."

Baldwin and I looked at each other, horror filling me. I turned to the older guard. "Tell them the prince wants to meet them in the drying shed."

Gerard's mouth dropped open. "Is he here?"

I pursed my lips. "Why, yes, he arrived this morning. No, of course not. Just get them to the shed. We'll take it from there."

Gerard returned the way he'd come while I tried to figure out my next step. I looked at Baldwin with a grimace. "Show time."

"Oh, no. No, no. I know that expression. You are going to do something dangerous or d—er, reckless."

"You were going to say dumb."

"But I did not."

Right. "I'll be back."

He grabbed my arm. "No, it is too dangerous. I will go."

"And how is that better?"

Asha and Sorsha approached us. At the sound of raised voices, I looked behind them, stunned to see a long line of people snaking toward the waiting area.

Sorsha gave me a pleased smile. "This is the biggest group yet."

I swallowed. "That's not good. Gerard just told us some guards are returning. But we told him to tell them the prince would meet them at the drying shed."

Asha's voice stayed calm. "What is your plan?"

"She does not have one." Baldwin gave me a glare.

"I will by the time I get there, thanks." Sweat beaded on my neck and slid down my back.

We turned at a shout from the field behind us.

"No more time." Baldwin put his hand on his sword, his voice grim. "The guards are coming."

Half a football field away, guards ran, their whips out and their faces angry masks. Gerard must be a terrible liar.

The people closest to the portal surged toward the clearing, toward freedom, while those on the path turned and fled back to their homes.

Asha stepped forward. "Back up."

The green trees along the path bent low, trunks flexing and palm leaves flapping, blocking the men's progress. As the guards ran around obstacles, ropy vines rose into the air, curling around each man before slamming them to the ground. A couple remained still while the rest struggled.

Wow. Disturbingly effective. "Did you kill them?" I asked.

Asha's smile was dark. "Unfortunately, no. Elyon does not approve of murder, although even that is too good for them."

As the few guards continued to struggle, long grasses flattened over them, muffling their movements.

Asha pursed her lips. "That should keep them busy for a bit."

Sorsha reassembled the people who had fled. Wading into the large group, Baldwin helped a few elderly women carry their bags to the clearing.

Asha's eyes narrowed as she studied the flailing guards. The ground around the captured men sank.

The scene was like a special effects disaster, fascinating and horrible. "What's your talent?" I asked.

She never looked away from the guards. "A Florabrand. I control plants. And right now, I would love to bury them."

The ground settled, and she pulled in a shuddering breath. The guards lay in a five foot-deep sinkhole.

She waved me on. "Go ahead. Help more people leave."

I helped Sorsha evacuate more families. After an hour, I scanned the field. Residents still headed for the clearing. I caught sight of the frown on Baldwin's face. "You okay?"

"Yeah. Have you seen Gerard?"

"No, why?"

He shrugged. "It is probably nothing. He left to check the entrance leading to the storage room. I thought he would be back by now."

"You don't think he skipped out on us?"

Baldwin shook his head and stepped forward to help a man struggling with a large bag.

"Do you want me to look for him?"

Baldwin didn't hear me, so I took that as a yes. I needed something to do anyway.

I hurried through the archway and emerged in the clearing. With a sudden roaring rush, water tumbled from the cliff high above, splashing into the blue-gray water of the pool. In minutes, the water began to empty, sucked away through the grated drain. The Alucin gas gusted from the ducts, a faint fragrance of lilacs scenting the air.

After peering into the other tunnels, I headed toward the back tunnel entrance. I entered it cautiously, my eyes adjusting to the dark interior. So help me, if I found him cowering somewhere...

He suddenly appeared in front of me. His eyes bulged as he grabbed hold of my arm, his grip painful. "He's coming. The prince. There's no more time."

"What? How do you know?"

With a shaking hand, Gerard held up a spiegel globe, a device that allowed an individual to view someone far away.

He drew in a rasping breath. "He just left the Half-Mile Down Trading Center and is headed this way. He's got an inspector with him."

Chapter Sixteen

FEAR CLAMPED DOWN HARD and twisted. Ten minutes—that was all we had left. I ran back to the clearing where a steady parade of residents still headed for the neighboring cities.

I flapped my hands, fear making me look like I was trying to take flight. "Everyone, go. Hurry. Rune's on his way."

The crowd gasped. Several women burst into sobs. The people surged forward, running for the closest exit. While guides tried to gather up stragglers, I ran back into Undertown Valley. The field of pale-green leaves undulated like a sea of split-pea soup. I skidded to a stop at the last row of plants, their spiced odor swirling through the air.

Closing my eyes, I muttered the Firebrand Creed under my breath. Although I wasn't an expert with pyrocharisma, I prayed for a flawless creation—a fiery, malleable net, each tiny square joined to the next and capable of burning this crop to the ground. I opened my eyes. In my palm rested a single mesh square which quickly mushed to a blob.

Groaning, I tried again, the weight of time pressing on my chest. My second effort produced the mesh netting fully formed in my hand. I flung it, but it only covered a portion of the plants.

I pulled in a deep breath as dread settled low. Did I have the time to create enough netting before Rune showed up? I was halfway done when Baldwin shouted my name.

He ran up to me, his cheeks flushed. "What are you doing?"

Dumb question. Leaves crackled and blackened, the full-throated roar of a monster as flames devoured the plants. "Burning this stuff to the ground, like I've dreamed of doing since I saw it. Now go away. You're messing up my vibe."

The flames snapped and popped. Baldwin raised his voice. "I do not know what vibe is, but we have no more time. When Rune arrives, you will have nowhere to run."

"Go. I only need another minute. I'll meet you at Mermaid Cove."

He hesitated, but I waved him on. Frustration filled his face, but he turned and headed for the tree line.

I created another piece of flaming mesh and threw it over the next portion of the field, the Firebrand Creed thrumming through my blood like a drum.

A straggling family of four emerged from one of the small houses. The father lugged a large bag while the mother scrambled to get the two children out the door. The girls' faces paled as they followed their parents. Sorsha appeared on the path, hurrying toward them. Although I couldn't hear her, her arms waved, urging everyone forward.

Despite the heat and smoke, my pendant blasted an arctic burn of cold against my breastbone. Two men stepped from the archway, and a horrified sob lodged in my throat.

Rune and Taurin.

I muttered the Firebrand Creed like a mantra. With a desperate draw of heat, the last fiery piece of netting materialized in my hands, and I tossed it over the remaining plants.

I crouched behind the growing flames and crept toward the tree line. Hidden among the greenery, Baldwin waited. Of course he hadn't headed to Mermaid Bay like I'd told him. My knees nearly buckled as Rune ran into the chaos of the once-orderly village. His face turned red, and his eyes latched on to the family and Sorsha.

Other residents who hadn't escaped scattered like rabbits, running to hide in the dense foliage or their homes. *No, head for the tunnels!* I wanted to shout. My heart rattled in my chest. They were trapped. And so was I. A sick tumble pitched my stomach.

Rune stalked toward the family. "Deserters! Who gave you permission to leave?"

The parents seemed to shrink, cowering into a small huddle, their children behind them. A flaming sword emerged from Rune's hand. With one motion, he sliced through the four people on the path. Blood spattered and their bodies crumpled, red crimson pooling beneath them.

I clapped a hand over my mouth to trap my scream.

He flicked a hand at Taurin. "Check for other traitors hiding nearby."

With a nod, Taurin headed down the path toward the houses.

Rune advanced on Sorsha, who met his gaze with a fierce look of her own.

No, no, no... My heartbeat thundered. Why didn't she run?

Rune's voice carried over the roar of the fire. "Brenna James! If you come forward, I will save this woman."

What? How did he know I was here? I couldn't breathe. Blood dripped from his fiery blade. There had to be a way out of this.

Sorsha's gaze met mine through the flames, and she shook her head. *Go,* she mouthed.

I couldn't move. But if I died here, Rune would win. I knew it, and Sorsha knew it.

She pressed her lips together and backed away, a mask of subservience replacing her proud expression. "I'm sorry, my prince. Please forgive me. It won't happen again."

Rune grinned, the smile a lethal slash on his face. "Of course it won't."

She turned and ran, but he was faster. He raised his blade. I didn't wait for him to complete the swing.

Dashing into the underbrush, I caught Baldwin's hand. We ran toward the archway. Snatching our bags from behind the rocks, we charged into the tunnel.

As we approached the fork, we veered to the Mermaid Cove tunnel, running, not slowing, feet pounding the stone, my breath hitching, tears streaming. The passageway curved hard and upward to the right. I pressed my hand to a stitch in my side, wondering if we'd have to run all the way to Mermaid Cove.

Finally, Baldwin slowed, his labored breathing loud in the passageway.

I wiped my burning eyes and tried to forget what I'd just seen. The family, their bodies collapsing like bloody rag dolls. Sorsha running, Rune's blade flaming as he raised it...

I choked on a sob. Baldwin pulled me into his arms. After a too-brief moment, he pulled away and shot a quick glance into the tunnel behind us. His reassuring grip on my hand was a lifeline as we continued toward Mermaid Cove.

The tunnel, carved of pale-pink stone, opened up the farther we walked. I dragged my hand against the pitted surface before realizing it was coral. The pathway continued to rise, small helli lights placed at regular intervals. For several minutes, we trudged, our breathing and footsteps echoing on the stone tiles.

Baldwin broke the silence. "Never ask that of me again."

I jerked at the steel in his voice. "Ask what?"

"To leave you behind. We are a team."

Stung, I pulled my hand from his. "When it comes to Rune, I can't protect you."

Wrong word. I knew it as soon as it left my mouth. As he sputtered, I tried again.

"Didn't you see what he did to that family and Sorsha? Nobody can win against him. Not even me. Sorsha had to sacrifice herself so we could escape." New tears came to my eyes, and I pushed at my lids, scrubbing away the sting. "So to live, sometimes we'll have to separate."

The conversation died, and our breathing came harder as the path angled to a sharper incline. Up, up, and up we climbed. Gradually, the path became layers of broken shells and white sand. The faint rhythm of breakers carried on a salt breeze came whistling through the tunnel.

We emerged from the corridor onto a wide stone ledge, the brisk breeze off the ocean ruffling our hair. I inhaled, the scent reminding me of Linneah and all I left behind. Would it ever truly be home again?

Blinking hard, I turned my attention to the beach below us. Or at least where the beach should've been. Instead, the ocean charged the rock shelf, waves beating against stone. Luckily, the ledge was big enough for a picnic table and a nice game of volleyball if we had the equipment.

Baldwin stepped closer to the edge and looked down. "Perhaps things will look different when the tide goes out."

"This can't be Mermaid Cove." I dropped my bag next to the high wall before checking the tunnel. "First of all, there are no mermaids, and second, there's no beach. We must have taken a wrong turn. Not that I—"

"Uh, Brenna?"

"—want to go back or anything." I squinted harder into the corridor. If Rune followed us, we were toast.

"Brenna?" Baldwin's soft voice made me turn.

My eyes rounded. At the ledge, a mermaid waited in the surf. A very beautiful mermaid, her golden-blonde and purple hair streaming behind her. A lavender-blue starfish was tucked above one ear. Several large pieces of seaweed had been twisted together to cover her abundant curves, and a purple tail flipped out of the water once before disappearing beneath the waves.

Baldwin couldn't tear his eyes from her as she clutched the side of the ledge.

Take a picture, bud.

Her violet eyes remained fixed on Baldwin. "Greetings, sailor. I am Marella."

"I am Baldwin."

I waited a beat. Cleared my throat.

"And this is Brenna," he blurted, his face flushing. He stepped closer and took my hand. "Is this Mermaid Cove?"

Face palm. No, this was the home of the Midnight Unicorn. I gave him a glare before turning to Marella. "Are you the keeper of the cove?"

She finally tore her gorgeous eyes from Baldwin. "No, that would be Queen Kevseri. Come with us, and we will introduce you."

"Us?"

"My sister Nautia always swims with me."

At her statement, another mermaid joined her at the ledge. Just as striking as Marella, she gave Baldwin a slow once-over. I gripped Baldwin's hand tighter and restrained the urge to punch her in her perfect nose. Blue streaks decorated her dark-brown hair. Baldwin's jaw was about to unhinge.

"Pull it together, sailor," I whispered in his ear.

He snapped his jaw shut.

"One minute, please." I gave them both a fake smile and dragged Baldwin back to the tunnel where my bag sat. Turning to him, I pushed down my jealousy and shifted my voice to a whisper. "You need to get a grip. Sorsha told me about mermaids. You can't trust them. They are shrewd, ruthless manipulators...and unfortunately, the only way to find the key."

"But we can use the Respiraqua to follow them." His eyes glittered.

I scowled, thoughts of our fight and breakup slinking through my mind. Maybe Baldwin had a deeper problem. Could he be happy with just one girl—namely, me?

My heart wilted. "Yeah, you're awfully excited about that."

"No, it is just, well, you know—"

I turned away, my lips twisting. "Yes. I know. They're absolutely gorgeous."

"No." He grabbed my hand and pulled me to face him. "First, I have never seen a mermaid. Many go their whole life without seeing one. I was surprised. Second, their offer is generous. The queen will be able to help us. If she is the keeper, she is the first person we should talk to. We have no other option." He paused, his expression suddenly uncertain. "Right?"

"Well, yeah. You just seem thrilled about the mermaids." I couldn't keep the sulky tone out of my voice.

He cupped my jaw, his thumb tracing a path across my cheekbone. "Never forget, Brenna, you are the one I am paired with."

"I know, I just thought..." My voice faded.

His voice was firm. "I almost lost you once. It will not happen again."

As I bit my lip, my heart puddled in my chest. I had to give him credit—the guy had a way with words.

I gave the sea creatures a side glance before removing my sheathed sword and boots. The mermaids were beautiful, and watching them swim and sway gracefully in the water made me feel awkward and yes, jealous.

Note to self: Don't compare yourself to a mythical creature. You will lose. Every time.

After placing the items next to my bag, I searched for the bottle of Respiraqua. It rested at the bottom. I pulled it out. "How much?"

"I think Abira said one or two teaspoons. It is listed at the back of the notebook."

A quick check revealed fuzzy writing impossible to decipher. "I can't tell."

He scrunched his forehead. "Maybe we should take one and a half."

"Okay." Sure. Why not? It wasn't like I knew the guidelines for using magical mystery liquids.

He removed his sword and boots as well and placed them next to mine.

"Baldwin, where is your boat?" Marella's voice drifted to where we stood at the tunnel entrance.

"We came through the tunnel."

"We have not had a man come that way in a long time. My sister and I are overjoyed for handsome human companionship."

Yeah, I bet.

Their eyes tracked our movements, their eyes predatory.

Baldwin voiced my thoughts. "Unfortunately, we cannot stay long. It is imperative we speak to the keeper, Queen Kevseri."

He opened the bottle and dribbled some of the liquid into the lid. "Good enough?"

That looked like the right dosage. Sort of. I nodded, and he downed it.

As he poured a dose for me, the odor of rancid water wrinkled my nose. I swallowed the liquid and gagged at the taste—the slime of dying plants, a significant punch of sulfur, with a slight aftertaste of mildew.

Baldwin wiped his mouth with a grimace. "Yeah, it is bad."

"Are you ready to meet our family?" Marella gestured for him to come closer, while Nautia held out her hand to me.

I slipped the bottle into my pocket and took Nautia's hand. Baldwin and I jumped into the water, breakers foaming over us.

The mermaids pulled us into deeper waters. Opening my eyes, the salt water stung for a few seconds before the pain dissipated.

As Marella and Baldwin pulled ahead of us, I began second guessing the old Respiraqua. This was a bad idea. We had no guarantee it would work. My lungs tightened.

I tried to pull away from Nautia, but her grip was firm, her webbed fingers like a vise. My oxygen eked away, and my mouth opened in a silent scream. Water flooded in, and with it, panic. It was over, I was drowning. But when I inhaled, the water was like silk in my lungs, and the ability to breathe underwater kicked in.

The mermaid sisters towed us past a kelp bed. A wall of tumbled rocks rose from the seafloor. After swimming around the rocks, we dove deeper still, and their world came into view. While the blue-gray water stretched before us into forever, a coral reef of a thousand colors exploded below us. A school of fish swam by, scales flashing.

Merpeople sat in groups, eating, working on the reef, and gathering seaweed while we swam past. Some ventured farther out, guarding the community, spears strapped to their forearms. A group of merkids chased each other, swimming in dizzy circles. This undersea village had no roof, so the sunlight pierced the water, dappling plants and colorful coral. But we would never have known the community was here unless we swam directly over it.

I opened my mouth to talk, but the sound was absorbed. A definite problem. How would we request the queen's help if we couldn't communicate? Nautia released my hand and gestured for me to follow her. I kept her colorful blue tail in view as I swam through coral arches, over purple sea urchins, and into a garden of brown seaweed. A school of brilliant red and yellow-spotted fish shot by. I blinked, and they were gone.

After a few more turns through the labyrinthine mermaid city, they led us into a cave only half-filled with water. A massive clamshell leaning against the wall stood open, a solid gold and pearl throne waiting in its center. I swam to a rock ledge, still waist deep in water, and squeezed the water from my braid. Baldwin stood nearby, Marella still holding his hand, her other curled possessively around his upper arm. I really disliked that chick.

Nautia turned to me. "Queen Kevseri has been notified of your arrival and will be here soon."

Marella murmured something to Baldwin and pulled him aside. A hollow feeling slithered through my stomach.

Moments later, a stunning mermaid swam in, a glittering gold crown on top of her green hair. Her torso was barely covered with thin strips of seaweed, and her tail was a beautiful swirl of blues, greens, and purples. Two muscular mermen followed her. One had long blond hair, while the other sported a short blue hairstyle. A second glance confirmed they were twins. Both of them stared at me until my cheeks heated and I looked away.

The queen slid onto the throne, her movements graceful. "Welcome to my kingdom of Liquiria. I am Queen Kevseri. We are thrilled to have such beautiful humans join us."

The merman with the blue hair gave me a flirty wink and moved closer. As I shifted away, I placed my hand on a protruding rock for balance. Smooth and round, kind of like—I recoiled in horror. It was a skull. A closer examination revealed several of them lined up like flowerpots on the stone ledge. I directed my attention back to what the queen was saying.

"—but I am prepared to hear your request before we decide what to do with you."

Wait—what? What did she mean by that? I looked over, but Baldwin—and Marella—were gone. I swallowed. "My companion should be here to discuss our request with you."

The queen gestured impatiently. "He is busy with my daughter Marella. Continue."

I'd have to hurt him badly the next time I saw him. "We're searching for the key to the Caelestis Staff. An evil man named

Rune is also looking for it. He plans to take over the Jasper Territory, join it to the Kasek Territory, and eliminate all other rulers, especially the female ones."

Queen Kevseri rubbed her chin. "That changes our plans. We were going to have you for supper. But if we do that, nobody will be left to challenge him. Did you come with an army?"

My face froze. That sounded suspiciously sinister. Unless I was overreacting? Maybe she meant we'd be their guests. "I—uh, no. It's just me and my friend."

She sighed. "And you looked so delicious, too."

Yep. Sinister.

The blue-haired merman floated up next to me. "No, I'd like to claim her, Mother."

I goggled up at him. Claim?

He gave me an appealing grin. "I'm Finn."

A hysterical giggle threatened to push past the confusion and alarm building inside. A merman named Finn? Of course. "I'm Brenna."

Queen Kevseri tilted her head. "I suppose that's acceptable."

Without warning, Finn slid a long piece of seaweed around my back and pulled me close, his eyes glittering.

Well, this was awkward. "Excuse me, but—"

I never finished my protest, because his lips covered mine in a salt-tinged kiss.

CHAPTER SEVENTEEN

TIME SLOWED, FINN'S LIPS moving over mine, his hands sliding to my back as he pulled me closer still. I placed my hands on his bare, muscular chest, his warmth slipping into my hands.

I could stay here forever in his embrace, kissing him, his arms holding me. Pulling away, I gave him a smile. He was absolutely adorable. His eyes drew me in, the green pools so much like Baldwin's. Baldwin?

I jerked, and the wet seaweed restraint snapped.

I was paired. To Baldwin. What had just happened?

Finn looked confused for a minute. Maybe he wasn't used to girls pulling away, which I totally understood.

I gave him a serious look. "You can't claim me."

He grinned, a gleam of sharp teeth. "Of course I can."

"I'm paired, to the guy I came with, actually."

On the far side of the cave, Baldwin and Marella had returned, but he wasn't looking at me. His adoring gaze was fastened on Marella.

"I don't think he's interested. You need someone who appreciates you." He punctuated it with another charming wink.

I gave Finn a polite smile and half stalked, half swam to Baldwin and Marella.

She looked at the queen. "Mother, Baldwin has agreed to be mine, and I've given him the Cherished Bequest."

Pain lanced through my chest. He agreed? What had happened while I was talking with the queen?

Queen Kevseri's eyes widened. "You cannot give a man something that important after such a short time, Marella."

Nautia rolled her eyes, and Finn shook his head.

Marella kissed Baldwin, and he swayed forward as she pulled away. "No, he's the one, I'm sure of it. And we'll be very happy." She reached up and caressed his face. Her other hand held a seaweed band wrapped around Baldwin's left wrist.

I wanted to slug her. "Excuse me?"

She looked at me, her lip curling. "What?"

"I do believe that's my boyfriend you've got. We're paired."

Smiling, she shook her head. "Impossible. He now holds my bequest."

The queen sighed. "Marella. If he's paired, truly, the hypnokiss band will break. We've talked about this."

She turned from her mother, her mouth set into pouty lines as she gave me a dismissive glance. "Find someone else, salt scum."

Rage bubbled up in my chest. No. Mermaid Barbie didn't get to set the rules here. I grabbed his right hand, and he tilted his head, confusion beetling his brow. Finn's kisses had done it to me. Maybe, just maybe...I reached up and pulled his head to mine, channeling all my heart into this one kiss.

When I pulled away, I opened my eyes to find his emerald ones clear, a smile lighting his face. "Brenna," he breathed. He pulled me close, and the seaweed band on his wrist broke with a wet snap.

"No!" Marella cried. "He's mine! I gave him the bequest."

"You should've made sure he wasn't paired when you gave it to him." Nautia's comment echoed in the chamber.

I moved to pull away, but Baldwin kept his arm firmly around my waist.

Queen Kevseri shook her head. "I'm sorry. My children are infatuated with humans. They'd much rather claim them than eat them. Which is too bad, because humans are so delicious." Her hungry eyes glittered.

My stomach recoiled. Marella stood in the corner, sobbing, her webbed hands covering her face. Nautia swam over and led her from the cave.

The twins trailed them, Finn pausing before me. "I could make you happy, Brenna."

Next to me, Baldwin stiffened, but I shook my head. "No, Finn, you really couldn't."

His shoulders slumped, and he swam from the cave.

As they left, I wondered if our refusal had sealed our doom. Should we have agreed to their demands to get the clues we needed? But the thought of Baldwin with Marella was killer.

The queen shifted on her throne, her tail swirling in the blue-green water. "Now that the family drama is over, the question remains. What to do with you?"

Duh. But I offered a respectful response. "Give us the location of the key, please."

Her eyes narrowed. "If I choose not to eat you and give you this valuable information, what will I receive?"

Baldwin and I glanced at each other as she continued.

"I like gold, silver, and precious gems. Humans are nice if you can find one, since they feed my family for a day or two. I will also accept servitude. If one of you stayed here for five times as my servant, you would be free to go when your service is up."

I barely suppressed a snort. Yeah, that wasn't happening.

Baldwin's grip tightened before he released me and stepped forward. "I can do that."

What? My heart ruptured into tiny pieces, and I pulled on his arm. "Baldwin, no. There's another way."

Her tail swishing hypnotically, the queen leaned forward.

He turned to me, his voice low. "How? We have no treasure, and we need that key. I can stay here for five times."

Pitching my voice to match his, I moved closer. "What if they do something to you in those five years? Or eat you? Or pull you in, the way Marella did? We can't trust them, remember?"

"Will you wait for me?"

My heart ached at his hopeful question. "You know I will, uh, would. But there's got to be another option."

A low, rolling roar rumbled through the cave. The queen sat up, her eyes bright. "Another human! My, this day just gets more and more interesting. Stand over there while we bring in the next guest."

The two of us floated to the side of the chamber. In moments, Nautia entered, dragging a large man behind her. When she stopped, he shot to the surface, gasping.

I covered my mouth, lightheaded. Taurin.

The man scrubbed seawater from his face and glanced around the cave, water streaming from his black braids. His expression grew thunderous as his eyes found me. "You! I should have known. A loudmouthed troublemaker just like your mother."

Setting my jaw, I willed myself not to react.

Baldwin's voice was as sharp as a steel blade. "You should be careful what you call the queen of Linneah, Taurin."

He laughed, the sound loud in the chamber. "Queen? I believe Rune is the ruler of Linneah now. Although he would be more than willing for you to serve at his feet, Firebrand."

Ignoring his last comment, I pushed down the anger building in my chest. "He was never chosen by Elyon."

"Rune does not need his approval." He turned from us. "Forgive me, my queen, for entering your kingdom, but I will remove the Firebrand from your presence and be gone."

He took one step toward us, and Queen Kevseri's voice sliced the air. "You will do no such thing until I decree it. Stay put, human. Do you have a name?"

"My apologies. I am Taurin Trennen, first in command to Prince Rune, the ruler of Linneah, Matana Island, and the Kasek Territory."

"And I hear you are on a quest?" She leaned forward, her tail a rhythmic blade in the water.

When Taurin hesitated, Nautia floated up next to him and ran a graceful hand over his muscled bicep. "I'm sure a man such as yourself is not satisfied by the ordinary. What exotic treasure are you looking for?"

Taurin turned into a moony-eyed idiot. His leer grew as he reached out to play with a long lock of her blue-streaked hair. "The key to the Caelestis Staff, my lovely. Rune is one step away from ruling the Jasper Territory and tying it to the Kasek Territory. With the staff, he will rule legions. I will have a prime spot in his kingdom. It would be my greatest pleasure to have you by my side after I return with the key."

"And what would I do in this kingdom?"

"A pretty little thing like yourself? Absolutely nothing. Your beauty alone is all that is needed."

Nautia's eyes narrowed. "I see. Are you strong and intelligent enough to find the key?"

"There is no puzzle invented that has been too clever for me."

"Of course not." Nautia ran her hands down his chest. "Mother, I believe we should have Taurin for dinner as our honored guest."

Queen Kevseri waved them on. "Show him to the dining room. I will take care of these two."

He shot us an arrogant grin, believing he was being given an award. I almost felt sorry for him.

Nautia led Taurin out of the cave, ignoring his gasp for breath as she tugged him off his feet and into the water.

Silence reigned in the chamber once they left. The queen eyed me before slipping off her throne and swimming closer. "You are the queen of Linneah's daughter?"

I nodded, afraid to say anything else. Would this work to my benefit or not?

"You should have told me when you arrived. I don't eat a royal's offspring. It causes wars. But I could use him for five times." She inclined her head to Baldwin.

"No." I swallowed my fear as her gaze sharpened. "We're paired. And you already have your payment."

She smiled, her pointed teeth a reminder to tread lightly. "How so?"

"Taurin followed us here. If we hadn't come with your daughters, you wouldn't have him in your dining room right now."

She pursed her lips, running a slim finger down Baldwin's arm. "True. Unfortunately."

Her comment fed my boldness, and I added another incentive. "And I'll make sure when I return home, my mother learns how you spared our lives."

The queen tapped her chin before sighing. "So be it. Follow me."

I exhaled a quiet breath. She swam from the chamber, and Baldwin and I followed. A guard dropped into place behind us as we exited the small cave. The queen's tail flashed green and purple in the sun-dappled water. As we threaded through rock archways and around seaweed beds, the coral reef dazzled with colors and shapes, an otherworldly backdrop.

Queen Kevseri swam into a massive cavern and bobbed up, her crown dripping with salt water like jewels. One of the rock walls of the cavern held a carved corridor opening, and she flicked a hand at it. "That leads to the charmed Room of Keys. It's the first opening on your right. You must solve the puzzle to find the correct key. After you make your choice, you'll find a freshwater pool. From there, it's only a short walk to the city of Lennor."

I shook my head. "We left most of our belongings outside the tunnel opening. And Baldwin left his favorite sword behind."

"As a show of goodwill, I'll have one of my guards leave your possessions at the freshwater pool. I've only ever had one searcher make it this far, and he chose the wrong key."

"What happens if you choose the wrong key?" I asked.

Smirking, the queen floated closer. "We'll have you for dinner after all. But knowing what's at stake, I'd like you to succeed. So I'll give you one clue. The staff and key were forged at the Oasisland's Lost Temple. The leaders always said, 'Follow the stars.'" She gave Baldwin a wink. "And if you ever change your mind, we can always use handsome servants."

With a splash of her gorgeous tail, she was gone.

I swiped water off my face. "So the temple was important, just not like I thought. 'Follow the stars.' That's it? Maybe she could've been a little more vague. You know, throw in a few hieroglyphics or smoke signals."

"We can do this." Baldwin swam to the edge of the cavern and pulled himself from the water before helping me climb out.

Standing at the edge of the corridor, I stared into blackness. A slither of foreboding crawled up my spine. I dried my hands, then created a small flame and held it aloft to light our way. Sand, driftwood, and shell bits lined the corridor, the walls hewn from the same pale coral.

Several yards in, a smaller tunnel branched to the right. A room half the size of a football field waited. As we walked in, our mouths fell open.

The floor boasted an intricate mosaic of cream and blue marble, silver medallions punctuating the tile pattern. Scattered pinpricks of light sparkled in the vaulted dark-blue ceiling. Rough, grainy walls were trimmed with a sparkling silver chain holding four keys at waist level. The chain was the only decoration on the coarse walls.

The slap of our bare feet echoed in the expansive room.

Baldwin broke the silence. "So we just have to pick the right key from the chain, right?"

I took a closer look at them. "They're all the same. Silver skeleton keys with a number embossed on the top."

"Hmm. What does the number stand for?"

"I don't know, but they only have numbers one through four." I blew out a breath and looked at the spangled ceiling. "We're never gonna get out of here, are we?"

Baldwin pointed to the far corner. "I will examine this side of the room. You take your bad attitude to the opposite side, and we will meet in the middle."

I glared his way. "But I don't even know what I'm looking for."

He blinked. "A key. Or a clue to choose the right key."

"Thank you, Captain Obvious. But how do I decipher the clue when I have no idea what the staff or the key looks like? For some reason, we don't want Rune to get it, but why? What does the key do? For that matter, what does the staff do? I get that it's powerful, but can he kill people with it? Call storms down from the sky? Finish crossword puzzles in ink? What?"

Baldwin's eyes widened during my tirade. "I thought Abira gave you Niklos's book about the staff."

Oh. That book. "Well, I must have missed that part. And the author didn't seem to know anything, just had a lot of guesses."

Baldwin crossed his arms.

"What?" I picked at a nick in my fingernail.

His lips quirked. "I read it. All of it."

Silence filled the room. He was going to make me beg for it. "And can you share what you read?"

He leaned a hip against the wall. "Maybe. What do I get for sharing information?"

I suppressed a grin. "A helpful partner rather than a clueless one."

He chuckled. "Fair enough. It is assumed the key will guide the owner to the Caelestis Staff. One end of the staff contains a blade and the other a weaving hook. It is full of power, allowing the holder to cut the fabric of space."

"My grandfather does that with his bo staff."

"Yes, but as a Traveler, he only makes minor cuts and then mends them afterward. With the staff, whole alternities can be cut free from space or woven together. Those that are cut off, collapse."

CHAPTER EIGHTEEN

A SICK FEELING SWIRLED in my stomach as I moved to the far wall. "I'll start over here."

An hour later, I settled on the floor and rubbed my eyes. "We're never going to figure this out. My brain feels like mush."

Absently, I rubbed at a silver medallion on the floor and felt a hole. A closer examination revealed each medallion held what looked like a lock at its center.

"Baldwin, these are all locks." I looked up at him.

He frowned. "Do we have to find the correct key to unlock each one?"

My mouth dropped open. "Oh, man. That'll take forever." Our job pressed like an anvil across my shoulders.

Baldwin settled next to me and put an arm around me. "You cannot give up. Perhaps it is easier than that."

I laid my head on his chest. "Just tell me it'll be all right." That's really what I wanted. Just five little words to create a light of hope in this dim, desperate situation.

"It will be all right. I promise." He pulled me close again, and we stayed that way for a few minutes, his heartbeat strong, his arm steady around me.

I pulled away with a deep sigh and let my head fall back to stretch my stiff neck.

Pinpricks of light glittered, some brighter than others. I tilted my head. Something struck me about the lights...why did they look familiar? Memories of dark nights spent with my dad and a telescope came to mind. Recognition stiffened my spine.

"Baldwin, those lights...I think they're constellations from Earth."

He looked up. "I failed to notice them when we arrived."

"I recognize the Big Dipper, Orion, Pegasus." Pointing, I identified each one. "Oh, and there's Scorpius. I don't recognize any of the others."

Baldwin squinted. "The Blood Spinner's Web, Drazil the Dragon, and Dal and Stormwing." He pointed to each one before turning to me, his eyes shining.

I quirked an eyebrow. "Stormwing?"

"The griffin who sacrificed his life to spend eternity with his rider, Dal."

"So now what?"

Baldwin shook his head, still studying the ceiling. "I know very little about our stars in Linneah. Do you know a lot about Earth's?"

"Well, some. Dad and I used to go out on weekends with his telescope. But you know what's weird? You won't find all the ones on the ceiling at the same time."

"Why not?"

"They show up at different times of the year. For example, Orion is visible in the winter. I remember a few years ago Dad and I went stargazing after a snowstorm." I grinned. "It was freezing, but the hot chocolate afterward was worth it."

Baldwin licked his lips. "Your dad makes *excellent* hot chocolate."

"And you can only see Pegasus in the fall." I was on to something, but I couldn't quite reach the answer. How were they connected?

Baldwin narrowed his eyes. "What about the other two?"

I bit my lip and thought back. "Scorpius is a summer constellation. I always found it when we had hotdog cookouts with stargazing afterward. And the Big Dipper is always visible, but brightest in the spring."

We were both quiet as we pondered the information.

An idea niggled at the back of my mind. "What if we're supposed to number the constellations in order?"

"How do you put stars in order?"

"Well, of when they appear. The Big Dipper would be first, right? Since it's always visible."

Still thinking, I walked to the chain. All the keys hung on hooks and could be easily removed. I gingerly removed the key with the number one embossed on it. Nothing happened. A small wave of relief swept through me. I returned to Baldwin. He stood under the Big Dipper, a silver medallion directly at his feet.

I knelt, inserted the key, and turned it, tumblers clicking. The lock sprang open, tiles peeling back like petals. In a small recession rested a clear glass cylinder holding a filigreed silver disc.

Unstopping the container, I shook the silver piece into my palm. "This doesn't look like a key."

"Maybe the following locks will be more helpful." Baldwin went to the wall and collected the remaining keys.

He met me under the constellation of Scorpius, and I used the second key. The lock swung open, tiles unfurling in the same manner. The glass container held a thin, silver stick as long as my index finger.

Doubt swirled inside. "This can't be right."

Baldwin's eyes held the same apprehension. "We are committed now. We might as well follow through."

As I scanned the far wall, the bottom dropped out of my stomach. The door had disappeared. Had we made a mistake? Or would another exit appear if we solved the puzzle? I glanced at Baldwin. Maybe I should mention that to—yeah, not happening. He was a bright boy. He'd figure it out.

I pointed to the stars forming Pegasus. "Fall's next."

Baldwin took the third key and unlocked the medallion in the floor.

Holding my breath, I prayed for the next clue to make sense. The tiles around the lock peeled away. Nestled in the clear bottle was a silver hook as big as Baldwin's thumb.

I didn't say what I was thinking—this mishmash of silver looked like junk. Expensive junk.

We moved to the last constellation of Orion. I inserted the key and twisted, and tiles shifted away to reveal a folded piece of paper in the glass container. I couldn't force myself to pick it up. We'd come all this way for three silver trinkets and a note? We never should've trusted the mermaids.

Baldwin pulled the paper out and unfolded it. "Eat this and learn," he read out loud. "With risk comes knowledge."

I threw my hands up. "There's nothing to eat. It's moldered away to nothing."

Baldwin touched his tongue to the paper. "No, I think we are supposed to eat the note."

"I don't trust those mermaids one bit," I grumbled.

"Me neither. But this is their puzzle and their rules." He popped the paper into his mouth, chewed, and swallowed.

I gasped. "What are you doing?"

"Solving the puzzle. Mm, tastes like root beer." Licking his lips, he reached out and caressed my cheek. "I could not let you risk yourself."

My heart melted a bit while the other part of me wanted to object. No fair. He shouldn't be simultaneously chivalrous and bossy.

Before I could respond, he fell to his knees. His face twisted in agony as he gripped his head and moaned.

"Baldwin?" I knelt next to him, my heart pounding, but I was powerless.

His moaning breaths were thunderous in the empty room. After a few seconds, he quieted and lifted his head, his eyes wide. "I know what needs to be done next."

I waved aside his comment. "Whatever. Are you okay?"

He visibly swallowed. "Yes, although I would rather not do that again."

Pushing aside my fear, I settled for squeezing his hand. "Next time, I'll eat the note. So what do we do?"

"Um. Well, uh." He opened his mouth. Closed it. And finally shook his head. "I cannot tell you. I just have to do it."

So typical. Shooting him a withering look, I crossed my arms. "You know, you don't have to be the hero every time."

"That is not what this is. The charmed paper is refusing to let me share the information. I have to complete the puzzle."

He gathered the pieces of silver and placed them in the glass cylinder. After replacing the lid, he put it on the ground and lifted his foot.

"Wait? What are you doing?" I held up my hands to stop him. He gestured to the cylinder helplessly. "I have to..."

"You're going to break it with your bare foot? Are you nuts?" He pursed his lips. "Do you have a better idea?"

Both of us were barefoot and unarmed, but a comforting weight rested against my leg. I pulled the bottle of Respiraqua from my pocket and wiggled it. "What about this?"

"Will we need it later?"

I looked at the bottle, then back at Baldwin before handing it over. "I think we need it now."

Kneeling on the ground, Baldwin lifted the bottle and brought it down on the entire package with a crunch. As cracks splintered up the bottle, the bottom broke away. A puddle of Respiraqua spread on the floor.

He sifted through the glass shards before pulling a silver object from the debris. "And here is the key to the Caelestis Staff."

The silver disc had morphed into a crescent moon and four wings. A silver chain wrapped around the key's length, star charms dangling from its links.

"It's beautiful." The sound of trickling water cut my admiration short.

An inch of water wetted our feet, slowly but surely rising.

A muscle ticked in Baldwin's jaw. "We need to get out. Now. Like I mentioned, I do not trust the mermaids."

"The doorway's gone." My heartbeat hammered. I hurried to the corner where we entered and ran my hands over the rough surface. My fingers sank into the now-mushy rock. "There's something weird about this."

Baldwin reached down to touch it. "Sea sponge. The entire wall is sponge."

A sudden geyser near the far wall shot high, spraying water. Another one split open across from us. We hurried for a dry corner.

"Let me try a fireball." I produced a flaming orb and shot it at the wall. The sponge sizzled, water turning to steam. A basketball-size hole remained. This would take too long. The water level slowly rose, climbing past our calves.

Tugging on Baldwin's sleeve, I pulled him back to stand with me. "Different tactic." With a deep breath, I created and shot four fireballs. *Bang, bang, bang, bang!* The section of wall exploded, bits of sponge flying and more steam filling the air. As the water escaped through the gaping hole, we did too.

A short hallway led to a vaulted opening with a pool in its center. Our belongings were piled neatly off to the side as promised.

Baldwin turned to me after strapping on his sword. "We can either bunk here or walk the mile to Lennor."

"Let's go to Lennor. We'll get a meal sooner that way." And a bath. My clothes hung stiff, and my scalp itched from salt water.

"Great idea."

I shouldered my bag, and we headed down the corridor toward Lennor. "So I'm curious. What exactly was the bequest Marella gave you?"

"Well, after she claimed me, she—"

The words rankled. "Yeah, about that. You just agreed?"

Baldwin looked uncomfortable and defensive at the same time. "She kissed me. You know how those hypnokisses work. Besides, I noticed you making out with Finn."

Indignation brought heat to my cheeks. "Excuse me. I wasn't making out. It was one kiss."

"A pretty long one."

I wasn't doing this. "The bequest?"

Relief flooded his face. "It was this glowing substance she pressed against my chest. It disappeared almost instantly. She claimed it would improve my sword skills."

"You're already really good," I said, referencing his past awards from swordsmanship competitions.

"Thanks. But it probably only works in the mermaid kingdom."

Falling silent, we continued walking through the stone corridor. Our passage ended at a silver gate barring our entrance into the town, secured by a lanky guard.

Baldwin approached the gate. "Pardon me?"

The guard jerked, his mouth gaping. He peered into the tunnel behind us before his gaze turned suspicious. "Nobody ever comes from Mermaid Cove."

Baldwin shrugged and offered him an affable smile. "We need a meal and a warm bed. Can you direct us to one?"

The guard ran a hand through his shaggy brown hair before opening the gate—slowly, all the while inspecting us. "The Bird's Nest is open until after midnight, so you still have several hours. Take this main road here, follow it until you come to a T, turn left, then right, then left. The Nest is on the left."

I repeated the directions in my head. *Left, right, left, on the left.*

Baldwin thanked him, and we set off. Darkness blanketed the town while welcoming lights glimmered from a few businesses and well-kept homes. The smell of beer and stale smoke slipped from a darkened doorway, a less-stellar establishment than what we were looking for. Houses were built on stilts, wood weather-worn to pale shades, sand and sea grass filling the yards. Helli lights near the doorways offered illumination, while the briny sea scented the air.

At a sudden idea, I perked up. "You know what? We should contact Lev and Arvandus. They could pick us up tomorrow morning, and we wouldn't have to take the travel portal back."

"That would be safer. I am also looking forward to renting a room."

"And a nice, long, hot bath to wash away all the salt."

He grinned. "Of course."

I contacted my griffin. Although it was late, I hoped he was still awake. He was such a grump if I interrupted his sleep. *Arvandus? Raven? Are you safe?*

Warm, yellow light spilled from nearby houses, and the sea breeze smelled like home. *Sure. Why?*

We were concerned about you.

Aw. Arvandus had his sweet moments, however brief. *We're fine. But if you could meet us at the Bird's Nest in Lennor, that would be great. Baldwin and I are going to stay overnight.*

The Bird's Nest? A hint of a smile crept into his voice. *Ask to see the owner.*

Why? Is it a dump?

Far from it. I will see you tomorrow.

Despite the night's darkness, we found the Bird's Nest. It was a two-story wooden building, also on stilts, with a large, partially covered rooftop balcony. Perhaps from there, an ocean view was possible. Helli lights glowed from windows and illuminated the stairs. As we climbed the staircase, I told Baldwin what Arvandus had said.

"I wonder why."

I shrugged. My griffin was often a mystery.

Inside the inn, the wooden walls were a weathered tan. A hallway running the length of the building led to rooms on either side of the entrance. Furnishings in the entryway were in tones of blue and cream, creating a rustic beach house vibe. A manned registration desk stood just inside the door. The clerk flashed us a friendly, if tired, smile as Baldwin stepped forward.

"Hi. We need two rooms for the night, as well as a meal, if possible."

"We have one room left," she said, her voice firm.

Her comment derailed my study of an ocean-themed oil painting. "But we—"

"That is fine," Baldwin said, interrupting me. "Thank you."

He handled the payment while I stood there trying to work out a sleeping arrangement in my head. I guess I could sleep on the floor, though I was really looking forward to a soft bed.

The girl handed him a key. "Second floor, Room 202. I'll have sandwiches sent up."

My stomach grumbled at her words. I put a hand over it. "Thank you very much."

After another set of stairs, we reached our room. I unlocked the door and stepped in. The small helli lantern on a table illuminated the room.

There was little space to bed down on the floor, just a cleared area to get from the bed to the bathroom. No couch either, but a hard, ladder-back wooden chair and a small table made up the rest of the room. Well, I'd think about the sleeping problem later, because right now I wanted a bath so badly I could taste it. I threw my bag in the corner and removed my baldric, which held my sheathed sword.

Baldwin sat down and started taking off his boots. "You can have the bathroom first. I know how badly you want a bath."

"Are you sure?"

He gave me a wink. "Ladies first."

With a thankful smile, I removed my second set of clothes from my bag and headed for the bathroom. Inside, I poured a hot bath and sank into the heavenly water up to my chin. A little bottle of shampoo and a miniature bar of soap sat on a small table near the bathtub. Both smelled of gingersnap cookies.

They could've smelled like broccoli, and I would've used them anyway.

After a good scrubbing, I rinsed and dried off, dressing in the only other clothes I had.

When I exited the bathroom, Baldwin was sprawled on the bed, fast asleep. A faint layer of stubble shadowed his jaw, his hair adorably tousled, his mouth slightly parted. I decided to explore and give him time to sleep and take a bath.

After scribbling a quick note, I swiped the room key and climbed the outside stairs to the balcony.

The brisk wind whipped off the ocean, tossing my damp hair. Unfortunately, with darkness covering the landscape, I couldn't see much except the stars and Petrus Rings glittering against a backdrop of midnight blue. When the air cooled, I headed back to the room to see if Baldwin had woken from his nap.

The bathroom door was closed, so I dropped to the bed. How would we handle the sleeping arrangement? Although we could sleep on opposite sides of the bed, it'd be a little awkward. And this bed was so soft...

I woke to Baldwin whispering in my ear. "Brenna, get up, love." There was that divine word again, the one that made my insides melt.

My eyes flew open, just as his lips touched mine. Relaxing, I slipped my arms around his neck because, really, there was no better place for them to be. In moments, the kisses shifted from playful to heated.

Baldwin left a trail of kisses along my jaw as his hand caressed my side, my waist, my thigh. "Brenna." Just my name, breathed as if the very word kept him alive.

At a knock at the door, he jerked away. "Room service for Room 202?" a faintly familiar voice called through the door.

"Yes, just a moment." He rose from the bed and opened the door.

"Let me put this tray here on the table for you." A dark-haired, heavyset woman bustled into the room.

I shot to my feet, stunned to see Abira's best friend. "Shiraz?"

"Brenna James? What an unexpected surprise! And with a young man?" Her voice pitched as her gaze bounced between the two of us.

Hurrying over, I gave her a big hug. "It's so good to see you. This is my boyfriend, Baldwin Marek. There was only one room left, and we were thankful to get even that."

"Hmm." Her eyes narrowed, and she tapped her chin. "We *are* full tonight. You should've told me you were here, chickie. I would've saved a room for you."

"It was a last-minute decision." Her words brought to mind Arvandus's enigmatic instructions. "I didn't know you lived in Lennor. You own the Bird's Nest?"

Her dimpled face lit the room. "I have for several times now. And I've got just the place for you to sleep. Unless you twined in the last few months?"

"No." Heat flooded my cheeks.

Crossing his arms, Baldwin only grinned.

"Good. I'd hate to miss your twining ceremony. I'll let you have your meal, and then Baldwin can sleep here. Since I have an extra bed, Brenna, you can sleep in my room. Ask the clerk for directions when you're done." With another beaming smile for us both, she left.

Baldwin picked up the tray and sat on the bed. "She seems like a nice person."

"She is. Tiny and I met her on the way to Kelda Hills several months ago. If it hadn't been for Shiraz, I never would've met Abira." I paused. "Wow, that's a depressing thought. If I hadn't met Abira, I never would've trained with her."

"You have a deep regard for each other. I hope I develop that with Niklos."

"You will. Give it time."

Baldwin raised his eyebrows. "He is a tough teacher."

Abira was no picnic either.

We ate our supper of sandwiches, content to enjoy each other's company. We tried to toss the pupkissberries into each other's mouth but failed miserably. The lighthearted meal was welcome after the last few tense days.

Baldwin sat back with a sigh. "You ever thought about being twined?"

Despite his casual demeanor, my relaxed feeling vanished. I swallowed and ignored the birds divebombing in my stomach. "Why do you call it twined?"

"During the ceremony, the couple braids, or twines, three cords together—a gold one, a silver one, and a purple one to symbolize the relationship of the man, the woman, and Elyon."

"That's cool. On Earth, teenagers don't often get married, or uh, twined. Some people wait until their twenties or even later."

"So you planned to wait?"

Pursing my lips, I considered what he was and wasn't saying. "I don't know. I feel older than my age sometimes. I've escaped death a few times and traveled across the territory and through Silvastamen. But I still think a few years' wait would be smart. And I wouldn't twine just because. I want to spend my life with someone I love."

Baldwin nodded, his eyes intent while my words floated in the room between us. "That makes sense." He cleared his throat and looked away.

Wow. Awkward. Maybe he wasn't serious about me, about us, although the thought hurt. Was he just hanging around for fun and adventure? *Yeah, spend time with the weirdo who's involved in the prophecies.* He could write it on a bathroom wall: *For a good adventure, call Brenna James.*

Standing, I brushed at the nonexistent crumbs on my shirt.

Baldwin looked like he wanted to say something as he frowned and slowly put our dirty dishes on the tray.

I broke the awkward silence. "Well, it's late, so I should probably find Shiraz's room."

"I will see you at breakfast, then."

Before I left, he captured my hands.

"You should know, I would never have asked anything of you tonight, only to sleep with you."

My eyes went wide, his words inflicting profound damage. So no twining but just sex? I wasn't okay with that. Not at all.

He closed my gaping mouth, his fingers gentle under my chin. "That is all. Only to hold you in my arms as we fell asleep."

My heart melted at his explanation. "Oh. That sounds...nice." Nice? Was that the best word I could think of? My brain blanked, and my nerves took over. "Well, some other time, I guess. I mean, not another time that was unplanned, but a planned time, maybe. Or not."

I rubbed my forehead, Baldwin's soft chuckle deepening my embarrassment.

"Good night, love. Sleep well."

The gentle brush of his lips on mine made it that much harder to grab my bag and leave the room. But I did just that, visions of his arms around me as we fell asleep swimming in my head.

Chapter Nineteen

With directions from the clerk, I found Shiraz's room. The woman put me to bed almost immediately, and despite my earlier nap, I fell asleep with no trouble.

The next morning I woke to two female voices floating into my bedroom. I got up and padded into the living area. Abira sat next to Shiraz on the couch, a traveling bag at her feet.

My mouth fell open. "What are you doing here?"

"And a good morning to you too, Brenna." Abira's voice was dry.

"I was getting to that. I just got up, you know."

She grinned. "I flew in on Arvandus. When he told me where you were, I decided a visit to Shiraz was in order."

I turned to Shiraz. "Yeah, how did he know you owned the Bird's Nest?"

"We talked about it when you visited Abira a few months ago. He's familiar with this area."

Of course he was.

Shiraz stood. "Give me a few minutes, and I'll have breakfast ready. Why don't you find out if your young man's hungry? And no friendly business."

I blushed. Sheesh.

Baldwin was up and dressed when I knocked on Room 202's door several minutes later. I led him to Shiraz's apartment where they exchanged greetings.

My mouth watered at the impressive breakfast spread—a large omelet bursting with fresh vegetables, two kinds of sliced meat, a colorful fruit bowl, and juice and milk to drink.

After a quick prayer, Shiraz eyed Baldwin across the table, her eyes narrowed. "So you are Brenna's boyfriend. What happened to Storm?"

Baldwin's shocked eyes found mine. "Storm? Storm Lee?"

Ignoring him and the little worm of guilt in my chest, I answered Shiraz. "Storm's involved with Phoenix, a friend of mine in Ginselwyn." At least I hoped he was.

"He seemed very taken with you when you two were at Abira's." Shiraz gave me a pointed glance.

Abira snorted. "Ridiculous."

The Jasper Territory could swallow me now. "Um, it didn't work out."

Baldwin shoved a forkful of omelet in his mouth and chewed, his cheeks flushed as he shot glances at me. I continued to ignore him, although I suspected he'd have more questions later regarding my time with the Lee family.

Abira leaned forward. "I'm assuming things went well in your travels."

I gave her a grateful smile, relieved at the subject change. "We found the key to the staff and some of the Lost Children."

Her eyebrows rose so high they created deep furrows on her forehead. "Tell me everything."

So we did. Baldwin finished by pulling the key out from under his tunic. It was strung on the leather holding his jasper. "Even though we have it, we are not sure what our next move is."

"We can think on that." She turned to me. "And you used your pyrocharisma? That's fantastic news."

"It wasn't easy. And I had a couple of false starts."

Abira swallowed the last of her juice. "Even so, I can give you the test and the next piece of the mark if you pass."

Shiraz brightened. "Ooh, could I see it? I so enjoyed the last one."

Abira tapped her chin. "We could do it on the rooftop. It would be private yet large enough to set up the marking area."

I fiddled with my silverware. "Sure. But sooner is better. I don't love the process."

"Late afternoon, then."

As Abira and Shiraz continued to talk, Baldwin and I excused ourselves.

In the hallway, he tugged on my hand. "Follow me to the roof?"

"Sure."

He was quiet on the way up, but I knew what was coming. My stomach twisted into a knot. This would be about as fun as a stroll through Silvastamen.

On the rooftop balcony, cool wind off the ocean ruffled my hair while the sun warmed the air. I shaded my eyes against the glare. Waves extended for miles, rows of white tops on cerulean-blue water.

When Baldwin sat on the bench, I sat next to him, and he slid his hand over mine, linking our fingers.

Still, several minutes passed before he spoke. "You were paired with Storm?"

It was easier to watch the surf than Baldwin's face. "No, he was just flirting."

"Shiraz said he was taken with you. That is not the same as flirting."

I swallowed. "It was nothing. He thought he was in love with me."

Baldwin frowned. "That is not nothing."

I rushed the next sentence. "But you can't fall in love with someone instantaneously, so...yeah."

"Did you kiss him?"

Pushing my irritation aside, I kept my response even. "I'm not giving you a play-by-play. You're jealous."

He paused for a moment before answering, his voice stone hard. "Yes. Absolutely. You and I are paired."

My attempt at patience snapped. "Yeah, now we are. But at the time, I'd seen Gari all over you and thought it was over, so I moved on."

"It was that easy for you?"

Hurt bloomed in my chest. "That's not fair. I thought you and Gari had gotten back together."

"Did you sleep with him?"

"What? No!" Shock had me yanking my hand from his. I stood and stepped away, needing to be isolated from the obnoxious question and the guy asking it.

He rubbed his hands on his pants and rose, a grimace twisting his face. "I am sorry. That was uncalled for. I did not know you two had been serious."

"We weren't, at least, not on my part." I pondered whether to share the next bombshell and decided to risk it. He'd find out eventually anyway. "He asked me to be his fiancée."

A muscle ticked in his jaw, and his eyes darkened. "That is serious."

I crossed my arms. "I turned him down because he didn't love me. Not really. And I didn't love him. Although his attention was flattering, the relationship never would've worked."

"Why?" His voice sounded like it had been pressed through gravel.

My voice escaped in a whisper. "Because of you. I was in love with you."

He took the few steps needed to stand next to me, almost touching. His fingers traced my cheek. "Was? Not anymore?"

Offering a shrug, I couldn't say anything, couldn't open myself up like that, where every thought would be exposed, raw, vulnerable.

His eyes searched my face. "I hope you figure it out soon, because I am in love with you."

I am in love with you... The words came from a long way off. I tried to breathe as a bud of hope unfurled at his words. "Yeah?"

He cleared his throat. "Well, yeah. You do not have to say it back. I just thought you should know how I feel. You know, in case anyone else asks you to be their fiancée."

A smile spread across my face. "Shut up. I love you too."

He gathered me close, his hand slipping under my hair to my neck. I squeezed my eyes shut and laid my head on his shoulder.

Laughter colored his voice. "I do not think you are supposed to tell someone shut up and I love you in the same breath."

"Baldwin?"

"Yeah, I know. Shut up."

Liquid warmth spread through my chest. He loved me. All the fantasies I'd spun in my head paled in comparison to the real thing, right here, right now.

Several minutes later, Arvandus and Lev arrived. While Baldwin greeted his griffin, I gave Arvandus a big hug, who nuzzled his furry head into my neck. We settled on the covered area of the porch and shared our adventure.

I ended with, "Now we just have to figure out where the staff's hidden."

Lev tilted his head and emitted a raspy whistle. "May I see the key, please?"

Baldwin pulled it out from under his tunic.

The griffin tilted his head again, his keen eyes studying the item.

Arvandus flicked his tail. "We will need to search for sources with information on the key. Perhaps legends, folk tales, songs."

Baldwin perked up. "I think I remember a song..." He shook his head. "I am not sure. Let me think about it some more."

"Let's take a ride on the griffins, then," I suggested. "I always think better in the air."

After a flight, we returned and had lunch, Shiraz again impressing us with her cooking. Thank goodness we didn't live nearby—I'd blow up like a balloon.

Afterward, I turned to Baldwin. "I hate to dump you, but I need some time to practice for my test."

"No problem. Shiraz has some books covering local folklore. Maybe I will find something about the key or the staff."

I doubted it, but we needed to look under every available rock. The only place where I could be alone was the rooftop, so I practiced there. By late afternoon, Abira, Shiraz, and Baldwin joined me on the balcony. Abira laid out the tattooing materials, and Shiraz propped a few pillows and a blanket on a chair. I pulled a piece of fypex gum from my pocket and popped it in my mouth.

When Abira turned to me, I pulled off my jasper and handed it to Baldwin. "Can you hold this for me?"

"You are not allowed to wear it?"

I shook my head. "Not for the test."

Shiraz and Baldwin sat, and he gave me a wink. A sudden attack of nerves hit as Abira sat across from me. "This will be a two-part test. For the first part, you must produce fifteen fireballs while I count to twenty."

Fifteen? Rolling my shoulders, I took a big breath. That was almost one fireball per second. I could do it. Her next words stripped away my confidence.

"Then you will create a form with pyrocharisma. The form must move and be stable for a count of ten before you shift it to another image. This second image must be bigger. It must also move and be held for a count of ten. The last created form must be as large as you can successfully stabilize and animate. You may begin the first demonstration when ready."

So glad she didn't make it too easy for me. Not.

Closing my eyes, I repeated the Firebrand Creed in my head. *Elyon within, guides my soul...* I gathered the heat quickly, then released fireballs in rhythmic explosions. My ninth one sputtered, and I scrambled to get my rhythm back. *Come on, come on! Ten, eleven...* I detonated the fifteenth one with a second to spare. Sweat soaked my back, and I panted as if I'd sparred a round with Baldwin.

Satisfaction glimmered in her gray eyes. "Very good. And the second demonstration when you're ready."

Nerves skittered through my stomach, but I pushed them aside. I couldn't think about failing. Heat slid into my hands, a quicksilver gathering, and I held out my palm. The image of a horse, fiery-red mane and tail whipping as he galloped, appeared in my hand. I counted to myself, straining to focus, to hold the image for the required time.

Taking another deep breath, I reassembled the flames into a school of fish, like the ones we saw in Mermaid Cove. This image filled a two-foot by two-foot square, and details mattered, especially at this size. Scales of yellow and red flashed, the fish moving in harmony...then the upper corner of the image shivered. I pulled hard on my focus, gritting my teeth as I counted down the seconds.

The third creation had to be my most impressive. Breathless, sweat stinging my eyes, I used both hands to form the image of a griffin, just like Arvandus. The griffin grew as I added more flames, until he was the size of a large Saint Bernard. Even at that size, the edges fuzzed. Unruly flames licked out as if tasting the air. I shrank it a bit and had the griffin ruffle his wings before tucking them against his sides.

Abira stood to my left, beyond my peripheral vision. Was I doing this right? Did it look horrible? What if I failed? My focus slipped and I squinted, adding more movement, the image panting and licking his chops. Near the end of my ten seconds, I allowed the creation to yawn before his eyes closed.

I held the image until Abira said, "Done."

Dropping my hands, the griffin dissipated in a shower of red sparks. The silence was deafening. My stomach flipped, and my knees weakened.

She smiled. "You've passed. Congratulations."

Baldwin and Shiraz clapped while I stumbled to a pillow and sat. Shiraz jumped up. "Let me get you comfortable, turtledove."

She plumped the pillows, and I lay on my stomach, this part of the ceremony being my least favorite.

Abira's voice came from behind me. "I assume you want secatic oil again."

"Yes, please." That was the one thing that made the whole experience bearable. I drank the offered glass with oil added to it and tied back my hair.

I caught Baldwin's eye. "Could you hold my hand?"

He settled next to me. "I will not turn down the opportunity."

Did I need him to hold my hand? No, I just wanted the reassurance that he was there, that I wasn't alone, and maybe, by some miracle, this whole adventure would have a happy ending.

Abira swabbed my back with secatic oil. A minute later, I moaned as the needle pierced my skin. It wasn't a big tattoo, but it was big enough.

Baldwin traced patterns on my palm. "I found nothing during my search this afternoon. No mention of the key or staff, although there was a long description of Mermaid Cove."

I hissed a breath into the pillow as the needle pricked my skin again, then carefully turned my head so my words weren't muffled. "How are we going to find the staff with no direction?"

Abira's voice was as steady as her hands. "Elyon will give us what we need when we need it."

If we were going to beat Rune to the staff, we needed to do it now. I squeezed my eyes shut and buried my face in the pillow, the smell of gingersnaps surrounding me. Baldwin's hand enclosed mine, his warm fingers now tracing patterns on my wrist. His touch sent tingles up my arm, which distracted me from the stabbing needle.

Abira finally sat back. "Done. Let me swab it with more oil. Wrap it tonight, but let air get to it tomorrow."

Baldwin helped me to my feet. As we followed the women downstairs, he gave me a questioning look. "Could Abira heal your mark?"

I gave him a wry smile. "No. Guild mark tattoos are to heal naturally. The individual is supposed to power through the pain like the Firebrand she is." I rolled my eyes and lowered my voice. "I wouldn't have minded the healing, though."

He gave me an understanding look and squeezed my hand.

Shiraz herded us into her kitchen where she provided a delicious celebratory meal topped off with pupkissberry pie. I ate too much of everything but didn't regret one bite.

Abira stopped us before we parted. "I think we should leave tomorrow morning."

I nodded. "I'll tell Arvandus."

Baldwin and I climbed the stairs to the roof to share our travel plans with our two griffins. They lounged on the deck as the sun hovered at the horizon, half of an orange ball.

I leaned against the railing. "Hey you two, Abira wants to leave tomorrow morning."

My griffin got up and stretched, his back arching. "I will hunt then."

"Sleep well. See you tomorrow." He leaped off the deck, Lev only seconds behind.

The Petrus Rings came into view, spanning the twilight sky. It was hard to enjoy, my mind spinning with confusion over the key and staff.

Baldwin moved closer, careful of my sore shoulder as his arm slipped around my waist. "Relax, love. You have that look on your face."

"What look?"

"The one that says you are trying to solve the world's problems. Are you worried about the key, the staff, or both?"

With a deep breath, I tried to relax into his embrace. "Both. We don't know anything."

"You will figure it out."

I gave him a questioning glance. "And why is that?"

"I have never met anyone as stubborn as you."

Although he was usually good at flattery, this one was falling flat. I pulled away a little. "Excuse me?"

"If you are confused about something, you keep pushing until you figure it out. It is not in you to give up."

"Oh. I guess." But underneath it all, pessimism bubbled. His confidence wasn't rubbing off on me.

We made our way back to our rooms. Baldwin and I lingered in the hallway outside Room 202 over goodnight kisses. After we were interrupted the third time by a neighboring room occupant, I said a reluctant goodnight and walked to Shiraz's room, my lips still tingling.

The next day dawned sunny and bright. After another delicious breakfast, the three of us thanked Shiraz for her hospitality.

She pulled me into a hug and whispered, "That boy's a keeper. Please invite me to your twining ceremony."

My cheeks heated, and I ducked my head, praying Baldwin hadn't overheard.

Abira joined me on Arvandus while Baldwin took the bags on Lev. It was a short flight to Starfall Rim, and we arrived at Declan's inn by lunchtime. Traveling always made me hungry. After promising to catch up with Arvandus later, the three of us made our way into the restaurant.

Behind the bar, Declan gave Abira a frown. "Good thing you're here. Some new students showed up for you. I've been feeding them, so I put it on your tab." He jerked a thumb at the back of the room.

Three teens sat at a corner table, talking and finishing their lunch.

New students? I reached up to tame the knots in my hair before giving up. Despite looking like a mess, I was curious about my new guildmates.

CHAPTER TWENTY

ABIRA INTRODUCED US TO the new Firebrand students. Fifteen-year-old Devarus was a Camlo with striking amber eyes. Etenia was a Welden with a quick, pretty smile rivaling her glowing aura. Hakan's angular features identified him as Kell, but he was either scared or overly serious. His expression hadn't changed once, almost like he was trying to figure out quantum mechanics in his head.

Abira patted my shoulder. "You and Baldwin have lunch, and I'll get the new students settled. Declan, can I have a sandwich to go? I'll settle my tab later."

After lunch, Abira found me in my room. "New lesson. Meet me in the backyard."

I stifled a groan but wove my hair into a messy braid and walked out to another exhausting workout.

She sat waiting in a wooden chair, her gaze determined. "You have two more lessons to gain Level Five status. I'd like to introduce the new exercises now rather than later."

"What about the other students?"

"I'm giving them the evening to get comfortable. Tomorrow I'll check their skill levels. Sometimes students arrive with some training—their parents have taught them a bit, or they've learned it from friends."

"Or from griffins." I grinned.

She nodded in agreement. "And it's a good thing he did, or the battle with Rune's forces would've gone very differently. Anyway, I'll give them a baseline test tomorrow and see where everyone is on the scale."

She walked to an area of freshly raked bare earth. All greenery was a distant memory.

"I'm going to show you a technique called Dragon's Breath. Just watch first, and then I'll explain it."

Extending her hands, she turned her palms outward. With a quick inhaled breath, a tall, rolling line of hot blue flames poured from her palms. She narrowed her eyes, focusing on the flames as they danced and licked higher. When she withdrew her hands, the flames winked out as if someone had flipped a switch.

My mouth was hanging open, so I snapped it shut. "That was wicked impressive."

She inclined her head in thanks. "Much like pryocharisma, focus is paramount."

Of course it was. I fished a piece of fypex gum from my pocket. "Why does it burn so hot? Those flames were blue."

A glass of water waited on the table, and she took a large swallow. "With Dragon's Breath, the flames burn hotter than any other creation. But each person's Dragon's Breath will be a different color. Gray, blue, green…I've seen quite a variety."

While I chewed, she continued. "You gather the power, but rather than releasing it all at once, you dispense it in a long continuous stream like syrup from a bottle. The Level Five lessons all deal with self-regulation. I'd like you to try."

I exhaled and shook out my arms. Closing my eyes, I murmured the Firebrand Creed and prepared to pull in a massive amount of heat.

In moments, the power waited to be discharged, heavy and pulsing. I'd never tried to slow fire while I released it, and my arms quivered with strain. A three-foot flame popped from my palms with a bang, then another and another. *Bang, bang, bang.* One more like a cherry bomb firework—*bang*—and I pursed my lips. Epic fail.

Abira stepped forward. "On the plus side, there was a lot of power in your attempt. On the minus side, you had no continuity. This time, try to release a continuous amount of fire, but don't worry about temperature. Once you've mastered the flow, we'll focus on heat."

After two hours of attempts, a massive headache pounded from temple to temple. My last effort had been better, a mostly continuous unspooling of flames, but they weren't very hot or very tall. When Abira dismissed me, movement from one of the bedrooms caught my eye. Three faces peered out, the new students all viewing me like a caged zoo animal. I gave them a weary wave, and the curtain dropped back into place.

In Abira's bathroom, I found the medicus syrup and poured myself a dose, hoping the pounding in my head would ease.

Despite my attempts to relax, the headache followed me for the rest of the evening, and I went to bed early.

The next day, Abira had me assist her with the new students, although every time I drew near, they clammed up. Were they all shy? Afraid? After their baseline tests, Abira began to instruct them in basic creation exercises.

Devarus broadened his stance. Holding his hands in front of him, he squeezed his eyes shut. A ball of fire shot from his hands and blasted the ground next to a pile of wooden sticks.

"Saints and sinners," Abira muttered under her breath. "Devarus, it helps if you keep your eyes open. Try again, please."

While Abira dealt with Devarus's power issues, I checked on Hakan, who'd produced a two-inch writhing flame in his palm. No smile on his face, but pleased satisfaction simmered in his eyes.

"Wow, good job, Hakan. On your next effort, pull in a little more heat to make the flame larger."

I moved on to Etenia. The girl clutched her hands to her chest. I showed her how to hold her hands like she was cupping a baby bird.

"And the fire will just show up there?" She blinked rapidly, and her aura dimmed to a sickly yellow glow. "I don't think that's a good idea."

"That's your gift, right?"

"Yes, but what if I hurt someone? Burn someone? Kill someone?" Her voice squeaked higher with each question.

"Etenia, what's going on?"

"N-nothing." She hesitated, then whispered, "I don't want to hurt people."

"You won't. That's why you're learning control now." I pulled one of her hands up to hold her jasper. "Close your eyes. What do you feel?"

"Heat." Her voice was a breath of sound. "And a kind of itch, but like one I can't scratch."

"Right. Elyon put this ability in you—*you*, Etenia. He gave you the ability to create your own fire, and it'll be special, just like you. So don't be afraid of what He gave you. He doesn't make mistakes, okay?"

She bit her lip, and her eyes opened. "Okay."

We tried again. She cupped one hand, held her jasper with the other, and a small flame sprang to life in her palm. She gasped but kept it burning. After a few seconds, it went out.

Joy sparkled in her grin. "I did it."

"You did awesome."

Abira clapped her hands. "All right, everyone. Water break. We need to stay hydrated."

The students rushed for the kitchen door, and Abira walked over to me. "You did well with Etenia."

I shrugged. "Poor kid was terrified of her gift. I just wanted her to feel more confident."

"You ever thought about being an instructor?"

I wrinkled my nose. "I haven't really given much thought to what happens, you know, after."

"You'd do well teaching others. You're empathetic, and you re-member what it was like when you came into your talent with no warning. That's an asset, especially with students like Etenia."

The thought of a future waiting for me was too much. "But doesn't everything depend on how the future plays out? If things go badly, I'll be dead. Probably."

"How about thinking positively, hmm? It's a lot less depress-ing." Abira walked past me into the kitchen.

Yes, but dashed lower expectations were easier to deal with.

After more practice and a quick lunch, she dismissed everyone except me to Niklos's guild hall.

I furrowed my brow. "Why would you send them to Niklos?"

"He has a conference room we're temporarily using for acade-mic studies. The Builderbrands are drawing up plans for a conser-vatory."

She filled a basin with soapy water to wash the lunch dishes. "Go on outside and practice your pyrocharisma to warm up. Then start practicing Dragon's Breath."

I'd rather do the dishes.

I walked outside, choosing to stay in the roof's shade instead of under the blazing sun. My pyrocharisma creations came easier—a helicopter, a flashing sword, and finally, a little man doing the moonwalk. I especially liked him.

After enjoying his cool moves on my palm and up my arm, I let him disappear and moved to the bare earth area to work on Dragon's Breath.

I unwrapped a piece of fypex gum and popped it in my mouth, closing my eyes as the raspberry and vanilla flavor teased my taste buds. The sun warmed my bare shoulders and baked through my white tank top. I murmured the Firebrand Creed and let the heat gather. How much could I hold? More, more, and a little more. Heat and power built, my forearms buzzing with my talent waiting to be released. I opened my eyes and gasped.

My forearms were on fire.

CHAPTER TWENTY-ONE

RED AND YELLOW FLAMES licked from my glowing, orange skin. My mouth hung open. No pain, but I definitely had a Human Torch-vibe going on. I'd never seen anything so fascinating and horrible in my life.

"Brenna! What are you doing?" Abira's voice came from the porch.

I couldn't look away from my arms. "No idea. Um, should I be worried? Cause I kinda am."

"It looks like this would be a good time to go over the final lesson of level five. Exhale and push out the power—slowly."

As I exhaled, several large fireballs flared into being with a *whoosh* before disappearing, my control still problematic.

Abira walked closer. "Incendior is becoming the fire itself. And it's very, very dangerous."

"Why?"

She folded back her sleeves to well above her elbows and drew in a deep breath. Flames flared, flickering from her fingers and growing to consume her hands. She turned her hands over, each finger and palm alive with fire. "If I don't regulate this, I can burn up from the inside out. A lucky Firebrand may escape that fate, although their ability can burn out." She released several swirling flames, her hands normal once again.

"What's the purpose of Incendior?"

Abira pressed her lips together. "Aside from a good demonstration of control? It's the only technique that can withstand Shadow Power."

Dread punched low. I had to learn this, then. The memory of the crop we'd burned filled my mind. Maybe Rune wouldn't have any extra Shadow Power, and he'd have to use his own unenhanced talent? Yeah, I wouldn't be that lucky.

I tuned back in to Abira talking. "...too dangerous. Just focus on Dragon's Breath for now."

After drinking water from the glass on the table, I walked back to the spot of bare earth and tried again.

Over and over for the next several hours, I tried to create a rolling line of fire in a slow, controlled stream. My last attempt before supper was okay. The fire still wasn't as hot as I'd like.

All the students including Abira and me ate at the kitchen table. Etenia sat on my right, full of a story about meeting one of Declan's light wolves. Hakan and Devarus spent the meal arguing about whether hippogriffs or griffins were faster.

After supper, Hakan and Devarus handled cleanup. I headed outside to enjoy the cooling evening air. Dropping into a chair, I leaned my head back, a light breeze scented with cactus flower brushing my cheeks. Practicing Dragon's Breath had wiped me out.

I had a feeling Incendior would do the same.

Despite having found the key, none of us had any grand revelations regarding our next step. Since Baldwin's room was constantly being invaded by younger students, he'd given the key to me. I hid it deep in my bag, tethered to an inside strap, so I didn't lose it. The rest of the week and into the next, I worked with students during the day, helping with basic Firebrand skills. Surprisingly, I liked it. And the kids lost most of their shyness around me, making the relationships more comfortable.

In the evenings, I added Incendior creation to my rotation of practice skills. My control issues improved with practice, and Dragon's Breath came easier. I'd learned to infuse more heat and power into the exercise. Incendior was still tricky.

On Friday evening, Abira met me outside and dropped a bundle of cloth into my lap. "Try that on for size."

The silver cloth shimmered in the twilight as I unfolded it. "It's gorgeous. What is it?"

"Dragonscale silk. Rare and, of course, made from the scales of dragons."

I paused in slipping it on over my tank, the shirt hanging off one arm. "For real?"

"Yes. Impervious to all fire, it's a necessary addition for anyone practicing Incendior. Wear it whenever you practice."

"What about pants? Or doesn't Incendior take over the legs?"

"No, it's possible, but as you first learn, just your torso is affected. Your boots—are they rason leather?"

I glanced at my boots as if I'd never seen them before. "I don't know. Why?"

Abira ran a finger over the leather. "They feel like it. Rason leather doesn't burn, so they won't need to be fireproofed."

After tying the matching belt into a knot, I smoothed a hand over the material—glossy like satin. "I love it. Thank you."

She smiled. "You're welcome. And for what it's worth, it looks fantastic on you."

I spent the next few hours practicing. My last attempt at Dragon's Breath was after Abira went to bed. Closing my eyes, I allowed the power to gather in my hands, then let the flames leak out in a slow stream. Fire flashed, a rolling tide, and I released more power into the flames. They climbed chest high, the crackle and roar like a living beast. As I continued to feed the fire, it turned deep violet, heat coming off the flames like a blast furnace.

I let the Dragon's Breath die out. Wiping my forehead, I gave myself a mental high five and walked into the kitchen to get a glass of water.

After a quick shower, I dropped the Dragonscale shirt in my bag. I'd put it away later.

As I turned to walk away, the glistening key caught the light, and I pulled it from my bag. Lying on my bed, I turned up my helli lantern to inspect the metal key. A silver moon. Four metal wings. The perfect hook at the bottom. The metal warmed in my hand, and as I fiddled with the chain, little marks on the barrel caught the light. I squinted.

Tiny notches marched up the length of the silver barrel, slashes like hieroglyphics. A closer inspection revealed they were microscopic letters, but I'd need better eyes to read them.

Clutching the key, I hurried downstairs to the living room. A decorative yet functional spiegel globe rested on a pedestal. Could I use it like a magnifier? No, it only curved the key like a funhouse mirror. Letting the globe warm in my hand, I focused. The glass turned a light blue, and an image of Baldwin appeared in the center. Although in his bedroom, he was still awake as he lay on his back.

I set the spiegel globe down and hurried out the door to Baldwin's guild house.

Over the past few days, I'd learned the location of his room, so I grabbed a few pebbles and aimed for his window. The first one missed. After looking around for witnesses, I tried again. Although

I wasn't technically doing anything wrong, something told me most instructors might not be happy about my actions.

The next stone pinged against Baldwin's window. After another well-aimed pebble, his curtain shifted, and his face appeared. I gestured for him to come down. He disappeared, and I stepped into the shadows to wait. In moments, he showed up on the porch dressed in soft, loose pants and bare feet. A T-shirt was slung over a shoulder.

He padded down the steps. "Hi."

I stepped forward. "I'm glad you're still up. I used a spiegel globe to make sure."

"Is everything all right?" As he drew close, the scent of oranges mingled with leather drifted over me.

Swallowing hard, I tried to ignore his muscular biceps and concentrated on his collarbone. No one had told me being in love would make focusing more difficult. With my ADHD, I had enough trouble as it was. Of course, his lack of a shirt didn't help.

"Hey, put a shirt on, would you?"

He grinned and propped his hands on his hips. "Why? Am I distracting you?"

Heat filled my cheeks. "Shut up." I yanked the shirt off his shoulder and shoved it at his chest.

Chuckling, he tugged the shirt over his head.

I held up the key. "I think I might've found a clue. But I need a magnifying glass."

"I have one in my room. We can use the lantern on the back porch at your guild. I will meet you there."

"Okay." I hurried back to the Firebrand guild.

Baldwin arrived only a minute later. Claiming a chair next to mine, he turned up the lantern, setting it between us. I pulled my chair closer to the table, suddenly realizing I was wearing only a camisole and pajama pants. Hmm, I'd been a little too hyperfocused on the key. A blanket lay over a nearby chair, so I draped it around my shoulders.

"Look." Pushing aside the chain, I held the key up to the lantern. "On the barrel of the key here it looks like letters. But I can't read them."

Squinting, he held the key closer, then put it under the magnifying glass. "For the innocent."

"What?" Exhilaration swept through me. Another clue!

"That is what it says."

He held it closer to me, and I looked through the glass, reading the microscopic letters.

My sudden excitement shriveled into a heavy lump in my chest. "What does that mean?"

Baldwin continued to frown, his eyes unfocused. "The innocent," he repeated. His face suddenly cleared. "Remember when I mentioned a song? I remember now. It was so long ago when I heard it. I was maybe six or seven times old."

I suppressed a grin as my mind conjured up an adorable little boy with bright, inquisitive eyes and messy hair.

He turned to me. "Some of my father's friends came to our house. They were celebrating. My mother had me go to bed early, but I crept down the stairs to watch the men drink and sing. I do not remember the verse, but the chorus goes, 'The innocent will take the key and cut the kingdom free.'"

The distinct, creepy feel of eyes on me froze my question in my throat.

Baldwin saw me stiffen. "What?"

I lowered my voice to a whisper. "Someone's watching us."

"Where?" His eyes shifted to the dark shadows ringing the backyard.

"You are correct, Brenna." Arvandus materialized from the shadows, and I exhaled, relief leaking from my pores.

I favored him with a glare. "Really, dude? Do you have to skulk in the shadows like that?"

"Firstly, I am not a dude. And secondly, I do not skulk."

"Whatever." Semantics hardly mattered while my heart drummed within my chest.

"What are you discussing this late at night?" Arvandus settled next to our seats, his golden eyes glowing in the darkness.

"There's a clue on the key," I said, waggling the item.

"Brenna's observant eyes found it." Baldwin gave me a wink. "It is written in tiny script on the barrel of the key. 'For the innocent.' It reminded me of a drinking song I heard when I was very young."

"Ah, the Ballad of the Innocent." Arvandus blinked once. "An old, old song, it is the story of a monster that invades the kingdom of a wealthy man. The monster throws the man, his family, and his servants into the man's own dungeon. His youngest daughter escapes and finds the key to their cell. She frees them, then lures the monster onto an isolated island. When he follows, she takes her enchanted knife and severs the island from the rest of the kingdom. The daughter sacrificed herself to save the kingdom and her family."

I sat back in my seat, disappointed with the ending. "That's so sad."

Arvandus tilted his head. "Yes, it is. Although no family in history recorded this event, so it seems to be a myth."

That made me feel better. The story slipped through my mind, connecting all the other information I'd gathered. *The innocent will take the key and cut the kingdom free...* "What if the key leads the innocent to the staff?" Images of a zombie-like person clutching a key while blindly roaming the countryside filled my head. "Never mind. That makes no sense."

Blinking once, Baldwin sat straighter before he slumped again. "We are missing something."

As usual. I didn't want to say that out loud, though. We were all doing the best we could. "Any idea who the innocent is?"

Arvandus spoke. "Someone who has not come into their gift yet."

"Oh." I raised my eyebrows. I hadn't thought of that. "Can we test the theory?"

"No." Baldwin's tone left no room for an argument. "Everyone here has already come into their gift. And it would be impossible to test it and keep it a secret. Before long, someone would inevitably share the information, and Rune would arrive to steal it."

Arvandus stood. "Excellent job, both of you. But you should go to bed. We can talk about this tomorrow."

Baldwin said goodnight and headed back to his guild. With a yawn, I stretched and put the blanket on the chair.

Arvandus ruffled his wings. "I need to hunt. Go to bed, Raven. It is late."

"I know. Goodnight, Arvandus." I patted his neck before he prowled to the other side of the porch and disappeared into the darkness.

Back in my room, I tucked the key into my bag and snuggled under my covers. The new information we'd discovered made it hard to relax even though my body was tired. I shifted to my side, pulling my pillow more fully under my head.

I woke to a difference in the air. Had a sound roused me? A smell?

I sat up, my jasper freezing my skin. In the dark, the odor of rancid spices drifted through my room. My pulse spiked. I crept to the window and peered out.

Rune stood one hundred yards away, his body an emaciated shell. The black cloak flapped open, exposing a bony chest and rib cage, his heart a faintly glowing blob pulsing in the night. I gagged, blinked, and looked again.

He wasn't there.

But the greedy sound of crackling fire came from far below. I leaned out my window. In the grass, a line of high flames licked at the wooden boards of the guild, golden fingers illuminating its fiery path.

CHAPTER TWENTY-TWO

SHOVING MY BOOTS ON, I grabbed my bag and shoved my sword inside. I dashed from my bedroom and took off down the hall. "Fire! Everyone up! Wake up! Fire! Everyone out!"

As I pounded on doors, the scent of wood smoke grew stronger. A faint gray haze wafted up the stairs and gathered near the ceiling. Etenia, Hakan, and Devarus stumbled out of their rooms, rubbing their eyes.

Devarus headed down the stairs but returned seconds later, coughing. "Fire's blocking the exit."

Etenia started to cry, and Hakan awkwardly patted her back.

Arvandus! Fire! We need you!

Raven! Where?

The guild hall. Top floor.

Which window?

The big one at the end of the hall. Please hurry!

I turned to the students and swallowed past the rock in my throat. "My griffin, Arvandus, is coming. He can fly us to safety. Head for the big window."

The students scurried down the hallway and clustered in front of the window. Devarus undid the latch and pushed the pane open. I placed my bag near the window.

Smoke collected near the ceiling. Pungent and thick like pea soup, with the scent of burnt spices—it was the product of Shadow Power. My heart pounded. I shook out my cold fingers. If I used Incendior, I could douse this fire. Ignoring the ache in the back of my throat, I hurried to the stairwell and faced the wall of smoke.

I reached for my gift, words from the Firebrand Creed jumbling in my head. My mind raced, jumping from one bad scenario to the next—smoke inhalation, fifth degree burns, death. Flames ignited from my fingertips, withered, and died.

My arms trembled as my stomach plunged.

Devarus's question pulled me from my failed attempt. "Where's Abira?"

Noting her closed bedroom door, I dashed over and pounded on it. "Abira, get up!"

She opened her door, her white hair loose and mussed, her eyes unfocused. "What's going on?"

"Guild hall's on fire. Exit's blocked." As I spoke, my pendant froze again. I swallowed a sob. He was back.

Pushing up her sleeves, she waved me away. "I'll put it out."

I grabbed her arm. "It's Rune's Shadow Power. He's here. Somewhere." I sucked in a painful breath.

She paled. "Get everyone to safety."

"Arvandus is on his way."

"Good. I'll take care of the fire at the source." She turned and fled down the stairwell.

My mouth dropped open. Gagging on smoke, I yelled after her, "We have to go. Now! There's no time."

In seconds, sounds carried up the stairs—explosions, hisses like steam, the roar of fires igniting. The hallway popped and cracked beneath my feet. Far away, Abira shouted. Maniacal laughter followed.

My chest grew tight. I pulled my shirt over my mouth, but I couldn't leave the top of the stairs.

My pendant warmed. Abira returned a minute later, her night-gown scorched, the sleeves in tatters. "Rune started two fires for every one I extinguished. He's gone, but the building's a loss. Have Arvandus pick me up at my bedroom window. I've got to get something."

I grabbed her arm as she turned toward her bedroom. "Everyone needs to get out."

"And I will. Now go." She nudged me toward the end of the hall, her face set.

Hurrying toward the window, I squinted against the overpowering smoke, relieved to see Arvandus had already carried Hakan and Etenia to safety.

As Devarus climbed onto Arvandus, I turned at a whoosh of fire, transfixed by the bright flames consuming the stairs and taking over the hallway. Sweat pooled under my arms, soaking my torso.

Raven, hurry. The fire is too intense.

My eyes watered from the dense smoke and flames. I turned back to Arvandus. "But Abira—"

Now, Raven. Metallic sparkles erupted from my griffin's wings, his eyes boring holes into mine.

Grabbing my bag, I climbed onto his back, careful not to bump Devarus. *Abira said you should pick her up at her bedroom window.*

I will get her next. He dove from the burning building.

Flames danced high, a glowing nest as they climbed the guild-hall walls. The whole first story shimmered and glowed, and fire licked out of second-story windows and crawled along the roofline.

Arvandus deposited us a short distance away and streaked back toward Abira's bedroom window. I ran around the corner of the guild to watch for her. A box shot out of her window like an arrow. Sailing past the griffin, it bounced safely away from the burning building. My stomach twisted. Forget the box—where was she?

Her form backlit by the fire, Abira finally emerged onto the ledge. She inched forward to climb onto Arvandus. With a massive crack, the roof gave way. Abira tumbled, her arms extending as she disappeared into the burning house.

My breath stalled. "No!"

I reached out, not caring I was too far away to catch her. My heart ripped, ash and pain mixing. I couldn't believe it. This wasn't happening. She was fine. She'd crawl from the gaping hole.

Arvandus flew closer, but flames shot up and forced his retreat. Still, my griffin hovered, dodging flames and peering into the burning building. I watched. Waited. Prayed.

After several long minutes, he returned and settled in front of me, his eyes watering. His breath came in ragged pants. "I am sorry. Her fall was fatal."

My knees collapsed. This had to be a nightmare. I'd wake any minute now. Abira would shake my shoulder and tell me to pull myself together.

With a gasp, Etenia began to sob. Devarus hugged her as Hakan moved to her other side, the three of them clustered together.

"Brenna? Where are you? Brenna!" Panic filled Baldwin's voice.

I peeked around Arvandus's bulk, and Baldwin closed the distance between us.

His voice shook as he pulled me to my feet. "Are you hurt?"

With his arms tight around me, I inhaled his familiar scent, his embrace giving me strength.

Pulling away, I swiped at my wet cheeks. "Abira. She's..." Grit coated my throat. "She's gone."

His eyes widened. "What happened?"

My eyes stung from the rancid smoke. Still, I stared at the burning guild, willing Abira to appear around the corner. "The roof collapsed."

He tucked me close, and I leaned into his strength, refusing to look away from the fire.

This isn't real, can't be real. Not happening.

Shock numbed everything into a fuzzy hallucination of shadows and flames. Nobody tried to save the guild—it was a lost cause. Instead, Weatherbrands encircled the building, controlling the wind surrounding the blaze. Several Warriors fanned out to search for the arsonist. I could've told them he was gone. As flames engulfed the structure, the gathered crowd stood back to let the guild burn to the ground.

Declan found us, rooted near the Wisdom Trainer guild hall. His eyes swept our group before he frowned. "Where's Abira?"

My throat clogging, I shook my head. "The roof—" I couldn't say more.

Declan's eyes grew wide, and he scanned the area. "No. No, she's a Firebrand. A fire can't kill her." He turned to stare at me, waiting for an explanation, unbelief stamped on his face.

I swallowed hard against the ache in my throat. "She tried—Shadow Power—she fell..."

My words seemed to sink in. "No!"

Hearing Declan's cry, Niklos stepped forward and led him away.

Turning from the carnage in front of me, I walked to where Abira's all-important box had fallen and picked it up. But didn't open it. As I shuffled back to the group, I held the box tight against my chest as if to ward off pain.

While the Weatherbrands directed wind currents, Waterbrands doused the surrounding area. I could only watch, my heart a bruised, broken mass. If Rune's fire escaped the Weatherbrands, no amount of water would protect the other buildings. None of the other talents could affect Shadow Power. And I had failed miserably.

It was a while before Niklos returned to collect us. "Come. We will house you at our guild. Devarus and Hakan will be in one room, and Etenia and Brenna can share another."

Arvandus and I shared a hug before he left for the griffin house.

Baldwin stepped into place next to me. Silence reigned for a few moments as we walked, then, "What is in the box?"

I cleared the scratchiness in my throat, soot and spoiled spices still thick in the air. "I don't know. A-Abira was determined to save it." I was terrified to open it—it was Pandora's box housing all the bad things, including the realization she was gone. If the box stayed closed, Abira would return to claim it.

When we reached the guild, a healer was brought in to examine the students. He checked our lungs and examined our bodies for burns. After a thorough exam, Etenia and I were ushered into a room at the guild hall, but we didn't talk.

I placed the box under a nearby table where it was barely visible. A rush of fatigue swept over me, clearing all thoughts from my mind, except those involving sleep. As I lay down, Etenia's whimpers drifted through the room, but I had no words of comfort.

In fact, I joined her, burying my face in my pillow to muffle the sobs.

The next day, I didn't wake until noon. After a shower to remove the smoke from my body, I dressed in a donated outfit and fiddled with my hair.

Baldwin stopped by my room. "How did you sleep?"

I pulled a comb through my wet mane. "Fine." Not really. The loop in my head wouldn't stop playing—fire climbing the walls, smoke filling the hallways, flames everywhere, Abira reaching, then gone...

Baldwin rubbed my shoulders. "Get something to eat. I have training now, but I will see you at supper, okay?"

I mumbled a reply, and he left. The scent of smoke still hung in the air, its acrid odor unavoidable even in the kitchen. Out the window lay the view of the decimated, smoldering remains of the Firebrand guild. I turned away, made a snack of cheese and crackers, then left for the quiet of the guild library.

Other students seemed to avoid my company, which was fine, because I kept seeing Abira fall, the image on replay in my mind. I should've done more, forced her to leave everything behind. Why hadn't I?

Later in the day, Niklos put me on kitchen duty. Helping prepare supper for the guild residents kept my mind off recent events. Because of my supper responsibilities, Baldwin and I only had time for a quick exchange. He squeezed my hand, his eyes worried before he sat down to eat. I took as long as I could washing dishes. Once my job was over, the hours until bedtime stretched in front of me like a hollow, endless tunnel.

After trying to practice Dragon's Breath in the backyard, I headed to my room. It was quiet, too quiet. I gave up and walked to a secluded stand of sweet nessian trees. In the privacy of the small glade, I freed the tears pushing for release all day. After several minutes of crying, I developed a headache but still sat, wiping my eyes and letting the purple shadows settle around me.

"Devarus said to look for you here." Niklos appeared beside me, his dark shirt and pants blending in with the night.

Using the tissue clenched in my hand, I wiped my eyes.

"May I have a seat?"

I shrugged. There was no nice way to say *Go away*.

He lowered himself to the sandy ground and leaned against a thin tree trunk of his own. "It is a beautiful night."

So help me, if he wanted to talk about the weather, I was going to smack him. His words broke through my irritation.

"Abira and I are—were—friends for several times before I became an instructor. I will miss our talks. But don't mourn her absence. You will see her again."

His cliché made everything worse. My reply burst forth. "But it was my fault! She fell because I didn't make her come with me."

Niklos shook his head. "It is an instructor's job to put students first. She did that. And your griffin did an excellent job as well, but Abira's choice to delay was hers alone. We have Warriors searching. They'll find the person who set the fire."

"Rune." My recollection of his withered figure and eerie grin, the black cloak flapping around him, was seared into my memory.

"How do you know?"

"I saw him outside, right before I discovered the fire. Abira went downstairs to fight him during the fire. She said he left, but the guild hall was beyond saving. But—" I stumbled to a stop. "He looked different. He's almost like a skeleton, bony, with this weird glowy-heart thing." I shuddered at the memory. "I don't get it, because he used to look normal."

Niklos turned his gaze to the landscape. "That was a theory Abira and I had discussed. Rune's the Skeleton King. He's employed illusions for a while to pass as human. But his experiments developing Shadow Power and the massive amounts he uses have eaten away at his humanity, and he no longer uses illusions. What you're seeing is his true self."

A group of people left Declan's inn, their voices carrying on the breeze before growing fainter.

The sandy valleys were gray smudges, the brilliant sun a distant memory. I fisted my hands in my lap. "I hate him. I hate him so much. I'll find him and make him pay for—"

"Brenna, revenge isn't the answer. Rune has committed so many atrocities, it would take him several lifetimes to make restitution for them all. Once he's captured, the authorities will deal with him."

Not if I got to him first.

Standing, Niklos brushed off his pants. "Don't forget our guild has a midnight curfew."

After several seconds, he walked away.

I still sat, allowing the shadows to gather, to cover me and make me numb. The darkness to my right moved, and I turned. Arvandus emerged from the shadows and settled next to me.

After several moments, he spoke, his voice heavy. "Raven, I apologize. Abira's death rests solely on my shoulders and—"

"No. Stop." I laid a hand on his neck. "Have you been avoiding me?"

His golden eyes never moved from the landscape. "I have spent my day in thought. I should have demanded Abira ride with the rest of you."

"I don't think she would've listened."

He said nothing, just stared into the darkness.

My griffin was wicked stubborn. I tried again. "Arvandus, you don't have to apologize. Without you, everyone in the guild hall would've died."

"Even one death is too many."

"Yeah, I know." I sighed, feeling the truth of his statement deep in my bones. "You did everything you could."

He finally looked at me, his eyes like lasers. "I feared you would blame me."

"No, buddy." I slipped my arms around his neck. "You're a hero."

His low voice was quiet. "I do not feel like one."

"My guess is most heroes don't." I scratched behind his ear. "Just don't—don't avoid me, okay? I need you."

He nodded and leaned into me.

We sat together for a while longer before I finally stood. "I should get back to the guild. Niklos will lock me out."

"Perhaps we could fly together tomorrow."

Up in the air, just the two of us, where I didn't have to think about loss or sadness or the future...it sounded like paradise. "I'd like that."

"Has anyone told you about the funeral?"

I jerked at the word, my hands shaking. "Funeral?"

"Yes, they recovered her body. She died of a broken neck. They are planning a funeral for the day after tomorrow."

Tears leaked out, a sob lurking in my throat. He walked me to the guild in the darkness, and I patted his shoulder before he walked away. Shadows swallowed him. The cool wind dried my cheeks, offering a few breaths free of the omnipresent smoke. I didn't go in right away, choosing to sit on the porch steps instead.

I dropped my head into my hands. Everything felt so wrong.

Someone stepped from the guild and onto the porch. I raised my head as Baldwin spoke. "I was just leaving to find you."

Sheesh, I was popular. Three visitors in one evening. "I'm not running for the razor blades or anything."

"Sorry?"

I slid over for Baldwin, and he settled next to me. "Niklos found me earlier. Then Arvandus. Now you. Everyone seems to think I need supervision."

"Are you okay?"

I released a laugh that sounded like a sob. "Probably not. Everything's messed up. Abira was supposed to be here. What do we do now? I'm confused and upset and sad and angry. I want everyone to go away, yet I want someone to hold me and make everything better." My voice thickened, tears welling.

"How about a hug?"

A tear slid onto my cheek. "You're going to get tired of me crying on your shoulder."

"Hardly. Come here."

I slipped into his arms, curling into them, making myself smaller. Warmth, safety, comfort—his arms made me feel strong, although I knew I was numb, fragile—a heartbeat away from breaking. After several moments, I murmured against his shoulder, "I just miss her."

"Yeah, I know. We will figure everything out. Did you know they are planning a funeral for the day after tomorrow?"

It was too soon. It still felt like she'd show up any minute, walk around the corner of the guild hall, and demand a practice session. "Yeah, Arvandus told me."

"Well, after that, we can decide what to do next. I believe Abira would want us to keep moving forward."

Moving forward? At this point, I didn't even know how to do that.

CHAPTER TWENTY-THREE

THE DAY OF ABIRA'S funeral dawned bright and clear, although the service was planned for twilight. I frowned at the sunny landscape. It was surreal—the sun rose and set and people lived their lives while my small part of the universe had imploded.

Life moved on.

Keeping busy helped me ignore the pain living in my chest. That afternoon, I practiced my fire skills. Because of a lack of focus, my results were unimpressive.

After supper, I made my way to the area behind the guild houses. The dark river providing water to the houses rushed nearby, its faint splashing a soothing backdrop of white noise. In front of a table holding a long wooden box, people filled rows of chairs set up like soldiers.

Guild students sat up front, and to my consternation, the Firebrand guild and close friends were in the front row. Shiraz had shown up minutes before the service began, hugged me hard, and then proceeded to cry quietly. His expression shattered, Dr. Jivin Winward, Abira's doctor friend from Syeira, arrived and sat between Shiraz and Declan.

A minute later, the religious leader began to speak. Tall and broad-shouldered, the leader's bass voice originated from a place deep inside, and his long white robe made me think of ghosts and spirits, rather than angels and heaven. As he began a long monologue about death being the beginning of a different journey, I focused on the sandy landscape behind him.

He didn't know Abira, not like I did. Abira would've thought he was as boring as toast.

When he was done, Niklos, Devarus, Hakan, and a guild instructor I didn't know walked to the front to move the box.

Declan stood, his shoulders drooping as he wiped his eyes. He turned to the gathering. "Thank you all for coming to honor Abira. I was blessed to have a sister like her. She'll be greatly missed." His voice broke on the last word. He lowered his head and followed the box and its carriers out of sight.

After the service, I stood, eager to be away from the cloud of grief hanging over the group. Baldwin walked with me back to the guild houses. I appreciated his quiet strength and the way he didn't feel the need to fill the silence with small talk.

When we reached the guild, he touched my arm. "Niklos wants to meet with the Firebrand students tomorrow after lunch. Probably has something to do with an instructor for the guild."

I closed my eyes for a long second. "Already? I can't. I just—"

He gripped my hands. "Relax. He wants to talk to the students before he plans anything."

"Right." I gritted my teeth. Everyone was in such a hurry to move ahead. Shouldn't there be a mourning period, a chance to adjust?

We parted in the hallway, and I walked up the stairs to my room. Etenia wasn't there, so I had some welcome privacy. I plopped on my bed, my gaze landing on the box Abira had risked her life for. It taunted me from its hidden position. What was so important that it was worth dying for? Nothing could replace her, especially not a useless box.

Refusing to open it wouldn't bring her back. The tight feeling in my chest strangled me, and I heaved in a great lungful of air. Through tears, I wrestled the box from under the table, running my hand over the stiff cardboard. I also grabbed the half-finished bottle of verum waiting in my bag and headed for the stand of sweet nessian trees.

Once I found a comfortable spot, I uncorked the glass bottle and took a swallow of alcohol, allowing it to burn all the way down. My heart pounded as I held the box. My stomach roiled, but I swallowed hard and pulled off the lid. A thick layer of tissue paper hid the contents, and I shoved it aside.

A folded pile of cloth shimmered in the fading light. I reached inside to pull it out. The thin, glossy material tumbled out, and I choked out a gasp. Dragonscale silk pants. Why would that matter more than anything else to her?

I let the pants fall into my lap. After another burning drink of verum, I moved the box off my lap, but something clunked inside. Another search revealed a square object the size of a card deck. Made of embossed metal, the case featured smooth rounded corners with one edge sporting five metal studs across. Each one was labelled—Note, Review, >>, <<, and Stop. Underneath the studs, the metal surface was clear and shiny with no embellishment.

I shook it but nothing rattled. The cool bulk of it weighed heavily in my grip, as if it anchored me to the ground. Without it, I'd float away, disappear into nothing. I leaned forward and rested my head on my knees.

Supplemental notation...

Abira's voice drifted on the breeze. I lifted my head. What?

Just a few notes this time.

Ridiculous optimism built in my chest as I frantically scanned my surroundings. A soft glow from the metal item in my hands caught my eye. Abira's image smiled from the smooth surface. Despair slammed into me, crushing the hope inside.

I fumbled with the square case, squinting to see what I was doing. After a few stabs, I found the metal studs were actually buttons. I hit the stop button, then hit the << and waited.

In seconds, Abira's face appeared, and she leaned forward. *Just a few notes this time. The new guild students, Devarus, Etenia, and Hakan are doing well. Brenna's a big help, instructing them in beginning skills. She'd be a great instructor. But saints and sinners, that girl is stubborn.* One side of her mouth kicked up in a rueful smile. *Kind of like me. It's a good thing, too. That persistence will serve her well as events become more dangerous. She's working on Dragon's Breath and Incendior. By the time I discover Rune's location, she'll be ready. Then we can bring him down. I know she doubts herself. Although the battle with Rune will be tough, she's enough.*

The image disappeared, the screen silent. I rewound it again. Tears dampened my cheeks as I watched her image, listened to her repeat the words. I reviewed her notes at the very beginning to see when this started.

A much-younger Abira gazed at the screen. *Jivin gave me this dhakira box to remember important events in my life. While I'll use it, I can't comply with his other request. Stop teaching? I don't think so. He said it like it was easy, like it was something I chose to do, not a calling that runs in my blood. For some reason, he thinks this will keep me safe, safe from Rune and those who follow him. But to ask me not to teach...it's what I'm supposed to do. And I could do it anywhere, even here, so we could be close. But his ultimatum was clear—him or teaching.*

A tear tracked down her cheek. *I'm going to stay with Declan for a while. I hope we'll be able to work through this. But right now, it just hurts.*

The screen went dark. I searched for more references to Rune, but there weren't any. I reviewed other entries, watching a few more recent ones. I couldn't give up this connection to Abira, her thoughts and memories so alive, although she was gone.

When I finally turned off the dhakira box, sunset was a distant memory. The Petrus Rings sparkled in the sky. The risen moon glowed pale yellow, illuminating the landscape.

Folding the pants, I placed them in the box, laying the device on top before replacing the cardboard lid.

The simple act cracked me open. Ugly sobs tore from my chest, wracking my body. I wrapped my arms around my knees and let it all out.

After a few minutes, I picked up the bottle of verum, but my nose wrinkled from the strong odor as I brought it to my lips. Was this what I wanted? Did I enjoy drinking? How much did I want, *need*, to function? The answers remained just below the thin surface of daily living.

I inspected the bottle as my thoughts spun. Was I enough without the verum? Abira's last note was embedded in my heart. *She's enough.* Even the Sahale believed it. My gift was enough.

Rolling the cool glass bottle over my hot cheeks, I stood. Could Abira hear me? I tilted my head back. A few rogue tears leaked into my hairline as I looked for the brightest star.

"I miss you, so much. I can't believe you're not here. You were supposed to be. You were supposed to be here so we could take Rune down together. Every time I thought about how this would end, I imagined you standing right next to me."

Heaving out a breath, I wiped my cheeks. "I don't know how to do this alone. Even though you said I'm enough. How do you know? Because I don't feel like it. I'm the one who gets distracted, remember?"

I swallowed hard, the ache in my chest growing. "I get what you said about the calling being in your blood...I feel it too. I was put here for this, to fight him, no matter what. Even if I fail. I promise you I'll do my best to defeat Rune, but I don't think I can be a great Firebrand. So I won't shoot for that. I'll just shoot for enough."

Tilting the bottle, I allowed the remaining alcohol to water the sandy ground. I corked the bottle, tucked it into the cardboard box with the Dragonscale silk pants and dhakira box, and headed back to the guild hall, feeling wrung out. Maybe this time by myself hadn't had all the formalities of the earlier service, but I think Abira would've liked it just as much.

The next day after lunch, I met with Niklos downstairs in the study. Hakan and Devarus were waiting when I arrived, and Etenia came in shortly after I sat down.

Once we were all seated, Niklos leaned forward, his dark-eyed gaze including each of us. "This is a difficult time for all of us. But we can't stop your training. Therefore, we've arranged for another instructor to teach you."

My nose twitching, I fought the sneer. I didn't want another instructor. Maybe I could go home and practice. But then how would I take the test for the last level? Who would give me the mark?

"The Builderbrands have already made plans to build a new guild. We'll house you here until it's ready. Any questions?"

Nobody spoke. Hakan and Devarus inspected the floor while Etenia twisted her hands in her lap. The idea of a new instructor didn't sit right with me, probably because I'd been so close to Abira. I was the least unbiased person in the room, so I kept my mouth shut.

He dismissed us, and I slipped from the study. After putting on the Dragonscale silk shirt, I practiced in the backyard—reviewing old skills, then newer ones. I forced a rolling line of flames, my Dragon's Breath steady and constant as the fire turned purple. Incendior was still a struggle. I'd been able to ignite my torso, but barely, and that was it.

Baldwin walked into the backyard, his sword strapped to his hip, followed by a cluster of students as my hands burst into flame. I immediately extinguished them, not wanting the distraction or the audience.

"Sorry, I didn't know you needed the space. I'll clear out."

"No, stay. We will just use this area over here." With a wink, he smiled and moved away.

I walked to the shaded porch. The students paired up, and Baldwin instructed them according to their skill level. After an adequate amount of practice, he moved among them, correcting stance or flaws in their movements. When he was done, he dismissed them, and I blinked, realizing I'd sat through his hour-long class.

The last student left, and he walked over. "Cannot keep your eyes off me, huh?"

I snorted. "Right. You're modest, too."

He gave me a quick kiss. "Absolutely."

"You know what I noticed?"

"My sculpted abs? My menacing gaze? My flawless execution with the blade?"

Sometimes this guy just killed me. "Uh, no, no, and yes."

The teasing grin slipped from his face. "What do you mean?"

"I mean, the Cherished Bequest is a real thing. You've improved quite a bit, Baldwin, and you were already wicked good to begin with."

He raised one eyebrow. "Everything feels the same. In fact, I feel normal."

"Well, the bequest is there, even if you can't feel it. But I don't think you need to return to thank Marella. Maybe you could send her a nice thank-you note and a bouquet of sea sponges."

He smirked and pulled me into his arms. "No, there is plenty here to keep me busy." His gaze heated and dropped to my mouth.

A low bark followed by a howl interrupted the moment. Luna waited at the edge of the building. I hurried over, Baldwin behind me. The fo-li planted her butt on the ground and continued to pant. "You have a message, Raven."

After fishing the message from her collar, I unfolded the note. The simple message was written in a hard hand, dark slashes of ink on white paper.

I have an innocent, Silver Lee. I believe you two are acquainted. Bring the Caelestis Key to Linneah, or I will kill her. For every week you refuse to follow my instructions, another young girl will die. ~Prince Rune, Ruler of Linneah, Matana Island, and the Kasek Territory

"Baldwin?" I couldn't breathe. As I handed him the note, the paper fluttered as if it had grown wings.

He scanned the message then looked up, his face pale but determined under his tan. "When are we leaving?"

Not when was *I* leaving, but when were *we* leaving. I fell in love with him a bit more with that one question. "As soon as possible."

"If he is asking you to come to Linneah, that is where he will make his stand. I will send a fo-li to the Linneans in Syeira."

"Send an invisible one. And send one to Ginselwyn, Hamlin Bay, and Lennor. Can we get one to Fallon?"

"I will find out." He turned to Luna. "Thanks, Luna. I will send the messages with other fo-lis so you can rest." They both turned toward Declan's Inn.

"Don't forget to tell Niklos," I called to Baldwin.

Raising a hand in reply, he hurried away with Luna trotting at his side.

My reminder was the wrong thing to do, as I found out fifteen minutes later.

I'd hurried inside to pack my bag while messaging Arvandus. *Hey, we have to leave. I just got a message from Rune. He's kidnapped Silver Lee and is threatening to kill her unless we give him the Caelestis Key. I want to get there as soon as possible.*

I will be ready when you are.

Thanks, big guy.

As I shoved the last item in my bag, a firm knock rattled my door. "Come in," I called.

Niklos walked in. Baldwin stood in the doorway, staring daggers at his instructor, a muscle twitching in his jaw.

The guild instructor crossed his arms. "I won't sanction this trip."

My mouth fell open. "Um, excuse me?"

"Neither of you is trained for warfare."

Reining in my temper, I held up a hand and ticked items off on my fingers. "First of all, we both fought Rune's forces in the battle against Linneah a year ago. That's warfare right there. Two, I'm one step away from being a Level Five Firebrand. Three, he's holding my best friend's little sister hostage. And last of all, in the past, he tried to kill me, my friends, and successfully killed my mentor. I'm. Taking. Him. Out."

Or I'd die trying.

His face settled into hard lines. "I told Abira I'd protect you."

"She's the first one who would've sent us to handle this."

"I forbid it!" His voice was cold steel.

My control broke. "Look, I'm not asking you, I'm telling you! I'm going to Linneah and taking that monster down!"

He held out a hand. "Give me the key."

My gut roiling, I looked him in the eye and fed him the biggest lie I'd ever told. "I have no idea where it is. Sorry."

He set his jaw and pointed a finger at me. "If you walk out that door, you won't be permitted back in."

Closing my bag, I grabbed my sword. "Good thing I'm not a Warrior then."

I shot an apologetic look at Baldwin, then brushed past Niklos and headed for the griffin house.

CHAPTER TWENTY-FOUR

ARVANDUS PACED IN FRONT of the griffin house, silver flickers flashing from his wingtips. A saddle was already on his back, and I waved my thanks to the caretaker standing in the doorway.

I attached my bag to his saddle. "How quickly can we get to Linneah?"

He knelt. "Even if we fly hard, we will arrive after dark."

"Let's do that." Nerves skittered under my skin. I wanted to be there now, although I had no idea what to do once we landed. I'd form a plan while we flew.

"Wait!" Running up, Baldwin skidded to a stop next to me. "We should fly together."

"What are you doing here?"

He frowned. "We are going to Linneah, right? Or did something else happen?"

"What about Niklos? He said—"

His voice was firm. "I am going with you. Period."

"But your training—"

A solid kiss stopped my objection. He pulled away, his green gaze steady. "I can replace Niklos. I cannot replace you."

My heart melted into a puddle.

Lev walked over, and Baldwin attached his bag to the saddle and mounted the griffin.

Despite my concern over Baldwin throwing away his opportunity for training, I spent the travel time mulling over the situation waiting for us in Linneah. What would happen once we arrived? Should I give the key to Rune? Because even if I did, Rune wouldn't release Silver. But if I kept the key, he'd kill her. The questions spun, making my head hurt. Finally, I stopped trying to puzzle it out. Maybe Baldwin had some ideas.

Our stopover was on Hamlin Bay's beach. I waited on the shore in a secluded cove with Arvandus and Lev while Baldwin headed into town to pick up supper. The minutes stretched long. I looked for shells and walked along the water's edge, trying and failing to breathe deeply. Stress knotted my shoulders.

Farther down the beach, a few people stood in the water or walked the edges of the waves. Thankfully, they never drew closer. I didn't want to talk to anyone or try to explain why I was hanging out on the beach with two griffins.

Lev left to hunt. When he returned with an unidentifiable carcass to share, I swallowed hard. Ick. I moved closer to the waves so the griffins could eat in peace. An hour later, as the sun set in the bay, Baldwin returned.

Hunger made me snappish. "What were you doing? Growing the food?"

He grimaced. "Few establishments were open, but I found a street vendor selling meat and cheese pockets. Rune's men are patrolling the streets. I wonder what they are looking for."

"The Lost Children?"

Baldwin tilted his head. "Maybe. Or perhaps more men for his Life Shade army?"

My stomach cramped, and what little appetite I had disappeared. This was really happening—war. What would Linneah be like afterward? Would it even exist? Or would it collapse after being severed by a madman?

Baldwin pointed to the untouched meat and cheese pocket on my lap. "You have to eat."

"I feel sick. We're rushing to a war in Linneah with no plan. What happens when we get there? We won't be able to just waltz in. The soldiers will stop us, arrest us, and throw us into the dungeon. Oh, that's right. They'll take the key first."

Baldwin chewed slowly, his meat pocket almost gone. "We should approach this like a military strategy. Make camp across the New River. Scout it out, see where their patrol is weak."

I sighed. "You won't be able to get close enough, not without being discovered."

"What about that thick stand of pines on the Wildamek side of the river? You can see the castle perfectly from there."

My stomach flipped. "Is there enough cover for us and the griffins?"

Baldwin bit his lip. "I think so. If not, another stand of pines is farther upriver. We could split up."

Divide our group when we were about to face the biggest enemy ever? Bad idea, but I'd keep it as a backup, a plan B. We consulted with Lev and Arvandus after they finished their meal.

My griffin licked his muzzle with a large pink tongue. "I know the area. It will be dark when we arrive. Perhaps a quick flyover to identify the number of guards is the best approach. Afterward, we will land close to the trees. But we should leave now."

In short order, we took to the air. As the sun disappeared below the horizon, the Petrus Rings glittered and the air cooled. I scanned the landscape below, desperate for any encouraging signs. A thrill shot through my heart—several troops moved west toward Linneah, although I couldn't see where they were from.

Arvandus, look below! Reinforcements! Ooh, are they from Fallon? I had learned our allied city had a large military force, complete with dragon riders.

That is Hamlin Bay's small army. Regarding Fallon, I fear the message will not reach them in time.

I fell silent. The assistance of the legendary army would've been a nice reassurance.

We skimmed the mountains as they shifted from purple to dark gray in the coming night. Before long, the first few stars were joined by their brothers, and Indermitt Lake glimmered below. The dense copse of pines was a fuzzy smudge of black.

We approached the castle. In the dark night, we were flying shadows. Two guards walked the lower perimeter of the castle. They'd be our most pressing concern. Four more guards had been stationed near the main entrance and along the balcony. It wasn't an enormous number, but we'd have to be careful and quiet.

Lev and Arvandus landed behind the trees. Baldwin and I dismounted, and the four of us slipped among the trees, a tight squeeze for the griffins. There wasn't enough room for all of us to stay clustered together, so the griffins each found a roomier place to settle.

I am right behind you, Raven. Alert me if needed.

Despite the hours sitting on his back, I was exhausted and strung out with a wonky mix of worry and fatigue. I leaned against one of the trunks. *Thanks, Arvandus. I just need to rest a bit.* The rushing of the New River filled my ears.

Baldwin peered through the thick branches before kneeling next to me, his breath brushing my cheeks as he spoke. "They have no idea we are here. If we stay quiet, all will be fine. You should try to sleep before morning."

"What about you?"

Baldwin gave a shrug barely visible in the dark. "I have skipped sleep before. I can keep watch while you rest."

"I'll try." The long hours before dawn stretched before me. Sleep wasn't a bad idea. As he stood to get a better view through the trees, I settled on my side, my bag under my head.

But sleep didn't come. Instead, my gaze was drawn to the lit areas of the castle, visible between tree trunks. A guard regularly came into view during his patrol, each sighting cinching the anxiety around my stomach tighter. Was he looking this way? Could he see us? Hear us?

I don't know how long I lay there, apprehension filling me. It was late, and I was so weary. My vision grew fuzzy. *I should close my eyes, think happy thoughts.*

From another stand of trees across the river, a soldier led a line of individuals. As they moved into the light near the castle, I gasped.

All the people who meant the most to me—Mom, Dad, Grandma Helen, Grandpa Takacs, Baldwin, Tiny, Anna—shuffled toward the castle, heads bowed, their wrists bound and bloodied. Rune followed, his black cloak flapping open to expose the skin and bones body beneath. A crown on his head, he held a sword dripping crimson as he shadowed the line of prisoners.

From my vantage point, his voice seemed to come from every corner. "You will watch me kill them one by one, Brenna James. Until it will be only you. And you will be mine." His low laugh echoed, filling the air until I couldn't breathe.

I blinked. My vision cleared, my breath wheezing in short bursts. The line of people was gone. As before, only two lone guards patrolled the area. What had I seen? A vision? A dream? Clammy sweat dripped down my neck, and I shivered. Wrapping my cloak around myself, I stood and scanned the area for Baldwin. After slipping around another tree, I found him, still watching the castle. Relieved, I dragged in a shaky breath.

I slid to the ground. Just being near him convinced me that everyone was okay. Shakes wracked my body, and I squeezed my eyes shut. How could I shut off the images I'd seen?

"Brenna?" Baldwin knelt next to me, his fingers finding mine in the dark.

"Sorry. I—I couldn't fall asleep." Despite his firm grip, my hand shook in his.

He brushed my hair back from my cheek. "You are shaking. Did you have a bad dream?"

It didn't feel like one. "No. Maybe. I don't know. Minutes ago, I saw Rune taking prisoners I knew to the castle. When I blinked, they disappeared." Rune's words still echoed, his threat sitting cold and heavy in my memory.

Baldwin's thumb caressed my knuckles. "Once we resolve this thing with Rune, the nightmares and visions will go away."

But dread still held my heart in an iron grip. After a few minutes, I glanced up at him. "Baldwin, what happens if everything goes wrong? What if Rune somehow gets the staff and then cuts the territory apart?"

He sat next to me. "That will not happen."

The darkness allowed me to voice every terrifying doubt I'd carried for the past few days. "But what if you die? What if I die?"

He stilled, then shot another glance at the castle. "I do not allow myself to think like that."

"But it might happen."

He sighed. "Yes, the world, our lives, might end tomorrow. Anything is possible. But I prefer to assume we will defeat him." He leaned closer, his finger tipping up my chin. "After all, I have an excellent reason to remain alive."

My free hand stopped worrying the edge of my cloak. "Yeah? Me too." But my vision from Rune had cemented a rising fear—in order to win, I'd have to give up something. Or someone.

Baldwin cupped my cheek and kissed my forehead. "It is still late. You should try to sleep."

The thought of another vision nearly paralyzed me. I couldn't do that again. "Baldwin? Could you—I mean, if you don't mind, maybe you would, um—?" I cleared my throat. "Could you just hold me until I fall asleep?"

He nodded, and I released the breath I was holding. When he settled next to me and drew me into his arms, I let the vision and dark threat slip away. In his embrace, I could almost pretend the coming war, the key, and everything else was a bad dream too—almost.

It felt like Baldwin woke me from my dreamless sleep minutes later, his low voice in my ear. "Brenna? Wake up."

I drew away, stiff from sleeping in one position. The promise of dawn lay at the horizon in shades of beige and gray.

Standing, I stretched out my stiffness while Baldwin checked the guards' positions. We reunited with our griffins behind the trees, our voices low.

Baldwin frowned as he handed out packets of dried meat and nuts. The breakfast of champions it wasn't. His worried eyes met mine. "The guards are gone."

"What?"

"Nobody is on guard."

The handful of nuts I'd tossed in my mouth seconds earlier nearly choked me. "He knows we're here."

If anything, Baldwin's expression darkened further.

Gloomy clouds hung low, their gray undersides scraping tree-tops. A cool wind smelling of the ocean mingled with the scent of pine.

I patted Arvandus's furry neck. "What do we do now?"

"Find Rune. He is almost certainly in the castle, waiting."

Everything in me resisted seeing Rune face-to-face. "If we could find Silver, we could rescue her first. Then we wouldn't have to worry about him bringing about the apocalypse."

Lev ruffled his feathers. "He would only find another innocent. He must be dealt with."

Baldwin put his hand on his sword's hilt. "I am ready."

Rune's words flashed through my mind, filling my chest with ice. *You will watch me kill them one by one...* "Um, I'm going by myself."

Baldwin's eyes grew flinty. "Absolutely not."

Of course. I loved arguments first thing in the morning. I steeled my resolve. "It makes more sense. If we both get captured, we're done. But if only I get captured, you're still here to get help."

"No. I am not arguing about this." His face set, he turned his back to me.

I rubbed my forehead. With his stubborn jaw and crossed arms, he looked like a two-year-old a few seconds away from a full-blown tantrum. I touched his shoulder. "It's the wisest choice."

He turned, his face flushed. "I told you to never ask this of me again. How can I protect you if we are apart?"

"I don't need protection."

His eyes were fierce, the unyielding glare of a Warrior. "He will not be alone. I can engage his men. We are talking about Rune, not your average enemy." He swallowed hard. "Please. I cannot stay behind. The thought of you facing him, alone..."

I wasn't thrilled with the idea either. A small part of me, the cowardly part, wanted company. "All right. But don't die. Or I'll kill you."

Baldwin raised an eyebrow. "O-kay."

Guilt flooded me. I hoped I hadn't just signed his death certificate. "I need to change before we leave."

Grabbing my bag, I returned to our sleeping area in the pines and pulled out the silver Dragonscale shirt and pants. The glossy material slipped through my fingers, shining even in the gloomy light. As I changed, the silk slid against my skin, soft as the lightest touch. After tucking the pants into my boots, I grabbed a piece of fypex gum and shoved my old outfit back into my bag.

My hand brushed the key, and I pulled it out. Even in the overcast light, it glittered like the supernatural treasure it was. I clenched my fingers around it before dropping it into my pocket.

CHAPTER TWENTY-FIVE

I CLIMBED ONTO ARVANDUS, and our griffins launched into the sky. Once in the air, we could see troops fighting, Rune's men pushing our allies into a retreat. My worry grew, despite seeing armies from other regions approaching from around Linneah. More blue-uniformed soldiers from Wildamek joined troops in red and black from Lennor and Hamlin Bay.

In the sky, dark specks flew in from the north. They grew larger with every passing second, and my heart lifted as I recognized them. *Griffins, Arvandus! Linneans!*

The griffins flew past, several carrying two or three soldiers each. Behind them trailed massive birds, embers flying from stunning red, orange, and yellow feathers, each carrying another solider.

I closed my gaping mouth. *What are they?*

It is a blaze of phoenixes, Raven. It is good they have come to help.

Of course it was phoenixes. Yet another mythical being that actually existed here. But even with phoenixes, it looked like Rune's forces had us outnumbered.

Near the portal, Arvandus and Lev touched down, and I dismounted, trying to ignore the shivers creeping up my neck. The portal fountain wasn't running, its stones bone dry.

Baldwin's indrawn breath was harsh in the silence. His eyes narrowed at something behind me. At the snap of a twig, I spun to find my worst blast-from-the-past nightmare. Four towering praying mantises advanced, obviously the beefier, angrier cousins of the Largamants killed months ago when I first came through the portal.

Each one was six to seven feet tall, their kelly-green bodies covered with modified black armor. Foot-long spines on their forearms peeked from behind black metal bracers, while rugged tubes protected their upper legs. A shield, embossed with the serpent that was Rune's calling card, covered their vulnerable abdomens.

I pulled my sword, mentally doing the math. One for each of us—good odds, although terror iced my blood. Arvandus engaged one of the bugs while another Largamant crawled toward me with its wings flaring and its mandibles clicking.

"No, you've got a different Brenna this time, pal." I feinted right, then took a swing at its left side, which he blocked with a forearm.

Moving back, I gritted my teeth. I could do this. I knew my way around a sword now and was more experienced. Just step forward and—

A metal-covered forearm slammed into my stomach. My breath whooshed from my body, pain doubling me over. Arvandus roared, hundreds of silver sparkles erupting from his wingtips as he swiped at the mantis.

Everything hurt—standing, breathing, thinking. I forced myself up, noting Baldwin and Lev had dispatched a Largamant already. Sheathing my sword, I cradled my stomach as I moved toward the other bug. Arvandus advanced from the other side, growling and still shooting dozens of flashes from his metallic wingtips. I opened my palms and created a fireball, a fiery orb of orange flames.

When the Largamant tilted his head, I released it. In seconds, the bug toppled, its face burning. Arvandus attacked its unprotected back, tearing its wings from its body.

Baldwin and Lev leaped at the last Largamant. The mantis stretched a forearm to knock Baldwin aside, but Lev struck, raking his talons across its face. As the bug twisted its wounded head aside, Baldwin brought down his sword across the unsuspecting Largamant's neck, severing its head from its body.

In seconds, all was quiet, and I hissed out a shaky breath. The Largamants lay dead, all of them oozing a green, viscous liquid. Aside from the headless one, two were in pieces, courtesy of the griffins, and the other was burned and mangled. Baldwin wiped off his sword, and I gingerly rubbed my aching stomach. If those bugs were our first deterrent, I hated to imagine what was inside the castle.

I approached the griffins. "Can you check the perimeter for any other enemies? I don't need any more surprises like that."

Arvandus nodded. *May Elyon be with you, Raven.*

The two griffins took to the air as my shoulders tightened. It would've been nice having Arvandus next to me, but at least I wouldn't worry Rune would kill him to hurt me.

We hurried toward the castle. As we reached the stairs, my pendant froze, a span of cold spreading across my collarbone. The double doors swung open. Rune stood in the opening, an amused smirk twisting his face. A gold crown sat on his head. His black cape hung from his emaciated shoulders, a snake medallion holding the material together at his neck.

He stepped forward, his presence a punch to my gut. Nausea surged, and my limbs twitched. A massive creature with oversized horns and the face of a wolf trailed him, its clawed hands balled into fists.

Raising his hands, Rune clapped slowly. "Bravo, Brenna James and Baldwin Marek. Really quite extraordinary entertainment from you. I'll have to reconsider my original plan of killing you and instead keep you on hand for amusement."

When we said nothing, his grin grew.

"Why so quiet? I assumed you would have amazing things to share with me. Perhaps like the illusion I revealed to you last night?"

"Shut up." The words exploded from my mouth unchecked.

With a flick of his wrist, he discharged a fireball that detonated at my feet. My toes curled at the heat leaking through my boot soles. His eyes were black pools of hate. "As your king, I deserve your respect."

I clenched my teeth. *Learn to be disappointed, scum.* "You sent me a fo-li. I'm here. Where is she?"

He took another step closer. "In the castle, protected. Do you have the key?"

Its comforting weight rested low against my hip. "Maybe. What do I get if I give it to you?"

His eyes widened. "You get to live. Hand it over."

"Why? It's just a key."

His eyes glittered with a terrifying, gleeful madness. "That key will allow me to fulfill my father's dying wish for a great kingdom. Perhaps you'd care to join me?"

Baldwin stiffened next to me. My brain stuttered. "What?"

"I've watched your immense power increase. As my queen, your rise to power would be complete. And with our two Firebrand talents twined as one? We would be unstoppable."

His queen? I suppressed a shudder and swallowed hard against the bile in my throat. "Yeah, not happening."

"Such a waste of power." He sighed. "No matter. I have a plan for your city."

Dread coated my stomach.

Baldwin spoke. "Whatever it is, it is unnecessary."

Rune ignored him. "That key will lead us to the Caelestis Staff. We will find it, then Silver will cut Linneah away from its earthly portal forever. After its slow, painful disintegration, we'll marry and I'll rule the Jasper and Kasek Territory as it was meant to be. Now hand over the key."

He was going to marry Silver? My stomach heaved. She was only eight. "For something this valuable, I want more. Trade me Silver for the key."

Rune's eyes never left my face as he descended the stairs. The scent of Shadow Power filled the air. "Please. That's insulting. Silver's my precious future bride, too valuable. If anything, you owe me."

Baldwin snorted. "For what?"

He ticked the items off on his skeletal fingers. "You burned my crops at Undertown Valley, freed my slaves, and killed two of my guards."

A smug seed of satisfaction warmed me. "I didn't kill your guards."

"You encouraged the Florabrand to kill my guards."

"Your reports are skewed. That's not what happ—"

"Quiet!" He pointed a bony finger at me. "Give me the Caelestis Key, and I'll release you from your debt."

I narrowed my eyes. "What's my alternative?"

In the blink of an eye, he was next to us, one hand clutching Baldwin's throat and the other seizing mine. Baldwin's face paled as Rune's thin fingers dug deep. "I'll kill everyone you love, Firebrand. You, I will keep for amusement."

I couldn't swallow against his iron grip and could only manage shallow breaths. "You won't get the key then."

"Apparently, you need more motivation." He squeezed harder, then pushed me away but held on to Baldwin. He opened his other hand, a fireball growing in his palm. "Give me the key, or I'll kill him."

My heart stopped. Here it was, my nightmare come to life. And I was out of time. Rune was done talking and wanted action.

As I hesitated, Baldwin laser focused on me. "Do not do it, Brenna."

Rune shot Baldwin a disgusted look and squeezed tighter, making him choke. "I'll cut out your tongue. You talk too much." His fireball morphed into a dagger.

"No!" My heart slammed in my chest. I held up my hands, willing to beg and grovel. "I'll give you the key. But if you hurt him, I'll bury that key so deep you'll never find it."

Rune sneered, and the dagger morphed into a fireball. He shoved Baldwin away, who collapsed, gagging and coughing. With a flick of his wrist, he tossed the fireball to the ground. It spun around us and became a fence of dancing flames. "First, allow me to retrieve my exquisite fiancée."

Leaving us, Rune spoke to the creature waiting at the castle's double doors.

Baldwin shoved to his feet, coughing. He visibly swallowed, fingerprint-sized marks on his throat red warning flags. Coughing again, he rasped, "Of course. Trapped."

The horned wolf disappeared inside. Rune watched him go before turning back to watch us, his black cape whirling around him like a shadow.

How could I work this situation so nobody died? Save Silver. Save Baldwin. Save Linneah. Kill the bad guys. The puzzle made my head hurt.

Arvandus broke through my grim thoughts. *Raven? There are no other enemies or traps laid for you. We are returning.*

No! Please don't. Rune will kill you, and I couldn't bear it. Just stay close, okay?

Brenna, it would be an honor to help you bring down this monster.

I almost smiled. My griffin was the bravest animal I knew. *You'll get your chance. Just be patient.* I didn't say more, but he needed to wait until I came up with a clever solution, a cunning scheme...something. Anything.

My shoulders curled forward, and I dropped my chin to my chest. After solving one problem after another, I'd failed. I had no behind-the-scenes strategy, no grand final plan, no unique outside-the-box tactic to defeat the biggest threat of all.

Rune drew closer, inspecting me like a bug under glass. "You're carrying the key, aren't you?" He laughed.

My stomach tightened. Why had I thought it was a good idea to keep the key on me?

He snapped his fingers, the fire guttering out. He grabbed my forearm. As Baldwin drew his sword, Rune created a flaming dagger and pointed it at my chest. The scent of rotting spices curled around me. "Stop right there, boy. Not another move, or I'll carve her open in front of you."

I closed my eyes briefly. The nightmare from last night had been an omen, only the sacrifice was me. Although I didn't have a problem with paradise, I wasn't leaving this world with Rune still alive. If I was going down, he was too. I fisted my palms, ready to release an inferno.

The castle doors swung open. The horned wolf creature led Silver forward, its clawed hands tight around her small arms. I pushed down the power gathering inside. If I attacked now, Rune would hurt Silver.

Keeping me in his grip, Rune gestured at Silver with the flaming knife. "There's your evidence she's been well cared for."

Silver's straight-blonde hair was in disarray, violet smudges under her eyes. "Brenna?"

"Hey, Silver. You doing all right?" I gave her an encouraging smile as if we weren't all being held hostage by a madman.

"I'm fine." Her blue eyes moist, she blinked a few times, her jaw jutting out. Her delicate appearance, white-blonde hair, and bright-blue eyes hid an inner strength. She'd need every ounce of it.

Baldwin was a statue, his sword drawn, his knuckles white.

Rune's fingers tightened. "I've reached the end of my patience. You will kneel before me."

He viciously twisted my arm. Pain knifed through my elbow and shoulder. Gasping, I dropped to my knees.

"And the last act you will do is hand me the Caelestis Key."

All I had to do was reach into my pocket and give it to him. But I couldn't. Knees aching, I studied the grass, each blade a precise point of green.

Time stretched. One breath, two breaths…I risked a glance at the monster. Rune's face twisting, he backhanded me, and I fell. Before I could recover, he'd pinned one of my arms to the ground with his knee. I struggled, my free arm swinging as I slugged his jaw. He trapped my other arm in his icy fist.

My cheek throbbed like a heartbeat. The deafening crackle of the fire dagger was a terror-filled soundtrack.

Before I could escape, agony blanked my mind, and I screamed as he swiped the blazing dagger up my forearm.

Rune laughed and leaned closer, his breath a sour blast against my cheek. "It will be a pleasure to hear you beg while I slowly kill you. But the key comes first."

Collapsing the dagger, he plunged his hand into my pocket and ripped out the key.

He sat back on his haunches, and his eyes widened, an unholy glee filling them.

Sobbing and with my arm dripping blood, I released a fireball. He stumbled up, finally tearing his gaze from the key. I scrambled to my feet and fired another fireball at his hands, but he blocked it.

Rune clenched a fist, his voice full of deadly promise. "Do that again, Firebrand, and I'll slit the innocent's throat."

White faced and visibly shaking, Baldwin pulled me to his side and muttered in my ear. "I am so sorry. I should have—"

"He would've killed you. You did the right thing."

We all had. But Rune had still won.

While Rune focused on the key, I tried to mend the vicious slice to my arm. The burn went deep, the stinging ache nestled in folds of muscle. While I healed some of the blisters, the Shadow Power blade had done damage only time could repair.

"Finally." Rune's voice filled with wonder. "Finally, I'll rule the territories as they were meant to be governed. But first, I'll punish this rat's nest of a city."

He walked over to Silver. "Hold this, my dear. This will be your scepter when you rule beside me."

Silver shuddered, her blue eyes flat. "No, thank you."

"Hold it! Now!"

She gasped as he jerked her forward and thrust the key into her hand, crushing her fingers over it so she couldn't escape.

Immediately, the metal thickened and lengthened into a four-foot staff. From the top of the pole, a metal crescent moon gleamed and metallic wings glittered, their edges razor sharp. At the bottom, the hook became more prominent.

Everyone's eyes fastened on the Caelestis Staff that hadn't been seen for over a hundred times.

Rune's grin almost split his face. "Walk to the center of the portal and plunge the staff's head into the ground. You'll see the beginning of the end of Linneah."

When she shook her head, he grabbed her and created the fire dagger again. He held it to her neck, the blade sizzling. The little girl whimpered.

"To the portal. Now."

He shoved her forward. Silver scuffled toward the fountain, tears tracking down her cheeks.

As she reached the center of the portal, she grabbed the staff with both hands, spun, and heaved it toward Baldwin. The staff spiraled from her hands, and she took off running. Baldwin grabbed for it but missed as the glittering staff sailed overhead. Continuing to twirl, the staff slashed several holes in the air, revealing a purplish-blue, spangled void beyond.

After a couple more spins, the staff shrank into a key midair and dropped without a sound into the high grass.

Chapter Twenty-Six

"No!" With a snarl, Rune swung toward the guard. "Get the girl, now!"

Baldwin sprang into action, his sword swinging. As he engaged the guard, I turned to Rune and released a wall of fire.

He took a step back and threw something toward me. I flung up an arm. The flamer beam seared my wrist, and I yelped.

The clash of steel and mini explosions filled the air as Rune and I exchanged fireballs. In a swift move, Baldwin plunged his sword through the guard's midsection. As the guard crumpled, he yanked out his sword and ran after Silver.

My heart dropped to my stomach as Rune focused on Baldwin. With a sick grin, he threw a fireball. It landed in front of Baldwin, its deadly flames igniting his clothes. As he dropped to the ground and rolled to put out the flames, Rune flicked a finger and the flames morphed into a cage. Standing, Baldwin turned, his chest heaving. A muscle ticked in his jaw as he eyed the bars surrounding him.

Arvandus, Silver escaped. Can you find her?

Raven, are you sure?

Silver knows you. You need to take her to safety.

I felt his sigh. *Very well. Be careful with Rune.*

Rune and I circled each other. He pulled a pill from his inner pocket and popped it into his mouth. He grinned, and my skin crawled. "I saved a small amount of Shadow Power for myself. Your destruction of my crop was merely an unfortunate incident. After I kill you, I'll be the last powerful Firebrand. I'll reclaim my slaves and build a bigger estate."

"With what?"

His sneer grew. "I can plant more, repeat my steps for success."

I released a fireball in response and flicked a glance to my left. Baldwin stood in his fire cage, his face a study in horror as he watched Rune and me circle each other. My chest went hollow, but I turned away. I could only handle one problem right now, and it stood in front of me.

I created another shield of flames.

Rune's voice rose over the crackle of the fire. "Is that the only skill you know? How regrettable your instructor didn't live long enough to train you better."

I gritted my teeth so hard my jaw ached, his words like arrows impaling my heart. The words of the Firebrand Creed filled my head, and I pulled power into my free hand.

Rune extended his withered arms, and a rolling line of flames crawled toward me.

My breath lodged in my throat, and I lowered the shield to protect myself. The heat from his fire seared my face. Above the shield, the blaze danced, turning black. I grimaced. An appropriate color for Rune's Dragon's Breath.

I peeked around the shield. He advanced, drawing closer, flames climbing, heat building.

He laughed, and flames jumped higher. "Still hiding, Brenna the Firebrand? Still cowering? After all your training, the hero's still a coward."

Releasing the power in my hand, my Dragon's Breath met his with a fierce crackle. With a grunt, Rune jerked back. Frowning, he poured more energy into his flames. Heat intensified, my face baking from the temperature. I continued to feed my violet line of fire until my collected power was drained.

The odor of Shadow Power swirled around me. My head ached, and my nostrils stung. Although the flames slackened, I was afraid to drop my shield.

Rune continued to circle me while he released fireballs. "Give up. It's over. Or perhaps you'd prefer burning to death?"

A large group of men crested the hill, Rune's soldiers tangling with the troops of Linneah and Lennor.

He looked up, his black eyes sparkling from the deep holes of his skull. "It's a bad day to be Linnean. Their troops are inadequate against my men, and I've all but defeated their heroine." As he spoke, his hands began to glow. Flames exploded from the tips of his fingers and climbed his arms and torso.

Backing up, I allowed my shield to dissipate and began gathering power. *Elyon within, guides my soul...* Heat flooded my body. Warmth and energy licked through my veins. *Leads me on, makes me whole.* Fire erupted from my hands.

I gathered more heat, and fire raced up my arms, my chest. *Fire within, ignites my heart.* My face warmed, flames curling from my skin. *Lights my way, my counterpart.* With a deep breath, I smiled as fire engulfed my legs. I burned, a living inferno.

Rune snapped his mouth shut as his eyes filled with anger. "Nice try, Firebrand, but you are nothing. And you will always be nothing."

His words rattled inside, but I refused to let them settle. *I am enough.* As I moved forward, energy vibrated through me. I created a fireball and released it, which Rune deflected.

The fire around his body shot high like a flaming geyser, and he laughed. "I'll enjoy watching you burn like the Firebrand guild."

Anger flooded me, and my flames flickered. I couldn't let his mocking get to me. Clearing my mind, I reached for the always-slippery focus.

While I struggled to limit my release of power, to hold some back, Rune let loose. Devastating flames of black and red exploded from his hands. His expression froze into a crazed mask. A few of his shots went off target, but several more found me. The powerful strikes slammed through my Dragonscale shirt.

He blocked my shots with a created shield. It flickered, then in rapid succession mutated into a wall, a cage, a fence before he screeched and let it disappear.

He circled me again. I moved past Baldwin's cage, and as I passed the strange cuts made by the staff, a powerful tug caused me to stumble, and I fell to my knees. Rune threw several fireballs in rapid succession. One landed with a punch to my arm, but I never felt its heat through the Dragonscale silk.

The rents in space exerted a strong sucking force, and I crawled away before standing so it wasn't behind me. This area around the portal was a war zone. Edges of the split made by the staff had ignited, fire burning midair. Areas of high grass had been incinerated to dust. Blazes pockmarked the ground around the portal. Smoke hung in the air, while ash and soot coated everything that wasn't burning.

Although I moved as far from the glittering holes as possible, Rune continued to track me. His fire trembled, pulling inward before flaring out like solar flares. He grimaced, his hands stuck into claws as the blaze gathered. Behind him, the cuts hanging midair pulsed, the strange space beautiful yet dangerous.

With another sudden surge, his fire exploded upward in a rush of heat and chaos. Even cloaked with Incendior, I flinched and shielded my face with my arms. Immediately, his flames returned and gathered around his shuddering body. Pacing, he got too close to the tear.

With a roar, he stumbled and fell. His fire disappeared into the void. He never paused, only pushed to his feet and advanced toward me, surrounded by his own Incendior.

My heart leaped. Could I do it? Could I maneuver him closer to the tear in space?

Squinting, I gathered more power. *Come on, Brenna—imagine a bow and arrow.* Our eyes met. His throbbing heart glowed through the ribcage's thin skin, and I released a flaming arrow. It plunged into his chest, forcing him back. Grinning, he yanked the arrow out.

I gasped. Couldn't he be killed? In desperation, I shot two more bolts, each one pushing him back farther but never fatal. The last arrow sank deep, forcing him to take another step back—into the sparkling vacuum waiting behind him. With a cry, his leg disappeared up to his knee. His smile vanished. He reached out, grabbing for an anchor.

He caught the edge of Baldwin's cage and latched on.

The cage of fire wasn't heavy. Instead of securing him, the cage slid closer to the tear. Baldwin's eyes met mine, a sad resignation resting in them.

Oxygen disappeared. My heart stopped beating. I needed a miracle.

Desperate, I created an arrow instead. With my eyes gritty and burning, I concentrated on my target and let the arrow fly. The arrow struck true, piercing Rune's wrist.

Screaming, he let go. Both of his legs disappeared into the tear. His bony hands caught the edges of space. The ragged borders held. Grappling for a better grip, he managed to get a foot back through the hole. His gaze found mine, and he shot a fireball at me. I refused to let go of the bow and arrow. The fireball hit my legs like a train, the force hammering me to my knees. Groaning, I pushed aside the pain and loosed one arrow, then another, aimed at his wrists.

I was not losing this fight. Rune would never harm anyone, not ever again.

As the arrows embedded in his bones, he gasped, a sonic boom of sound. His fingers slipped. Time slowed to seconds. One...two...I aimed for the area between his eyes and let another bolt fly.

The arrow struck. He jerked, and with a shriek, he vanished into the abyss.

I blinked, panting. Had he really been pulled into space? Or would he show up somewhere else?

Despite my questions, I pushed to my feet and limped to Baldwin. He stood tall, his face blank, although hope flickered in his eyes.

The cage shifted toward the cuts, the void pulsing.

My eyes widened. I glanced at Baldwin. He moved closer, ignoring the bars of flame. His gaze locked on mine. "I love you, Brenna. Never forget that."

But it didn't sound like a reminder. It sounded a lot like goodbye.

As if in response, the cage slipped closer.

Clenching my jaw, I lunged for the bars, fire meeting fire with a sizzle. But no pain. What?

My conversation with Abira echoed in my head.

"What's the purpose of Incendior?"

"Aside from a good demonstration of control? It's the only technique that can withstand Shadow Power."

Although I held tight to the bars, my feet slid. The force beyond the slashes tugged me closer to the glittering void.

Baldwin stood tall, his shoulders back. "I am not afraid to die, love."

I shook my head. Not listening. To defeat Rune and lose Baldwin—no. With a great heave, I pulled the cage away from the dangerous force. A few more tugs and the cage rested a safe distance away.

Setting my jaw, I grabbed the bar again with both hands and imagined Rune's neck. The bar snapped with a whoosh.

That's for Abira, scum.

With hope lightening my heart, I did it twice more, for all the other people he'd hurt and killed. The opening widened, and Baldwin escaped with a shaky sigh of relief and wobbly legs.

Arvandus? Rune's gone. He was sucked through the hole cut by the staff when Silver threw it.

Are you well?

Cheers from the hill behind me drew Baldwin's and my attention. Rune's soldiers fled. Sounds of victory faded as I struggled with my new problem.

My body still burned, a column of fire and blazing intensity. I gritted my teeth, trying to grasp the slippery control I'd dropped.

Um, I used Incendior. I'm still burning.

Raven?

Baldwin's expression shifted, his brows drawing together. "Brenna?"

Little by little, I tried to reel in the power and heat. I dispelled a few fireballs, but there was still too much. My body shook. I couldn't breathe, and my vision twisted like a funhouse mirror.

I was dying.

What had Abira said? *I can burn up from the inside out...*

Stumbling to the portal fountain, I waved my hand to turn it on. Nothing happened. Rune must've turned it off somehow.

Turning to Baldwin, I shook my head. *I'm so sorry.*

"No. No!" He reached for me but couldn't touch me. I backed away, flames leaping from my body like explosions.

I'm sorry, Arvandus. Fly true.

Raven!

So hot, I was out of control. My blood turned into rivers of fire, and heat built. I moaned as a swell of power surged up my torso, broiling my lungs, scorching my throat. Swallowing hard, I fisted my hands, but it didn't help. The next surge slammed my head back, and I opened my mouth to scream.

Instead, fire blazed from my mouth. Massive flames erupted from my hands. Tongues of fire burst from my body.

A red haze coated my vision as I detonated.

CHAPTER TWENTY-SEVEN

I SLITTED OPEN SANDY eyes. The dim room held a faint scent of lemon, cloves, and cinnamon—the cleaning agent the castle staff used. A warm glow emanated from the helli lantern in the corner. The familiar stone walls didn't quite look like the infirmary's. Maybe I was somewhere else in the castle.

I looked to my right, the sheets downy soft on my cheek.

Baldwin sat asleep in a chair next to my bed, his chin on his chest. His hair was tangled, and dark stubble covered his cheeks. My eyes watered. I took a deep breath, savoring the miracle of being alive. Had Baldwin stayed with me the whole time? How many hours had I been out? Did I still have my gift?

Pulling my hand from beneath the sheet, I brought up a tiny flame on my palm. A single tear slid into my hairline. It was still there. Another miracle.

"Brenna?"

I looked up, and the small flame flickering in my palm went out. Baldwin straightened, his eyes glittering with hope, love, and everything else I needed that I couldn't quite name.

"Hey, you." My voice cracked, as dry as old tissue paper.

His breath whooshed out, and he ran a hand over his face before leaning forward to grab my hand. "Love, I am so glad to see you awake."

I tried a smile. "It's good to *be* awake."

"I was afraid you were—well, Renke prepared us for the worst."

Something about the way he said it... "How long was I out?"

He swallowed hard and looked at the floor. "You were unresponsive for five days."

His words stole the breath I'd marveled over minutes earlier. "Five? What happened?"

"Y-you exploded. That is the only way to describe it. I have never seen anything so terrible. I thought—" He took a shaky breath. "I thought I had lost you. By the time Arvandus and Silver returned, your fire was gone, but you were unconscious and too hot to touch. Silver got the portal working again. I stayed with you as the portal took us to Cloverdale, and the water brought down your temperature. By the time we arrived back here, Arvandus had retrieved Renke to care for you."

He rubbed a calloused thumb over my hand, the simple touch causing butterflies to take wing in my stomach.

"What happened with the war?"

"After we recovered you, Rune's troops retreated and then surrendered with his death. The Fallon army eliminated the force on Matana Island."

I perked up. "Are they still there?"

"They left yesterday."

Darn. I'd missed seeing a dragon again. "Any news on Rune?"

"After Takacs inspected the slashes, Silver recovered the staff and helped him seal it up. He said anyone disappearing into the tear would be lost."

Nerves jittered under my skin. What if Rune had made it? It seemed impossible for him to be dead. "But Grandpa Takacs can cut space and appear somewhere else."

"Yeah, but he knows how to navigate it. If you need further evidence of Rune's passing, my Time Reeler talent returned. We believe it is somehow tied to his death."

I let out a slow breath and gave him a smile. "Congratulations. And I'm glad you found the staff, too. That thing's wicked dangerous."

"Right now, they are keeping it with the Sacred Veil while they decide what to do with it." After a moment of silence, he grinned and stroked my cheek. "I am hesitant to leave you, but I need to tell Renke you awakened."

He left and returned with the physician moments later, Mom leading the group.

She covered her mouth with her hand, her eyes welling. "Sweetie, you're awake." Leaning over, she gave me a hug, her scent of lily of the valley and vanilla enveloping me. "How do you feel?"

"Kind of tired."

She moved out of the way as Renke proceeded to look into my eyes, ears, nose, throat, listen to my lungs, and just in general prod anything and everything.

When he proclaimed me fine, I shifted up in bed. "Can I come down for a meal?"

Mom looked at Renke, who shrugged. "If she is able."

"I'll take it slow, I promise."

Mom pursed her lips. "That's something you almost never do."

Baldwin spoke, my hand encased in his. "Do not worry, Queen Sarah. I will make sure she does."

"Thank you, Baldwin." She turned to me and gave my other hand a squeeze. "We will see you for supper then. Maybe I can have the cook make Kunkelsteuchen for you."

My mouth watered at the thought.

Baldwin helped me out of bed and continued to hold my hand as I made my way downstairs. Not that I really minded. Although part of me was glad to be up and out of bed, my muscles ached, and navigating the stairs was exhausting. After a quick supper, I went back to bed.

I woke late the next day but wrangled a brunch from the kitchen staff. Afterward, I sought out Arvandus, who met me at the castle steps instead of the griffin house.

"It is a mess, Raven." He growled, his nostrils flaring. "They used our quarters for livestock. Livestock! Barbarians."

"I'm sorry, Arvandus. Are they cleaning it up now?"

"Yes. It should not be long before it feels like home."

"I wanted to thank you. Baldwin said you and Silver saved me."

"You are welcome." He looked away, his gaze fastened on the silver sea shimmering in the distance. "Please take adequate time to recover. I will need to recover, as well, from the horror of that day."

At the thought of what I almost lost, I teared up. I slipped my arm around his neck. "I'm sorry. I didn't want it to end like that."

He pressed his head against mine for a minute before pulling away. "I will repeat myself, although I am not sure why—in the future, refrain from reckless behavior."

I grinned. "Rune's gone, so I think we're safe."

Arvandus didn't return my smile. "There will always be those who prefer the dark. It is our responsibility to shine the brightest light possible."

Hopefully, it'd be a while before I met those people.

After lunch, Niklos found me in the library. I put aside my book and met his serious gaze. We hadn't talked since I'd stormed out of the guild house.

"May I have a seat?" he asked.

I gestured for him to sit. Something deep inside urged me to offer an apology, but I wasn't sorry for what I'd done. Very few could've taken on Rune and lived. I almost hadn't. Did apologies count if you weren't sorry?

He took a deep breath. "I heard what happened between you and Rune. Congratulations."

"Thank you. I'm sorry for the way I left the guild." There. An honest apology.

He dropped his gaze. "I overstepped. What you said when you left was true. Abira never once doubted your ability to fight Rune. But my promise to keep you safe made me forget."

"All my training had been for that moment. Rune wouldn't wait for me to finish. And when I got the fo-li he'd taken Silver? That was it. I couldn't wait."

"I didn't see you two fight, although a Firebrand from Lennor did. He was in the battle near the portal. From his report, you're eligible to pass the fifth level. Do you want the last piece of the mark?"

"I don't have to take a test?"

Niklos shook his head. "The fifth test is dangerous. The only requirement is a display of control."

Yeah, I'd done great on that prerequisite. "I exploded."

"You didn't explode. You quenched your Incendior by releasing the power. That's part of the test. Also, while you fought Rune, you used Incendior and pyrocharisma simultaneously."

I squinted. "I almost died."

"That's why the fifth test is dangerous. The test usually occurs with a Waterbrand in attendance."

Sheesh. How did anyone ever become a level five? "Well then, yes, I'd love the last piece."

I bit my lip. Abira wouldn't be giving it to me. Niklos seemed to read my thoughts.

His tone was gentle. "Is there anyone you'd prefer to give you the mark?"

"I don't know any other Firebrands."

He stood. "A Firebrand does have to administer it. Rune did his best to kill many of them. If there's no one else, I know a Firebrand from Lennor named Fenix. I'll ask if he's available."

I nodded and studied the carpet. He wasn't Abira, but it was better than nothing.

CHAPTER TWENTY-EIGHT

NIKLOS'S MESSAGE ARRIVED SEVERAL hours later. The ceremony was scheduled to take place on the beach in two hours. Although I would've preferred the Linnean Gardens, Rune's soldiers had used it as Party Central. It was wrecked.

After notifying my family, Baldwin, and Arvandus, I changed into a white tank, added a tunic, and headed for the beach. With my lack of time management, it'd be better to be early just in case. The upcoming ceremony filled my thoughts until a familiar voice called my name from behind.

I turned with a smile.

Baldwin approached me. "Hey. You are supposed to be on the shoreline. The ceremony is about to start."

Yep. Lousy time management.

"Allow me to escort you, Lady James," he said with mock formality.

Faking a curtsy, I took his arm. My thoughts pulled the grin from my face. "You know what? Although getting the tattoo hurts, I really wish Abira were here to give it to me."

He squeezed my hand. "I know.

I swallowed the lump in my throat and took the stone steps leading down to the beach. The mild breeze off the ocean whipped up only a few whitecaps today. On the sand, a couple of blankets had been laid out, and Niklos and another man waited at the front near a separate blanket.

My parents and grandparents were closest to the front. Baldwin's parents, Mariel and Keel, sat behind them. A few castle employees hung near the back. Reggie, the portal guard, gave me a friendly wave, which I returned.

With a massive flapping of wings, Arvandus touched down as we reached the beach.

I raised an eyebrow. *Cutting it kind of close, aren't you?*

As are you, Raven.

Sassy griffin.

Baldwin whispered in my ear. "Do you need me to hold your hand? I am completely available."

"No, I'm good." For some reason, this was something I wanted to bear by myself.

He gave my hand a final squeeze and sat on the blanket next to his parents.

Niklos gestured for me to approach, and as I did, he introduced the other man. "Brenna James, this is Fenix Vianey, a Firebrand instructor from Lennor."

"Hello, Lady James." Fenix wasn't as old as Abira, although ages were hard to guess in the Jasper Territory. A little gray mixed with his light-brown hair, and despite his stocky, muscled build, he had kind brown eyes. "Abira Edan was a great instructor and a fine individual. She'll be missed."

At his comment, my eyes stung, but I managed a nod.

He continued. "Where's your Firebrand mark?"

"My right shoulder." I stripped down to my tank top and lay on the blanket facedown.

While I got comfortable, he turned to the crowd. "Brenna James is here to take the fifth and final mark of the Firebrand. This is a highly coveted position attained through precise training of each skill. She completed her training with an admirable display during the recent Jasper Territory War."

I squirmed a little, uncomfortable with the praise.

He turned to me, his voice lower. "Would you like some secatic oil?"

"Yes, please." I didn't see a glass, so I hoped the topical application would be enough.

Turning my head to the side, I waited for the first prick and then closed my eyes. His touch wasn't much different from Abira's, but while he worked, a massive lump resided in my throat, hurting every time I swallowed.

From the moment I met Abira to Starfall, to each training session, to the last moment I saw her before she fell—the memories filled my head, my heart aching. I hoped somehow she knew I'd completed my training and was proud of me.

When Fenix was done, I sat up. "Before you put that away, could you give me another mark?"

He frowned. "That's highly unusual. What kind of mark?"

I cleared my throat. "I'd like to have Abira's initials. Just a small AE on the inside of my right wrist."

Fenix's face softened a bit. "We can do that."

He swabbed the area with secatic oil, and I closed my eyes. As the needle pierced my skin, a few rogue tears leaked from behind my closed lids. The physical pain was a distant ache while the absence of Abira overwhelmed everything. I swallowed hard and let the breeze dry my tears.

When he was done, he wiped it, as well as my shoulder, with more oil. Both stung, but it fit the bittersweet event.

As I stood, a round of applause filled the air. Everyone stood to leave. My parents came forward, and both Mom and Dad gave me careful hugs.

Mom cupped my face. "We're so proud of you, sweetie. We're having a celebratory meal in an hour. Are you coming up?"

"Not right away, but I won't miss the meal."

"I didn't think you would." She grinned and linked hands with Dad before turning to Fenix. "Lord Vianey, we'd love to have you join us for the meal."

"Oh, I don't want to impose."

Dad gave him an encouraging smile. "Please. It's the least we can do. The cooks made pupkissberry pie for dessert."

"Well, I suppose another delay won't hurt." He gathered his supplies and followed them toward the castle.

Each grandparent gave me a hug before walking back. Grandpa Takacs's hand rested in the small of Grandma's back. The small gesture gave me hope they'd make their relationship permanent again.

Even Arvandus gave me a feline nuzzle, his golden eyes gleaming with pride. *Well done, Raven.*

I scratched his ruff before he turned and padded down the beach.

Baldwin lingered before coming up to me. "Do you want to be alone?"

"Not really. But the castle will be all, you know, people-y."

"That is not a word."

I gave him a mock glare. "It is. My word. It means full of people. And the castle will be."

"True. Your family knows how to celebrate." He gestured toward the beach. "Do you want to walk?"

"Sure." We removed our boots and socks and walked along the surf as it surged and retreated, wetting our feet.

A few seconds later, his hand intertwined with mine, and I sighed. "I never thought this day would come."

"What day?" he asked.

"One where the horror of Rune wasn't waiting. I can actually breathe and relax."

He nodded. "It is a little strange, but in a good way. What happens next for you? Back to school?"

"Well, school starts soon, but I'm not going back. My parents agreed to let me complete schoolwork on my own to get my high school degree. Some of the work I can easily do from here, although the rest will have to be completed digitally. Grandma Helen has a computer, but since Dad quit his job at the college and is Mom's advisor, there's nothing in Cloverdale for me."

"Are you planning on living here then?"

"Oh yeah, no doubt about that." Rocks and massive boulders blocked our walk. Baldwin climbed onto the first few rocks, pulling me up beside him. The light breeze ruffled my hair, and I pulled it behind me. My shoulder stung a bit at the action.

The water glowed blue and green in the sun, waves foaming as they rolled in. Baldwin settled onto the rock, patted his pocket, shifted, picked up a few pebbles, tossed them at the surf, shifted again...

"What's wrong?" I sat next to him.

He blinked several times. "Why would something be wrong?"

"You're acting weird."

He took my hand. "You make me crazy."

"Yes, that's lovely. Thank you." I pulled my hand away and shot him a mock glare.

He grabbed my hand again and faced me more fully. "You do. Crazy in love with you. You, Brenna James, are my heart."

"Oh." It was barely a whisper. Baldwin turning poetic? My eyes welled as my heart fluttered in my chest.

He pulled an item from his pocket. "I wanted to wait for the perfect moment. Soft lighting, faint music..." He shrugged. "But perhaps that is right now. I cannot imagine my life without you. Would you be willing to be twined to me?"

My mouth dropped open, my fluttering heart stopping, as he held out a ring. Two silver bands were connected with an exquisite scrolled ivy pattern.

My fingers itched to take the ring, but I found my voice. "I'm still a teen."

Baldwin's loving smile faltered. "Is that a no?"

"No! Of course not. I love you. But I don't think I'm ready to get married now." The admission hurt and made me feel even younger. This is where Baldwin would give up and walk away, disgusted at this stupid child—

You are enough. The thought interrupted the vicious hater that sometimes filled my head.

"But are you ready to be engaged now?" His eyes glittered with hope. "I know we are both young, but Linnean engagements are usually long. My parents were engaged for five times."

"Five, wow. That's a long time." I tilted my head, getting lost in his earnest gaze.

Was it any wonder I'd fallen for him from our first meeting? Thoughtful, kind, understanding—and over time, he'd captured my heart. The thought of walking away was crippling. I wanted him by my side—for everything.

"I can do an engagement, but maybe not that long. Is the offer still open?"

He slipped the ring on my right ring finger. "For you? Always." His kiss was warm, his lips slightly salty from the ocean breeze. Pulling away, he smiled as if he had a secret. "I have had that ring for a while."

I studied it again. The ivy leaves sparkled in the sun. "It's gorgeous. Where'd you get it?"

"Niklos's brother is a metalsmith and is opening a smithy near the guilds. When he came to visit, I asked him to make a ring for me. The ivy leaves hold crystals from the medallion you gave me."

I jerked, studying the ring again. "Wait. The Stones of the Spring? Can you do that?"

"They cannot use them anymore. Niklos's brother felt this would be a better use than leaving them in the medallion."

I brushed a finger over the design, a tingle zipping through my veins. "It's beautiful."

He pulled me to his side, his lips brushing mine. "Not as beautiful as you."

CHAPTER TWENTY-NINE

(*THREE TIMES LATER*)

The gray stone of the new guild hall sparkled in the setting Linnean sun. I still couldn't believe it was mine, all three stories of it. The students would arrive in two weeks.

Arvandus ruffled his wings and settled next to me. "It is a beautiful building, Raven."

The balmy breeze caressed my cheeks. A warm front was moving in. "Thanks, Arvandus. Are you sure you won't mind having it close to your griffin house?"

"It is not *my* house. And I do not mind at all. It seems fitting to have Firebrands training close to the griffins."

"The Warrior guild isn't happy about it. They wanted to build first. And if the instructor had been able to get the money, they'd be your neighbors instead."

Amazingly, I hadn't blown my Starfall money. It seemed perfect to spend it on this, a new guild for Firebrands. Abira's comment so many times ago had stuck with me. After tutoring a few kids, I found it was a good fit.

Arvandus sniffed, bringing me back to the present. "They are bullies and will have to build elsewhere."

I crossed my arms. "Easy. My soon-to-be husband is from that guild."

Although Baldwin's Time Reeler talent had returned upon Rune's death, he'd bested the Warrior guild's top blade instructor. Thanks to the mermaid Marella's Cherished Bequest several times ago, he was now the Warrior guild's top trainer.

Hands grabbed me from behind, and I squeaked in surprise.

"Evening, love." Baldwin kissed my cheek and nuzzled his face into my neck, making me hunch my shoulders.

"I will see you later." Arvandus padded off to the griffin house.

"Is it bad luck here to see the bride on her wedding day?" I pulled away from Baldwin, goosebumps still on my skin from his tickling.

He raised an eyebrow. "No. Why? Is that a superstition on Earth?"

"In America, yeah."

"Superstition would not keep me from seeing you."

"You're sweet." And distracting. Although his comment made me realize I should probably be at the castle, I had no desire to leave.

His next comment confirmed my suspicions. "Your mother told me to find you and drag you back."

I wrinkled my nose and gave him a smart salute. "Yes, sir."

With a grin, he tugged me toward the castle. "I could get used to that."

"Yeah, don't."

He laughed and fell into step beside me.

"So now can you tell me where we're going on our honeymoon?" I'd bugged him for two weeks, but so far, he'd not said a word.

"Well, I could. But my track record with this secret has been amazing."

"Come on. Pleeease?"

Rolling his eyes, he relented. "Okay. I have planned a trip to the Fallon coast."

I squeaked. "To see the dragons? Really?"

At his nod, I threw my arms around him and gave him a tight squeeze. "You're so sweet—you remembered!"

He returned my hug before pulling away. "And I contacted a guy who raises and trains them. He agreed to meet with us."

I bit my lip, my heart pounding. "That is amazing. *You're* amazing. I can't wait to see them."

His warm smile was full of promise. "And I cannot wait to share them with you."

We reached the castle, and Baldwin followed me in.

Mom paced in the foyer, her cerulean-blue dress swishing against her legs. Silver and gold embroidery on the bodice glittered in the light. She saw me and pounced. "Thank Elyon you're here. Upstairs, right now. Baldwin, go get ready. You'll see her in a couple of hours." She shooed him away.

He winked and left.

My gown, gorgeous in its simplicity, waited on a hanger in Mom's room. I loved it with all my heart. Long layers of the palest blue chiffon with a deep V on each side were captured at my waist with a silver filigreed belt. Delicate crystals and silver chains draped across the back of the dress like a reverse necklace. An ivy design in silver made up the circlet for my hair and a silver band for my upper arm.

After I wrestled the dress on, Mom asked the servant Dabeer to do my hair.

After a half hour, Dabeer huffed out an exasperated breath. "My lady, please sit still. I am almost finished."

I shot Mom a pleading glance. She ignored me and called for a servant to check the setup in the Linnean Garden.

Grandma Helen came in, wearing a striking burgundy gown stitched with silver flourishes. "Ah, my beautiful granddaughter. Today's a big day."

I grinned and tried to not move.

Finally, Dabeer stepped back. "Is that acceptable?"

Mom and Grandma wiped away tears while I inspected her work in the mirror. I would've been happy with a simple braid, but Dabeer had worked a miracle with a style that swept the hair off my neck in an elegant, braided updo.

"It's fantastic. Thank you."

After she left, Mom embraced me. "You look so beautiful. And happy."

Grandma patted my cheeks and wiped away her tears.

I eyed the two of them. "Why are you both crying?"

"Because you're growing up," Mom said with a watery smile.

I rolled my eyes but pulled them close for a group hug as someone tapped on the door.

Dad poked his head in. "Wow—three of the most beautiful women in the Jasper Territory. Here's the bouquet for the stunning bride. It's time to go. The quartet has started playing."

I smoothed a hand over the yards of chiffon and readjusted my belt. The group of musicians tucked into a corner of the Linnean Gardens started the last song. Where was Arvandus?

I leaned against a stone pillar to wait, my thoughts even more of a chaotic mess than usual.

Mom and Dad strolled up next to me.

"You're beautiful, sweetie." Giving me a misty smile, Mom adjusted the tiara on my head.

Dad pulled me close to his side. "Baldwin's a lucky man."

I kissed his cheek rather than voice my thoughts. I felt like the lucky one. Despite my ADHD tendencies to zone out, mismanage time, and forget things, Baldwin remained understanding and supportive. Although it seemed impossible, I loved him more than I had three times ago. Would it always be like this? Love growing and my heart expanding?

Peeking through the ivy curtain, I could make out the rest of my family and friends waiting for the ceremony to start. The rows of chairs were arranged into an enormous square, divided into four sections. Two intersecting aisles met at a large cleared platform in the middle.

My grandparents had claimed front-row seats with places next to them reserved for both sets of parents. Behind them sat Phoenix and Storm Lee and Anna and Erhardt, both couples who were now married or twined depending on the word one used.

Tiny settled next to Liam, her fiancé, their hands firmly joined. They planned to be married next month. That relationship was a surprise—but if anyone deserved it, it was Tiny. Kersen was cuddled next to his newest girlfriend, a pretty blonde I didn't know very well.

And true to my promise three times ago, Shiraz perched at the end of the aisle, laughing and talking with Gareth. His wife and two little boys sat next to him. The crowd was way bigger than I'd planned, but Mom and Dad's ties with everyone compelled them to invite them all.

Arvandus prowled up to me, his approach silent.

I turned to him, nerves skittering under my skin. "Where have you been? I didn't want to walk the aisle without you, but it's almost time."

"You worry too much, Raven. This day is a time for happiness."

"If you were on time, I would be happy."

He flicked his tail and sat, ignoring my comment.

The song ended, and I blew out a breath, suddenly nervous. Arvandus stood, ready to walk down the aisle on my left as my parents flanked my right. Baldwin waited on the other side of the gathering with his parents and Lev. We would walk toward each other, our parents moving to their seats and the griffins veering to the left as we met at the platform in the center.

This was really happening—marriage to my best friend, the love of my life. I tugged at my neckline, a little self-conscious about the deep V, even though I was completely covered.

The first, clear notes of a woodwind instrument hung in the air before the strings joined in. My entourage and I stepped out from my hiding place and began walking toward Baldwin and Lev.

Our eyes met, and his widened before he gave me the look that melted my heart. I couldn't prevent my answering smile. His white suit made his skin even more tan. Dark-blue embroidered swirls decorated the jacket sleeves, and silver chevrons representing his guild instructor status adorned both shoulders. Three thick silver cords draped diagonally across his chest from left to right.

As I reached the center, the griffins moved to their positions while our parents took their seats. I climbed the steps of the small platform to stand beside Baldwin. At each corner of the platform, a cluster of thick white candles burned, the arrangement wrapped with lengths of ivy and decorated with flame flowers. The lilies' petals glowed, shifting from red to orange to yellow, their sweet aroma mixing with wax and the ocean breeze.

Murray stood in front of us, smiling, as we waited for the music to stop.

"You look stunning." Baldwin's gaze was like a physical touch, his comment pitched for my ears only.

I bit my lip, nerves getting to me. Still, I couldn't pull my gaze from his. "So do you."

Murray cleared his throat, and I focused on the faun. No zoning out. It was the last thing I needed, even if it was because I was crazy in love with my soon-to-be husband. Twining ceremonies were short compared to conventional wedding ceremonies. I could focus and get through this, knowing when it was over I would be Baldwin Marek's wife.

Murray's voice rose to address the crowd. "Thank you all for coming together for this very special twining. Brenna James and Baldwin Marek have agreed to a traditional Linnean pledge."

He turned to us. "Will you recite it together, please?"

As we joined hands, our voices blended, Baldwin's lower baritone with my husky alto. "Today I promise myself to you. I will hold your hand, protect your heart, and share your life. May our love grow stronger as we honor the One who brought us together. Forever and always, I will be yours until Elyon snuffs out the stars."

Even though tears blurred my vision, I'd never been more sure of a decision in my life. Baldwin winked, and a lump grew in my throat as the faun spoke again.

"As tradition dictates, we will have the couple complete the Twining to signify how their lives will twine with Elyon's power to become a strong foundation."

The musicians began a quiet melody as Murray produced a fist-sized bronze ring already threaded with the dark purple cord that stood for Elyon's part of our twining.

Reaching into the pocket of my gown, I withdrew the silver cord. Baldwin pulled a gold one from his pocket. We looped our cords around the ring and carefully began braiding them together.

I bit my lip and squinted as we wove our cords together. We'd practiced this at least half a dozen times over the past week. The braid wasn't overly complicated, but I desperately wanted to do it right. I hadn't grown up here, but I wanted my braid to look exactly the same as any full-blooded Linnean's. Silly? Maybe, but Baldwin had humored me.

When we finished, Murray took the braid and dipped the end in melted wax to prevent the braid from unraveling. The musicians ended the song, notes suspended in the air like mist.

Murray handed the finished braid to Baldwin. "By Elyon's power, I pronounce you twined as Lord Baldwin Marek and Lady Brenna Marek."

The crowd burst into applause, and Baldwin pulled me into his arms. A lifetime of love waited in his green eyes. "Hi, Lady Marek."

My heart fluttered at his husky voice. "Hey, how's it going, Lord Marek?"

"Never better." He leaned down, claiming my lips with his.

I wrapped my arms around him and held on tight to my love, my best friend, my rock. The two of us would set the world on fire—together.

THE END

Where do Brenna and Baldwin go from here? Read on to learn what happens next to the couple in the short story, "The Helix."

THE HELIX

LATE MORNING SUN STREAMED through the living room windows. I scooped up Aurelia before she reached the yawning staircase leading to the first floor. It was such a hazard now that she was walking.

Baldwin pulled her from my arms with a smile. "Good catch. The carpenter promised the baby gate would be ready tomorrow. I can install it first thing."

"Thank you. You're sure you're okay watching her?" I asked as he followed me downstairs.

He gave me a mock offended look as Lia babbled in his arms before smacking his cheek with her little hand.

"No hitting," he said to her before turning to me. "I can handle this angel. Nothing to it."

I smirked. "Right."

He captured my hand before I stepped out the door. "Are you forgetting something?"

"Ma-mum-mum-mum-mum," Lia demanded, her efforts drawing my attention.

"Yes!" She was so close to saying my name. "Can you say Mama?"

"Mum, mum, mum, da-da."

I sighed, and Baldwin grinned.

Shaking my head, I kissed her cheek, but Baldwin didn't release my hand.

"I get one, too." He slipped his hand behind my neck and pulled me close.

Lia gently patted my cheek as I finally pulled away from his kiss.

I gave him a smile. "Twined for three times and you still make my heart race. You are a dangerous man, Baldwin Marek."

"Yes, but who else would remind you to take your notebook with you?"

"That's what I was forgetting!" I grabbed the notebook from the kitchen table. "Thank you!"

Baldwin's chuckle followed me out the door.

I'd been on pins and needles since I woke this morning. Earlier this week, Story Shapers had put out a request for griffin courtship stories. All of them would be bundled into an anthology for the castle library. Even though I didn't consider myself a storyteller, Astraya, Arvandus's mate, had agreed to share how they'd met and become a couple—I was determined to get the entirety on paper.

The two griffins waited for me outside near the Linnean castle steps. While they were both mutants, mostly big cats with wings, they were gorgeous together. Their coloring was like night and day, with Arvandus's black fur and Astraya's golden pelt.

Arvandus gave me a dark look. I think the only reason he agreed to share their story was because Astraya had bullied him into it.

As if sensing my thoughts, she caught my gaze and gave me a wink.

The portal fountain sparkled in the sunlight, glittering drops of water spraying up before falling in a gorgeous curtain.

I settled on the steps, trying to ignore Arvandus's glare. Finally, I gave up. "You know, if you're going to sit there glaring the whole time, this will be unpleasant for everyone."

"No one is making you do this, Brenna."

Ooh, *Brenna*. He was using my given name instead of my nickname, Raven. He must be more annoyed than I thought. Before I could speak, Astraya butted him with her head. "Must you be so irritable this morning, carus?"

"This complete story is unnecessary." He didn't respond to the affectionate name meaning *beloved* Astraya often used.

"But it is our history. Brenna is willing to write it down for us. It will be good to have this recorded."

Arvandus said nothing, so Astraya turned to me. "We will answer any of your questions."

Two servants from the castle walked by, and I gave them both a smile and a wave.

"Thanks. Um, maybe you could begin by telling me how you met?"

Her golden eyes brightened. "I noticed him first."

Arvandus perked up. "That is untrue. I noticed you before you were available."

"Available? What does that mean?" I opened my notebook and began taking notes.

Astraya fluffed her golden wings. "A griffin is considered available when he or she can choose a mate and raise a cub, usually around twelve times. Arvandus was twenty, regarded as an elder mate."

Arvandus snorted.

Biting my lip, I smothered a grin.

A few silver sparks drifted from his wingtips. "Elder? I had not found an acceptable mate. I ignored Riothamus's lectures and bullying."

I tilted my head. "The griffin leader bullied you?"

Arvandus sniffed. "He told me I had wasted too much time. I was to fulfill my responsibility to choose a mate and produce offspring. That was about the time I met you, Raven. I told him I was too busy."

"With what?"

His gaze was steady. "With my responsibility to my high-risk rider."

"Right." I jotted down a few more sentences. My pen skittered to a stop as his words registered. "What do you mean? I'm not high risk."

"Raven." He paused, his golden eyes like lasers. "You have traveled through the dangerous forests of Silvastamen, battled a man-eating serpent, and fought a madman with massive amounts of Shadow Power. I have rescued you from drowning, from horrifying creatures, and from death-defying falls. You are the very definition of a high-risk rider."

"But that was in the past. I haven't done that for several times." And if it hadn't been for Rune, I never would've signed up for all the danger in the first place.

"True. Your offspring has calmed you a bit. I pray your recklessness does not return."

Favoring him with a glare, I ignored his smirk and turned to Astraya. "What made you notice him? I can't imagine it's his personality."

Both of us ignored Arvandus's growl.

The golden griffin tilted her head. "As my time of availability grew near, I watched the male griffins. Not all behave as honorably as Arvandus. He was kind to elder griffins, gentle with young cubs, and protective of those who needed it. His bravery during Linneah's battle against Rune was legendary. And I found his stunning silver wingtips very attractive."

Arvandus sat a bit straighter at her words. "I knew there were other males who noticed her. How could they not? But I waited for the Gathering."

At my questioning look, he continued. "It is a yearly event for griffins to meet and choose mates. I was hoping she would not mind I was not deemed a 'true griffin.'"

"Ridiculous." She shook her head and turned to me. "When the Gathering started, I watched him. Before long, he approached me." She nosed his neck and leaned into him. "He was so chivalrous."

Arvandus chuffed in response. "You could have chosen a more acceptable griffin, one with more eagle-like qualities."

She sniffed. "But I am the same. Do you consider me unacceptable?"

My eyes widened. Oh, boy. Arvandus needed to be very careful with his response because I was *not* getting into a domestic griffin dispute.

Arvandus jerked back. "Of course not. You are perfect."

Mollified, Astraya sniffed once more and settled back at his side.

Glancing at my notebook, I winced. I'd forgotten to add to the story as they talked. Quickly scrawling a few notes, I shifted on the hard stone steps. "So that was it? That's how you two became a couple?"

My griffin shook his head. "No, it was not so easy. There was a challenger wanting Astraya's affections." Arvandus's eyes glowed, his voice a low growl. "Drabek. But Astraya was true with my heart, and I fought the contender."

I frowned. "It wasn't a fight to the death, was it?"

Astraya looked down at the ground before her eyes met mine again. "That is not the goal, although it has happened in the past. The rules state the fight continues until one pulls back from the Helix."

"What? What Helix?" Frowning, I combed through the memories when I'd lived with one foot in Cloverdale and one foot in Linneah. I would've remembered Arvandus telling me about this. Right?

I rubbed my forehead—mom brain was a thing. What had I eaten for breakfast this morning? I paused. Had I eaten breakfast? Lia had woken up before sunrise...

Astraya's words broke into my thoughts. "It is when—"

Arvandus cut her off. "It is unimportant. The important point is we are together."

He'd paired with Astraya the spring before I took the trip through the travel portal to Ginselwyn. But I was pretty sure he'd never mentioned a fight or a helix or anything like that.

She bumped him with her shoulder and favored him with a glare. "That was ill-mannered, carus. Do not interrupt me. Brenna needs the complete story."

I sure did—there was a lot more here than two griffins getting together to start a family.

Shifting forward, she ignored Arvandus's sullen glower. "Drabek had been stalking me for weeks before my availability. When he issued his challenge, I was afraid for Arvandus. Although he was strong, I had never seen him fight."

She gave a distressed purr. "The challenged griffin chooses the fighting ground. After Drabek issued the challenge, Arvandus chose the Helix on the southern side of Mount Gibor. The next day, the two met on the summit. A frigid wind whipped colder on the mountaintop, but I barely noticed."

The sunny Linnean day dimmed a bit as she talked. Mount Gibor lay further north. While searching for the Sacred Veil and my mother, Arvandus and I had flown over it. Its forested and forbidding peak offered little comfort.

Astraya leaned against Arvandus. "Many of the griffins were there to watch. But I feared for his safety. What if something happened? What if Drabek was the victor?"

Giving her a side glance, Arvandus snorted.

His mate ignored him. "Drabek spent several minutes strutting back and forth on the mountaintop, shouting insults. Suddenly, he leaped at Arvandus. The two rose into the air, the fight intense. Drabek slashed at Arvandus's chest, and the two descended into the icy chasm. The strong wind currents carried them up, then their fight plunged them down. Up and down, over and over. Arvandus struck Drabek, who then lodged his talons in Arvandus's fur. And that is when the two spiraled into the Helix. One of them had to give up."

Astraya paused and looked at the ground. The silence grew long. Tension scraped its fingernails across my neck, and my stomach went hollow. My eyes widened, and I finally blurted out my question. "Well? Who gave up?"

She looked at Arvandus and nodded, as if encouraging him to tell the rest of the story. His voice was quiet. "The plunge took only seconds, but while I fought, I thought of only Astraya—and you, Raven."

I blinked once. "Why me?"

"Do you know what happens when death separates a griffin and his bonded rider?"

I swallowed hard, preferring not to imagine my life without Arvandus. "I assume there's a long period of grieving."

"Yes. Because of the vinculus. And rarely does a previously bonded rider or griffin later bond with another." He sighed. "Although winning Astraya was important, so is my relationship with you. I feared this would be a fight to the death. I had so much to lose. But I would never give up."

"Of course not. That's not who you are." I gave him a warm smile. His unflagging loyalty, strong will, and extraordinary stubbornness concealed his tender side.

Arvandus continued. "So before you ask, yes, Drabek died. I did what I could to prevent his death, but once he had his talons latched into my fur, he refused to let go. The chasm grows narrower at the bottom. As we neared the depths, I tried pulling away, but he was intent on killing us both."

I could barely breathe. "What did you do?"

"Pumped my wings once and flipped. He was at the bottom when we landed."

"Oh, Arvandus," I breathed. My eyes stung. To be without my griffin was unimaginable.

A sudden thought intruded, and I blinked. "Wait a second... You chose to fight on Mount Gibor?"

Arvandus nodded, his gaze suddenly wary.

"Something tells me it's pretty dangerous, correct?"

Astraya jumped in. "It is *the* most dangerous fighting location there is."

I narrowed my gaze. "Yet you labeled me a high-risk rider?" I snorted. "I'm not the only adrenaline junkie here."

Chuckling, Astraya gave Arvandus an affectionate lick. "I think she knows you well, carus."

Humor lurked in his golden eyes. "Like you, I have left that dangerous tendency far behind."

I scribbled a list of important details to jog my memory for later before I looked up at the couple. "So how long did you wait before you started a family?"

Astraya answered. "Three months. And we have had a litter every two times."

As if the topic conjured them, another griffin approached, the three cubs bounding behind. The adult griffin looked at Astraya and emitted a high-pitched cry before leaving. Although I didn't understand, Astraya shrugged. "They wanted to play outside."

"It is fine," Arvandus responded as two of the three griffin cubs climbed over his back.

Astraya nuzzled one of the black cubs as it tumbled off its father. "This is Erion. The other black one is Keziah, and the tan one is Torr."

I bit my lip. All were adorable balls of fluff and feathers. The two miniature griffins like their father shimmered black in the afternoon sun while a golden Torr nestled next to Astraya.

Standing, I brushed off my pants. The ocean glimmered in the distance, the sun so bright the white tops disappeared. "Well, I'll let you two enjoy your family time. Thanks so much for sharing your story. It's amazing, full of true love and dangerous thrills." I shot a stern glance at Arvandus, who as usual, gave me an impassive stare.

"Ma-mum, mum!" I turned to see Aurelia tottering toward me.

Baldwin walked close behind her. "The beautiful day drew us outside. Do you need more time?"

Lia threw her arms around my legs, and I almost fell over. "No, I got all of it. It's quite the story."

I picked up my little girl, her tiny body warm, her unruly dark brown curls a glorious halo. Her scent of powder, sunshine, and earth tickled my nose.

Baldwin drew closer. "Hello, Astraya, Arvandus."

Both griffins nodded.

He grinned. "I will have to stop at the griffin house later. Yesterday, Lev promised me a flight."

Lia squirmed to be let down, and I swung her to the ground as Baldwin continued to chat with the griffins. Lia's eyes were wide as she approached the two griffin cubs. "Mum-mum?"

Smiling, I crouched down. "Be gentle with the kitties."

Arvandus growled at my words.

"Sorry. I mean, be nice with the baby cubs," I amended.

"Ba-ba-ba." She reached out, and I bit my lip. What if one of the cubs swiped at her? Though they were tiny, their claws were like little knives.

Erion, one of the black cubs, took a step closer to her outstretched hand and nosed her fingers. She giggled then patted the cub's neck. Relaxing, Erion sat facing her. My breath caught as the two stared at each other, both sets of bright blue eyes connected.

"Arvandus?" My voice was a whisper. "Can griffins choose riders at any age?"

He eyed his cub. "Although early ties can be made, riders are not chosen until griffins have reached the age of at least five times."

He paused, his gaze softening. "But I pray whoever Erion and Aurelia bond with, they will be blessed like I have been."

My mouth fell open at the unexpected compliment, a warm glow surrounding my heart. I pulled him close for a hug. "Thanks, big guy. My feelings exactly."

THE END

Anna's Island Slang

- **Chasing sea glass:** searching for the impossible
- **Danced the drift:** died
- **Drift talk:** nonsense, rambling
- **Foam talk:** empty words
- **Foamed out:** excellent/awesome
- **Low tide behavior:** sneaky & underhanded
- **No drift about it:** no doubt
- **Reef logic:** confused thinking
- **Reefstars:** expression of awe/wonder
- **Ride the curl:** travel on/keep going
- **Riprider:** hero
- **Rogue wave:** terrible situation
- **Salt it down:** relax; take a breath
- **Sea spray:** daydreaming/ unfocused
- **Seagull:** obnoxious
- **Seaweed spun:** crazy
- **Shell fine:** good; perfect
- **Shells and shimmer:** exclamation
- **Shimmer:** magic
- **Skim the blue:** take off; leave
- **Slick as a reef eel:** agile & fast
- **Stone deep:** sincere; heartfelt
- **Storm tossed:** bad
- **Surge boss:** attractive guy/girl
- **Tail-tied:** stuck in a bad situation
- **Tide called:** destined
- **Wave hung:** crushing on a guy/girl
- **Wavekeeper:** friend
- **Whitecapping:** angry
- **Wind slick:** charismatic and smooth

THANK YOU!

THANK YOU FOR READING the Firebrand Chronicles! I hope you enjoyed it. For more fun, head to my website (https://jmhackm an.com/) to find Firebrand Chronicles freebies, learn more about my other books, and to sign up for my newsletter, True North. I'd love to stay connected! The once-a-month newsletter is packed full of book recommendations, occasional freebies and giveaways, and behind-the-scenes reveals into upcoming books. Hope to see you there!

PLEASE LEAVE A REVIEW

Reviews can help other readers find good books and can create more exposure for good books by indie authors. Plus, all authors treasure reviews!

If you enjoyed this book, please consider leaving a review on Amazon, Barnes & Noble, Goodreads, or even a post on social media! A line or two is all that's needed. The information below can give you a few more tips.

Writing an Easy Book Review

Writing a book review can be hard, but it doesn't have to be.

Review Template (pick one):

Not sure what to say? Just copy, paste, and fill in the blanks! Your review can be as short or as long as you like – but every word helps this book find new readers.

Option 1: Quick + Easy

I really enjoyed [Book Title] by [Author Name]. If you like [genre/theme], you 'll love this. My favorite part was [a scene, a twist, a character]. I'd recommend it to anyone who enjoys [similar books/authors or vibes].

Option 2: Feelings First

[Title] made me feel [emotion: hooked, heartbroken, hopeful, etc.] I couldn't stop reading because [reason]. I especially loved [character/scene]. I can't wait to read more from this author.

Option 3: Vibe Reader

If you're into books that are [adjective: dark, romantic, twisty, cozy, fast-paced], this one is for you. [Book Title] gave me major [vibe: fairytale, dystopian, small town, enemies-to-lovers] energy.

Option 4: Combo Review

I loved [Book Title] by [Author]. It was a(n) [adjective] tale that left me [emotion]. I loved [scene, character, twist] and can't wait for more from this author. If you like [similar book/vibe], check out [Book Title].

Ready to leave a review? Please go to my Amazon author page (https://www.amazon.com/stores/J.-M.-Hackman/author /B01K9PJMPE), click on the book you want to review, then scroll down to leave a customer review. Thank you so much!

Acknowledgements

AND HERE WE ARE at the end. I view *Burn* with equal parts joy and sadness—joy that I've been privileged to write this series, but sadness that it's over. I've learned so much, met so many amazing people, and enjoyed sharing Brenna, Baldwin, Arvandus, and all the other characters with you. Having them ride off into the proverbial sunset is difficult. So is writing acknowledgements! I'll try to remember everyone.

My family deserves an enormous thank you. They'll brainstorm, discuss strange topics, and help me stage fake fights to make the scenes read correctly. They've also become used to me trailing off in the middle of a conversation before I mutter, "I've got to go write that down." Thank you for putting up with all my oddities and cheering me on. I love all three of you more than words.

Loving thanks to my mom and dad, and my mother- and father-in-law who encouraged, supported, and prayed for me. They reminded me to take care of myself despite my tendency to get wrapped up in my stories.

Thank you to all the bloggers, reviewers, and readers. Each kind word and review kept me writing, and I'm grateful you've read and enjoyed my stories. Thank you to my beta readers for your keen eyes and feedback. And thank you to C.S. Hackman for the new beautiful covers!

Thank you to my Lord and Savior, Jesus Christ. When I questioned what I was doing, You gave me the words and consistently encouraged me to "Write the story." I love You and couldn't have done it without You.

About the Author

J.M. Hackman, the award-winning author of the Firebrand Chronicles and the Stardust Hearts series, loves thunderstorms, fuzzy socks, and thick chocolate milkshakes. Her engaging fantasy and soft science fiction stories are threaded with hope and end with a happily ever-after. While her characters are fearless, J.M. is afraid of spiders, wasps, and the crowds at post-Christmas sales.

Her short stories have been published in the anthologies *Crowns*, *Encircled*, *Tales of Ever After*, *Mythical Doorways*, and *Realm-scapes*. When she's not writing, she reads, crafts, watches football, and adventures with her family in the mountains of rural Pennsylvania.

www.ingramcontent.com/pod-product-compliance
Lightning Source LLC
Chambersburg PA
CBHW020555120726
47903CB00001B/263